CW01512002

The Colony

The
COLONY

DANIEL POLLOCK

Published by Daniel Pollock
Copyright © 2025 Daniel Pollock
First published April 2025

All rights reserved. No part of this publication may be reproduced,
stored in a retrieval system or transmitted in any form or by any
means, electronic, mechanical, photocopying, recording or otherwise,
without the prior written permission of the publisher.

Type by BookPOD
Cover design concept by Daniel Pollock.
Elements of this cover have been generated with the assistance of AI.

ISBN: 978-1-7640662-0-4 (pbk) 978-1-7640662-1-1 (eBook)

A catalogue record for this
book is available from the
National Library of Australia

For SG, Pook and Smeep

CONTENTS

PROLOGUE

In 1603, following the Union of the Crowns, James VI of Scotland also became James I of England. From that point Scotland was shamefully ignored by its London based monarchs and became progressively poorer due to limited trading opportunities and devastating failed harvests.

By 1688 the ruler was the Dutch Protestant, William of Orange who had overthrown his Roman Catholic father-in-law James. However, Willian remained suspicious of his subjects in the North especially the powerful Jacobite lobby which was intent on restoring James to the throne.

Fuelling the Scottish resentment was the fallout from the Massacre of Glencoe. On February 13th 1692, the King's troops had slaughtered thirty eight men, women and children of the Macdonald clan as they slept in their beds.

In 1695, to temper the growing ill-feeling, William assented to an Act which allowed for the creation of a Scottish trading company which would have an exclusive monopoly on Scottish trade and be permitted to establish an overseas colony. This became known as the Darien Scheme.

EDINBURGH

CHAPTER 1

Jamie Buchanan peered out of the carriage window. "What in the name of God am I doing in Edinburgh?" he muttered. But he was only too painfully aware of the answer.

As soon as the horses were reined to a halt, he pushed open the carriage door. Even in late May a blast of bitter Arctic wind hit him hard. He glimpsed the Castle, half-lost in the chimney smoke that drifted down to the street before it was whipped away in the wind. At least he was in the right place.

His mood wasn't improved when he stepped down from the rig, slipped on some wet cobblestones and watched his left shoe disappear into a pile of dung. Grabbing his bag, he glanced back down the street. There was no other carriage. He hurried down a stinking close and was soon standing before a three storey sandstone building. The brass plate read, 'The Company of Scotland.' He chapped the lion rampant knocker and glanced up at the rainclouds which clung to the rooftops like children at their mother's skirts. It would be wet again soon.

The oak door was opened by a skinny youth dressed in a crimson uniform which hung off him like it was his big brother's. Buchanan said he was here to see the Company Secretary and was escorted up a flight of stairs into a brightly lit office overlooking the main street.

A slender, sallow man in his early twenties with eyes as grey as a wolf came round from his desk. He extended a bony hand. "I'm Roderick Mackenzie. Pleased to meet you, Mr. Buchanan." His voice was taut and reedy.

"The pleasure is mine, Mr. Mackenzie," Buchanan replied, as he tried not to crush the clerk's spindly fingers.

"Please call me Roderick," he said.

"Roderick it is. Please call me Mr. Buchanan."

Mackenzie's eyes widened. Buchanan grinned. "Just a wee bit of Glasgow humour there to keep you on your toes."

Mackenzie gave a nervous laugh and offered Buchanan a drink. "How was the journey?"

"Bloody awful. I sat wedged against the door by a giant with thighs like two sides of beef and across from a sanctimonious little clergyman who droned on for hours about his parish, its parishioners and the Good Lord."

Another laugh, this time less forced. "One of the hazards of modern day travel. Anyway, we're pleased you're here. Your father's group is well regarded."

Buchanan let out a little snort. "Well, I imagine their money is. How else would someone like me get to become a director of this Company?"

"What do you mean?"

"You're seriously telling me that a Glasgow criminal lawyer is an obvious fit for your Board?"

Mackenzie sniffed. "Ah. I wouldn't worry too much about that. Few of the current lot are here on merit. They're either part of the aristocratic elite or rich merchants who've bought their way in."

Buchanan cocked an eyebrow. Mackenzie began to stutter a retraction before Buchanan raised his right hand. "We'll get along much better if we avoid any bullshit."

This prompted a genuine smile. "Fine by me."

"What's the next step then?" asked Buchanan

Mackenzie gave him a sly look. "You'll find that out tomorrow."

Buchanan cocked his head. "Tomorrow?"

"Your first Directors' meeting."

CHAPTER 2

William Paterson wasn't happy. He wasn't happy at all. The knives were out and he was an easy target. It was bad enough that he'd had to high tail it out of London but to now have to sit here and be judged by these overstuffed buffoons was too much. Christ almighty. He'd been the figurehead of the whole bloody Company and now these pricks were going to hang him out to dry.

He was summoned just before ten. Picking up his black felt hat, Paterson pulled back his one good shoulder and hirpled into the boardroom. It was ablaze with the welcome shafts of spring sunlight pouring through the windows. A quick head count showed that there were twenty directors plus Mackenzie. He knew them all personally except the new chap from Glasgow.

Sitting on a raised dais were the two main Company powerbrokers.

Lord John Belhaven was almost as round as he was tall and looked like he'd been poured into his straining white breeches and forgotten to say 'when'.

Sir Robert Blackwood on the other hand had a face like a bird of prey with hollowed cheeks and sunken eyes. Despite this, he favoured the sartorially flamboyant end of Knoxism and today had a bright purple kerchief protruding from his jacket cuff.

Paterson sat in front of them with the remaining Directors arranged in two rows facing each other. He felt like a mouse caught in a trap.

Belhaven placed his chubby diamond encrusted paws on the table and spoke in the measured tone of a man accustomed to being listened to. "Mr. Paterson. Thank you for your attendance today."

Paterson nodded but said nothing.

Belhaven scratched under his wig at some irritant and then proceeded. "We all know why we are here. The embezzlement of near six thousand pounds of Company of Scotland funds has been sorely felt. While the Board is satisfied that you were not party to the actual fraud we cannot ignore your ill-judgement in bringing the culprit into the heart of our Company."

Paterson cast his eyes to the floor and remained silent.

Belhaven then dropped the hammer. "Given the matter's wide publicity, the Company must be seen to take action. Otherwise it will be accused of condoning the failures which led to this catastrophic outcome. Accordingly, it has been decided that you be removed from the Board, any Company stock forfeited and your place to sail with the Fleet revoked."

Paterson clenched his jaws tight and looked across at Mackenzie, whose head was now bowed. Belhaven continued. "However, the Company will seek no other restitution from you."

Paterson fingered the edge of his hat. On the one hand they had stripped him of all status and potential wealth and denied him the opportunity to be part of the colony in Panama. On the other, he wouldn't end up in a debtor's prison and leave his family destitute.

Looking at the light pouring down between him and the dais, Paterson watched the little particles of dust dart and wheel around the rays. Then some memory deep within his soul catapulted him back to another time. As a boy, he would sit with his father at the end of those long summer days on their farm. He remembered the sun, the warmth of the soil, the musky smell of his dad after an honest day's toil and the sheer happiness of the moment. But most of all he recalled seeing the dust jumping in and out of the shafts of sun. The image flooded over him and brought a singular tranquillity.

His reverie was interrupted by Belhaven's sharp voice. "Mr Paterson? Can you hear me?"

Paterson looked up to see all faces turned towards him. "Your Lordship. I'm grateful for the Board's consideration of this matter. While I might not agree with its conclusions I have too much respect for you and the

Company to do anything other than accept the decision." With that he fell silent again.

Where all present had been anticipating an outraged response, Paterson had just rolled over and acquiesced. An awkward quiet descended until Belhaven gave a grunt and brought down the curtain. "In that case I suggest we adjourn for an early lunch."

As the Directors filed out some stopped to shake Paterson's hand and express their sorrow at the outcome. These were not unreasonable men and knew that the toll would be significant.

Mackenzie walked over to Paterson and said in a near whisper, "Jesus, we all thought you'd curse Belhaven and the directors to Hell and back."

"Yes, I'd rather expected that myself."

"So why didn't you?"

'The dust in the sunlight," said Paterson.

"Eh?" Mackenzie just stared at him.

With that Paterson pulled on his hat and walked out into the bright Edinburgh morning. He took a deep breath and closed his eyes. There was too much still to be done and the Company of Scotland could not possibly succeed without him.

CHAPTER 3

In his first week or so Jamie Buchanan was kept busy enough as a Company lawyer but any Director's duties didn't seem to involve much. Then Mackenzie asked him to lunch at a nearby inn.

A serving girl arrived and set down two anaemic looking pies. Mackenzie plunged his fork into one of them and a greyish substance oozed onto the plate. After chewing away manfully at a mouthful he took a swig of beer and fixed Buchanan with his vulpine eyes.

"We've got a problem."

"What kind of problem?"

"Belhaven and Blackwood want to reconsider the location of the Colony."

"Why, for Christ sakes?"

"Because Paterson was the main driving force behind the current choice. Anything with his stamp on it is now being questioned."

"Oh, for fuck's sake. I thought everyone was sold on Panama. So was it all just guff then?"

"Was all what just guff?"

"You know, about creating a trading route between the Atlantic and Pacific so that ships wouldn't need to navigate Cape Horn."

"No, that's still the plan."

Buchanan shook his head. "Until it might not be the plan."

"Well let's hope it doesn't come to that."

"So what'll happen now?"

"Blackwood has arranged for an expert on Panama to come and meet with the Board."

"And what if they don't like what he has to say?"

"Then we look somewhere else for a Colony."

Buchanan blew out his cheeks. "Brilliant. Absolutely fucking brilliant. Let's just see if I've got this right. As things stand the Company has a Fleet anchored in the Firth of Forth, warehouses fit to bursting, hundreds of settlers itching to start a new life but now no confirmed destination?"

Mackenzie smiled. "I knew you were a fast learner, Jamie."

Buchanan looked at his glass. "I think I'm going to need another one of these."

"Aren't you having any pie?"

He eyed the debris on Mackenzie's plate. "I'm suddenly not particularly hungry," he said before draining his pint.

"Well, you'll have to get used to all kinds of food on the voyage."

Buchanan splattered the last of the beer over his jacket.

"Did I say something funny?" asked Mackenzie.

"Roderick, there is more chance of King Billy becoming a Catholic than me being part of the Fleet."

"So how are you going to monitor your father's investment?"

"From a soft leather armchair in Edinburgh is how."

McKenzie gave a faint smile but didn't reply.

CHAPTER 4

Lord Belhaven negotiated himself up the three stairs to the dais and sank into a carver chair which seemed to let out a groan as the weight landed. He banged the gavel with his wooden hammer and the room fell silent. "Gentlemen, we are here today to review the earlier decision to locate our colony on the Darien peninsula in Panama. To assist us in this task we have secured the expert services of Mr Lionel Wafer."

Buchanan watched as a tall, pallid man stood up. He was perhaps in his late fifties with deep set eyes which were almost impenetrable under their hooded lids.

"Very good of you to join us, Mr. Wafer," trumpeted Belhaven.

Wafer responded in a voice which had lost little of its Welsh accent. "An honour to be in such august company, your Lordship."

Belhaven acknowledged the expected sucking up with a slight nod of his head. "Perhaps as an entrée you could give us a brief summary of your connection to Panama."

"My absolute pleasure," he replied, giving a little theatrical bow. Buchanan smiled at his chutzpah.

Wafer spoke with a mellifluous drawl. The type of voice you trust. "I was part of a privateering raid headed by William Dampier across the Isthmus of Panama in 1680 to plunder Spanish treasure. The raid was successful but my leg was injured and I stayed behind with the local Indians to recuperate. During the nine months I was there I learned about their customs and studied the local wildlife and topography. The following year I was rescued and reunited with Dampier in the Bahamas."

This elicited muttered approval from the directors before Belhaven turned to Blackwood. "Sir Robert, would you lead the questioning?"

Blackwood nodded and flicked through some notes. "Mr. Wafer, we understand the Spanish have created a trade route across the isthmus. If the Company were to settle further south in Darien could a similar route be established?"

Wafer rubbed the side of his face. "I can't answer that definitively as I only travelled the Spanish trail. But I do know they used the Chagres river to cut through the inland mountains which are extremely high."

"But do you think it could be done?" Blackwood persisted.

"Well, most anything can be done. It is just a question of whether you're prepared to pay the price in money and lives." Then he hesitated.

It didn't escape Blackwood. "Was there something you wanted to add?"

"Aren't you concerned that the Spanish will take umbrage?"

"Not at all. They'll know the Company of Scotland has the King's protection under the Act. Why risk conflict with the English over a trifling piece of land which they've no intention of settling themselves?"

Wafer raised an eyebrow but made no comment.

Blackwood, ran a finger down his notes. "Now, do you know if there are any resources on Darien which can be profitably mined or harvested?"

"I'm not aware of any gold, silver or tin in Panama itself. But then again we never had to look as the Spanish were kind enough to give us theirs."

This brought a round of laughter before Wafer continued. "No, the money would be in the Nicaragua hardwood. I only saw a few trees myself but the Indians spoke of vast numbers further inland."

Excited chatter fizzed around the room. Buchanan had heard that William Paterson had called them the El Dorado of the Forests. Cut them down and a fortune would fall into the Scots' laps. But Buchanan was concerned that the directors hadn't listened to what Wafer had actually said. He had only seen a handful of the trees not the actual forests. But given that it was so early in his tenure, Buchanan bit his tongue

Blackwood scribbled another note. "Tell us, are there any particular pitfalls the Scots should be aware of in Daren?"

The old sailor puffed out his cheeks. "Well, bear in mind that for the land to be so fertile it obviously rains a great deal."

Blackwood snorted. "Mr. Wafer, we live in Scotland. Do you think we're unused to rain?" This raised a communal guffaw.

Wafer gave a faint smile. "I'm sure that's so. But I'm talking about rain that doesn't stop for days and the skies empty with such a force that you'd swear another flood was coming. Marry this to the heat and you have a steaming cauldron so humid you think your skin will never be dry again."

"But surely structures can be built withstand these conditions?"

"No doubt, and if all you need is protection from the elements that'll be fine. But if you want to farm your lands and carry on business then you'll have to venture outside from time to time don't you think?"

"Quite so," replied Blackwood, apparently unconcerned by the answer. "Anything else Mr. Wafer?"

"Well, there's the yellow fever and malaria. The bastard mosquito has killed more Spanish than the Indians ever managed."

Blackwood sniffed. "Some illness is only to be expected and we will have excellent medicines and doctors. Wherever in the Indies one goes, pestilence, extremes of weather and alien landscapes will be encountered. Of course, if we could establish a trading entrepôt in Holland then all such hurdles would be absent but then again so would the prospect of any worthwhile profit." This brought more laughter. Wafer said nothing.

The grilling went on for another hour during which Buchanan became increasingly troubled that nobody had thought to ask why the Spanish weren't sipping red wine on Darien's beaches. After, all they'd colonised every other corner of Panama. But again he kept quiet.

When the directors had exhausted all avenues of questioning, Wafer was thanked for his time. He gave another bow, turned on this heel and as he exited Buchanan saw him pat the little pouch of gold guineas which constituted his handsome fee.

Belhaven then took over. "Gentlemen, I think we have all the confirmation we need." The others nodded obediently.

Buchanan looked on, astonished by the arbitrariness of the decision. Wasn't there going to be some debate on what they'd just heard?

Mackenzie glanced across at him and imperceptibly shook his head to indicate that this was not the time or place to question the outcome.

"Excellent," said Belhaven. "Now, there is one other matter. Our London informants have heard the name Darien bandied around the English East India Company offices. This means either loose tongues in our midst or something more malign."

This triggered worried glances among the audience.

"Whatever the case, the need for secrecy is now absolutely paramount. To achieve this, the final decision on our exact destination will be entrusted to a select committee. The location's particulars will be placed in sealed orders and given to the Fleet Captains for opening only when the ships are ready to sail. Does anyone oppose the proposal?"

No voice was heard or hand raised. But Buchanan thought it utter madness for even the ships' captains to be in the dark about the destination until the eleventh hour.

"Splendid," boomed Belhaven. "Time for luncheon, I think." That this was not up for debate was reinforced by the florid faced noble levering himself to his feet and heading directly towards the Company's oak panelled dining room.

Given the famine which had gripped Scotland these last five years, Buchanan couldn't avoid the thought that the orgy of food and fine wines seemed entirely incongruous with the Company being the self-proclaimed champion of its people.

CHAPTER 5

As preparations for the voyage increased the city began to buzz with anticipation. Buchanan was happy to be a part of it. He'd taken easily to Edinburgh and, most importantly, felt safe. But if you're a Scot nothing good lasts forever.

July 8th had been a stifling day by Scottish standards and by the time Buchanan had finished work, he needed a drink more than a thirsty camel. The Doric Inn on Market Street was packed and Buchanan had to push his way through the throng to get to the bar. The first beer slipped down his throat in a few gulps and the second didn't take much longer.

By the time he had the third in his hand, he began to enjoy the cheerful noise and the easy banter of the pub. Edinburgh had become the melting pot of Scotland and accents from all parts of the country surrounded him, including the guttural intonations of his home town. Even if telling a fairy tale, Glaswegians still managed to sound threatening. But all that mattered was that you had something to say, preferably funny, and were happy to stand your round.

Suddenly in the midst of all of this gaiety Buchanan froze. Strange how you always sense when you're being watched and some ancient instinct prepares your body for the unseen danger. There was nothing tangible but Buchanan knew. He just knew. His eyes darted furiously from one group, one face, one voice, to another. Then he saw them. Two small wiry men dressed almost identically in grey sleeveless tunics, black trousers and black stockings. Totally anonymous and unlikely to stick in anyone's memory. But both had the lazy, hooded eyes of a cobra. They were not here by accident.

Buchanan immediately started pushing and shoving his way towards the nearest door causing beer and wine to spill from the jolted hands of anyone in his path. As Buchanan's eyes flitted back to his pursuers he saw they had slipped into the wake created by his stumbling exit. Locked in on their prey they were gaining quickly. He groped for the cane inside the lining of his coat but in the confined space couldn't get at it.

As he made a last desperate lurch for the door Buchanan collided with a massive, kilted Highlander. The contact resulted in the man pirouetting one hundred and eighty degrees so that what he saw was not the actual cause of the impact but two ugly dwarves trying to move past him at speed. Concluding that they were the culprits he grabbed one by the neck and lifted him up like a paperweight. The second pursuer had no option but to stop to resolve the situation. This he did by sliding a stiletto into and then out of the Highlander's side. Such was the speed and efficiency of the movement that no-one other than Buchanan seemed to register it happening.

The Highlander let out a sharp scream and dropped the first man from his grip. He grabbed his side and staggered sideways causing the pathway between Buchanan and the killers to be temporarily blocked. Seizing the chance, Buchanan forced his way out and in seconds was on the main street. Off this branched a honeycomb of narrow closes crammed with spiralling grey tenements.

He darted down one of these little side streets but running blindly stumbled over a dog which let out a yelp. An oil lamp attached to the disembodied arm of a resident emerged from a window. Buchanan knew he would now be silhouetted for his pursuers but at least he'd have some light to see where he was going. Then his heart sank. Shit, he thought, this isn't the way to the High Street. It's a fucking cut-de sac. He could bang on the nearest door but by the time it opened, if it opened, they'd be on him.

He slid out the heavy brass headed cane and prepared to defend himself. As the predators edged closer Buchanan shouted at them hoping that this might draw attention from the neighbours. "Something I can help with you with, lads?"

One of them spoke in a strained high pitched voice. Buchanan assumed he'd been the one grabbed by the neck. "Don't you worry about that Mr. Buchanan. You're helping us plenty by just being here," he squawked.

"Oh aye, and how's that then?"

The second let out a cackle. "You're wur wee pension plan. Dae the business here and then we collect the ten pound bounty on yer heid."

Buchanan tried to stall them. "So, just out of interest boys, how did you find me?"

"No' that hard really" said the second one. "Wur boss has contacts everywhere."

"And here was me thinking I'd got all invisible."

"Aye well, unless yer a mirage I don't think it's worked."

"Don't suppose there's any use in trying to buy you off?"

"Nae point at a'. It gets out we let you live, then that'd be our reputations up the Clyde. Gottae maintain our professional standards 'n that. Nothing personal, you understand," said Squeaky boy, his sneer exposing a mouthful of broken yellow teeth.

"Oh, that makes me feel much better. Fine, if I'm gonna go, I'll take one of you wee bastards with me."

He pulled the cane from behind his back and tapped its end on the cobbles. He saw their eyes narrow for an instant but they kept coming. The dance was nearing its climax. Buchanan saw the long, thin knives glint menacingly in their sinewy hands. So this was it. What a fucking way to die, down some shite-filled dead end filleted by two wee cunts from Glasgow.

Then out of the darkness came a deep, melodious voice. It belonged to the Highlander.

"Weel now. If it isn't our little friends from the tavern. Sorry you had to rush awa' before we became better acquainted."

The killers swivelled round astonished by the interruption. How had they not heard the approach of this giant? Squeaky curled his upper lip. "Fuck off you Teuchter cunt. This hus got nothin' tae dae wi' you."

"Tut tut, laddie. Whit would your mother think if she heard you use such language." The Highlander was obviously not the least bit perturbed.

"Just piss off," sneered the second one.

"Now that's no' very friendly, especially since one of you left me a wee gift earlier." He pointed to his side where he revealed a bloodstained shirt visible under the thick plaid cloth of his jacket.

Squeaky spat his response. "Oh for fuck sake. Want me tae buy you a new shirt, you dumb prick?"

The Highlander shook his head from side to side. "You're really not very nice people are you?"

Squeaky snapped a few more words. "Look, I know you've probably got some mental disease aff a goat, but just get tae fuck."

"Aye, well now, I'll no be doing that. You see I'm a great believer in the teachings of the Bible. The Old Testament is ma favourite and I particularly like the idea of an eye for an eye. Very popular with us folk, you ken."

That prompted four more giant men to emerge from the shadows as if following a carefully rehearsed choreography. All were bearded and kilted. All of them were holding a blackjack and a hunting knife.

Buchanan watched the blood drain from the faces of the assassins. The Highlander switched his gaze to Buchanan. "Weel now, I don't ken who you are meester but I reckon that given the scenario here, you'll no be in league with these gentlemen."

Buchanan nodded and Highlander continued. "That being the case I suggest you move along so that we can take care of things here in private."

Buchanan edged past the killers and took off up the close as fast as his legs would carry him only stopping when he got to Market Street. When he looked back all was darkness, but he could clearly hear the blood curdling cries of the assassins as they were gutted by the Highlanders.

Providence had intervened in the unlikeliest of forms and saved him this time. But Buchanan knew when news filtered back to Glasgow there would be another time and then another until the job was done.

CHAPTER 6

The next morning Buchanan stirred from a broken sleep and watched the first faint sliver of dawn's light leach across the rooftops. Edinburgh had suddenly been transformed from a sanctuary to a place where every look carried a threat. Maybe he could flee to another part of Scotland. But would that be enough? Perhaps he could change his name and live in the shadows but that was no existence. Europe would be safer but how would he make a living? No, there was only one viable option.

Buchanan hurried to Milne Square. It was barely light but Mackenzie would be at his desk. He knocked on the half-open door.

Mackenzie jerked his head up from his papers. "Jamie, what brings you here at such an ungodly hour?"

"An urgent matter, I'm afraid."

"What's wrong?"

Buchanan sat down and looked dead at Mackenzie. "The real reason I left Glasgow wasn't to monitor my father's investment here."

Mackenzie's eyes narrowed. "Go on."

"About two months ago I was in a pub and got into a stupid argument with a little prick named Cullen. Next thing I know we're outside and I was knocking seven shades of shit out of him."

"Isn't that just another Saturday night in Glasgow?"

"Aye. Well, the problem is that Mr Cullen is part of a crime family and didn't take kindly to being given a doing in front of his associates. Next thing I know I'm a dead man walking with a ten pound bounty on my head."

"You're kidding."

"I wish I was. But life's cheap in Glasgow and there are plenty willing to risk the gallows for money like that."

"Jesus Christ."

"Anyway, word of the contract got back to Cullen's father. He knew it wouldn't be good for business if I was summarily butchered in the street so I was given four weeks to get out. After that it would be open season."

"But you left before the deadline."

"Aye, but turns out Cullen Junior is not one to forgive and forget."

Buchanan then proceeded to narrate the previous night's events. Mackenzie's eyes widened in disbelief. "In the name of God. Why didn't you tell me about this?"

"I thought that once I was away from Glasgow it wouldn't come back to bite me."

"Christ, Jamie, did you really believe you could outrun it?"

"Yes, actually. But obviously I underestimated the malice of that wee gobshite. I'd thought that being warned off would have been enough."

"So, what are you going to do?"

"As I see it, the only place that's going to be safe is on one of those ships sitting out in the Firth."

Mackenzie let out a sputtering laugh. "But you said there weren't enough wild horses in Christendom to get you onto the Fleet."

"Well, apparently circumstances change Roderick."

A smile played over Mackenzie's lips as he rustled among the papers on his overflowing desk. Finally he found a letter and began reading aloud. " July 7th 1698. Dear Mr. Mackenzie, it is with the utmost regret that I must advise that as a result of a change in personal circumstances I can no longer to take up my position on the Fleet. Yours faithfully, Daniel Mackay."

"What, the Colony lawyer?"

"One and the same. A severe case of cold feet I suspect. Anyway, he's no great loss."

"Have you replaced him yet?" asked Buchanan.

"Not a hope. No lawyer worth his salt wants to forsake his plush office and Gentleman's club for a tortuous voyage to God knows where in a ship full of desperate settlers and ex-servicemen. Well, not unless he's running for his life. Know anybody?"

Buchanan's face broke into a grin. "I might do."

Mackenzie ran a hand through his thinning hair. "There will be one caveat, Jamie."

"What's that?"

"I have to be sure that this vendetta won't follow you onto the Fleet."

"It's a fair question, but look at it this way. If I sail, then any man wanting to kill me would also have to be part of the Fleet. Even if that were possible the assassin couldn't then just toddle back home for his dinner. He would be stuck where he was and only able to get off at the next port of call. And God knows where that is. Most importantly, Cullen would still need proof I was dead before he paid out. And that's pretty damn tricky without a body or at best, reliable witnesses."

Mackenzie, raised his eyebrows. "You've thought it through pretty thoroughly haven't you?"

"Believe me, it was a long night of soul-searching."

"Then there's the other thing."

Buchanan's raised his left eyebrow. "What other thing?""

"Whoever is the lawyer on the Fleet will also be part of the Council for the colony."

"What the hell do I know about administering a colony?"

"Fuck sake, Jamie, if we were prepared to give the job to Mackay, who has about as much common sense as a dead sheep, then you'll be a big improvement."

Buchanan tugged at this left earlobe. Knowing he had no option, he forced a smile and said. "I'd be honoured."

CHAPTER 7

The increased numbers of soldiers and sailors milling around Leith was the most obvious indicator that the departure date was fast approaching. Recruiting the soldiers had been easy. The end of the Nine Years War in Europe meant that most had lost their sole employment. Robbed of the opium of combat, they personified the sad reality that war doesn't determine who is right but who is left. And for many, a glorious death in battle would have been preferable to the ignominy of living out their remaining days in poverty.

There was also no difficulty crewing the vessels as the end of the War saw Leith infested by scores of unemployed seaman willing to accept almost any terms to get back on board a ship.

The civilian settlers had also begun their descent on Edinburgh. The economic desperation sweeping Scotland had resulted in a clamour to respond to the Company advertisement seeking applicants for its colony 'in the Indies'. Despite having no idea of their destination those chosen were happy to put their faith in the Company to transport them to a new Eden.

Nine hundred civilians along with three hundred soldiers and sailors would form the First Fleet to establish the colony with the Second Fleet leaving six months later to transport the rest of the settlers and supplies.

The company warehouse at Leith now resembled a Caledonian Aladdin's cave and was crammed with all manner of goods and supplies. The transfer of its contents into the holds of the Fleet was orchestrated by a gangly Fifer named Sturrock. He well knew that crime and docks went hand in hand and along with the two sentinels who'd apparently won the Company giant-measuring contest, did what he could to prevent the light-fingered from cashing in on this once in a lifetime opportunity. With his comically long strides he daily patrolled the dock perimeter like a suspicious giraffe banging his spindly arms against doors and checking warehouse walls to ensure that no new openings had been created.

Three ministers of the Kirk were to be enlisted to protect the souls of the Colonists and preach the Presbyterian gospel. How the dour and prescriptive teachings of John Knox would play out with the carefree natives of Central America was anyone's guess.

As it transpired the prospect of leaving their snug manses meant that there was little enthusiasm among the clergy. So eventually, only two ministers, Adam Scott and Thomas James, joined the Fleet and only after both were heavily pressurised by the Church. Crucially, it was through the Reverend James that William Paterson would be given the chance to come in from the cold.

One afternoon in early July Mackenzie poked his head around Buchanan's office door. "Got a minute, Jamie?"

"Of course."

"As you're a Councillor there's something you should know."

"Go on."

"One of the other Councillors, William Vetch, may be too ill to make the voyage."

"I'm sorry to hear that. "

"Yes, we all are. He's a good man and will be sorely missed." Mackenzie hesitated for a moment. "So here's the thing. If he can't make it then the likeliest person to take his berth is William Paterson."

Buchanan snorted. "I thought Paterson had been ostracised."

"Aye, well. He was. But one of the Reverend James' demands was that his old friend be part of the Fleet."

"Did Belhaven agree?"

"The great Lord is usually not a man who takes kindly to a gun to his head. However, there's been a softening in attitudes toward Paterson recently and Belhaven has indicated that he'd have no objection if Vetch doesn't make it."

"Is Paterson aware of this?

"What do you think? He knows everything that's going on even though he's been in Kirkcaldy these last few weeks bothering the poor Fifers."

Buchanan smiled. "Would Paterson take Vetch's role on the Council?"

"Christ no! That'd be a step too far. He'll just be there as a rank and file settler albeit with Vetch's cabin."

"On which vessel?"

"The Unicorn."

Buchanan laughed. "I'm to get a new shipmate then?"

"So it would appear."

CHAPTER 8

The great day finally arrived on July 14th 1698.

In the preceding week Buchanan had been careful to remain out of the public spotlight for fear of another attack. He dined at home, stayed away from taverns and didn't walk anywhere.

As his carriage neared the port, he could see the docks seething with the thousands who had poured into Leith to farewell the Scottish Armada. Some were loved ones and relatives, some were investors, and some were there to take advantage of the criminal opportunities which any large crowd presents.

The Fleet of five vessels bobbed at anchor, their enormous masts glittering in the sunlight and their prows a blaze of gold, scarlet and blue.

A path cleared through the throng. The gilded carriages of the nobles had arrived. They included Belhaven, now so fat that he had to be helped down from his rig. Behind him came the rich merchants who still had to adhere to the established pecking order even if their purses far outweighed many of the nobility.

Small tenders ferried passengers out to the ships along with their baggage. For those travelling in cabins this would include the ornately designed sea chests containing their fine clothes and bed linens.

This was in marked contrast to the sailors who boarded with not much more than a wooden box containing their plate, mug, knife, tobacco and pipes along with a tinderbox. Ordinarily their only clothes would be whatever they had on their back but the Company had mandated that they be provided with a fresh shirt and trousers.

As Buchanan stepped out of his cab he was greeted by the deafening roars of the spectators. For a brief moment he enjoyed the transient glow of celebrity before clambering onto the little rowing boat which would take him to his new home. For the first time in days he felt secure, finally out of reach of Cullen.

As the little tender moved away from the dock, Buchanan got a better perspective of the legion of cheering people lining the shore from every possible vantage point. Saltires were waved and choruses of patriotic songs rang through the still morning air.

He caught sight of Belhaven sitting on a raised wooden platform. The corpulent noble seemed very comfortable receiving the plaudits of the adoring masses which he acknowledged with a desultory wave of his fat, bejewelled hand. In an ostentatious display of wealth and position he was dressed in a cloak of scarlet silk trimmed with ermine and gold.

As the little boat paddled out into the Firth, Buchanan saw the entire Fleet up close for the first time. The nearest was *Saint Andrew* the flagship. It was moored against the dock allowing its passengers and crew to embark across a thick gangplank. The leviathan's hull seemed to erupt from the water and Buchanan had to tilt his neck at an almost ninety degree angle to take in her majesty. As they moved slowly past, he couldn't help but let out a cheer along with his fellow passengers.

The Unicorn, while smaller, was still astonishingly impressive and dwarfed any ship which Buchanan had boarded. But given that was the ferry across the River Clyde, the bar wasn't set particularly high.

When they came alongside the passengers were hoisted aboard on a broad wooden bucket seat attached to a rope and pulley. As Buchanan was hauled skywards he felt he was being transported to Olympus itself.

The Captain, Robert Pincarton, was waiting to greet him. Pincarton was broad and tall with a muscular build which was the perfect clothes horse for his blue uniform jacket and white britches. Intelligent brown eyes crinkled to slits when he smiled and a full head of black hair was slicked back into a single ponytail. He seemed possessed of an effortless grace and polish.

"Welcome aboard the Unicorn, Mr. Buchanan."

"A pleasure to meet you, Captain. Thank you for the reception."

"Think nothing of it, especially as it's a courtesy I bestow on every new arrival, not just our august Councillors." His eyes twinkled mischievously and disappeared as he grinned.

Buchanan returned the smile. "I'm grateful you don't discriminate."

"Always plenty of time for that once one gets to know people better." Again the twinkling eyes. "Now Mr. Robertson here will show you to your quarters where I believe your belongings have already been stowed."

The little barrel shaped bosun nodded a confirmation. He led Buchanan up some stairs to the aft deck which sat higher than the rest of the vessel and afforded a view not only of the decks beneath, but of the wider vista.

The bosun then guided him down some narrow internal stairs and into the gloom of the interior. They stopped in front of a small wooden door which opened outwards. Robertson then gave a salute and excused himself.

Inside wasn't exactly a cabin, more an oversized cupboard. The exterior porthole cast enough light for Buchanan to make out a wooden bed which hung from the ceiling by four chains. Under this sat his chest and a chamber-pot. Squeezed into the corner of the cubicle was a small table and a stool. On the table sat a candle together with a wash basin, flannel, pitcher of water, pewter goblet and a bottle of French claret. Buchanan slipped his satchel from his shoulder and tested the bed with his hand. To his delight it housed a well-padded mattress, fresh linen sheets, a thick top blanket and a plump pillow filled with goose down. So, verging on the claustrophobic, but nonetheless quite acceptable. Buchanan wondered that if these were the quarters of a dignitary what did those further down the pecking order have to put up with?

Stowing his gear he made his way up to the aft deck from where he surveyed the bustle all around him. The throng on the dockside; the small vessels flitting around the queens of the ocean like dragonflies; and the frenzied activity of the crews, working round the gawking passengers hanging over the rails waving goodbye to loved ones, friends and, in some cases, creditors.

After about half an hour Pincarton emerged and stood on the curved poop deck from which he would control his floating dominion. He looked like a modern day Jason, standing heroically with arms folded and legs astride. When he issued orders, Pincarton hardly seemed to raise his voice and any direction sounded more like a polite request than a command. His calmness seems to communicate itself to the ship's company who buzzed in an efficient synchronicity to the prompting of the orchestra conductor.

Then the moment arrived. The tide would wait for nobody, not even the Company of Scotland. But nothing apparently was more important than seeking the blessing of the great God Almighty. A bell rang out from the Saint Andrew and the process was repeated on board each of the other vessels.

On the Unicorn, the Reverend James clambered up to the poop deck and a hush descended over the company. He was an austere chap, stooped by age and so full of asymmetric angles that he looked like he'd been stuffed in a fearful rush by an incompetent taxidermist. His thin voice matched his physique but he gave it his all as he beseeched their Maker to watch over the Fleet and show bountiful mercy to their daring venture. When he had finished, a resounding Amen echoed around the ship.

This was soon followed by the boom of a cannon from the Saint Andrew to signal the ships to weigh anchor and unfurl their massive sails. Buchanan thought the complicated rigging looked like an impenetrable spider's web but when the call came to release the lines, the waves of canvas fell freely as if from the heavens. Drums rolled and trumpets sounded from the shore as the odyssey began with the Saint Andrew leading the way. Buchanan watched her prow cut proudly through the waves, her sights set on a new horizon. On her main mast the Saltire fluttered proudly and beneath it the red, yellow and black horizontal stripes of the Company flag at the bottom of which emerged the rising sun emblem.

While the ships slowly gained speed, those on deck watched the well-wishers slowly evaporate into the Scottish mist. As their cheers continued to resonate, tears and excitement mixed in equal measure.

The cool grey of the dawn was dissipating into a beautiful summer morning, the sky's purity untarnished by a single cloud. The light breeze caressed the Fleet and ushered it gently on its way. A more auspicious beginning one could not have imagined. This was a moment to savour. A golden east coast morning when all was right with the world and everything seemed possible.

CHAPTER 9

It turned out the departure from Leith was only a ceremonial precursor to the start of the actual voyage. The intention was to make a grand exit amidst all the fanfare and then drop anchor a few miles up the coast to allow for all last minute preparations, checks and loadings to be completed in relative peace.

Buchanan used the time to get to know the other elite travellers over dinner in the Great Cabin. This was a large room at the rear of the ship with full length windows allowing for maximum visibility. Buchanan thought that the 'Great' was a little flattering, but then again everything was relative on a sailing ship. During the day it was the mess and chart room but in the evening fine wines and food were served on a table laid with china, silver and crystal.

There were three civilians other than Buchanan. The first was the Reverend James who made John Knox look like a libertine. In keeping with many of his brethren, James' thin spare frame seemed constantly in want of a good meal. Buchanan supposed this ascetic look spoke of restraint, self-denial and all the other presbyterian virtues which brought a man nearer to his God.

The second and third were Mr. and Mrs. Archibald Russell from Edinburgh. He was a merchant who had invested his way onto the voyage and wanted to ensure that his monies were being properly spent. A pompous little man cocooned in soft fat, Russell was no stranger to his own opinions and Buchanan soon realised his company would have to be tolerated rather than enjoyed.

His wife on the other hand was a different proposition. Constance Russell was slim and alluring. Reddish-gold hair framed a heart shaped, softly freckled face painted with egg white alum. Long tapering fingers were festooned with sparkling rings which were no doubt part compensation for marrying Archibald Russell. Her pale blue eyes wordlessly conveyed to Buchanan that Mr. Russell was not providing her with everything she needed.

During the lull in the voyage Buchanan had asked Pincarton if he could explore the ship. Pincarton didn't hide his surprise. "That's a bit of an unusual request, Jamie."

"Why?"

"A ship's not exactly a democratic environment. Segregation is well understood, certainly among the crew and soldiers. As far as civilians go, what you've paid for is generally where you stay. And believe me you'll be glad to be housed on the upper deck when we're halfway across the ocean."

"So is that a 'no' then?"

Pincarton smiled. "Tell you what. I've got to check over the ship anyway. Why don't you tag along?"

He also asked the Russells if they would care to join. Mr. Russell looked as Pincarton as if he'd just taken a shit in his dessert. "Thank you, no. And Mrs. Russell will remain too," he said, jutting out his chin. Mr. Russell obviously did not care to mix with the villagers.

Pincarton began at the top and worked his way down. The ships officers and elite passengers shared the upper deck. Each had cabins similar to Buchanan's although Pincarton's private quarters were slightly larger. Those passengers could enjoy the aft deck and Grand Cabin as their exclusive domain.

Beneath the cabin deck sat the general passenger quarters. These were more dormitories than anything with hammocks suspended from the ceiling, but at least there was adequate light and air from the numerous portholes. Around these were dotted the areas designated for tradesmen and next to them was the surgeon's room. Also on this level was the galley which was heavily lined with firebricks to stop any stray spark from setting fire to the wooden vessel.

Below this were housed the sailors. Their quarters were devoid of natural light unless the gun ports were open. Even in the mild Scottish days the air here felt heavy and rank. But Pincarton said they were well used to the life and in any event spent most of their days above decks working.

But under all of them, next to the great storage holds, were billeted the soldiers. This space felt like the bowels of a massive beast and was completely dark except for the dim light that came from a few candles.

"Are the soldiers and sailors always kept separate?" asked Buchanan.

Pincarton smiled. "Soldiers and sailors don't mix well. A bit like gun oil and saltwater. Just wait until we hit some bad weather and the gun ports are closed."

"What happens then?"

"The sailors open the hatches down to the soldiers' deck to void themselves."

Buchanan laughed. "Aye, I can appreciate how that might create some friction between the Services."

Buchanan quickly came to understood the merit in having status on the Unicorn. This even extended to the ship's latrines. Buchanan had the luxury of a chamber pot. An alternative for the upper deck passengers was the heads. These were nothing more than two broad planks extending beyond the prow of the ship with a circular hole cut in them and a canvas tube extending downwards for about three feet to reduce the undesirable impact of any updraught of wind or sea spray. There was also a modesty curtain which could be pulled across for the more sensitive during devotions. For those on lower decks this facility would be over the stern of the ship but almost entirely public in nature and exposed to the elements. An optional bum-cleaning extra was to haul up the line that trailed in the seawater and apply its frayed end to ones behind before tossing it back into the ocean. Apparently in rougher conditions it was not unknown for an unsuspecting user to be thrown overboard mid-shit.

The inspection over Pincarton had asked, "Seen what you need to see?"

"Aye, thank you Captain. And if you ever hear me complaining about my lot feel free to give me a kick up the backside."

"Duly noted, Mr Buchanan."

CHAPTER 10

The first couple of days spent bobbing at the new anchor continued to feel like a grand adventure but as the third day dawned the novelty began to wear off. Buchanan knew it would be better when they were properly under way. At least there would be a change of scenery and sense of progress. But for most not occupied in the management of the ship, sitting in a floating wooden box going nowhere proved painfully tedious.

Buchanan busied himself with his writing and reading but even that sustained for only so long. The claustrophobia of the ship began its slow creep. Most travellers were unused to the confined conditions and Buchanan wondered how those below were coping. Mercifully the weather was kind and during daylight hours the decks overflowed with passengers and soldiers enjoying the sunshine.

The little supply boats finished their work near the end of the third day. However, the Fleet still remained at anchor. When Buchanan quizzed Pincarton he answered, "The captains only received their sailing orders when we weighed anchor in Leith. That's when we learned our first port of call. Each Captain has his own view of how to get there so at present we're trying to coordinate a single approach."

Buchanan burst out laughing. "You've got to be kidding! So where is the first destination?"

"Madeira. Apparently to give the impression that the Fleet is bound for the East Indies rather than sailing West."

"Oh for Christ's sake. Every man and his dog knows that we're heading for Panama. Where do we stand?"

"I'm going back to the Saint Andrew today for another meeting. But finding common ground hasn't been easy, especially since there's no love lost between Pennicuik and Drummond."

"I've not met either of them yet."

"Aye, well, that's a pleasure in store for you. Pennicuik captains the Saint Andrew and is Fleet Commodore. He's capable enough but is a cruel bastard. Drummond's not much better. He was kicked out of the English navy but family connections got him the captaincy of the Caledonia."

"Isn't there a Drummond in charge of the soldiers?"

"That's his brother, Thomas. Now there's another prick of a man. He was part of the King's regiment at Glencoe. The story goes that when others baulked at slaughtering the Macdonalds in their beds Drummond didn't hesitate."

Just then they were interrupted by a shout from one of the sailors "Boat approaching on the starboard side!"

Buchanan screwed up his eyes. "Captain, hand me your telescope would you?" Buchanan fixed the glass on a small rowing boat which was gamely making its way through the chop of the sea towards the Unicorn. And there was Paterson, his twisted silhouette turned gallantly towards the prow of the little vessel like a Caledonian Don Quixote. At the stern sat a woman and a young man and in the middle two local worthies tasked with getting them out to the ship.

As they came alongside the Unicorn, the family Paterson and their baggage were hauled aboard using the precarious pulley. Mrs Paterson was most put out by the ordeal and for such a mousey woman used language which would have made a brothelkeeper blush. Her son just sat there, the poster boy for glaikit Scottish youth, obviously overwhelmed by the entire situation.

Pincarton watched the scene with a wry smile. "And who do we have here?"

"That is the great William Paterson and family."

"Is that a fact? A grand man for an entrance is he?"

"So it would appear."

"Then let us go and greet His Eminence."

By the time the two of them had reached the main deck a small crowd had gathered. In the vanguard was the Reverend James who enthusiastically clasped Paterson's hand in his bony grip. It had been his championing of the disgraced Paterson which had paved the way for this moment.

As Pincarton made his way towards the new arrivals the crowd parted respectfully. "Mr. Paterson, I presume," said Pincarton.

"The very same," came the reply.

The round robin of introductions was undergone and on seeing Buchanan, Paterson's eyes narrowed. "I believe we nearly met once before."

"I believe we nearly did."

Paterson gave a wry smile. "Well, better late than never."

"Indeed. Welcome aboard the Unicorn."

This prompted Paterson to rummel about in his inside jacket pocket before pulling out a sealed envelope. "Captain Pincarton. This is for you."

Pincarton looked at the red wax insignia. The circular imprint was marked "Blackwood." Pincarton broke open the letter and scanned its contents. "I see," he said in a neutral tone. Naval men were used to receiving all manner of news and learned to take it all in their stride. Pincarton handed the document to Buchanan who read it quickly.

Dear Pincarton,

It is with regret that I must advise that Mr. Vetch is too unwell to travel with the First Fleet. It has been agreed that his berth on the Unicorn might be most expeditiously filled by William Paterson and his family. Could you please arrange these accommodations? Please note that Mr. Paterson holds no position of authority within the Company and as such there is no compunction to afford him any other preferential treatment.

Yours sincerely,

Sir Robert Blackwood.

He handed it back to Pincarton who raised a single eyebrow. "Well, given Mr. Vetch's indisposition, you are to have his cabin Mr. Paterson. It may prove to be a tight fit for the three of you but they are excellent quarters."

Paterson thanked him and Pincarton ordered that Mrs Paterson and the boy be shown there immediately. He asked Paterson to tarry a moment.

Then in his quiet assured way, Pincarton said, "Mr. Paterson, while I am happy to welcome you on board, can I make it clear that in light of Sir Robert's letter this does not give you any special rights."

Paterson fixed him with his shrewd blue eyes. "Noted Captain. Rest assured that my sole goal is the success of the Company."

Pincarton nodded, believing that the proper tone had been set. However, that moment of respite was fleeting.

Paterson fumbled again in his jacket and after a second or two pulled out several sheets of paper. When unfolded these contained a series of lists with a line down the middle. Paterson handed them to Pincarton. "I think you should be aware of these."

Pincarton examined the documents. "And, Mr. Paterson?"

"The column on the left represents the inventory of stocks recorded as received into the warehouses."

"And the column on the right?"

"That represents my estimate of what has actually been stowed in the holds of the Fleet."

Pincarton's eyes widened. "How did you come by this information?"

"I've been working with Roderick Mackenzie auditing goods received into the warehouse. Hence, the first column. My contacts among the warehousemen led me to the second."

Buchanan surveyed the figures. "Jesus Christ. Are you sure about this?'

"As sure as I can be from the information I've received. And I trust that information."

Pincarton slowly shook his head. "You need to accompany me this afternoon to the Saint Andrew for the captains' meeting. We can raise the matter then. Jamie, you should also attend."

Two hours later, the three men were rowed across to the flagship. Pincarton introduced Paterson who then proceeded to outline the situation. Pennicuik, as Commodore, had ultimate say in matters to do with the Fleet.

However, in choosing Pennicuik, the Company had appointed a man devoid of any attractive character traits. He made enemies easily and aroused antipathy with a cocktail of self-righteousness, belligerence and out and out rudeness. His response reflected this. "Nonsense. Utter nonsense. What proof do you have, Paterson?"

"Carry out an inventory of the ship's stocks and you'll have your proof."

"What, on your say so?"

"Well, yes. That and the list in front of you," answered Paterson, in the surprised tone of a man unable to comprehend why his word alone wouldn't create an immediate call to action.

"You expect me to order an inspection of the Fleet's entire inventories based on that? Do you have any idea of the delay it would cause?"

"I'm not sure I follow your logic. If I'm correct, then the entire venture is headed for disaster."

"Oh, you think so? I'm aware of your recent history Paterson and to be frank your opinion carries little weight these days."

Buchanan could see Paterson bristle. "Aye, well that may be your view, but don't make the mistake of letting it get in the way of the facts."

"The only 'facts' I see rest on what you have presented here. In the absence of any independent verification I will take as read the inventories which appear on the ships' manifests."

"Don't be a fool, man. At least conduct a trial stocktake on one vessel."

Pennicuik exploded. "Who the fuck do you think you're talking to? I'm Commodore of this Fleet and unless you can show me otherwise you're just another passenger. If you were on the Saint Andrew I'd send you back to shore where you belong. So, kindly get the fuck off my ship and back to your hutch."

"Gentlemen, gentlemen," said Pincarton. "Let's all take a step back. May I suggest that I organise an exploratory examination of the Unicorn's inventory to see if there is any merit in Mr. Paterson's comments?"

"You can do whatever you want Pincarton," said Pennicuik, "but don't expect me to waste my crew's time on a wild goose chase."

Another of the Captains, Robert Drummond then piped up, seizing on the opportunity to undermine the pompous Commodore. "Excellent idea, Pincarton. I'll dae the same. After a' we wid never want it said that we wur forewarned of a potential disaster and did nothing tae avoid it."

Pennicuik snarled. "Just don't come crying to me if you're not ready to weigh anchor when the signal is sounded tomorrow."

With that Pincarton nodded to Buchanan to escort Paterson back to the Unicorn leaving the Captains to work out how the hell they were going to get to Madeira.

CHAPTER 11

When Pincarton returned to the Unicorn an hour later he ordered his First Officer, David Robb, to carry out a preliminary check of the inventory to test Paterson's claim.

"An interesting meeting?" asked Buchanan.

"You could say that. It was like herding cats trying to get consensus on a route. Drummond kept banging on that if the Fleet had sailed from the West Coast we'd have taken at least a week off the journey."

"Well, wouldn't it?"

"Of course it would, but no way were the Company potentates having us leave from anywhere other than Leith. I can tell you though, I'm not particularly looking forward to taking virgin passengers up round the North of Scotland."

Buchanan, one such virgin, swallowed hard. "Can't say I'm exactly champing at the bit myself."

"You'll be fine, man. It's the poor wretches on the lower decks who'll suffer most."

"How's the weather looking?"

"Set fair at the moment, but there's not much wind so we'll just dawdle up the east coast."

Buchanan gave a little smile. "Sounds fine to me. When do we start?"

"Pennicuik wants to sail on the morning tide."

"But what about the stores?"

"Don't jump the gun, Jamie. Let's see what the initial survey throws up and take it from there. One thing you'll learn at sea is that there are real problems enough without manufacturing others."

That the ship was obviously being readied for departure created a buzz of excitement among the passengers. But it all got too much for some young seamen. Word had reached the Unicorn that a couple of Kirkcaldy lads had been unable to bear seeing their house on the nearby shore and had gone over the side of the Saint Andrew and swum for it.

Pincarton had let it be known that this would not be tolerated and that the consequences would be dire for any absconder who was caught. But even with this warning ringing in his ears, fifteen year old Dougal Thomson decided that homesickness overrode any potential punishment.

As the sun started to go down he leapt over the side of the ship and into the water. That's where his luck ran out. As he thrashed manfully towards the shore he ran right into a row boat which had been coming from the Caledonia. Dripping wet he was marched before Pincarton, crying like a newly pupped wean. Much as Pincarton felt sympathy for the lad, discipline was crucial. So he gave the boy a fierce dressing down but, taking into account his age, spared him the cat. Instead, Thomson was put in chains and given only bread and water for twenty four hours.

Pincarton then turned his attention to the news from the Caledonia. He was handed a folded piece of paper which said simply. "Paterson correct. Stores greatly overstated. Drummond."

"Dammit," he cursed. He turned to his second officer, a skinny youth whose spotty face was partially hidden by his first patchy attempt at a beard. "Can you ask Mr Robb if our check of stores has been completed?"

"Aye, Captain," he answered, and rushed off to find the first officer.

Pincarton collared Buchanan and Paterson in the Great Cabin and filled them in. Robb, a gangly specimen with wide brown eyes that looked a size too big for his head, appeared a few seconds later.

"Well?" asked Pincarton.

He hesitated for a second. "There appear to be some discrepancies, Sir."

"Go on," said Pincarton in an even voice.

"The thing is, the numbers of barrels and boxes seem right, but when we opened them some were only half full."

Paterson banged his fist down on the large oak desk. "I knew it,"

"Mr. Paterson, this is not a time for celebration," chided Pincarton.

"Sorry. It wasn't meant that way."

"Uh huh," said Pincarton. "Thank you, Mr. Robb. Please arrange for a full stocktake first thing tomorrow?"

"Aye, Sir," he replied displaying no trace of the frustration at the task which lay ahead.

Pincarton then penned a quick note for the sailors from the Caledonia to give to Drummond. It read, "Similar finding here. Conducting full inventory tomorrow. Pincarton."

He then turned to Buchanan and Paterson. "It appears there's something rotten in the State of Scotland, gentlemen."

Buchanan raised his eyebrows. "Never a dull moment."

CHAPTER 12

The next day dawned like the several before it. But as the sun burned off the haze there was the hint of a breeze which promised to fill the Fleet's sails.

Aboard the Saint Andrew, Commodore Pennicuik was about to order the signal to weigh anchor when he saw a small boat come across from the Unicorn. Perched uncomfortably in the back was Robb. It was difficult to tell whether his discomfort was due to his lanky frame being ill-fitted to the space or the imminent reaction to the document which he held in his right hand.

Pennicuik was clearly not pleased at the interruption. "Yes Mr. Robb. What pray tell can we do for you today?" he growled.

Robb was no stranger to Pennicuik, having had the misfortune to serve under him during the Nine Years War.

"A message from Captain Pincarton, Sir," replied Robb with a straight bat.

"Must be important if he's sending his chief lackey on the errand."

Ignoring the barb Robb, replied, "Your urgent response is requested Sir."

"Is it now? Well, let me get out my dancing bear and we'll both do a jig to Pincarton's tune," he sneered.

Pennicuik ripped open the letter and read its contents.

Pennicuik. Supplies on Unicorn and Caledonia grossly understated. Suggest delay to allow full inventory and necessary replenishment.

Pincarton.

Pennicuik's face reddened and Robb thought he was going to have a seizure. Instead the Commodore ripped up the note and tossed it at

Robb's feet. "The damned impudence of the man! Tell that ass Pincarton if he has allowed his vessels to be so poorly stocked then perhaps he should consider his position. If he needs to carry out an inventory then he can do so when we're under sail because the Fleet leaves this morning."

Robb took a deep breath. "I shall convey that message, Sir."

"Yes, you just do that. Now, toddle off back to your little ship and let the real sailors get on with their job."

Robb gave a curt salute and clambered back into the rowing boat. A few strokes into the return trip he heard the boom of the Saint Andrew's cannon sound the imminent departure of the Fleet.

Pincarton, Buchanan and Paterson were waiting as Robb came back aboard the Unicorn. Pincarton spoke with a gentle humour which was the antithesis of the brutish Pennicuik. "Let me guess. He invited you for tea and scones and suggested that a thorough examination of the cargo holds was an eminently sensible idea?"

"Not exactly, Sir."

Pincarton smiled. "I think the departure signal may have given the game away, Mr. Robb. "

"Yes, Sir. The Commodore suggested that a stocktake be conducted as we sail." Robb then paused.

"Come now, Mr. Robb. What else? You will only be repeating his comments not making them yourself."

Robb coughed and repeated verbatim what Pennicuik had said.

Pincarton just laughed. "The man really is an imbecile if he thinks only two ships have been impacted. Well, if that's the way of it Mr. Robb, proceed with the more detailed search of the barrels and boxes once we are under way."

"Aye, Sir," said Robb who then left to supervise the ship's departure.

Pincarton looked at Buchanan and Paterson and shook his head. "This is the calibre of the man charged with leading our Fleet."

Paterson was incandescent. "What a complete fool. He must be stopped."

Pincarton eyes narrowed. "Mr. Paterson, while I am grateful to you for drawing the anomaly of the stores to our attention, please remember your somewhat fragile status on this voyage." The upbraiding hit home and Paterson nodded his acquiescence.

Pincarton then turned to Buchanan. "What do you think, Jamie?"

"Is there really a choice? Staying behind will detach us from the rest of the Fleet. It looks like we have to count our chickens and other provisions as we go."

"Welcome to the Company of Scotland," smiled Pincarton.

"If there is a verified shortage, what are the options?" asked Buchanan.

Pincarton gazed out at the reassuring skyline of Kirkcaldy before responding. "The Orkney Islands are on our way so if we can convince Pennicuik that there is an issue we can make a detour there."

"Will they have the supplies we need?"

"Well, if you don't mind a diet of mutton for a few weeks we should be fine."

They then focussed their attention on the grand spectacle of the Fleet leaving port. Slowly, the massive sails began to fill with the southerly breeze and flap like white sheets on a clothes line. As the now familiar horizon began to gently recede the real adventure was finally under way.

THE VOYAGE

CHAPTER 1

The Fleet plotted a course along the East Coast, past Elie, Anstruther and Crail, all neat little towns with a Main Street about the length of a musket shot. At each one cheering crowds lined the shore, shouting and waving their arms or whatever articles of clothing were to hand.

Sadly, the breeze didn't last long. On the third morning, about fifty miles north of Aberdeen, a haar descended and shrouded the ships in a dense fog so thick it could be cut into blocks. The Fleet was becalmed and all visual contact lost. Pincarton ordered the bell to be rung to signal the Unicorn's position and this was followed by tolls from the other ships.

The Fleet sat dead still in the middle of the North Sea. For all the terrifying stories Buchanan had heard about giant waves and fearsome winds, this seemed comically anomalous. Other than the gentle rocking of the swell he could as easily have been sitting in the parlour of his father's house.

On the upside, the calm conditions did allow the stocktake to be carried out fairly quickly. Pincarton was in the Great Cabin staring into the impenetrable mist when Robb handed him the report.

"In the name of God," Pincarton muttered. "Are you certain, Mr. Robb?"

"Yes, Captain, we double checked," replied the first officer.

Five minutes later, Buchanan and Paterson were sitting round the Cabin's oak table.

"Well Paterson, it appears that you were correct," said Pincarton. "The long and the short of it is that we only have provisions for five months and not the mandated nine."

Paterson nodded his head, silently smug in his vindication.

"Obviously," said Pincarton, "we'll need to restock. Food and water shouldn't be too much of an issue. We can put in to the Orkneys for those."

"Which begs the question as to what might be an issue," said Paterson.

Pincarton handed over the report. Paterson quickly scanned it and hissed. "Bastarding Munro."

Buchanan was puzzled. "Meaning?"

"Meaning, Dr. John Munro's the sanctimonious Edinburgh prick responsible for arranging the medical supplies. We've about enough medicine on board to fight an outbreak of the common cold."

"You're kidding," spat Buchanan.

Paterson shook his head. "I wish I was. But if these figures are correct our surgeries are woefully understocked and friend Munro has lined his pockets with the rest of the budget. I doubt we'll be able to get what we need in Orkney."

Pincarton nodded. "We'll have to send word to Edinburgh to arrange for replacements."

"How long will that take?" asked Buchanan.

Pincarton shrugged. "Rough guess, about seven days."

"What a complete balls up."

"Well, I think that about covers the science, Jamie," laughed Pincarton. "Mr Robb also drew my attention to some of the actual goods we're carrying."

"Such as?" asked Paterson.

"Apparently there are dozens of boxes of wigs. Now, who exactly do we think might be in need hairpieces in the Tropics? The odd native with alopecia?"

"I think these may have been meant for trade with the North America colonies." suggested Paterson.

"Is that so. But have you seen the actual hairpieces?"

"No, I wasn't involved in their purchase."

Pincarton reached behind this chair and held out a mid-length peruke. "Notice anything peculiar?"

Buchanan guffawed. The hairpiece was bright red.

"Made with hair harvested from the heads of Highlanders."

Paterson gave a rueful smile. "A Sir Robert Blackwood fire sale perhaps?"

Pincarton continued. "Next on the list. I know that Mr. Knox's legacy is a powerful one. But do we really need to be taking two thousand Bibles?"

Paterson answered, "The Board came under considerable pressure from the Kirk and agreed to take quantities of the Good Book."

"Aye well, there's 'quantities' and 'quantities'. I'm not quite sure what the Kirk thinks its success will be in converting the locals, but my guess is that if any of them were for turning, the Spanish and their Papism will have already beaten us to it."

Buchanan was still laughing. "I suppose we'd better work out what the hell to tell our august Commodore."

Pincarton grinned. "Aye, but perhaps leave out the wigs."

Over the next hour the three men fashioned an analysis of the situation to be presented to the other Captains. The practical issue would be how to get them all together since in the fog meaningful contact was next to impossible.

"We'll just have to wait it out, Gentlemen" said Pincarton, finally. "In the meantime I think our labour deserves some small reward." Minutes later his steward appeared with two bottles of French claret.

CHAPTER 2

The following morning the haar had lifted and an hour later Buchanan and Pincarton were being rowed across to the Saint Andrew to discuss the provisioning crisis. Paterson had insisted he attend, but had been quickly put in his place by Pincarton who had once again painted in stark colours that Paterson was aboard under sufferance and would not be a party to the discussions.

The emergency meeting comprised all Councillors along with the other Captains not holding this office. As they entered the Great Cabin of the Saint Andrew, Buchanan registered that Pennicuik had installed himself at the head of the table. No question about who the Commodore thinks is in charge, he thought.

The various representatives from the other ships shuffled in and soon, even the spacious Cabin became uncomfortably cramped. Buchanan was pleased to see Roderick Mackenzie. The two exchanged nods but both knew that this was not the time nor place to be seen to be allied with anyone. It was going to be a rough meeting.

Pennicuik opened proceedings with no thought for pleasantries. The deep lines on his face were creased into a scowl. The voice matched the demeanour. "How the fuck was this allowed to happen?" Then a pause for effect. "For Christ sakes can anyone explain to me why I'm sitting here today?"

It was Captain Robert Drummond who picked up the verbal gauntlet. Here was a man not cowed by anyone. He was only medium height but his barrel chest and tree trunk legs brought significant physical gravitas. "I think several of us are wondering why you're sitting there today, Captain."

The room went completely silent and as pregnant pauses went it was a very long confinement. Pennicuik looked like he was about to self-combust. "What did you just say, Drummond?"

"I think you heard me well enough." The absence of any pretence at civility conveyed the measure of the two mens' contempt.

"You impudent prick. I'm Commodore of this Fleet and if I wanted, I could have you thrown in irons."

"Aye that you could, and then you'd have my brother and the entire soldiery tae contend with."

"Are you threatening me, Drummond?"

"Well bugger me, that's rich coming from a man who just said he could throw me in irons."

If a pin had dropped the noise would have been like the bells of Notre Dame. Buchanan stifled a laugh thinking that all that was needed to complete the Parisian scenario was for the hunch-shouldered Paterson to be present.

Pennicuik and Drummond glared at one another with unconcealed hatred. It was the phlegmatic Pincarton who broke the poisonous silence. "Gentlemen, may I remind you that we're here to try to resolve an issue which could derail our entire venture. Perhaps best to put any personal issues to the side for a moment and address the current problem as best we can."

His measured words had the desired effect.

"Right, let's get on with it then," said Pennicuik in a slightly less antagonistic tone. "Mr. Mackenzie, you've collated all of the inventories. Let's have your assessment."

With his bottle top eyeglasses perched on the end of his nose, Mackenzie fussily arranged his papers before sweeping back a stray hair from his balding pate. He then reeled off the reports from each of the vessels and concluded in a sombre tone. "What it comes down to is that we only have about half the food we need and limited medical supplies."

A baleful murmur filled the crowded room. Pennicuik moved to reassert his authority. "A damnable disgrace. I'll make it my mission to hold those responsible to account."

Buchanan shook his head at the empty rhetoric. It was beyond him how Pennicuik was going to unravel the corruption in Edinburgh from onboard a vessel bound for the other side of the Atlantic.

Pennicuik thumped the table. "We shall make for the Orkneys and take on what we can including any available medicines. The Second Fleet can make up any shortfall."

Drummond couldn't resist the opportunity to have another dig. "Aye, well of course if you'd listened to myself and Captain Pincarton when we were still in Kirkcaldy we wid huv bin able tae comfortably re-stock there and then."

Pennicuik glared at Drummond. "I had strict orders from Edinburgh to proceed without delay to Madeira. Anything else would have been to fail in my duty."

Drummond snarled. "Any sensible man woulda reportit the issue tae the Company and sought further advice. Now wur faced wi' berthin' in the God-forsaken Orkneys for Christ knows how long."

"We'll put into Kirkwall for as short a time as possible," said Pennicuik through gritted teeth.

Pincarton again intervened. "While we can get food there, it would be folly to continue without the necessary medicines. We'd only be creating a rod for our own backs."

"Oh you think so! Well, what do you suggest then?" growled Pennicuik.

"That we request a supply ship from Edinburgh make for the Orkneys with the necessary provisions and await its arrival."

"No, quite out of the question. We can't afford such a delay."

"Why not?" pressed Pincarton.

"Don't dare challenge me! I have my orders which do not include waiting for a fucking supply ship to arrive in Kirkwall."

Clearly Pennicuik was not a man to listen to reason. However, knowing he needed support he embarked on a systematic bullying of the weaker elements in the room. More fearful of Pennicuik's wrath than the displeasure of the objectors, they fell into line, agreeing that orders were orders and that since Pennicuik was Commodore, his directions should be followed.

This brought more protest from Drummond. "Wi' the greatest of respect Commodore whit on earth is the point of huving a Council if they dinnae determine matters democratically?"

"As far as I'm concerned the Council has no currency when we are at sea. And you can take your 'greatest of respect' and stick it where the sun doesn't shine."

This served to kick off another furious shouting match. The arguments raged well into the afternoon but eventually the discussion ground to a frustrated standstill. For all the squabbling, the only thing actually resolved was that the Fleet would berth in Orkney for a period yet to determined.

CHAPTER 3

Even before the dawn of July 24 arrived with all its savagery it was clear that something had dramatically altered in the weather. The gentle zephyr had vanished, replaced by a cold malevolent wind blowing down the North Sea from its big brother, the Arctic Ocean.

The first indicator of the change came in the bowels of the ship where the hammocks began to swing and bang into one another like human Newton's Cradles. Sleep was impossible but much worse was the stomach churning effect of the wave surges. Most of the passengers, unused to the sensation, began to wretch uncontrollably. And to make matters worse, there was no escape. The decks were now slippery death traps and any attempt to go above was blocked by the crew.

Even Buchanan, in the relative comfort of his cabin, was grateful that his bedpan was within easy reach. When he was able to make his way to the Great Cabin he could see the other ships bobbing like corks on the ugly grey sea. A sudden wave knocked him off balance and he banged into the dining table.

"Listing a bit to leeward there, Mr. Buchanan. Been at the grog already?" laughed Pincarton.

Buchanan tried to turn round but only succeeded in falling into one of the bolted-down dining chairs. He thought that this perhaps was a good option in the circumstances. "I'd feel a damn sight better drunk than I do at present."

"Aye, you'll get used to it, son. By the way, this is nothing to what's coming in an hour or so. I suggest you get something in your stomach now as you'll not feel like it when the storm hits."

"This isn't the storm?"

"You have lived a sheltered life haven't you? No, this is just a wee aperitif."

"I can't tell you how happy that makes me."

"Well, at least you made it up. Other than Paterson, your fellow passengers are unlikely to surface."

"So where's William then?"

"Looking after his wife and wean. Some dreadful noises coming from inside that cabin."

"And the Russells?" asked Buchanan.

"Both a bit poorly but not enough for Mrs Russell to miss the chance to lambast her husband for dragging her off to this 'floating shit hole.' Her exact words incidentally."

Buchanan smiled. An odd coupling those two. Then, taking his lead from Pincarton, he filled a plate with some eggs and bacon but after picking at it for a while gave it up as a lost cause. Pincarton on the other hand wolfed his meal and when finished, excused himself to go prepare the ship for the tempest as if it was just another day at the office.

Then it began. A series of gales swept in smashing against the hull of the ship with a force of a giant hammer. Titanic breakers, their crests rising up like giant towers, crashed into the ship and deluged the decks. It shuddered and bucked violently in protest but each time the game little vessel was dumped by the impact, it bounced back up for more punishment like a punch drunk boxer.

Up above, Pincarton was barking orders to the sailors as they raced around like dervishes trying to tie down anything which could be washed overboard. For them there was no respite from the stinging rain and bitter cold which sliced through their sodden clothes like an ice knife.

On the passenger decks, people huddled together as the freezing waters of the North Sea bullied their way through the gaps in the deck planks. They tried to demonstrate the stoicism which they had heard preached from the pulpit, but the pews of the Sunday kirk were a far cry from this the maritime roller coaster. No amount of prayer could overcome their terror as the ship continued its seemingly impossible quest to remain afloat.

The soldiers cowering in the dark belly of the beast suffered most. Their hammocks, bedding and clothing became drenched and as the salt water sloshed beneath them, it mixed with the shit and vomit already caked on the floor. Some cowered in their sodden bunks while others took refuge in their drink rations, allowing the alcohol to numb the horror.

As the visibility deteriorated, the sails of the other ships vanished from view. Pincarton knew that it was impossible for the Fleet to stay close when a wind like this was blowing. It was every vessel for itself. The storm would eventually blow itself out and if nothing else, they had orders to make for Madeira. If they survived they might pick each other up somewhere along the way or in the port itself.

There was no reprieve for two days and nights as the ships were blown around the north coast of Scotland like bobbins in a whirlpool. The howling winds tore at the ship and the sailmakers worked flat out to try to patch the savaged canvas. Every time the Unicorn lurched into another wild pirouette, the lookouts, perched high in the masts, clung to the rigging like the parents of a returned lost child. And on the deck, the crew, lashed to the railings, peered through the horizontal rain searching for the rocks which would sound the death knell of their vessel.

Eventually on the third morning the squalls abated and the raging seas became calm. A flash of blue sky signalled better weather and was soon followed by the first sunshine in days. All around the ship, passengers and soldiers emerged from the bleak oubliette of the lower decks, blinking like startled moles in the milky light.

Pincarton made his way into the Great Cabin and slumped into one of the dining chairs. Buchanan poured him a stiff drink. Draining the glass in a single gulp, he looked up, his face grey with exhaustion. "That was fun."

"We obviously don't share the same sense of enjoyment, Captain."

Pincarton smiled. "Aye. Whichever fool made us sail round the north of Scotland wants his head examined. I'd been praying for good weather for this part of the trip more than any other, but when that blow sprang up I knew we were in trouble. Scapa Flow is one of the worst sea passages in the world in normal conditions. In what we just when through, it's a maritime hell."

"Glad I didn't know that at the time." Buchanan said, trying to lighten the mood.

Pincarton moved to get up but his balance betrayed him momentarily and he slipped back into the seat. He laughed at his frailty. "Maybe another of these might do the trick," he said, motioning towards the empty glass.

They sat in silence for a few moments until Buchanan asked, "Where exactly are we, Robert?"

Pincarton let out a little laugh. "I'm not exactly sure. We'll have been catapulted somewhere west of the Orkneys."

"So what about the supplies? Do we go back to Kirkwall."

"Not in my lifetime. Once you've got your head out of a tiger's mouth you don't stick it back in."

"What do we do then?" pressed Buchanan.

"We'll have to trim the rations until we get to Madeira. Plenty of food and water there if they let us have it. But you can bet we'll be charged handsomely. For now what I need more than anything is some sleep. I'll work out exactly where we are in a few hours. In the meantime, take in the view and thank whatever God you worship that you're here to enjoy it."

CHAPTER 4

Buchanan didn't realise how tired he was himself until Pincarton left. He gave his bunk another chance and was asleep almost as soon as his head hit the pillow. When he woke it was still light but through the porthole he could see the sun beginning to fall. He got up, splashed some water on his face and went into the Great Cabin.

Standing with his back to him was Pincarton, wearing what appeared to be a freshly laundered uniform. Buchanan feeling shabby by comparison, buttoned his jacket, smoothed down his hair and rubbed a finger over his teeth.

Mr and Mrs Russell had also made an appearance and were casually sipping sherry as if they were visiting the country house of one of their landed friends. He was buffering on to Paterson about some business venture but Buchanan paid him little heed as, not for the first time, he was struck by the elegant Mrs Russell.

On hearing him enter Pincarton swivelled round. "Aha. The bold Buchanan released from Morpheus' grip at last!"

"Greetings all. Have I missed much?"

Mrs Russell answered. "Only if the same view of an endless ocean is something to be missed." Mr. Russell gave her a reproving look which she returned with interest.

Pincarton filled him in. "Well, two significant developments. First is that we sighted the Dolphin this morning. Captain Malloch was kind enough to slip across for morning tea while you were having your beauty sleep."

"What about the rest of the Fleet?"

"No idea, nor does Malloch. Looks like the two of us will be making our way to Madeira in reduced convoy. All being well, the others will meet us there."

"And the second thing?"

"Despite the hurricane, I think I've worked out where we are."

He gestured to the map table, strewn across which were several charts. On top of these sat a long wooden instrument about three feet in length which had four different moveable pieces. Pincarton picked up the strange looking object and moved it around in his hand. "This is a cross-staff. By holding it to my eye I can take the altitude of the sun or a star above the horizon to determine latitude."

Buchanan nodded, but was totally mystified by this apparent sorcery.

"Anyway," said Pincarton, "once I have the latitude I can determine the longitude using these maps." He tapped his right index finger on the rolled out scrolls on the desk. "These were invented by a rather clever Flemish chap called Mercator."

Again, Buchanan was completely lost. "Robert, I'm just a simple lawyer."

"How could I forget! Well the long and the short of it is this is where the Gods deposited us." Using a different map he pointed to a spot north and west of the Outer Hebrides.

"So how far are we from the islands?" asked Buchanan.

"About fifty miles," said Pincarton.

"So do we head to this one to re-provision?" Buchanan pointed to the largest land mass.

"What, you mean Lewis and Harris?" said Pincarton.

"No, the big one," replied Buchanan signalling again the large island.

"That is Lewis and Harris," laughed Pincarton.

"But it's only one island."

"Yes I know that, but the islanders are more than a bit tribal. One clan live in Harris and other in Lewis and never the twain shall meet. So the single island in effect becomes two."

Buchanan shook his head. "Utterly bizarre. Anyway, are we going there?"

"The short answer is 'No'. The long answer would involve explaining tides, winds, sailing times and seasonal storms but given your failure to grasp how this wee stick works that would be wasted."

"So, next stop Madeira then, Captain?" asked Mrs Russell.

"Indeed, Madam."

Just then there was a knock on the door and the steward appeared with tea. Buchanan sat down and watched as Mrs Russell insisted on being mother, making a point of brushing Buchanan's hand as she slid the fine china cup towards him.

CHAPTER 5

For the next few days the wind was a zephyr and the sun shone clear and bright. The downside to the halcyon conditions was the slow progress made by the Unicorn. This wasn't helped by having to trim its sails from time to time to allow the smaller Dolphin to keep pace. It lagged behind like an absent minded little brother but Pincarton accepted its dawdling with a philosophical shrug of his shoulders.

On the second day after the storm a cry of "Land Ho!" came up and the passengers rushed onto the decks. About five miles to port sat a tiny set of islands which looked like they could be covered with a few good sized rugs. Pincarton told them this was St Kilda, the westernmost of the Outer Hebrides, inhabited by around one hundred and fifty hardy souls. However, the sea cliffs and capricious surf made it inaccessible for vessels their size.

As the archipelago faded from view, few among the passengers knew that this was the last land they would see for weeks. All that awaited was mile after mile of ocean stretching endlessly to the horizon.

Buchanan quickly came to appreciate that the pivotal punctuation points of the day were mealtimes. For passengers below decks breakfast was bread and porridge. Lunch would be salted meat or dried fish of some sort, apples or prunes, beans or peas and the staple of the hardtack biscuits. Dinner was usually the leftovers of the day and as with all the meals was washed down by beer or water.

Three feeds a day were a luxury for those passengers who had suffered through the recent devastating years of famine. But the less disadvantaged soon became weary of the monotonous diet and the increasing need to check their food for signs of the unstoppable maggots and beetles.

For those eating in the Great Cabin, life was very different and courses of meat or fish would be supplemented by vegetables followed by cheeses. All were accompanied by fine wines. However, Buchanan had not fully anticipated the devastating tedium of the same featureless watery panorama. The company on board, limited though it was, proved diverting enough for a few days. But familiarity soon bred indifference and the close quarter living caused some friction especially when the opinionated Paterson or Russell got onto their soap boxes. He could feel his mind becoming gradually more inert and most afternoons he just sat on the aft deck looking out at the rippled summer sea.

Then about a week into the crossing, life took a turn for the better. As he lay in his bunk one cool starless night, he heard a quiet knocking. Easing open the door he found Mrs. Russell standing in the passage wearing a white cotton night-dress. She carried a candle in one hand and shielded the flame with the other. Her eyes were wide in the light and her teeth shone like pearls against the ruby of her full lips.

"Are you alone?" she whispered.

"Would I be anything else?"

"Sorry to disturb you, but I can't sleep."

"And Mr. Russell?"

"Comatose and snoring like a pig."

"Must make life difficult."

"It does, but that's not why I can't sleep."

"Is that so?" said Buchanan feeling distinctly uncomfortable but aroused at the same time.

He glanced along the passage and seeing no movement stood aside as she brushed past him. Setting down her candle, she climbed into his bed. She opened the covers and smiled provocatively. "Come on, then."

Buchanan looked at her, beautiful in the flickering shadowy light. He knew this was a very bad idea.

"There's nothing I'd like more, but what about your husband?"

"Don't give that a second thought. Mr. Russell isn't interested in me or any other woman. His pursuits lie elsewhere."

Buchanan nodded. "I see, but isn't this…"

She placed a finger against his lips. "Our marriage is an arrangement pure and simple. I have security and position and he has a trophy wife."

"And sex?"

"We turn a blind eye to the other's peccadilloes. I don't resent his young men and he is not jealous of my needs. And I am a much nicer person when I've had a good fucking. So, come and make me a nicer person."

She wriggled backwards to make room for him. Buchanan sat on the edge of the suspended bed, momentarily testing its robustness. It seemed untroubled by the extra weight.

He stood up and with his back to her began to remove his nightshirt. He was fully erect now.

"No need to be shy," she said.

"I'm not. Just don't want to turn round too quickly and poke your eye out."

She laughed, a deep throaty, dirty laugh and immediately he placed his hand against her mouth to stop the noise carrying. Now naked, he slipped under the sheets and put his arms around her. But then she pushed him away and sat up. His first thought was that she had been stringing him along but the movement was only so that she could ease the nightdress above her hips and over her head. She watched his eyes take in her body, hair cascading over her shoulders to frame the small round breasts which sat firm and proud.

"One minor compensation for not having children." she said.

"Not so minor if you're lying where I am," he replied. "This might be tricky."

"Don't worry. I'm very imaginative."

Constance Russell was true to her word and totally uninhibited. She arranged herself on top of Buchanan with a practised skill which spoke to the fact that this was not her first carnival ride.

She let her soft full body sway and rock in unison with the ship's roll over the ocean. Buchanan began to keep time but she put a hand on his chest and said, "Just you lie still, look pretty and keep what's between my legs good and hard until I've finished." Placing Buchanan's hands on her gyrating buttocks she gave instructions for him to squeeze them with varying degrees of pressure. Very soon she arched her back and her whole body went rigid. She moaned as she came and then her long hair fell over his face as she slumped on top of him.

He could feel the heat from her and the sweet smell of her breath. He tried to kiss her but she pulled away. "This is just sex, Jamie. No need for intimacy."

Buchanan nodded. "Suits me perfectly, Mrs Russell. Now before we try for your second coming do you think we could focus on my first?"

"But of course. This is a tit for tat deal after all," as she placed his hands on her petite breasts.

When they had finished she slid off him and silently replaced her nightdress. Then she kissed his nose and whispered. "Thank you. I needed that."

He was still smiling as she slipped away, back to where her snoring husband lay dreaming about cabin boys.

CHAPTER 6

The journey to Madeira took a further four weeks. For Buchanan, the boredom of the days was offset by the delicious diversion of Mrs Russell's nocturnal visits. Lost in their fevered coupling, they would crash about in the tangle of his sheets and be transported to a place far from the hardship of the voyage.

Pincarton was aware of everything that occurred on his vessel and delighted in teasing Buchanan about the clandestine shenanigans. At any breakfast following a night time visit, Pincarton would invariably comment on how well Mrs Russell was looking and that the sea air must be agreeing with her. He would then turn to Buchanan and remark how exhausted he appeared. All this was said with a twinkle in his eye as Buchanan squirmed uncomfortably beside the oblivious Mr. Russell.

Then in the course of that four weeks, the inevitable occurred. Disease reared its ugly head. When it took hold it spread quickly and didn't discriminate between high born or low.

When reports of ill-health began to percolate Pincarton had sent Robb to inspect the passenger quarters. His report didn't make for easy listening. Scurvy was running riot and conditions were deteriorating quickly. The stench of excrement and vomit hung in the stale air and despite the presence of the voracious ship's cat, the rat population continued to grow.

Scurvy began with swollen gums and black blotches beneath the skin before the afflicted lost all energy and slipped into a torpor. The only available treatment was a diet of sauerkraut, meat soup and malt extract.

Pincarton immediately instituted a stricter hygiene regime. Everyone had to wash regularly or be denied their rations. An increased rota for scrubbing the quarters was implemented. Bedding and clothes were laundered by tying them in a bundle which was tossed overboard on a line and towed behind the ship so that the turbulence of the wake could wash them clean. Although this caused the materials to become abrasive from the sea salt, they were at least free from lice and shit.

After a week the scurvy outbreak had improved only to be superseded by the dreaded dysentery or 'flux'. This brought on excruciating belly cramps, diarrhoea and fevers. It claimed its first victim in the last week of the voyage to Madeira. Word came late one afternoon when the ship's doctor, a young man called Ritchie, was ushered into the Great Cabin. He looked dog tired.

"Good afternoon Mr. Ritchie," said Pincarton.

Ritchie glanced at Buchanan and Paterson, prompting Pincarton to add. "You can speak freely."

"Right you are, Sir. I'm sorry to report that a soldier has died from the flux."

"Was he one of the quarantined?" asked Pincarton.

"Yes, Sir. "

"Well, that's something. Any sign of it spreading past the isolation quarters?"

"Not yet."

"Good. Do all you can to keep it that way. Under no circumstances let anyone other than essential personnel in there."

"Aye, Captain. There's a guard posted to do just that."

"Well done. Ritchie. Come and sit down. You look all in. Will you take a dram?"

"Thank you, Sir."

The young medic took a tumbler from Pincarton and the amber liquid disappeared in a single swallow. Pincarton refilled the glass. "Go easy this time son, as you'll not be getting any more."

Ritchie smiled sheepishly.

"How many cases are there?" asked Buchanan.

"Fourteen. Well thirteen now," said Ritchie.

"What's the treatment?"

"Treatment? God, I wish there was one. A soul's no sooner taken with the flux than he looks upon himself as dead. I'm just trying to keep them hydrated. We mix a pint of water with half a teaspoon of salt and six teaspoons of sugar and try to get them to swallow. Apart from that we clean up their shit and vomit and keep them away from everyone else."

"So, is the body prepared?" asked Pincarton.

"It is, Sir."

"Aye well in that case let us go and show our respects. Come on, Mr. Buchanan and see how we do things at sea."

They left the Great Cabin and walked onto the top deck. Two soldiers emerged from below carrying a long heavy-looking sack. Buchanan got a jolt when he saw it. "What the hell?" he exclaimed.

The body was inside the sown up canvas but the head left partly exposed. One of the rough stitches went straight through the poor unfortunate's nose. Pincarton could see Buchanan's confusion. "We put the last stitch through the snout to prevent us sliding someone overboard who might only be unconscious."

"You're joking."

"Not at all. A coma can be a strange creature, Jamie. Bodies can give every outward appearance of being corpses but are actually still alive. I'll guarantee that if you go to any pub in Leith or Portsmouth you'll see more than one scarred snuffler which has been the salvation of the lucky prick who'd otherwise be fish food."

"Sweet Jesus," muttered Buchanan, shaking his head.

Pincarton nodded. "Aye. Well we're not finished yet."

Buchanan watched as the sack was carried three times round the main mast. The Reverend then said some solemn prayers and the ship's bell was tolled. One of the soldiers beat out a mournful eulogy on a drum as the body was rolled from a plank into the waiting arms of the ocean. The sack was weighted with a cannonball to prevent defilement by sharks and all present bowed their heads as the corpse hit the sea with a sorrowful splash.

Pincarton looked at Buchanan. "Let me guess your next question? Why three times round the mast?"

"You're a mind reader."

"Sailors are the most superstitious creatures on God's planet. They believe that if the funeral isn't conducted exactly this way then the deceased's soul can't be at rest and will return as a massive wave."

"Fair enough. I'd rather have three times round the mulberry bush than a freak tidal wave," smiled Buchanan.

"Let's hope this is last one before Madeira," said Paterson.

"Aye," whispered Pincarton. Then after a pause he turned to the doctor. "Carry on, Mr. Ritchie and do your best to keep the numbers down."

"I'll try, Sir," he replied, saluting as he took his leave.

Buchanan lingered in the fresh air after the others had left. The sun was beginning to fall in the blue Atlantic sky and he could feel the change in the wind. This was no longer the chill crisp breeze of the North Atlantic. It now carried a gentle warmth and was infused with a different smell redolent of exotic herbs and spices.

He craned his neck hoping to somehow usher in an earlier arrival at Madeira. But that would be another five days away, during which the drum roll would sound eight times more.

CHAPTER 7

It started as a low rumble and began to build. Buchanan was lying in his bunk, letting his body wake in its own time. Mrs. Russell had been particularly energetic the night before but a gentle entrée to the day became impossible when he heard the sound of feet running past his cabin and excited voices fill the air. It could mean only one thing.

Everyone had known in the last couple of days that they were getting closer. Birds had landed on the deck looking for scraps and it was only a matter of time until the Unicorn found its way to their land.

Buchanan got up quickly, cursing as he banged his knee against the corner of the bunk. He dressed hurriedly and shoved open the cabin door nearly taking out Robb as he rushed past. Collision avoided, he looked at the animated face of the first officer. "Madeira?" asked Buchanan.

"Madeira!"

The two men raced onto the aft deck where they found Pincarton and the other elite passengers. In the distance an island rose jaggedly from the ocean. Even from this distance it appeared lush and dramatic, its peaks seeming to fall straight down onto the beaches as if it couldn't be bothered with the nuisance of foothills.

Every deck was packed with seamen, colonists and soldiers, all anxious to get a glimpse of this exotic paradise. The preceding six weeks had been the hardest many of them had endured and the prospect of being able to feel solid ground beneath their feet was something most would have given their eye teeth for. Although in fairness there weren't too many still possessing those bargaining chips.

Pincarton acknowledged Buchanan with a nod and Paterson slapped him on the back with uncharacteristic glee. "We've made it, Jamie. That's the worst of the trip done."

"So, no more storms then?"

"Certainly not like that monster we got in Scapa Floe."

"That's alright then," grimaced Buchanan, not quite sure if he was reassured or not.

Pincarton then disappeared into the Great Cabin and asked Buchanan to follow him. Spread out on the chart table was a large relief map of Madeira. Pincarton jabbed a finger at a spot on the south east of the landmass. "That's where we're headed, Jamie."

Buchanan peered at the map. "Funchal?"

"One of the prettiest places on Earth."

"Think we'll get a good reception?"

"We should do. The Portuguese own it and should have no quarrel with us Scots."

"Should?"

"Well, Portugal and England have been thick as thieves since their alliance in 1373. Never waged war against each other since then."

"Pretty chummy, then."

"You could say that. There's a large English community on Madeira and even a Consul."

"Think he'll queer the pitch for us?"

"Can't say, but I'm sure you flashing the Company's Act at them should do the trick."

Buchanan smiled but then a thought occurred. "If Pennicuik isn't in port are you going to wait for him before going ashore?"

"Seriously, Jamie? Thought you had more common sense than that. First off, if none of the other ships has made it, how do we know that they'll even arrive? For all I know the Unicorn and Dolphin are what's left of the Fleet."

"Fair enough. And second?"

"Ever seen a mutiny? Not a good thing I can assure you. If I tell these good folks that they have to stay on the Unicorn until the rest of the Fleet turns up they'll jump ship."

"But most of them can't swim," said Buchanan.

"Don't worry. The fall would probably kill them anyway."

Buchanan laughed, pleased to be in the hands of this affable mariner. "You been here before?"

"A couple of times. Lovely place but the people are not Braganza nobility if you get my drift. They'll steal the eyes out your head if you're not careful."

"How long do you think we'll be there?"

"Enough time to get everyone healthy and the ship re-supplied. So maybe a week or two but not so long that their passion for this grand endeavour wanes and we get folk wanting to stay on Madeira or hop on a ship back to England."

"There'd be a good few in that camp right now."

"Right now, that's how nearly everyone is feeling. But trust me, after some time ashore the fire returns to the belly. Remember, they all signed up voluntarily, so they've more desire to see it through than most."

Buchanan gave a wry smile. Well, not all of us, he thought. Bastarding little Cullen.

"Come on, let's get back on deck," said Pincarton shoving him out of the Cabin. "You don't want to miss this."

How right he was. As the Unicorn drew closer, the spectacular landscape of Madeira came into view. The island represented just the tip of a massive underwater volcano. A towering mountain range covered in greenery formed its spine and was bookended by vertiginous cliffs plunging down to the sand. But what most took Buchanan's breath away were the explosions of colour from the extraordinary flowers which chequered the emerald canvas.

CHAPTER 8

The Unicorns' log showed that it reached Funchal on August 20th 1698, almost six weeks after it had left Leith.

The port nestled in a natural amphitheatre under towering peaks which seemed to brush the sky. Pretty white and blue houses encircled the harbour and overlooking them stood the castle that housed the Portuguese governor's residence.

There were, however, two immediate causes for concern. The first was that no other Scots vessels had arrived in the port. The second was that the one other ship which was anchored was a large man-of-war flying the Genoese flag.

"This might be interesting," said Pincarton. The crowds on the decks below him were oblivious to the issue and continued with their excited cheering and waving. "Mr. Paterson and Mr. Buchanan would you please prepare to go ashore? And Gentlemen, please dress well. We will only get one opportunity to make a first impression on the Governor."

Pincarton then addressed his first officer. "Mr. Robb please prepare the pinnace and signal the Endeavour to hold its position."

Pincarton then disappeared into his cabin emerging ten minutes later in full dress uniform, wig and tricorn hat. He cut a dashing figure as he eased himself into the pinnace, swiftly followed by Buchanan and Paterson both in their Sunday best. The oarsmen all wore clean white trousers, dark blue shirts and caps badged with a silver unicorn.

As the little boat made its way into the port, the trumpets sounded on the Genoese ship signalling the trundling out of its cannon for any possible engagement. As the pinnace passed, Pincarton made great play of standing up and saluting the vessel and then doffed his cap in a show of amity. When he'd sat back down he turned to his companions. "Obviously no-one has been expecting us. I also imagine they'll never have seen a vessel flying the Saltire before."

"Well, isn't that just lovely " said Buchanan. "Come all this way and then get blown out the water just because someone forgot to say we were coming for lunch."

After a few minutes of steady rowing the little boat reached the jetty. Awaiting them was a reception committee of local dignitaries, dressed in silk suits and fine wigs. Behind them stood an armed militia of perhaps a dozen men dressed in the grey uniform of the Portuguese army.

Pincarton was first ashore and saluted the group. Standing at its head was a short, almost gnomish man who returned the gesture. Pincarton then offered his hand in greeting. "Captain Robert Pincarton, commander of the Unicorn, in the service of the Company of Scotland."

The rotund little chap stuck out a chubby mitt and in heavily accented English introduced himself as, "His Excellency, Joao de Vasconcelo, Governor of the island of Madeira and loyal subject of his majesty King Pedro the Second of the house of Braganza."

He was obviously a man for whom appearance, status and title were of the utmost importance.

"An honour to meet you, Your Excellency," said Pincarton. "May I introduce senior representatives of the Company of Scotland, Mr. Jamie Buchanan and Mr. William Paterson."

Buchanan thought that Paterson's name seemed to trigger a flash of recognition in de Vasconcelo's eyes but the Governor said nothing to confirm the suspicion. However, it was clear that he was somewhat bemused. "Captain Pincarton, I am sorry but I have some trouble in comprehending. You say you are from The Company of Scotland?"

"That is correct," replied Pincarton.

"You will excuse my puzzlement but how can it be that Scotland can possess two ships of such size and grandeur but does not fly under the English flag?"

"Your confusion is most understandable, Your Excellency. I would be happy to explain, but perhaps somewhere a little more conducive to discussion." He cast his eyes up at the hot afternoon sun to indicate that the 'somewhere' would preferably be cool and shaded.

"Ah indeed, Captain. Can I suggest we repair to Government House and take a glass of Madeira wine?" Although said with a smile, de Vasconcelo was clearly not convinced as to the Scots' intentions.

The short ride was taken in an open top landau and as the horses clopped along the pretty cobbled streets the three Scots took in the sounds and smells of this paradise. Birds of all hues darted past and the roadside was lined with blue agapanthus and orange proteas. The air was balmy but the humidity made tolerable by the gentle breeze feeding off the ocean. Buchanan wondered that if Darien was in any way, shape, or form like this, then perhaps having to leave Glasgow would turn into one of life's great blessings.

They entered the whitewashed building through an interior courtyard. De Vasconcelo ushered them into a large cool room which was illuminated by shafts of bright sunlight diffused through the slats of cream plantation shutters. He invited the trio to sit and gave some instructions to a servant. The Governor was happy to wait in silence until the man returned carrying a silver tray laden with fruit and wine. De Vasconcelo nodded his head and four glasses of dark red Madeira were poured.

De Vasconcelo took his glass and raised it in a toast. "To the intrepid gentlemen of Scotland." The others followed suit and took a sip of the delicious wine.

"Now, please tell me what you are really doing here?" de Vasconcelo asked sharply.

Pincarton replied. "Your Excellency, I can assure you that we are who we say and represent the Company of Scotland. The only surprise should be that the English Consul in Funchal has not advised you of our existence."

"And why should he have done that, Captain Pincarton?"

"Simply because the English Government and its trading houses have been following our every move since King William provided Scotland with a Royal Charter to found its own colony."

"Pah. You mock me, Captain. Why would the English do this when they have a stranglehold on trade in your Islands?" de Vasconcelo scoffed.

"Perhaps I should defer to the architect of the Scheme. Mr. Paterson, would you care to provide His Excellency with some background but perhaps in an abridged format?"

"I would be delighted," said Paterson, almost salivating at the opportunity. He then proceeded to narrate the history of the Company and did not disappoint when it came to describing his key role in events. When this had finished de Vasconcelo stroked his chin, obviously deep in thought. "Mr. Paterson, I have heard of you in respect of your work with the Bank of England."

Buchanan swore that Paterson's head swelled to double its size.

"However," continued de Vasconcelo, "what proof can you provide that this Company exists, and that you are not some outlaws fleeing William's navy?"

"Mr. Buchanan, if you will."

Buchanan reached into his leather satchel and produced a copy of the Company Act which he handed to de Vasconcelo. "This, Your Excellency, is the document which validates all we have said."

The Governor scanned the papers and slowly his demeanour changed. "Well, Gentlemen, it appears that you are not brigands and since you fall under the guardianship of a friend of Portugal, please be welcomed to Madeira."

"Your Excellency is too kind," said Pincarton. "We may shortly be joined by others of our Fleet and trust they will be equally well received."

De Vasconcelo bowed his head. "Most certainly Captain. Madeira thrives on trade and I expect we will be able enter into some mutually beneficial dealings. In the interim, please make yourself comfortable in our town. I am also sure that the English Consul will be eager to meet with you."

The three Scots exchanged glances but it was Paterson who spoke. "By chance is the Consul either Samuel Brooking or Edward Potter?"

"You know these men?" asked a clearly astonished de Vasconcelo.

"Our paths have crossed."

"Well, why did you not say so earlier? They are both highly regarded merchants in Madeira, and indeed, Sir Samuel is the consul," said de Vasconcelo, now visibly impressed by the calibre of the men before him. "I shall arrange for us all to take dinner together."

"Thank you for that," said Pincarton with a little bow.

De Vasconcelo drained his glass. "Now, before you return to your ship, please come to the balcony so that I can officially welcome you."

He led them out onto a large veranda which overlooked the entire port, summoned one of his guards and muttered a few words into his ear. Five minutes later there came from below the boom of a twelve gun salute indicating to the townspeople that the new arrivals were welcome guests.

Pincarton, aware in advance of the form, looked out towards the Unicorn. He searched the poop deck which was barely visible from this distance but then saw the reflection of the sun on Robb's telescope lens. At this, he took a white kerchief from his pocket and held it in front of him. Thirty seconds later there came from the Unicorn the thunder of twelve cannonades in reply.

De Vasconcelo dipped his head in acknowledgement and walked out with the Scots to the waiting carriage. As they made their way back to the jetty Buchanan turned to his companions. "You both never cease to surprise me."

Pincarton smiled. "It is not my first dance, Jamie. But William, what a trump card to play. A friend of the English Consul, no less."

Paterson was quiet for a second before replying. "I didn't exactly say how our paths had crossed."

Pincarton laughed. "So, are we in trouble then?"

"Not as long as we have the King's protection."

CHAPTER 9

As soon as he got back to the Unicorn, Pincarton asked Robb to assemble the entire ship's company on deck. Most of them were already there, tantalised by the prospect of strolling on Madeira's white shores and bathing in its warm water.

Pincarton rang the ship's bell to call for silence and after a few seconds the hubbub died down. "Ladies and Gentlemen, I am delighted to advise that the Governor has given us permission to go ashore."

A cheer shot up and Pincarton had to raise his arms to restore quiet. "However, let me make several things very clear to each and every one of you. We are here as ambassadors for Scotland and our Company. As such, any behaviour which brings either into disrepute will not be tolerated. If you are a civilian and you cross the line then you will be sent back to England on the next available ship. If you are under my command as a sailor or soldier you will be severely punished. Is this clear?"

There was an uneasy silence before Pincarton shouted. "Is this clear?" A muffled chorus of acknowledgement ensued. "Understand also, that even though Madeira is Portuguese owned, there is a strong English presence here. Their spies will be watching and reporting back to London, so don't give them any cause to criticise us."

Pincarton allowed the import of his words to sink in before adopting a softer tone. "Now, our time here will be an opportunity to rest and recover after the difficult voyage. I want to congratulate all of you on your fortitude and resolve in getting here." This triggered another round of cheering. "When in port we will undertake a thorough cleaning programme. Be aware that my men are not your servants, so when it comes to your living quarters I expect you to do the lion's share of the work."

He then wound up his address. "We anticipate being here for at least a week and hopefully our sister ships will find their way to safe harbour during that time. So, enjoy the break, get yourselves healthy, eat well, but please watch the drink. The Madeira wine packs a punch. Right, off you go."

Pincarton then told Robb to ask Captain Malloch on the Endeavour to deliver the same message. The first officer saluted and hurried off. Pincarton turned to the elite passengers standing beside him. "I don't suppose I need to tell any of you that the same rules apply."

"Even the cleaning?" asked the Reverend James.

Pincarton fixed him with a look that left no doubt as to the answer but saved the clergyman's blushes by replying. "I'd always been told that Kirk Ministers possessed a dry sense of humour. Thank you for confirming it. Now, who wants to pay a visit to the English consul? I'm in the mood to ruffle some feathers."

Buchanan and Paterson showed willing but the others demurred, preferring the other pleasures awaiting ashore. When they'd left, Buchanan asked Paterson. "William, before we go knocking on his door shouldn't you tell us how you left things with Sir Samuel Brooking?"

"Let's just stay that he came off on the wrong side of a business deal I was involved in."

Pincarton cocked an eyebrow. "Well, if it was just business then that's fine. I thought you were going to tell us you'd fucked his sister."

Buchanan exploded into laughter followed, somewhat reluctantly, by Paterson who always seemed a little uncomfortable around the topic of sex.

But for all that, Buchanan thought it interesting that even though Paterson had a dubious history with the consul it wasn't going to prevent him being one of the party presenting the Company credentials. The man's ego was a small planet in itself.

CHAPTER 10

Sir Samuel Brooking was a slim man who stood so erect one would have been forgiven for thinking that a rod had been inserted up his arse. He had deep set eyes and a long aquiline nose together with that peculiar patrician air which comes from being the King's representative on a far off shore.

The Consul's office was gloriously lit by bright sunshine which pierced the half open shutters. Brooking came round from his mahogany desk and offered his hand. His smile seemed genuine and his manner friendly, although Buchanan noticed that when he came to Paterson his eyes took on the cautious look of a dog being offered a scrap of food by a stranger.

Brooking then ushered them to the sitting area in the middle of the room. "I trust you're recovering well from your voyage?" he asked, while pouring some Madeira.

Pincarton took the lead. "A little early in the process, Sir Samuel. But fresh food and clean water are a welcome tonic. Coupled, of course, with fine hospitality." He tipped his glass to the Consul.

"I'm pleased to hear that, Captain. The north Atlantic crossing is never easy." He hesitated as if he weighing up whether to say any more. But he did. "Especially when one starts from Leith."

There it was. No question the English were watching them.

"Not if that's where one's Fleet assembled," parried Pincarton.

"Quite so," said Brooking. "However, I do find it curious that you chose to sail round the north of Scotland rather than take the Channel. A strange route for your intended destination." Brooking was too well bred to be overtly inquisitive, but his eyebrows weren't. They bobbed up and down full of questions.

Pincarton ignored the eyebrows. "Our intended destination?"

"My apologies, Captain. None of my business, I'm sure."

Pincarton looked at his colleagues. Here was a golden opportunity to lay down a smokescreen. He nodded to Paterson who picked up the thread.

"A perfectly appropriate question, Sir Samuel," said Paterson in a fawning tone.

Brooking's eyes narrowed. "Kind of you to say so, Mr. Paterson." His guarded response indicated that the last thing he expected out of Paterson's mouth was anything vaguely complimentary.

"We're well aware of the advantages," said Paterson, "which the Scots Act affords."

"But about which not everyone is too pleased," said Brooking.

Paterson pursued his conciliatory approach. "Yes, I can quite understand why existing interests might feel threatened by a new player in the game."

Brooking looked at him warily. "I'm glad you appreciate the delicate dynamics, Mr. Paterson."

"Dynamics can either work for or against parties."

"Something we know only too well, sir," said Brooking, a little more curtly.

"Yes indeed, commerce is like that," said Paterson before dangling the carrot. "But every situation is different and new possibilities will always arise."

Brooking paused. "Go on."

"Well, given the strategic location of Madeira, it may well be that this would be the perfect staging post for our Company's future voyages."

"Might it?"

"Of course. Anyone sailing to west Africa would see Madeira as an obvious port of call."

"West Africa? Don't tell me Scotland has seen the light and is embracing the slave trade?"

"Never that, but there is far more to West Africa than slaving."

"I'm sure there is, but not enough to warrant it being a destination for your grand Fleet."

Paterson continued to lay the trap and laughed the nervous laugh of one who has been uncovered. "You have me, Sir. But for all that west Africa will still be another useful stopping off point for…" Paterson cut himself short, as if he had said too much and desperately wanted to take back the words.

"Well then, Mr. Paterson," said Brooking, "that can only mean one thing."

Pincarton stepped in to play his part in the charade. "I think that Mr. Paterson may have misspoken, Sir Samuel," he said, levelling a scowl at Paterson.

"Perhaps so, Captain. But we both know that if you are stopping here and in West Africa the only logical destination will be the East Indies," crowed Brooking.

"You may surmise that Sir Samuel," said Pincarton, as he fired another false death stare at Paterson, "but unlike others I can keep a confidence."

Paterson looked away as if embarrassed. Buchanan suppressed a smile at the game which was being played out. No doubt Brooking would deem this a splendid turn of events. His old adversary humbled and he in possession of information which would place him in good stead with his masters in England.

Brooking adopted the magnanimous tone of the victor. "Don't worry Gentlemen, your secret is safe with me."

"Thank you," replied Pincarton. "Now, Mr. Paterson, perhaps you might get back to what you are good at and broach with Sir Samuel some mutually beneficial trade."

The apparently chastened Paterson then spent the next half hour negotiating some excellent deals with Brooking, who one felt had almost taken pity on his erstwhile foe. Buchanan had come to learn that Paterson could talk a starving dog off a meat wagon and the discussions saw some of the Fleet's more questionable trading goods being bartered for fresh food and three thousand gallons of Madeira wine.

When it came time to leave, Brooking left the last farewell for Paterson.

"William," he said, using Paterson's Christian name for the first time. "I appreciate that we have had our past differences. Hopefully we can put those behind us and use today as a platform for the future."

"I'd like that, Samuel," replied Paterson as he grasped the Consul's outstretched hand.

As the Scots made their way back, Buchanan began to laugh. "Very well played, Gentlemen. Seems that we have a new friend."

"Well, until he finds out where we're actually going," said Pincarton.

Buchanan grinned, "But think of all of that lovely wine going aboard our ships. Something decent to trade at last."

"Indeed," said Pincarton. "Now, all we need is for the rest of the Fleet to turn up."

CHAPTER 11

Their prayers were answered four days later. A cry came from the deck of the Dolphin that three ships were approaching Funchal. When confirmation came that these were the Saint Andrew, Caledonia and Endeavour, wild celebrations broke out and Pincarton ordered six cannons be fired to welcome the stragglers.

He then sent Robb to advise Commodore Pennicuik that a bridgehead had been established and the Scots were welcome to berth. Pincarton had expected the response to be peppered with a little gratitude. Instead, when Robb returned he wore the haunted look of a man who knew he was about to deliver bad news and would give anything for someone else to do it.

"Mr. Robb, by your demeanour can one assume that Commodore Pennicuik's reaction was not what we'd anticipated?" asked Pincarton.

"No, Sir," said Robb, little beads of sweat beginning to form on his brow.

"Well, don't keep us in suspense."

Robb cleared his throat and read from a piece of paper. "I took the liberty of writing down the Commodore's exact words to avoid anything being lost in translation."

"A savvy move, Mr. Robb."

He began to read. "Tell those pricks Pincarton and Malloch to get their arses onto the Saint Andrew toot vitesse and bring with them any fucking councillors they can find."

"That's it?"

"Yes, Sir."

"I see. Thank you, Mr. Robb. Please alert Captain Malloch."

"Yes, Sir," replied Robb, now breathing a little more easily.

Pincarton turned to Buchanan. "Let's go and find out what all this is about. No doubt it'll be Pennicuik feeling affronted about something."

Buchanan nodded. "Maybe William should join us given his relationship with the Consul?"

"Fine by me. What say you Paterson?"

Seeing the limelight beckon, Paterson jumped at the chance. Thirty minutes later the trio came alongside the Saint Andrew and found Captain Malloch already being hoist aboard. He had with him his First Officer. Whether this was for moral support or as a reliable witness was anybody's guess. Inside the Great Cabin they found the remaining Captains and Councillors.

The newcomers to Madeira looked tired and haggard especially compared to those who had already spent five days convalescing. Buchanan thought this would do little to soothe Pincarton's savage brow. The Commodore's opening remark confirmed this. "At last. Sorry if I had to drag you away from your siesta. I thought you were never going to arrive."

Pincarton retorted with an easy grace which disguised the punch. "Indeed, Pennicuik, we've been thinking the exact same of you. It comes as a great relief to see you all."

"Well, quite. But it would have been a deal easier if I hadn't these mutinous vipers to contend with."

He stabbed a finger in the direction of Captain Robert Drummond and his brother, Thomas, one of the military men. Buchanan saw Thomas make a move toward Pennicuik but he was restrained by his sibling.

Pincarton spoke calmly. "Mutiny is a serious charge Pennicuik. What are the grounds?"

There then followed a litany of accusation and counter accusation from the different factions. It emerged that the issues were twofold. The first was Pennicuik's allegation that Robert Drummond had deliberately lagged the Caledonia behind the Saint Andrew. Drummond fiercely rejected this, explaining that his vessel was far smaller and slower than the flagship and in any event what possible reason would he have to prolong the voyage. Pennicuik rebutted that it was done out of petty spite.

The second was that when the ships had lain motionless in the doldrums off the coast of Portugal, some ships officers had gone aboard the other's vessels to socialise. During one of these visits it had been alleged that the Drummonds had discussed plotting to oust Pennicuik and seize command of the Saint Andrew. The Drummonds threw scorn on this notion and fired back that the source of these allegations should be carefully considered. The agent provocateur was Lachlan MacLean, one of the soldiery. His hatred of the Thomas Drummond stemmed from Glencoe and he would do anything to discredit him.

The argument continued to blaze for the best part of fifteen minutes and deteriorated into a slanging match. Buchanan watched it all play out with a mixture of fascination and dismay. That most of these men were to constitute the Company's representative body on the Colony was terrifying. The schisms were already acute and they had only reached Madeira, for God's sake.

Roderick Mackenzie silently implored Pincarton to intervene. However, it appeared that Pincarton was enjoying the spectacle too much to intercede directly. He did what any astute Pontius Pilate would do and passed the buck. Winking at Buchanan, he said, "Seems to me that we should ask the Company lawyer to determine the procedure to be followed."

Pennicuik was the first to seize on the suggestion. "Well, Buchanan? Surely there's enough evidence to have these men stripped of their rank and sent back to Scotland."

"That'll be right," said Robert Drummond. "The only thing there's enough evidence of is your unfitness to command a row boat never mind the Company's flagship."

This kicked off another round of abuse. However it gave Buchanan some breathing space and when the shouting eventually stopped he was ready. "Gentlemen, if I may," he said in a sharp voice which indicated that this was not really a request. He had had enough of this bullshit. "It's clear that this matter isn't going to be resolved by continuing down the current path."

The statement was an obvious one, but struck a chord. "Firstly, the

Council has the power to determine if a breach of Company rules has occurred sufficient to warrant dismissal from the expedition. Agreed?"

Of course, nobody other than Buchanan and perhaps Mackenzie had the faintest notion as to what the Company rules might say, so there was no push back. "I'll take silence as agreement. In short, the situation is that the allegations against the Drummonds must be crystallised and a vote taken."

The precise dispassionate manner of Buchanan's delivery deterred any objections. "The motion can be distilled to this, that Robert and Thomas Drummond have planned or incited mutiny against Commodore Pennicuik and should be dismissed from the Company with immediate effect."

The stark articulation of the position generated fresh uproar. Again Buchanan waited for the furore to subside. "Gentlemen. Let us be absolutely clear. This is the nub of what has been discussed. If matters are not brought to a head and concluded then this will fester like an open sore."

Buchanan could see Pennicuik and the Drummonds doing the arithmetic about how the Council members might vote.

It was at that point that Paterson asked to be heard. "Gentlemen, while I completely agree with Mr. Buchanan's legal framing of the issue, can I suggest a caveat which might help find a middle course?"

"Go on, then," snapped Pennicuik.

"It's acknowledged that Edinburgh entrusted Commodore Pennicuik with command of the Fleet for the duration of the voyage."

"Their mistake," said Thomas Drummond, "was giving it to the useless prick in the first place."

This set off another barrage of insults before Pincarton bellowed. "Enough! Let's hear Paterson out." When Pincarton bellowed everyone listened.

"I propose," said Paterson, "that the Motion be amended to read, Robert and Thomas Drummond have been accused of planning or inciting mutiny against Commodore Pincarton and should be dismissed from the Company with immediate effect *unless* they agree to submit to Commodore Pennicuik's authority while the Fleet is at sea."

The factions entered into hurried whispered discussions. For Pennicuik it would allow his authority to be restored. For the Drummonds it would remove the uncertainty of a negative vote.

Pennicuik was the first to speak. "Agreed."

Robert Drummond sought some clarification. "Mr. Paterson when you say 'while at sea' does that mean when we reach our destination his authority ceases to apply?"

"That was the intention." He then turned to Pennicuik, "Commodore, is that in line with your view?"

"Believe me, Paterson I will want nothing to do with those two when we reach that point."

The amended Motion passed without objection. It laid down a marker against the Drummonds but let them continue as part of the travelling circus provided they towed the line. On the other hand, Pennicuik's authority was confirmed but its boundaries now set. For the second time that week Paterson had proven himself in the heat of a tricky negotiation.

CHAPTER 12

Funchal proved to be a much needed salve for the ragged tempers and tired bodies of the travellers. The Portuguese proved to be amiable hosts. The air was full of exotic aromas and its warmth and humidity eased their aches and pains, bringing smiles to even the most Presbyterian countenances.

But on the other side of the ledger, Funchal represented the first time that most passengers had been confronted with the harsh reality of slavery. Madeira, as a principal staging post, contained a sizeable number of slaves who had been bought by the locals. The Scots saw the poor cowed souls, eyes blank like automata, just trying to get through each day. Mrs Russell was particularly affected and was little comforted when Pincarton advised that compared to the West Indies and the Americas, the treatment of the slaves in Funchal was benign.

However, the most significant development during the stopover came four days after the arrival of the other ships. Buchanan, Mackenzie and Paterson were lunching in a small tavern at the far end of the harbour where Mackenzie had been entertaining the others with tales of life under the bizarre command of the autocratic Pennicuik. The Commodore presented as an insecure megalomaniac seeing conspiracies all around him and treachery in the soul of every man. The Drummond incident had been a prime example.

Then three bottles of wine in, Mackenzie said, "I know this may not be my place, but having seen some of our Councillors at close quarters I think we're going to be in trouble when we reach Panama."

Buchanan couldn't help but laugh. "I think the debacle on the 'Saint Andrew' demonstrates that we're in trouble now."

Mackenzie paused for a second. "No offence when I say this, Jamie, but currently there's nobody on the Council who has the slightest idea of how to oversee a commercial venture."

"Couldn't agree more," said Buchanan.

Mackenzie blew out his cheeks. "Thank God for that. Now, given we're a Councillor short due to Mr. Vetch's illness there should be no objection in theory in proposing a replacement."

"But we're not dealing in theory," said Buchanan, "so just cut to the chase, Roderick."

"Fine. I think the Company needs William on the Council."

"And I think you're right. What say you, Paterson?"

Paterson responded with as much modesty as he could muster. "If others think me fit, then I'd be honoured. But how can it happen?"

Buchanan grinned. "Well, if you can keep that gigantic ego yours in check, it may actually be easier than you think."

The old Paterson would have railed against the comment but now just gave a wry smile. Buchanan continued. "Let's test the water with Pincarton and if he's on board then we can approach the others with some momentum."

"Do you think he'll be receptive?" asked Mackenzie.

"Well he's seen the better version of William over the last two months and his stock has certainly risen since we left Leith."

Two hours later Pincarton had endorsed the proposal and they had written a note to each of the other Councillors. On the back of these, a meeting was convened that evening in the Great Cabin of the Saint Andrew. There wasn't a single dissenting voice when it came to the vote. Some of the Councillors might be involved in their own vendettas but they appreciated that at the end of the day they were all in this together and there was a far better chance of success if William Paterson was at the heart of it. His return from the wilderness was now complete.

CHAPTER 13

The Fleet left Funchal on September 2nd, its holds reasonably stocked and its passengers healthy and rested. The ships had been sanitised and the dysentery brought under control. In the short term, the main challenge for the doctors would be treating the inevitable souvenirs of any stay in a foreign port. Mercifully, there was enough mercury to handle the gonorrhoea but otherwise the medicine cabinets remained woefully under-provisioned courtesy of the venal negligence of Dr. Munro and his Edinburgh cronies.

Before their departure, Buchanan had written several letters and placed them in the hands of de Valasceno. The plump little Governor, for a modest sum, had promised to arrange for any correspondence to be placed on the next ship headed to England. This was not de Valasceno's only such transaction that day and Buchanan reckoned that he probably made more money as a postmaster than as a diplomat.

Shortly before the Fleet set sail one of the ships' surgeons, Walter Herries, had also gone ashore one last time. He had returned with some herb extracts and potions for the medical stores but had also left behind several letters with the English consul for forwarding to his principal employer, the English East India Company.

As the five ships weighed anchor, Buchanan watched the beautiful town slowly disappear from view. A new horizon beckoned and at last the Fleet knew its final destination.

That morning the Captains and the rest of the Councillors had gathered aboard the Saint Andrew to open the identical sealed orders from Edinburgh. Pennicuik did the honours, ostentatiously slicing the wax on his own document with a silver letter opener and making great show of reading the contents aloud.

"You are hereby ordered to make for Crab Island, and if you find it free, to take possession in the name of Scotland. From there you are to proceed to Golden Island in the Gulf of Darien and establish a settlement in the bay located behind this. Executed in Edinburgh, the twelfth day of July, 1698."

There had been a few puzzled frowns in the room. Drummond asked the question on most lips. "Why the hell are we going to Crab Island if Darien is where we're building the colony?"

Maps were hurriedly laid out and pored over. They quickly located Crab Island which sat about eight miles east of the Puerto Rican mainland.

"Anyone know anything about it?" The questioner was Robert Jolly, Captain of the Endeavour. His last command had been several years ago and he'd spent much of the interim stoking his expanding belly. His was another appointment that came largely on the back of contacts and availability.

"It's a Danish protectorate," said Pincarton. "They've a permanent base on Saint Thomas and stuck their flag in Crab Island for good measure. Christ knows why Edinburgh thinks we'll be able to claim it."

"Is it of any value?" asked James Montgomery, one of the soldier Councillors.

"Questionable," said Pincarton. "Geographically it's strategically attractive. But it's next to Puerto Rico so there's the constant fear of the Spanish kicking them out."

"Does that mean they'll cede it us?" continued Montgomery.

"Why of course," Pennicuik sneered. "We'll just turn up and they'll say, 'Welcome Scotsmen, we've been hoping someone would come along to take this pile of shit off our hands!'"

The atmosphere changed immediately. Montgomery's reputation as a fearless combatant in the field was not matched by his intellect and so far he'd felt cowed by Pennicuik's bullying in the unfamiliar environment of the ship. However, revived from the stay in Funchal and infuriated at being humiliated in public, Montgomery exploded. "Who the fuck do you think you're talking to Pennicuik? I've had enough of you and your snide put downs."

The room became electrified by this unexpected rebellion. Montgomery was now in full flow. "All I've heard from you this entire voyage is your negativity and sniping. Are you so pathetically insecure that you have to attack anyone, no matter how innocent their question?"

The outburst took Pennicuik by such surprise that he had no immediate response, allowing Montgomery to continue his diatribe. "I may not be a seaman or know about maps or navigation but I do know about men like you. Lording it over others and swanning about totally oblivious of how much they're detested. They're all pricks, but you're the prick's prick. Well, I'm done. I'm off this ship today."

By this time Pennicuik had gathered himself. He looked around the other faces and realised that Montgomery's words registered as true. But instead of doing the smart thing and try to retrieve the situation, he blundered ahead. "You can do what the hell you want Montgomery. After all you're only here because you were spat out of your high born father's dick. You've added nothing from day one and I'll be happy to see the back of you."

Buchanan doubted if Pennicuik saw the punch before it landed. Fortunately for the Commodore. Montgomery mistimed the blow so that the full impact was avoided. But it was still enough to send Pennicuik reeling back into those behind him. One of them was Robert Drummond who rather obligingly held onto Pennicuik's arm as Montgomery came at the Commodore again. But before he could connect a second time, Pincarton had jumped across the room and had him tight in a bear hug.

"Enough James, enough," he said into Montgomery's ear. "I think you've made your point."

Drummond, seeing that there was no more fun to be had, released Pennicuik.

"I'll have to you court martialled for that, you bastard," Pennicuik snarled.

"Oh Aye. Is that right? Well good luck with that. Think you've got enough support left on the Council to pay you any heed?"

Pennicuik curled his lip. "Get the fuck off of my ship."

"With pleasure, you ridiculous turd." And with that Montgomery stormed out of the room, swiftly followed by Robert Drummond who would be only too happy to extend an invitation for his newest ally to be quartered on the Caledonia. An eerie quiet settled over the rest of the group. After what seemed like an eternity it was Pincarton who snapped the tension. "Well, that was all rather exciting, But can I suggest we get back to the more boring business of finding Scotland a colony?"

Pennicuik still fuming from having nearly been put on his backside was in no mood to take the lead, so Pincarton continued, "Can anyone provide some clarity on these latest orders?"

Captain Malloch piped up. "Clear as mud, if you ask me. Even suppose Crab Island is free, what are we meant to do? Stick our flag in the ground and assert it's now Scottish? What then? Leave some settlers behind to build a separate wee colony before the rest of us toddle off to this Golden Island?"

This brought some much needed laughter but the truth of it couldn't be denied. Pincarton said, "Well, whatever the case we must follow the orders, however futile they seem."

All the seamen and soldiers nodded their approval. Orders must be obeyed. Pincarton then asked, "So, moving along, does anyone know the exact location of this 'Golden Island'?"

There was a worrying lack of response before Pennicuik found his voice. "Dammit man, it's obviously in the Gulf of Darien."

"But how good are your charts for that stretch of coastline?" asked Paterson. "Do any of them have a marking for Golden Island?"

This caused the assembly to jostle for position as they examined the maps. Fingers were traced down the Panama Coast and the Gulf of Darien but no-one could find Golden Island.

"In the name of God," spat Pennicuik. "How the hell did the brains trust in Edinburgh come up with a location which isn't even on our charts?"

Buchanan and Mackenzie both knew the answer. After the meeting with Lionel Wafer in Edinburgh, Lord Belhaven and Sir Robert

Blackwood had gone off and using the notebook sketches Wafer had left with them had unilaterally decided Golden Island was the ideal spot. No further discussion had been invited on the matter. Buchanan looked over at Mackenzie but the Secretary just gave an imperceptible shake of his head. What would be the point in saying anything? However, neither of them had any idea how Crab Island had also become part of the equation.

In the absence of any response to Pennicuik's question, Pincarton took up the baton. "Alright, let's break this down. There are two significant issues. The first is that we've serious doubts about being able to make a legitimate claim on Crab Island." This brought a wave of muttered agreement. "The second is that we don't know the exact location of our final destination. Personally I'm not overly keen to swan up and down the Panama coastline looking for a needle in a haystack."

"That's all well and good, Pincarton, but are you also going to propose any solution?" sniped Pennicuik.

Pincarton brushed off the jibe. "I suggest we plot a course for Crab Island as instructed. But then at a certain point the Fleet should split, with two vessels proceeding north to the Danish colony on Saint Thomas and the remainder to Crab Island."

"Why?" demanded the Commodore, now fearful that any division of his command might undermine his already weakened authority.

"Two reasons. The first to establish whether or not the Danes still assert a claim to Crab Island. The second to try to find a pilot who can take us to Golden Island. The added benefit of recruiting on Saint Thomas is that it's less likely that word will filter back to the English East India Company."

"Fine. But who's going to make the deviation to Saint Thomas?"

"That, of course, is your decision, Commodore, but it would seem to make sense if Mr. Paterson was a party to the discussions on Saint Thomas given his connections."

"But he's currently on your ship, Pincarton."

"Indeed he is, Commodore," said Pincarton playing a very dead bat. He could see Pennicuik weighing up each option. If he went to Saint Thomas then he'd have to put up with Paterson aboard the Saint Andrew.

If he chose Crab Island, then could he trust the group going to Saint Thomas?

Pincarton let him stew for a second or two before playing his trump card. "Of course, if Crab Island isn't claimed by the Danes then any ship going to Saint Thomas would miss out on the glory of planting the Saltire in its white sand."

The prospect of being the person to claim a new territory for Scotland was too seductive for Pennicuik to pass up. With the air of a man trying hard to appear reluctant about doing something he really wanted to, Pennicuik made his decision. "Yes, indeed, Pincarton. In light of the direct orders from Edinburgh I think that as Commodore of the Fleet it's incumbent on me to follow these to the letter."

"Valiantly said, Sir," declared Pincarton without a trace of irony.

"Alright," said Pennicuik. "You go to Saint Thomas and take the Caledonia with you as escort."

Doing this would allow Pennicuik to remove, at least temporarily, the thorns in his side which were the Drummond brothers.

"As you wish, Commodore," said Pincarton, delighted to be heading for the hospitality of the Danish West Indies.

"Well, it's settled then," pronounced Pennicuik, now restored to his self-imagined role of Supreme Commander of the Waves. "Back to your ships, Gentlemen and let's set sail."

CHAPTER 14

Mercifully, the Atlantic crossing was uneventful. The Unicorn surged along in the favourable trade winds, kissing the waves and leaving a glorious white wake.

Three weeks out from Madeira, the Fleet reached the splitting point. The Saint Andrew, Endeavour, and Dolphin sailed south west to Crab Island with the Unicorn and Caledonia heading north west towards Saint Thomas.

The journey to Saint Thomas only took two days and on October 1st, the two ships dropped anchor off Charlotte Amelie, the picturesque little capital, named after the Danish Queen.

Luminous blue water lapped gently at the shore which rose quickly through the verdant foothills to cliffs cloaked in a gentle mist. A massive watchtower, which rose up behind the town and fort, dominated the landscape. There was no doubt that it served its purpose. Before the Unicorn dropped anchor the sound of cannon split the air in greeting. It also didn't escape the Scots attention that they weren't the only ships visiting the port. Idling offshore sat three English sloops which were doubtless intrigued by the appearance of two vessels flying the Saltire and garish Company flag.

Pincarton, Paterson and Buchanan were rowed ashore and met at the harbour by a squat man whose eyes constantly darted from side to side as if he expected misfortune to jump out at any moment. He introduced himself as Johan Lorentz, the Danish governor.

Ten minutes later they were sitting in Lorentz's office with an uninterrupted view of the harbour. Rum arrived along with huge slices of pineapple and sticks of sugar cane. The Governor was evidently happy to have some fresh company and poured the drink liberally, not least into his own glass.

In excellent English, he asked. "So, tell me Gentlemen, to what do we owe your presence here?"

Pincarton responded. "In the interest of openness, we are part of a larger Fleet tasked with establishing a colony for Scotland."

"For Scotland, you say. Well I'll be damned. How did that come about?"

"That, Sir, is a long story but suffice to say we have King William's imprimatur."

Lorentz let out a nervous little laugh. "Well, I hope that we in Saint Thomas are not a target.."

"Not at all Mr. Lorentz. Our mandate only extends to territories not lawfully claimed by others," Pincarton replied.

"That's reassuring. But why sail here?" the governor asked, wary that there may be a sting to come.

"Well, if I tell you the other ships of our Fleet are headed for Crab Island, does that assist?" said Pincarton.

The truth dawned on Lorentz. "Ah! So you've come to find out if Denmark affirms ownership to it?"

"Precisely," responded Pincarton.

The Scots watched with some amusement as the little man's plump face began to twitch as if he was having some sort of medical episode. Eventually, he regained sufficient composure. "Gentlemen, strictly among ourselves, I would gladly hand over all rights to Crab Island tomorrow. However, my hands are tied and the instructions from my masters in Copenhagen are to continue to assert Danish sovereignty over it."

The strange response took the Scots aback. The Governor seeing their surprise sensed he had overstepped his remit. Perhaps the rum and the excitement of the new arrivals had gotten the better of him. "My apologies, gentlemen. I misspoke."

But Paterson was keen to pick at the thread. "No need to apologise Governor. We only ask since, like you, we are bound to follow the instructions of our overlords in Edinburgh."

This seem to comfort Lorentz. "Thank you, Mr. Paterson. Yes, it's never easy to have to follow the orders of those who sit many thousands of miles away divorced from the reality of a situation."

Paterson nodded empathetically. "I couldn't agree more. However, it would be a considerable obligement if you could shed some light on why Crab Island is so undesirable. This would allow us to report back to Edinburgh and avoid any recriminations that we didn't pursue the opportunity more diligently."

Lorentz let a smile play across his lips. He recognised what Paterson was doing. If his comments ever found their way back to Copenhagen and questions asked by his Danish superiors he would be able to advise that he cleverly deflected serious Scottish interest in Crab Island by exaggerating its pitfalls.

"Well, let me just say that between the Spanish constantly casting envious eyes in its direction, pirates using it as a hideout, and the land itself providing little in the way of bounty, there's not a great deal to commend it."

"Do you have a permanent settlement there?" continued Paterson.

"No, but we do visit regularly to ensure that no-one else has."

"So if we were to plant our flag in Crab Island it wouldn't be well received in Copenhagen?" asked Pincarton.

"I think you can safely make that assumption."

The Governor now content that the Scots were not aggressors was happy to continue to pour the rum and enjoy their company. Perhaps it was the fact that he recognised their underdog status in the grand scheme of European politics or maybe it was simply that they all liked a drink. But whatever the case, it was clear was that the Scots had found a kindred spirit in Lorentz.

Just before leaving Paterson asked a favour. "One last matter, Mr. Lorentz. Do you know of a pilot for hire in Charlotte Amelie who is familiar with Central America?"

Lorentz rubbed his podgy cheeks as he contemplated the question. "Can you be more specific Mr. Paterson?"

"You will understand that I am bound by some constraints in what I can divulge."

"Of course, of course. You have my word that I shall be discreet."

"I don't doubt that for a minute. But we have pledged not to reveal certain information. "

"Yes, always a tricky balance," nodded Lorentz.

Paterson paused to choose his words. "What we can say is that we need a man familiar with the stretch of land from Costa Rica to Colombia."

"Panama in other words,"

"You may say that but I couldn't possibly comment."

Lorentz grinned. "Well good luck with that. The Spanish believe Panama is their patch."

"The Spanish believe a great many things which are untrue."

"I'm sure they do, Mr. Paterson, I'm sure they do,"

"So can you help?" persisted Paterson.

Lorentz rubbed his chin. " What I can tell you is that there's a tavern in the town frequented by many of the old buccaneers who've been kicking around the Caribbean for years. That may be your best chance."

Paterson thanked Lorenz and the Scots said their goodbyes before heading back to the Unicorn. A visit to the inn could wait until tomorrow when the effects of the potent island rum had worn off.

CHAPTER 15

Taverns the world over have pronounced similarities. They serve alcohol; make more money if the barmaids are pretty; have a name, the source of which usually is lost in the mists of time; and generally are dens of intrigue where every type of business is transacted.

The tavern in Charlotte Amelie was no exception. Its name had been something Danish but this had been scored out and replaced with the misspelled but straightforward, "Admyrals Inn."

As Pincarton, Buchanan and Paterson entered from the bright sunshine, they felt every set of eyes on them. Not that every face had the full complement of peepers. Many of the clientele were outlaws so any strangers arriving in the small port warranted careful scrutiny. One wrong move could result in instant despatch to ones Creator without an eyelid being blinked.

Pincarton had chosen to wear his uniform jacket. He reasoned that the dark blue of Scotland would immediately set him apart from the English, Spanish, French or Dutch naval personnel all of whom would need to have a damned good reason to set foot across the Admyrals' threshold.

Pincarton sensing the tension, took the bull by the horns. In his finest Scottish brogue he announced, "A very good day Gentlemen. We are representatives from the Company of Scotland which would be delighted to buy all of you a drink."

The mention of Scotland and free drink served to take the temperature down. Anyone who had the balls to waltz in dressed like a tailor's dummy, proudly announce they were from some Scottish company no-one had ever heard of and shout the inn couldn't be all bad.

A pathway to the bar opened up for the trio. The landlord, a giant man with an unkempt beard and disconcerting squint, welcomed them with what looked like a smile. The first words out of his mouth were to demand payment for the drinks but once the lucre had been passed over he became the epitome of hospitality.

"What can I do for you gentlemen?" he asked, in a thick Cornish accent.

Pincarton answered. "We're looking for an experienced navigator."

"And where might you be heading then?"

Rather than go through the same farce that Paterson had played out with Lorentz the previous day he said simply, "Panama."

"Now what would the Scots be wanting down in Spanish territory then?"

"Who says we're going to Spanish territory?"

"Then it must be a different Panama. The Dagos have been there for years. I can tell you that because we've been plundering silver and gold from them for years."

This brought a great roar from the assembled listeners.

Pincarton laughed. "And I tip my hat to you for doing so. But, be that as it may, is there anyone here who knows the lie of the land and wants to make some money?"

Just then a grizzled bear of a man muscled up beside them. He had long straggly grey hair and a bushy black beard flecked with silver. Whether these flecks were orphan hairs or the remnants of last night's dinner was not easy to tell in the dim light. He had once been tall but his back was now slightly bowed with age. However his eyes were bright and quick, and set into a face weathered to the consistency of crocodile skin.

"At your service, Gentlemen," he said, in a surprisingly cultured voice, "Alliston is the name."

Paterson began to cough and splutter. After Buchanan had slapped him a few times on his back he recovered enough to croak, "Alliston. Robert Alliston."

"One and the same Sir. Have we met before?"

Paterson, now quite animated, continued. "Not personally, but I know of you from my days in the Caribbean."

"Is that a fact. And what is it that you know of me?"

"That you sailed with Morgan."

"Ah, the Captain. Splendid chap."

"Were you with him when he sacked Panama City?" asked Paterson.

"That I was Sir, that I was. And pray, how do they cry you?"

"William Paterson," he replied.

"Well in that case I'm happy to make your acquaintance." He struck out a large, gnarled fist festooned with gold rings. Buchanan stared at the misshapen fingers and could not help but think that the only way those rings were coming off was if they were cut off. Either that or the digits to which they were attached.

Alliston shouted over to the barman. "George, a bottle of rum, if you please. On the account of the Company of Scotland."

Alliston then bulldozed a path to a large table and commandeered it from the current occupants.

"So, Mr. Paterson, did you meet Morgan?" he asked.

"Sadly not, but his feats are legendary. Although maybe my young friend here is not so familiar with them."

"I only know his name. Thought he was a pirate." Buchanan answered,

"Ah well my son, that's where you are much mistaken" said Alliston. "The Captain was a privateer and had a commission from King Charlie to seize and plunder as many non-English ships and towns as he liked, He was smart enough to give a proper slice of the booty to his Protector and for that old Charlie boy made him Governor of Jamaica. Lived there in great comfort and wealth until he died about ten years ago."

"And they say that crime doesn't pay." smiled Buchanan.

"So, where in Panama are you fine fellows heading?" asked Alliston.

Pincarton replied. "We can only tell you more when we've agreed terms and you're aboard our vessel. Just accept that we can't risk word of our intended destination getting out."

"Aye, fair enough," said Alliston. "There are always those eager to buy good information. But at least tell me why you want to get to this secret place?"

"To establish a colony for Scotland," blurted out Paterson unable to contain himself.

Pincarton glared at Paterson but Alliston just burst out laughing. "Ah, Paterson, you might look like an undertaker, but man you've a grand sense of humour. A Scots colony in Panama. Very good," he said, as he continued laughing.

The three Scots glanced at each other before Buchanan asked. "We do like our wee jokes Mr. Alliston. But out of interest, why would such a venture be so derisory?"

"Well apart from the weather, the disease and the Spanish, absolutely nothing at all," he replied, sparking off another fit of laughter.

"I'm sure anyone taking on such a venture would be well versed in the issues," said Paterson, a little stung by the comments.

"I'm sure they would, Sir. But I'm also sure that they would bloody well know how to get there too." He chortled again. "All of which makes me even more certain that you've got something up your sleeves other than this cock and bull story about a colony."

There was silence from the Scots. Alliston thought this was just caginess so he went on. "Ah well, keep it to yourselves then. It's neither here nor there to me. I'll get you to where you want to go and then take the first ship back to Jamaica. Been a while since I was in Port Royal."

Pincarton responded. "Excellent. I take it that five Pounds is a fair price for your services?"

"Provided its English Pounds and not that worthless Scottish stuff," he said smiling.

"English Pounds it is." confirmed Pincarton.

"Well in that case you have a deal for ten Pounds, one half upfront."

Pincarton stared at him as if Alliston was asking for his first born. He would have been happy to pay twenty but wanted the old mariner to think he'd come out of the negotiation on top. "You drive a hard bargain Mr. Alliston. So be it, but no payment upfront."

"Ah well, then I'm afraid my services will be unavailable to you."

"Why, don't you trust me?" asked Pincarton.

"Not at all, Captain. It's simply that I have creditors on Saint Thomas who will need paying before they'll let me leave the island," he said with a crooked grin.

Pincarton mulled it over. "Fine. But if you're not on our vessel by sunrise tomorrow I shall bring my soldiery out for a little manhunt."

"You have my word, Captain," said Alliston placing his right hand on his heart.

The Scots now had their pilot. If nothing else it would be an entertaining voyage.

CHAPTER 16

As all this was going on the three English sloops anchored in Saint Amelie had made no attempt to contact either the Unicorn or Caledonia. However, Captain Drummond had readied his crew. He was no friend of the English and, despite the assurances under the Act, trusted them not an inch.

When the landing party got back from the mainland, he joined Pincarton on the Unicorn for a debrief. As the two Captains were conferring, Robb burst in to say that a signal had been received from one of the sloops asking permission to come aboard. Pincarton and Drummond looked uneasily at one another but the code of the sea meant that the request couldn't be denied.

They went out onto the deck accompanied by Buchanan and Paterson and watched as a little rowboat made the short journey across the calm waters of the bay. Paterson peered closely at the approaching figure and asked Pincarton to hand him his telescope. He fiddled with it for a few moments before exclaiming, "Unbelievable!"

"What is it man?" asked Pincarton.

"I know our visitor from way back."

"Are you sure?"

"Of course I am," said Paterson a little tetchily. "There can only be one man sailing these seas with a nose like that."

As the seaman was hoist aboard, those on deck were intrigued to learn what was so special about this man's snout. Paterson wasn't wrong. It was a nose of truly epic proportions, a giant beak dwarfing his other features and seeming to cast a shadow over the deck. The rest of him was unremarkable.

A medium sized, evenly proportioned man in his middle years. But that sneezer was a sight to behold.

Pincarton stepped forward. "Captain Robert Pincarton of the Company of Scotland."

"Captain Richard Moon of the merchantman, 'Caroline.' Very good to meet you."

"And you, Captain Moon. I believe that you are acquainted with one of my colleagues," said Pincarton turning in the direction of Paterson.

Moon's face erupted into a huge smile. "By the beard of Zeus. William Paterson!"

"It's been a long time, Richard."

"Too long, my friend," replied Moon, as he grabbed Paterson in an embrace. The Scot, never the most physically demonstrative, returned the gesture with ill-practised awkwardness.

The group moved into the Great Cabin. Moon took a sip of the Madeira which had been offered and looked at the glass appreciatively. "This is most excellent gentlemen. There is only so much rum a man can drink before tiring of its sickly sweetness."

"What brings you here, Richard?"

"Just re-stocking before heading to Curacao to sell the goods I picked up in New York."

"What are you looking to trade for these goods?" asked Paterson.

"Whatever is good and can be sold into another market. Supply and demand, William, the usual story."

"So what's your main cargo?" asked Pincarton.

"Well, first and foremost I have an abundance of the great narcotic of our age. Hogsheads of the finest Virginia Tobacco which with a few puffs will transport a man to heaven." Buchanan smiled at the patter.

Pincarton, who was fond of his pipe, asked the cost and was staggered to find that the leaf was currently as valuable as silver.

"So, what brings you Caledonian exiles so far from your frozen homeland?" asked Moon.

Even though he appeared a decent cove, Moon was still English, so Pincarton responded carefully. "Just some trade with the Americas."

"Splendid. Perhaps we can do some business? It would save me a great deal of time and effort if I could barter with you chaps rather than trudge down to South America. So what do you have?"

Pincarton continued to shadow box. If Moon had any malevolent motivations, it would be far better dealing with him far away from the other two English merchantman sitting in Saint Thomas. "Captain, we're part of a larger Scottish Fleet. The remainder is anchored off Crab Island and we leave tomorrow to rendezvous with them. Perhaps you could join us there to establish what business can be done."

Moon pondered this. "Well, you know I might just do that. Crab Island is more or less on my way to Curacao and I'm interested to see what you have. If this Madeira is part of it then I'm sure we can come to an accommodation."

The discussion then drifted to other matters and the afternoon slipped by convivially with Buchanan particularly interested in everything the Englishman had to say about the Virginia tobacco business. As the sun began to take its leave, the Scots bade the engaging Moon farewell with the promise to meet up again at Crab Island.

CHAPTER 17

As dawn broke the next morning Pincarton was relieved to see a small row boat approach the Unicorn. Alliston proved to be as good as his word, although it was apparent that he had made the most of his last night in Saint Thomas.

The dishevelled creature was given a dressing down, but seemingly well used to this took the haranguing in his stride before promising to stay sober for the voyage ahead. Pincarton asked Robb to find him a bunk to allow him to sleep off his wild spree on the town.

The journey south to Crab Island took two days and was remarkable only for the resurrection of the penitent Alliston and the first sighting of the shoals of flying fish. They launched themselves out of the water and arrowed through the air like a squadron of silver butter knives over the Unicorn. Not all of them made it and those that fell short proved to be good eating.

The arrangement had been for the Fleet to rendezvous on the more sheltered southern part of the Crab Island. However, as they approached from the north, Pincarton asked for his telescope and frowned.

"Is there a problem?" asked Buchanan.

"There's a small sloop anchored in that bay."

"Can you tell whose flag it flies?"

"Not as yet, but I have my suspicions."

These were confirmed as they got closer. Sitting in a little cove was a ship showing the red and white Danish flag.

Pincarton smiled. "The sneaky bastard."

"Who?" asked Buchanan.

"Governor Lorentz. While we were being wined and dined he

despatched this little chap to ensure Denmark's claim on Crab Island was reinforced."

"Got to admire his gall," said Paterson.

"Especially since he wasn't particularly enthusiastic about its worth. Still, must keep Copenhagen happy."

The Unicorn fired off a round to signal the Danish vessel and received an identical response. Buchanan swore that the sound of its cannon was almost apologetic. Like most things about the Danish it was ineffably polite and understated. The Scots could hear the laughter and high spirits of the sailors on the beach as they waved the flag above their heads.

"Pennicuik isn't going to be too happy when he hears about this," grinned Pincarton.

Indeed Pennicuik, was not best pleased. The Saint Andrew had reached the island four days previously. Having circumnavigated its mass and finding it uninhabited, Pennicuik had made great show of being the first to set foot on its golden beach, ostentatiously planting the Saltire and claiming the land for Scotland.

When he was advised by the new arrivals of the sighting of the Danish landing party, Pennicuik's reaction was predictably volatile. It was little tempered by the news that Alliston had been enlisted as their pilot and Moon would be arriving shortly with some trading opportunities.

Moon's sloop appeared later that day and berthed next to the reunited Scottish Fleet. As the disgruntled Pennicuik had set up camp on the beach, Moon was rowed ashore. The human proboscis was ushered into the Commodore's spacious tent beside the now redundant Saltire. Pincarton carried out the introductions. If Moon had expected a cordial welcome from the cantankerous Pennicuik then he was to be disappointed. The Commodore scowled in the corner like a petulant schoolboy whose milk has been taken away.

It was left to Pincarton and Paterson to show Moon some proper hospitality. A bottle of Madeira lightened the atmosphere as did Moon's unwavering good humour. In due course, the discussion turned to business and Moon asked to see the cargo manifests and some samples of the products on offer. However, when he was presented with a list of wigs, shoes, blankets, heavy woollen cloth, and stockings he almost burst a blood vessel guffawing, especially when he saw the proposed prices.

"No, seriously, Captain Pincarton, enough tomfoolery. Where is the real trading cargo?" he asked between bouts of spluttering.

Pincarton frowned. "I'm not sure I follow, Captain."

"These goods might be of interest to those living in the cold of the Northern hemisphere but we're sitting in the Tropics. So, come on, you've had your fun."

Paterson stepped into the breach. "Richard, I'd have thought that many of these would be of interest to you for your next trip to New York."

"Certainly if that was the direction I was headed. But I'm going south first and don't want to clog my holds. Besides there are dozens of ships coming in from Europe every month with similar items and dare I say it, a damn sight cheaper."

"I see. Well would some fine Scottish Linens be of interest?"

"Ah, now you're talking. Let's put all this inferior tat to one side and let me have a look."

At this Pennicuik emerged from his strop and banged his fist down on the table. "How dare you! If you think these products crafted by Scottish hands are "inferior tat" then you can take your miserable hide off this island immediately."

Moon stared at Pennicuik in disbelief. Was this man serious or was he involved in some bizarre Caledonian practical joke. But confronted by an apparently unhinged individual, Moon erred on the side of caution.

"My apologies if I gave offence Captain. But I'm here at the invitation of your colleagues to enter into some trade."

"Are you really? Or are you just an English spy? Tell me that Mr. Moon."

Moon stared open-mouthed at Pennicuik before turning to Paterson. "William, it was pleasure to see you again but I don't have to put up with this shit."

Appreciating the toxicity of the situation, Pincarton looked straight at Moon. "Can I suggest that perhaps we decamp to the Unicorn to pursue the matter further?"

Moon sized up what was happening and agreed. As he left Pennicuik's tent he heard the bellow of the Commodore's voice telling him to stay out.

Back aboard the Unicorn Moon asked what the fuck had just occurred. Paterson explained that the Commodore's dreams of colonial triumph had been thwarted by a fourteen man Danish ketch and he was not in the best of humours. Moon broke into a laugh. "I can only imagine his face when the news was delivered! But how the hell is he the Commodore of your Fleet."

Pincarton answered. "Well, despite his obvious lack of interpersonal skills he is actually a fine seaman. Beyond that it would be disloyal to comment further."

"I can only wish you good luck then, gentlemen. Hopefully he doesn't have to be rolled out too often in a public relations capacity." He then swirled the wine in his glass. "I'll take as much of this as you want though."

Paterson cast a glance at the others. Each nodded.

"As well as the Linens?" pressed Paterson.

"Yes, those too and any decent whisky. However, whoever advised on the rest of the cargo has sorely misjudged your target market."

This was the second time Moon had criticised the manifests and the gnawing sensation that Edinburgh had burdened the colonists with mercantile white elephants continued to grow. In the end, Moon was happy to exchange some tobacco and a few sorely needed medicines for a few bolts of linen, six barrels of whisky and a dozen barrels of Madeira. Before he left to continue on to Curacao, Paterson took him to one side.

"Richard, you'll have figured out that we're planning on establishing a colony."

"William, I'm not an idiot. How many nails, wood, hammers and other tools do traders need?"

"Yes, quite. Now, I can't tell you exactly where we're bound other than that it's near Panama."

"Panama. By God. The Señors won't take kindly to that."

"Yes, that's what we've heard a few times. But, be that as it may, can I ask something of you?"

"If it's within my gift and worth my while," said Moon with a smile.

"I can certainly guarantee the latter. If I leave word for you in Saint Thomas or Kingston of our location can you undertake to arrange for supplies to be sent?"

Moon pondered this. "How can I be guaranteed payment?"

"We can provide you with drafts on our Company agents in New York. They have funds from Edinburgh and will arrange for you to be kept whole."

"In that case I'd be happy to oblige," he said, holding out his hand to seal the bond.

The two men returned to the others and Paterson explained the arrangement. Buchanan drew up the necessary drafts which were then signed by both sides. Mackenzie would transmit word to New York confirming the validity of the agreement. The traded goods were then quickly transferred and the parties went their separate ways.

CHAPTER 18

The Scots left Crab Island on October 7th 1698. It was a scorching day with thunderheads gathering ominously in the distance. They were entering the Tropics and the weather would now be an entirely different proposition.

Buchanan stood with Pincarton on the top deck. "Am I imagining it, Robert, or has it suddenly become very hot? "

"Welcome to the Tropics, city boy. This is just the start. Wait until the humidity feels like it's slowly suffocating you."

Buchanan puffed out his cheeks. "And the good news just keeps coming."

As the days passed Pincarton's forecast proved deadly accurate. The sun beat down mercilessly, searing all in its path. Even the sails give little protection as most of their shadow fell uselessly on the water far from where it was needed. The surgeons had to deal with several cases of sunburn for those stupid enough to leave themselves exposed. But then again, it was a hard choice between the stifling claustrophobia below decks or fresh air and blistering heat.

The weather slowly ate into the travellers' minds. For several days there wasn't enough breeze to stir the dust and the ships' sails hung hopelessly limp in the enervating swelter. The only perspective other than the endless horizon was the convoy of other vessels. The boundless ocean stretched out in every direction, making the enormous Saint Andrew and her sister ships look like little model boats on a pond. There was no escape, no privacy. The cheek by jowl closeness magnified any irksome habits and tempers quickly became frayed.

Then two things happened.

Seven days out they ran into a storm of biblical proportions. Although it seemed to arrive from nowhere the sailors had known it was coming from the change in the atmosphere and the pods of porpoises scurrying quickly past in the clear blue waters. Even when the sky was still blue and the sea calm, Pincarton and Robb were barking out orders to batten down all hatches and for anything which could not be taken below to be lashed to the deck. The tallest mast was lowered and the sails furled on the others.

A hurricane was something to be feared. The preferred option was to try to outrun it to the nearest port but the Fleet was too far away from land. It would have to be met face on and ridden out. Alarmed by the activity, Buchanan ran up to the poop deck. "What the hell's going on?"

"'Hell' is the right word for what's coming," replied Pincarton.

"But it looks so calm."

"I know. That's why I'm a Captain and you're a lawyer. Have a look at the other ships if you're in any doubt." Pincarton handed his telescope to Buchanan who surveyed the rest of the Fleet. He could see that every one of them was a hive of frenzied activity in a mimed copy of what was unfolding on the Unicorn.

"So how long until it hits?" asked Buchanan.

"An hour, maybe less. The locals call it a "harey-cane." But the crew call it the Undertakers Wind. It comes off Jamaica and God help anyone in its path. So best get your pretty boy face out of harm's way and make sure your books are safely tied down."

"I'd prefer to stay up here to see it."

"Aye well, on your own head be it," warned Pincarton with a crinkled grin.

Within minutes the skies began to darken and every passenger was ordered to stay below decks. Then the peace was shattered. In an instant the hurricane smashed into the Fleet and hit with a vengeance which felt like the end of days.

Mountainous waves, black as night, rose up to the skies and crashed down on the ships. Their bubbling crests towered over the decks like giant ogres before unleashing their shuddering violence. Furious gales screamed like banshees as they whistled through the rigging. The Fleet was scattered like matchwood and visibility reduced to a few metres.

Buchanan, tied by a lifeline, clung onto the top deck with all his might and watched with a mixture of absolute terror and excitement. He felt the Unicorn rise up to the heavens and then plummet towards Hades with an unimaginable speed and force. But then it miraculously righted itself and began its ride up the grotesque big dipper once more.

Then, like an avenging Angel of Death, the hurricane passed just as quickly as it had arrived. An eerie quiet descended over the battered ship. It bobbed on top of the waves like a little cork coming to rest in a shaken bucket of water. The sun emerged tentatively from behind the disappearing black clouds and with a surreal suddenness the world was back to how it had been two hours before. The wind dropped to a whisper but the air had been cleansed and the oppressive humidity momentarily banished.

Buchanan finally let go of the deck rail. His hands were raw. He scanned the ocean. Mercifully none of the Fleet had been swallowed up by the storm. Untying the lifeline Buchanan could see Pincarton and Robb begin assessing the damage. He went below and as he passed Paterson's cabin could see him clinging on to his wife and son. Hannah Paterson's face was ashen with her son wrapped in her arms too scared to look up. Buchanan paused at the doorway and nodded silently to Paterson who returned the gesture.

Buchanan checked to see if there had been any damage to his own cabin and effects. Surprisingly, other than some items being tossed to the ground they had emerged unscathed. He changed out of his sodden shirt and breeches and then proceeded quickly to the Great Cabin. The Reverend James had beaten him to the malt. The clergyman's face reddened, but Buchanan was quick to put him at ease. "You read my mind, Reverend. If you're going to have another I'd be obliged if you could pour me a stiff one."

The Reverend stammered. "Of course. Just steadying the nerves you understand."

"After what we've just been through, even a teetotaller would need a little sensation to get the pulse down."

"Quite so. Praise be to God for our deliverance."

"Well, praise be to someone certainly. Personally I'd prefer to credit the fine German shipbuilders and our excellent Captain."

"Don't you believe in God then, Mr. Buchanan?"

"Perhaps this is not the best time to embark on such a discussion."

"Why ever not? Surely there can be no better time after He has spared us certain death."

"Or is it in dark times that the Devil tempts us to believe there is a God? I'd really prefer just to avoid the conversation, Reverend."

"You disappoint me Mr. Buchanan."

"Do I now?"

"Well, I would have thought that a man of your upbringing would embrace the Greater Power who created him."

That list the fuse for Buchanan. "The Greater Power? Really? What kind of Greater Power would inflict the misery we've seen on this voyage. That would bring disease onto our vessels, kill our countrymen, lash us with storms, and rot our provisions. What kind of Great Power allows children to die or humans to be enslaved?"

The minister was taken aback by the force of Buchanan's outburst but eventually replied with the age old fallback. "These are His tests sent to try us."

"Tests. They're not tests. They're punishments meted out regardless of wrongdoing. At least the Greek and Roman Deities imposed suffering as a punishment. Your God is randomly vindictive and merciless."

"But that is the purpose of faith. To believe even where there seems no earthly logic to His great plan. I suppose you're not religious either."

"Ha! Religion. That's even worse. If we are all God's children why draw distinctions and then fight Holy Wars to justify them? Would there have been the Crusades without religion?"

"But Saladin was an infidel and his Caliphate an empire of evil."

"Really? Many believe that Saladin was a great and benign leader. Who's to say that the Christian Crusaders who sacked, raped and pillaged their way through Europe had any greater moral right to the Holy Land than the Muslims?"

"That is blasphemy, Sir!"

"Well actually, it isn't blasphemy, but I can't be arsed going down that semantic rabbit hole. Just please don't preach to me about religion. Catholics are cowed by fear of the Church and eternal damnation. Presbyterians are paralysed by an inability to do anything which may be perceived as enjoyment. Jews are haunted by the belief they are persecuted. Which to an extent is true, but setting yourself up as the Chosen People will tend to do that don't you think?"

"So you're anti-semitic."

"Oh, for pity sake man. I'm not anti-anything. I'm for self-determination and the liberty to exercise one's beliefs. I'm for kindness and tolerance. I don't see very much of that in your religions and yet you all think you've got it right."

"So, you think you've got it right?"

"I never said that I did. But I don't go around trying to convince people that I am the truth, the light and the way and that if they follow my preachings a celestial welcome will await."

"I'm saddened that you think that way, Mr. Buchanan. My Church has always tried to preach acceptance and compassion to mankind."

"Well, that's fine as long as mankind is Presbyterian. And it's the same for the rest of the religions. If you are not one of us, then you're wrong."

"So you just sit there criticising us, smug in your beliefs?

"If you mean by "smug", doing no conscious harm to others and trying to help those in need, then the answer would be 'yes'."

The Reverend shook his head and gave Buchanan a pitying look. "I shall pray for you Mr. Buchanan."

Buchanan was about to fire back when a loud cough interrupted proceedings. Both men, totally engrossed in the exchange, had failed to notice that Pincarton had entered the Great Cabin and was watching them, arms crossed. "Quite a conversation, gentlemen," he said in an amused tone. "I do hope it will not lead to any rift which may cause us difficulties."

His calm voice brought Buchanan down off his soapbox. He realised that he had gone too far with this good man sitting in front of him.

"Please forgive my outburst Reverend. It was not meant as a personal attack. Sometimes I get a little exercised on the subject."

"Which is why you indicated that you preferred not to explore it?"

"Indeed," replied Buchanan.

"Well then, please forgive me in turn for forcing the issue."

"So, can we agree to disagree without it affecting our friendship?" asked Buchanan holding out his hand.

"I would hardly be a good example of what I preach if I did not," smiled the Reverend.

"Excellent," said Pincarton. "Now in the name of whatever God you follow or disavow, can one of you please pour me a very large whisky. I think I deserve it after what I've just endured. And I'm not talking about your little theological spat."

CHAPTER 19

When troubles come, they come not as single spies but in great battalions. The second thing that happened after leaving Crab Island proved to be much worse than the Undertaker's Wind.

Within a few days of the storm, passengers and crew on the Unicorn began to fall ill in alarming numbers. It was not alone. Signals transmitted from ship to ship conveyed the same desperate message. Dysentery was sweeping through the human manifest like a vengeful Pale Rider.

Ships doctors and surgeons raced from one sickbed to another trying their best to tend to the stricken. Civilian passengers, who had less resistance than the sailors, fell like ninepins and lay prostate and moaning as blood-laced shit flowed from their guts like sewer water. The worst affected writhed in agony as severe abdominal cramps, fever and delirium gripped them.

The medics initially thought that the seawater from the storm had spoiled some of the supplies in the hold, so ordered those afflicted to be kept hydrated but away from food. However, as the days passed, the death toll continued to rise and the sound of the canvas coffins plunging into the ocean became a solemn barometer of the tragedy.

Life below decks was appalling. Sick passengers lay listless in the thick fetid air praying for the heat of the day to give way to the cooler night. Around them rats and cockroaches scuttled about feeding off the faeces and growing stronger as their hosts inched towards their deaths.

For the sailors and the soldiers unexpected death was a normal part of their lives. For the colonists it was entirely different. At home, extended families would be there to provide support and somehow make sense of the circle of life. But here in the brutality of this alien environment, the suddenness and horror of it was unimaginable. As the drums rolled with each new death, the ship echoed with the agonised wails of the bereaved. Buchanan saw precious children slip away as they were cradled in a mother's arms and then watched the parents helplessly cling on to each other, their gaunt faces blank and emotionless.

Reverend James proved a tower of strength in the midst of the suffering, praying with the sick and counselling the bereaved. When the clergyman himself fell ill it was Buchanan who sat with him. The doctor left orders to keep James hydrated, but the more water he drank the worse he seemed to get. The Reverend, weak and soaked with fever, asked Buchanan to read to him from the Bible. This calmed James until the next spasm took hold, wracking him with pain.

Finally after twenty four hours, this kind servant of his God started to fade. He gripped Buchanan's hand and asked him to pray. James began to whisper the words he had offered up to so many of the dying in previous days, "The Lord is my shepherd; I shall not want. He maketh me to lie down in green pastures, he leadeth me beside the still waters."

His body contorted in agony and he squeezed Buchanan's hand even tighter. He gasped for breath. "Jamie please don't stop. I beg you." Buchanan looked into the watery eyes of the minister and softly continued, "Yea, though I walk through the valley of the shadow of death, I will fear no evil, for thou art with me…"

Then, before Buchanan reached the last line, a smile came to James' mouth and his face assumed a look of utter tranquillity. The preacher closed his eyes and unable to continue his struggle gently passed away into the arms of his Maker.

Buchanan gently released James' right hand and placed it across his body so that it overlapped with his left. Then as he sat in silence looking at the dead man something utterly irrational happened. The room became transformed from an agonising sweat box to a silent sanctuary where an inexplicable coolness descended accompanied by a sweet perfume of incense and eucalyptus. The light changed and little shafts of sun danced around the hollow shell of the diseased body. But in an instant it was gone and the heat and the noise and the darkness all returned.

Buchanan took it all in for a few moments before slowly getting up. He told Robb that James was dead and to make arrangements to prepare the body. Entering the Great Cabin he felt shaken but also strangely comforted. He poured a dram and sat quietly, trying to process what had just happened. His reverie was interrupted by Paterson who had been preoccupied in looking after his own sick wife. "Is he gone Jamie?"

"I'm afraid so."

Paterson sat down with a thud and cradled his head in his hands. "May God preserve his soul."

Buchanan thought about confiding in Paterson but realised he had more on his mind than the spiritual journey of a cynical lawyer. "I'm sorry William, I know what he meant to you."

"A great deal more than anyone realises." He paused as if he was about to say more but held back.

"How's Hannah?" asked Buchanan.

"Better than last night but still very weak. No matter how much water I give her it seems to do no good."

"And your boy?"

"Sad and confused. He's never seen his mother ill so just sits beside her, hoping she gets better. Sorry, Jamie I have to get back."

Buchanan took himself up onto the aft deck where Pincarton was issuing instructions to those crew members still healthy enough to work. Soon there wouldn't be enough fit men left to sail the ship and Buchanan could tell that even the implacable Captain was becoming anxious.

"Bad business this Jamie," scowled Pincarton.

"Seen anything like it before?"

"Aye, but never as severe. Usually the outbreak is contained."

"Any idea why this is different?"

"If I knew that my friend, I'd be doing something about it. With the current winds we're at least four days from land, so this will only get worse."

Just then a cry came up from below. One of the sailors shouted that a pinnace was coming towards them. Pincarton and Buchanan moved to the other side of the deck and as the small boat got closer they saw

Walter Herries, the surgeon, sitting in the back. A few minutes later he was hoisted aboard. He looked tired and drawn.

"Mr. Herries. How can we help you?" asked Pincarton.

"What have you been giving the sick?" he gasped.

"Water and malt extract."

"The water we took on in Crab Island?"

"Of course, it's the freshest."

"Maybe so, but it's also fouled. That's what's causing the sickness."

Pincarton grabbed his arm. "How do you know?"

"I've examined it using the Fleet's microscope. The water is contaminated with minuscule parasites invisible to the human eye. But under the lens they're everywhere. The water is the instrument of death."

"Christ almighty," exclaimed Pincarton. "So what do we do?"

"Throw all the Crab Island water overboard immediately and use the older supplies."

"But they'll be stale."

"Perhaps, but not corrupted. If there isn't enough water then beer will be better than nothing. Just keep the sick hydrated."

"Thank you, Herries. You look done in. Is there anything I can get you?" asked Pincarton.

"No, thank you. I need to get round the other ships to let them know."

"We're in your debt."

He nodded. "Think nothing of it, Captain. We're all in this together."

And that was the truth of it. When disease cast its deathly shadow there were no sides, just communal survival.

As soon as Herries had gone Pincarton issued the urgent instructions. Fifteen minutes later the contaminated water had been poured over the side and the older supplies broken out and given to the sick.

Within twenty four hours the change was miraculous. The death toll plummeted and the ill began to gradually recover. New cases dried up and light slowly returned to the ship. It was the same story across the Fleet as Herries' discovery proved the salvation. Had it not been for his microscope there is no telling what the final death toll might have been. But in those desperate days one hundred and twenty men, women and children had perished.

CHAPTER 20

The Reverend Thomas James was wrapped in a canvas shroud and buried at sea. Pincarton said a few words before the body was consigned overboard and Buchanan watched in macabre fascination as the minister's corpse hit the emerald water with a mighty splash. As it began its descent the fusiliers fired off four rounds as a mark of respect.

Buchanan had come to learn that the sea was a cruel, undiscriminating mistress. If you wanted to use her waves then there would a tariff. The sailors knew this and clung to their superstitions with the fervour of any religious man to his creed. Even with the Reverend's sad passing, there was a strange sense of relief among the crew, as ministers and priests were believed to bring bad luck because of their connection to funerals. But as Buchanan had also discovered, life on board a ship went on very quickly. The weather and ocean were impervious to mortality and there was little time for grieving.

With the dysentery outbreak now reaching manageable proportions, attention focussed on bridging the last leg to Darien. The only problem, and a not insignificant one, was that nobody had any great confidence about where to find Golden Island on the long, rugged, Panamanian coastline. Nobody that is, except Alliston.

Having sworn off the grog, the grizzled old navigator had proven his worth early on. The route which the Fleet would have taken without him to Panama was far different from the course he actually chartered. Alliston, logically and coherently, (which was a mercy given the state in which he had arrived from Saint Thomas), explained the tides and favourable winds of his preferred course. He had warned that they would almost certainly hit storms at that time of year- in which he had proved chillingly accurate-but that these would be even worse and more frequent on a more direct route. So the Fleet had skirted the coastlines of Puerto Rico, Hispaniola and Jamaica before turning South to make a beeline for Colombia and then west to Panama.

Then in the small hours of October 17th came a cry of "Land Ho."

Buchanan, thankful that Mrs. Russell was not visiting, dressed quickly and raced up to the aft deck where Pincarton and Paterson were engaged in animated conversation. Although the moon was bright, the view was compromised by dark clouds which scudded past at regular intervals. However, when they cleared, a great land mass became suddenly visible.

"Where are we?" asked Buchanan.

"At best estimate, we're looking at the cliffs of Cartagena," answered Pincarton.

Paterson agreed, "If we've kept to Alliston's course that should be the first land sighted."

"Aye well, we'd not be too welcome there," said Pincarton.

"Why not? Aren't we on the same side as the Spanish against the Frenchies?" asked Buchanan.

Pincarton shook his head. "Scotland is, but those bloody Jacobites threw in their lot with the French and the Spaniards weren't overly impressed."

Buchanan frowned. "But we're not Jacobites."

"Correct, but to all but the most discerning, 'Jacobites' equates to Scots. If you want to argue the toss with the Señors then be my guest."

"Surely that's not going to matter much in this part of the World?"

"It wouldn't have, except that last May, a French privateer caught the Spanish off guard, overran the city and spent the best part of a week plundering and sacking it. Once they'd had their fun, they buggered off back to France with their holds full of Spanish gold and silver."

"So we'll not be stopping in for tea and scones then."

"Exactly," answered Pincarton.

The assumption that this was Cartagena was confirmed as dawn lightened the sky and they could see the silhouette of the fort on the towering headland.

Buchanan couldn't imagine how anyone could possibly have mounted a successful attack on such an intimidating stronghold. But because the Frogs had done it, the little Scottish Fleet kept its head down and slipped silently past.

CHAPTER 21

The final leg proved excruciatingly slow. The winds and currents which had assisted on the trip south now conspired against them. The sea again resembled a millpond and the Fleet spent two weeks tacking against the feeble zephyr as it clawed its way, yard by agonising yard, along the Panamanian coast.

On October 25th, Pennicuik called a meeting aboard the Saint Andrew. When Buchanan arrived the Commodore was having a heated exchange with Alliston. It was clear that the old navigator was under attack but equally clear that he didn't give a shit about Pennicuik's status.

"I thought we'd paid you a king's ransom because you knew about the tides and winds, you clown," thundered Pennicuik.

"Well he'd be a pretty unpopular fucking king if that's what you'd consider his ransom."

"Show me some respect damn you," spat Pennicuik.

"I will when you've earned it," Alliston fired back.

Pennicuik slammed his fist down on his desk. "The first chance I get I'll have you off this ship and headed back to your whore in Saint Thomas."

The gnarled mariner looked at Pennicuik with a death stare. "Is that a fact, Captain. Well just drop me off at the nearest landfall and I'll get back and ask your mother if she's missed me."

The others erupted in laughter. Alliston, half expecting the Commodore to go for him, placed his feet apart and turned his body sideways. Pennicuik looked like he was going to have a stroke, his face crimson and a raised vein pulsing in his neck. But he made no move, which was probably a smart play, given the size of the navigator. Instead, he took a deep breath and turning his back to Alliston, addressed the wider audience. "You see what I'm dealing with here? Despite his repeated assurances Mr. Alliston has no clue how to find Golden Island." He spat the words "Mr. Alliston" as if he was ridding his mouth of snake venom he had just sucked from a wound. "Because of this, we're desperately short of potable water, the body count is rising and several of our ships need repairing. Now, we can either blunder on in the hope that this fool may be right, or find somewhere to take care of these issues."

Pincarton asked, "How far do you reckon we are from Golden Island?"

"The charts are vague so we have to rely on this oaf. At a rough estimate, maybe fifty nautical miles which with this damnable weather will take us at least another week."

The discussion went back and forward for several minutes but it quickly became clear that the best option was to make for the nearest anchorage.

"Aye, well best be careful," said Alliston. "Most of Panama's coastline is dotted with coral reefs. You want to keep a wide berth from these bastards. I've seen the surf take a ship and dash it like matchwood against them."

The Fleet edged carefully along the coast and at about four that afternoon, Pennicuik saw what appeared to be a small bay ideal for their immediate purposes. The Commodore signalled the Fleet to follow his course. Although there was little wind, the sea wasn't calm. Buchanan, standing with Robb and Pincarton on the top deck, felt the ship sway like a floating pendulum as it lurched from side to side in the powerful swells, the legacy of a far off storm.

"I don't like this Mr. Robb. I don't like this at all," muttered Pincarton.

"Nor me, Sir. Too dangerous a swell for my blood."

Buchanan gave an apprehensive look towards Paterson whose face was a mask of concentration. The canvas sails which hung limp from the timber yards of the mainmast almost groaned in pain, trying to find some life from the supine wind. Then came a shout from the lookout, "Reef to port side. Two hundred yards."

"Jesus Christ!" shouted Pincarton. "Mr. Robb, unfurl the rest of the sails and set course to starboard."

Buchanan watched mesmerised as the sailors leapt like agitated monkeys up the rigging. The canvas curtains plummeted towards the deck like hanged men but just dangled lifelessly, impotent in the still air. The swell was pushing them closer and closer to the reef which was waiting to bare its teeth. They watched in growing horror as the powerful waves lined up to be slammed with a deafening roar onto the coral, the boiling water spewing malevolently across the jagged surface.

But then, merciful God, the sails caught a breath of wind. Slowly the Unicorn inched away from certain damnation and edged past the riptide and surf. Buchanan felt a surge of relief, only to see Pincarton look past him and cry out, "Oh, My God. No!"

Buchanan spun round. Behind them the maimed Endeavour, crippled without a working mainsail, had been unable to trap enough wind in its remaining canvas and had continued its inexorable drift towards the reef. The other ships were safe, but now too far away to render assistance. They watched helplessly as Captain Jolly's ship remained in the magnetic grip of the swell. Its destruction became inevitable as each wave ushered it gently like a grinning mortician to its ghastly fate. The grounded ship would be pulverised by the destructive surf and most on board would die from the initial impact, drown in the maelstrom, or be sliced to pieces by the razor sharp coral.

But Jolly wasn't going to give up without a fight. Buchanan could see the ship's two pinnaces being hurled unceremoniously into the calmer water off the starboard side, quickly followed by twenty crewmen. When the sailors resurfaced, each clutching an oar above their head like an Excalibur, they scrambled into the little row boats and attached them with ropes thrown from the mother ship. They began to row for their lives, every muscle straining and sinew screaming as they tried to haul their stricken vessel to open water. But with no wind to assist them it was futile. Even their adrenalin-charged efforts weren't enough. All they were doing was slowing the progress of the vessel's gruesome end.

Buchanan could hear the cries and shrieks of panic from the terrified passengers on the main deck. Pincarton ordered the Unicorn's pinnaces to be lowered and rowed towards the Endeavour. By the time they got there it would be too late to save the ship but those who jumped overboard before the collision might just be able to swim far enough away to be rescued. The other ships were doing the same and the sea soon became dotted with the little boats heading to their stricken comrade.

Then, from nowhere a breeze sprang up. Buchanan felt it in his face and heard it in the rustle of the sails of the Unicorn. But he had felt this same breeze before and no sooner had it arrived, laden with promise, than it had departed. But this time it was different. This time it was delivering on its pledge.

Pincarton peered through his telescope and growled. "Come on, my beauty, come on. Fill her canvas damn you."

Buchanan could see the sailors on the Endeavour scampering about with renewed vigour, setting the remaining working sails to catch every ounce of the zephyr, while those in the pinnaces heaved with fresh energy. Then suddenly the Endeavour's foresail fluttered and caught the puff. Now stretched out, the canvas gathered more and more of the lifesaving breeze. Suddenly the rudder began to respond and gradually, ever so gradually, the Endeavour started to ease away from the reef's clutches.

After fifteen minutes of agonising uncertainty the Endeavour was in open water. As the reef retreated from view, cheers rang out from her deck and all the other vessels. For once the Gods had taken pity and given the plucky little ship another life.

CHAPTER 22

Two hours later Alliston spotted a secluded little bay which he declared perfect as a temporary anchorage. The Fleet moored almost without mishap. The exception occurred on the Caledonia. A young hand named Hughie Calder had failed to notice that the anchor rope had draped around his ankle. As the thick cord took the strain, it leapt up and grabbed his leg like a striking anaconda, wrapping itself around his limb in a death grip.

As the anchor disappeared into the crystal blue water so too did Hughie. He screamed as he was flung over the side and dragged down. The nearest sailors sprang into action and rushed to haul the line back on board. After a frenetic twenty seconds both boy and anchor hit the deck with an almighty thump. Knives slashed through the air to cut the rope, catching the sun and sending out wild flashes.

Eventually the leg was freed and the boy turned on his side. One old sailor banged repeatedly on Calder's back and after a few moments a spew of seawater spurted from the youth's mouth and splattered over the deck. Attention then turned to the limb. It had snapped like a twig, a compound fracture with part of the shattered bone protruding at a grotesque angle to the rest of his shin. The boy, having just regained consciousness, looked down to see the damage and immediately lapsed back into a dead feint.

"Haud on, Hughie, haud on, son," said one of his rescuers. "We'll get ye some help."

The ship's surgeon was summoned. He was a tough old buzzard who went by the moniker of "The Stump Man." This had been well earned given that many of the old salts hobbling around the taverns of Edinburgh with missing body parts had been at the sharp end of his saw.

The Stump Man opened his weathered leather case and his hand hovered uncertainly over a large serrated blade. By this time the boy had come round again and was aghast to see who was crouching over him. He screamed, "No ma leg Stumper, no ma leg," before once more passing out. Those gathered around looked at the surgeon. They all knew that taking half the leg was more likely to save the lad's life, but he was only fifteen, and at that age amputation was in many ways worse than death.

The Stump Man weighed up his options and with the words of the boy ringing in his ears, made his decision. "Aye, awright, Hughie. I'll dae ma best but I cannae promise you'll be dancing the Gay Gordons anytime soon."

He called for wooden splints, thick bandages and plenty of whisky to disinfect the wound, provide the boy with some relief, and allow a dram or three to steady his own hand.

Ordering two onlookers to hold the boy down he put a length of rope between the patient's teeth, instructing Hughie to bite down hard when the pain got too much. That wasn't long in coming as the surgeon manipulated the deformed limb one way and then another to try to re-align the displaced bones. The boy let out a gagged wail and once more passed out.

The respite from his struggling allowed the Stump Man to work unimpeded and he skilfully set the bones into something approximating a straight line. Taking another swig from the whisky bottle he moved around the leg examining it from different angles with macabre satisfaction. "Nae bad work, if ah says so maself," he muttered. The surgeon doused the wound with the alcohol and wrapped it delicately in clean bandages. He then tightly strapped several splints of varying lengths to keep the repaired fracture in place.

Well impressed with his efforts both in setting the bones and the inroads he'd made on the malt, the Stump Man ordered the boy to be taken below but for the whisky bottle to be left.

The rest of the Fleet caught its breath in the quiet bay, a sanctuary of transparent blue and green water. A broad belt of dazzling white sand framed the cove, behind which lay a pretty band of palm trees swaying in graceful rhythmic choreography to the afternoon breeze. At the rear of the palms some native huts nestled in the thick undergrowth but there was no sign of human life.

Pennicuik, ever keen to be the first Scot to set foot on terra incognito, was rowed ashore. The fact that the residents had not shown themselves caused him to be accompanied by two soldiers. They were under strict instructions to protect him -with their lives, if necessary- in the event that the locals showed up and demonstrated anything other than friendly intentions. On communication of this newsflash, the two soldiers looked at one another. If this prick believed that they would heroically throw themselves in front of an arrow, spear or blade, then the deluded Commodore had another think coming. Death might indeed be the final mystery but it wasn't one either of them wanted to investigate just yet. A quick exit stage left would be more their mark and the bold Pennicuik could look out for himself, thank you very much.

Of course, the reason there were no natives in plain sight was that they had fled in terror at the sight of the giant ships descending on their little bay. They watched from their hiding places as the pale faced man in the blue jacket with shiny buttons and a strange white mop on top of his head splashed onto their beach and stuck a blue and white flag in the sand.

Pincarton laughed at the spectacle. "There's Pennicuik claiming possession of another useless little beach for Scotland."

"Maybe there's a case of Saltires in the cargo hold," suggested Buchanan.

Pincarton chuckled away as the Commodore proceeded with the farce. Once finished he waved to the Saint Andrew. Its remaining pinnace and those from the other ships were loaded with the empty water casks and brought ashore. Within half an hour a fresh water source had been located not far from the beach. There was still no sign of the inhabitants but every sailor in the landing party was conscious of the hidden eyes upon them. So they went quickly about their business, filled up the wooden barrels and slipped back to their ships.

The hiatus also gave the carpenters aboard the Endeavour the opportunity to jerry rig a repair to the main mast. It was not ideal but would at least be workable until they could undertake a full replacement.

However, the most beneficial outcome was that it gave Alliston a proper opportunity to get accurate bearings. He had asked all the captains to convene in the Great Cabin of the Saint Andrew and to bring their cross staffs and maps. One of the peculiarities of navigation of the age was that each Captain had his own charts and these did not always conform exactly to those of others. Certainly the broad outline of a coast might be the same, but when it came to the detail, the differences could be pronounced.

The old navigator and the captains spread out the various maps on the large dining table and pored over the contents. Pincarton quickly compared the documents and turning to Robert Drummond said quietly. "Jesus, Robert, no wonder you have to follow me if these are the charts you've been using. You'd better tie a line to the Unicorn otherwise you'll end up in China."

"Aye, very fucking funny. Ah've no got lost yet, huv I?"

"I'm sure the Commodore wouldn't be too fussed if you did."

"Aye well, that cuts both ways, doesn't it."

Pincarton smiled and the two turned their attention back to the table. Allison was busy whittling down the maps and eventually alighted on Pincarton's Mercator chart and a hand drawn map of the coast of Panama which Drummond had purchased in Saint Amelie.

They all went outside and Alliston asked each of the Captains to take a bearing using the cross-staffs. The mariners held the strange device up to their eyes to take the altitude of the sun above the horizon. Then the results emerged. Malloch and Jolly were poles apart and Pennicuik made great show in advising of how he'd come to his conclusion.

Drummond, in the midst of Pennicuik's display, nudged Pincarton and whispered. "Whit did you get?"

"I'm not telling you."

"C'mon man. I think I'm miles out and don't want to look a twat."

"For fuck sake, Robert. Alright, but you owe me one," he replied, hastily scribbling some letters and numbers on a scrap of paper before slipping it across.

Drummond winked at him and took the precious information. After Pincarton announced his findings, Alliston had asked Drummond for his figures. Pennicuik smiled smugly at his foe in the expectation that he was about to make a fool of himself.

In a performance befitting a Shakespearian leading man giving his Lear, Drummond made great play of opening up the piece of scrunched paper. He nearly choked when he scanned what was written on it. 'We're somewhere in the Caribbean.'

Pincarton desperately tried not to burst out laughing. He then saw Drummond read the smaller lettering at the bottom. "Turn page." Drummond quickly flipped over the paper and Pincarton could see the relief flood his face. Jotted down were some figures which he then shared. Pincarton had been careful to amend these slightly from his own to avert any suspicion of collusion. The ruse robbed Pennicuik of his anticipated triumph and Pincarton chuckled silently as the Commodore's mouth fell slightly agape at the accuracy of Drummond's calculation.

Alliston issued his judgement. "Thank you, gentlemen. I agree most closely with the findings of Captains Pennicuik, Pincarton and Drummond. I was particularly impressed with Captain Drummond's skill given the inferior design of his cross-staff."

Drummond bowed theatrically which only served to rub salt in the wound for Pennicuik. Alliston then continued. "Now, given these bearings, the maps and the coastline which we've encountered, I'm confident that we're only about five leagues south of Golden Island."

A buzz of excitement fizzed round the group.

"Are you certain?" queried the sceptical Pennicuik.

"As certain as I can be."

"Well about time. Come on then, let's get to it."

But Drummond couldn't resist the opportunity. "Is there no time for a wee celebratory dram Commodore?"

Pennicuik had little option but to break into his jealously guarded stash but once the malt was downed the assembly dispersed to their respective ships.

Pincarton found Buchanan and Paterson waiting with bated breath. The Captain smiled broadly. "Five leagues to the north."

The long journey was finally coming to an end.

DARIEN

CHAPTER 1

It was difficult to say who was happiest when Golden Island came into view.

Perhaps the passengers finally reaching the promised land after so many months in their floating purgatories; perhaps the sailors ridding their vessels of the mewling, disease-ridden settlers; perhaps the soldiers, released from the stinking hell of the lowest decks and getting back to being useful; or perhaps the Councillors who could at last bring the planning and preparation to fruition.

But maybe above all of these stood Robert Alliston. Whether by design, skill, sheer dumb luck, or a combination of the three he had managed to fulfil his contract and navigate the Fleet to Golden Island. He would no longer have to suffer Pennicuik's haranguing and with the second half of his payment in his pocket could escape the lunatic Scots on the first passing ship bound for Jamaica.

Golden Island was a long barren strip of rock and in itself nothing to excite the senses. It was what it concealed which was of far more interest. When the Fleet dropped anchor Pennicuik had clambered aboard a pinnace and assumed his customary heroic stance in the stern as twelve sweating sailors toiled in the heat to take the Scottish Argonaut to his Golden Fleece.

What Pennicuik discovered couldn't have been more pleasing. On the landward side of the island sat a large natural harbour. Cliffs soaring like huge sentinels formed the heads of the bay and Pennicuik could see ribbons of white sand stretching along the shore. Smoke rose from a collection of mud huts set in front of a dense green hinterland which soon gave way to the hills which towered precipitously over the water.

The presence of the pinnace hadn't gone unnoticed. Peering through his telescope Pennicuik saw dozens of small dark skinned figures racing around pointing at the boat and shouting loudly enough for their voices to be heard.

Less assured as he moved further away from the protection of the Fleet, the Commodore ordered his men to stop rowing. The little vessel came to a halt and bobbed on the water, one half of a Panamanian stand-off.

Never one to risk his own neck, Pennicuik was about to order a return to the Saint Andrew when he saw what looked like a white flag. He jammed the eyeglass so quickly back up into this face that he banged it off the bridge of his nose much to the silent amusement of his oarsmen.

Once he'd focused it, his initial view was confirmed. A white cloth of some sort was tied to a long stick and was being vigorously waved by two of the natives. He thought that this was either one big fucking flag or else the inhabitants were midgets. Seeing the universal sign for safe parlay, he instructed the rowing to recommence. The little boat edged closer until it was about thirty yards from the shore. Despite the apparent detente, Pennicuik told his men to be ready to pick up the muskets which lay in the bottom of the tender.

Lining the shore was a welcoming committee of a dozen or so men holding lances and bows. A shout came from one side of the group and the men obediently laid down their weapons. Onto the beach and taking centre stage appeared the oddest sight. A small man-admittedly they were all small- strutted out in front of his warriors draped in a bright red military jacket fringed with gold brocade. Pennicuik recognised it as being Spanish but otherwise, the man was naked save for some strange metal cover over his privates. The little fellow raised a scarlet arm and waved. Pennicuik quickly scanned the boat and alighted on his chosen one. "Ralston, you speak a bit of the Spanish don't you?"

The crewman, not sure why he was being asked such a question, answered in the affirmative.

"Splendid. Well then, get yourself over the side and go and ask His Scarlet Lordship there if we can come ashore."

"With all due respect Captain, how am I supposed tae dae that? Ah dunny speak Indian."

"Ah yes, but chummy there in his fancy Hidalgo jacket probably has a few words of Hispanic doesn't he?"

"Aye well, be that as it may Sir, ah'm no too keen to jump oot."

"For God's sake man. I'm giving you a direct order. Do as I say or you'll face the cat when we get back."

"Captain, it's no that ah want tae disobey you but it's just that ah don't think ah'm the right man fur the joab."

"And why's that then Ralston?"

"Ah cannae swim Captain."

"Oh for fuck sake. Give me that oar."

Ralston handed over the oar which Pennicuik grabbed, turned upright, and plunged into the water. It hit the sandy bottom with a thud about three quarters of the way up.

"How tall are you Ralston? "

"About five feet five Sir."

Pennicuik examined the oar and then the sailor.

"Aye well you'll be alright then. Once you hit the bottom there'll be only about three inches of difference so I suggest that once your feet touch the sand you start running as fast as you can."

This brought gales of laughter from the other sailors who delighted in this solution to their crewmate's aquatic shortcomings. Ralston slipped off his shoes and tentatively perched on the edge.

"Off you go then, son," barked Pennicuik as he gave the trembling seaman a shove on the back with the oar.

Ralston squealed as he hit the water, spluttering and scrambling his way past the first deadly yards without taking anything approximating a conventional swimming stroke. But comical as it was, it proved effective. Soon, the bedraggled sailor was hauling himself onto the beach where, surrounded by the chattering natives, he briefly disappeared from sight. This would be the moment of truth. If the non-swimming guinea pig survived intact then all was well. Otherwise, it would be muskets at the ready and full steam back to the Saint Andrew.

After a few seconds, the hubbub subsided and Ralston emerged, apparently unharmed. He waved back to the pinnace and was acknowledged by Pennicuik who by now was congratulating himself on his excellent powers of delegation.

They watched as Ralston engaged in animated conversation with the Scarlet Chief. There appeared to be more sign language than actual dialogue but they were communicating. Eventually the shouting and waving stopped and Ralston took some tentative steps back into the sea. Anxious to avoid his messenger drowning, Pennicuik ordered the pinnace to move closer so that Ralston could enjoy the entirety of the return trip with his head above water.

After he was hauled aboard, Pennicuik asked what had transpired.

"Aye well, Sir, the lang and short of it is that thur awfy pleased wur no Spanish but dinnae ken whit Scottish is."

"And how did you enlighten them on that geographical conundrum?"

A puzzled frown creased Ralston's dripping brow. Pennicuik rephrased. "How did you explain what Scottish is?"

"Oh aye. Right well. Ah'm no sure if ah did tae be honest, Sir. Bit tricky tae explain kilts and bagpipes and that in Spanish."

"Oh for Christ sake. Is that how you explain being Scottish when someone asks you?"

"Aye well. It's either tha' or say ah'm English and ah'm naw daein' that."

Pennicuik looked to the heavens. "So what was all the chit chat about, Making arrangements for afternoon tea were we?"

"Naw, he never mentioned anything aboot tea, Captain, but it widda bin awfy nice if he hud."

"Oh, sweet Jesus, give me strength," blurted Pennicuik, "Just tell me what he said."

"Well, ah explained about wur ships oot past the big Island and he then hud a wee talk wi' his men." Ralston paused.

"And? Don't keep us in suspense man."

"Aye well, then he said he wid come oot for a wee visit tomorra mornin'."

"Oh he did, did he. That's big of him."

"Aye, ah thought so masel', Captain. Awfy nice wee fella."

"Oh, for fuck's sake. Ralston, in a village of village idiots, you would definitely be the village idiot. Just get into your seat and take me back to the Saint Andrew."

Ralston shot the Commodore a cold stare and Pennicuik could sense that the other oarsmen were less than happy with his treatment. Out of sight of the rest of the Fleet and alone on a small boat, this was perhaps not the best time to be too high handed. So he added, "Well done though, Ralston. Double rations of grog for the lot of you."

The atmosphere changed in an instant as the prospect of extra anaesthetic was always welcome. Emboldened by his adventure Ralston asked. "Permission to sing a sea shanty Captain?"

"Under absolutely no fucking circumstances." Pennicuik hated sea shanties. But then again Pennicuik hated a lot of things.

CHAPTER 2

The next morning, the Captains and Councillors, at the request rather than the command of Pennicuik, gathered on board the Saint Andrew in anticipation of the arrival of the Indian Chief. Pennicuik's unfettered authority existed only for as long as the Fleet was at sea and the second the anchors fell at Golden Island his autonomy evaporated. The dynamic of power shifted and now he would have to operate in an environment of consensus, a prospect which did not sit easily on his shoulders.

His most pressing issue though was whether or not the natives would object to him planting the Saltire and if they did, what steps were the Scots prepared to take to overcome it? The more belligerent among the captains and soldiers would have no hesitation in imposing a military solution. Against them would be stacked the moderates and God fearing Presbyterians. It was only to be hoped that the issue would not be put to the test.

At around eleven o'clock, a little flotilla of canoes rounded Golden Island but on seeing the Scottish ships, stopped and sat bobbing on the waves. Pennicuik grunted. "I see the majesty of our Fleet has given them pause for thought."

"Or did it cross your mind they don't know which ship to board?" asked Pincarton.

Pennicuik turned to his first officer and ordered that two men stand on the leeward side of the ship and wave flags. The officer responded that people on most of the other ships were already doing that.

"Well, fire off a couple of cannon rounds then." ordered Pennicuik. "And try not to hit anyone."

A few moments later the boom of the cannons resonated across the water. This had the desired effect as the canoes started towards his flagship. Only one of them came right up to the side of the Saint Andrew, with the others circling lazily twenty or so yards away. The occupants, including the scarlet coated chief, clambered nimbly up the overhanging rope netting. All except the chief was armed with a lance and long dagger.

Pennicuik took centre stage as they came aboard. By his side was a young seaman named Benjamin Spense who spoke reasonable Spanish. Wanting to make a good impression the captains were resplendent in their dark blue uniform coat. The civilians wore their jackets and all sported wigs. They must have appeared a strange sight to the natives who, other than Scarlet boy, were naked as the day they were born save for a string around their waist. Attached to this was a coppery metal cone which did a reasonable job of covering their genitals. All were nut brown.

With great flourish Pennicuik handed over some buttons and beads which he had been advised were much prized by the natives. However, the chief's eyes immediately shot towards the bottles of wine and whisky which were waiting to be drunk in welcome of the guests. The chief pointed towards these and mimed a drinking action. A marriage made in heaven thought Buchanan. Two nations obsessed with alcohol. What could be better?

Pennicuik, never the master of polite diplomacy, seemed thrown by this and it was left to Pincarton to step into the breach. He called for a tray of whisky to be brought over and offered this to the chief. The little man let out an excited giggle, grabbed one of the tumblers and downed the measure in a single gulp. He closed his eyes and that look of sublime pleasure which every whisky drinker knows spread over his face as the nectar hit the spot. The drinks were then offered to his entourage who diligently followed their leader's example. Darien was obviously not a land where puritanical missionaries had had much success.

There then ensued a disjointed dialogue, with Spense doing his best to act as go-between. It appeared that the chief's name was Andreas which he'd been given by the Spanish when involuntarily ferrying their silver across the peninsula. The Scots exchanged looks, pleased that here was someone who had actually trodden the path they hoped would unlock the gateway to the oceans.

Andreas had been a part of what the Spanish called its "native work program." At the first opportunity he'd high tailed it in the middle of the night and found his way back to his Tule tribesman accompanied by the scarlet coat which he'd souvenired from one of his overseers.

Buchanan noticed that every time the word Spanish was mentioned the other Indians seemed to tighten their grips on the lances. It was clear that they were no fans of the Conquistadores. After much mangled explanation, Spense finally succeeding in getting across to Andreas that the peculiar white men dressed in ridiculous clothes were neither English nor invaders.

Pincarton carefully led the conversation, assuring the Indians that the Scots came in peace and wished nothing other than to set up a trading post in the bay. Andreas consulted his comrades and amid much glottalised, staccato language and furious signing, an apparent consensus was reached.

The Tule would be happy for the Scots to stay provided they did not endanger or impact the life of the tribe. Andreas' eyes then alighted again on the whisky bottle. Pincarton willingly offered it to seal the deal, particularly since it came from Pennicuik's store.

After another hour or so the delegation left, all several sheets to the wind. One unfortunate fell into the water on the descent down the netting much to the amusement of his friends, who then decided it was a great idea and followed suit. All except Andreas who did not wish to tarnish his fine Spanish jacket.

Buchanan stood beside Paterson as they watched the canoe convoy paddle back round the island. "Can you credit how easily they agreed to allow us to set up shop?"

"Not really" replied Paterson. "Look at it from their angle. What's their alternative? Resist us? They've already been at the wrong end of the Spanish sword so better to open the door than have it kicked down."

CHAPTER 3

The Fleet eased its way into the wide bay the following morning. The decks were crammed with every man, woman and child desperate for a first glimpse of their new home. The initial impact didn't disappoint. Long beaches dotted the azure water like pearls in a necklace. These quickly gave way to the mountainous hinterland which was intermittently pierced by white waterfalls cascading into the sea like long bridal veils.

On seeing the billowing sails emerge, the Indians had jumped into their canoes. The Scots watched mesmerised as the dark, muscular, little men skilfully paddled out, shouting and gesticulating to the strange grey people. The Indians were as naked as the previous day's visitors and at first, the women averted their gazes and covered their children's eyes. But gradually curiosity became a more powerful driver than modesty.

As the Scots stood sweating in their European clothes under the baking sun it was evident that the Indians had the right idea. However, whether the Kirk or ingrained Scottish propriety would countenance such public displays of indecency among their own was highly debatable.

In no time, the ships were surrounded by dozens of little vessels buzzing like bees around multiple hives. In the distance on the palm fringed beaches, scores more natives stood waving to welcome their visitors. The Captains and Councillors would be first to go ashore. At the head of this vanguard would be the vainglorious Pennicuik undertaking his final act as Supreme Commander. Buchanan was squeezed into another pinnace beside Pincarton and Paterson. They were all struggling to keep their laugher in check at the sight of this ludicrous man trying to imprint himself on this seminal moment in Scottish history.

"Well, he's certainly dressed for the occasion," said Buchanan

"Wouldn't have been surprised if he'd wrapped himself in the bloody Saltire," added Pincarton.

Certainly Pennicuik had left no piece of his dress wardrobe untouched, including the tricorn hat which perched precariously on his powdered white wig. In his right hand he clutched the large blue and white flag but as the boat approached the beach he momentarily lost his balance. There was an instant when it looked like he would tumble ignominiously into the water but he grabbed the hair of the nearest oarsman and hung on for grim life. This elicited a squeal of pain from the unlucky sailor.

Buchanan spluttered, "Christ, I hope the Indians don't think this is some kind of ritual the Scots engage in every time we get out a fucking boat."

Pincarton guffawed. "Well, third time lucky for the flag planting. At least he'll have the speech off pat by now. Hope the natives don't twig that he's about to compulsorily acquire their land for bonny Scotland or else he might get one of those sharp wee lances up his arse."

"Won't bother them a bit," said Paterson. "They don't believe the land belongs to anyone and it's just there to be used by whoever needs it at the time. As long as they think they're not going to be kicked out, massacred or enslaved they'll be fine."

"Jesus, that's all a bit depressing William."

"Way of the world, Jamie, way of the world."

As Paterson said this Pennicuik finally let go the sorry sailor's hair, although such was his grip that a clump of it came away in his hand. This was then dropped into the sea by Pennicuik as he clambered out into the shallows.

Andreas was waiting in his Scarlet jacket and copper cock cover. On either side of him stood two curvaceous young girls, each with skin the colour of coffee, long black hair, dazzling teeth and small plump breasts which were displayed without a bit of self-consciousness. Their only clothing was a patch of material covering their pudenda. Pincarton smiled as some of the young – and not so young – sailors gawped open mouthed at these enchantresses.

Pennicuik splashed his way onto the shoreline, gave Andreas a peremptory nod and then with great pomp drove the Saltire into the sand. He then turned his back on his hosts and declared to his countrymen. "I hereby plant the flag of Scotland on behalf of our great nation and Company and take possession of this land in their name."

There was a momentary pause which then developed into an increasingly embarrassing silence. Pincarton revelled in the squirm-inducing moment and was disinclined to lead the applause which Pennicuik sorely craved. Ultimately, it was Captain Jolly who began to clap politely which then began the delayed cascade of acclaim from the others.

"His Julius Caesar moment," Pincarton whispered.

"Well let's just hope a bearded Dane doesn't jump out from the palm trees and fuck it up for him again," replied Buchanan.

Both men dissolved into a fit of sniggering wildly inappropriate for the grandeur of the moment when Scotland, the game minnow trying to wriggle free from the suffocating grip of England, finally laid claim to a colony of its own.

CHAPTER 4

The following morning the first meeting of the Council in Darien took place in the Great Cabin of the Unicorn.

This Council comprised the Captains Pennicuik, Pincarton and Jolly, together with Montgomery, Paterson, Buchanan and James Cunningham. The last of these, Cunningham was a seasoned soldier and staunch Churchman whose strong Presbyterian credentials worked in his favour. The fact he had never been outside of Scotland appeared to have been little impediment to his appointment.

The Council was to govern and administer the Colony until it became sufficiently established for democratic elections to be held among the settlers. Chairmanship of the Council was on a revolving weekly rota.

Montgomery, as current Chairman, opened proceedings. "Welcome, Gentlemen. I'm sure that some among us believed this day might never come." This was met with polite laughter. "However, it has and we give thanks to our Lord for delivering us safely."

Buchanan wondered just what Montgomery's definition of "safely" meant. It certainly wouldn't be the same as the hundreds of bodies they'd tipped over the side en route.

The first agreed task was to put a roof over the settlers heads. Templates of existing fortified townships were pored over and tradesmen wheeled in and out to give advice. The cliffs guarding the entrance would be the centrepiece in constructing the fort. The civilian settlement could then be built on the flatter land towards the far shore of the bay and cut back into the hinterland through the mangroves and forests. A plan began to emerge and sketches drawn up for this little Scotland on the other side of the world. Buchanan who knew nothing about building a sandcastle never mind a colony had little input.

The next significant issue was what to do with the passengers. They were all hungry, exhausted and desperate to escape their floating prisons. The Captains and crews were equally anxious to see them gone so they could reclaim their ships. But therein lay the rub. At first blush the land surrounding the bay provided little natural cover or protection so was ill-suited for habitation until the settlement was built.

Montgomery asked for thoughts, with Cunningham the first to pipe up. "Get them off the ships as soon as possible. It's only a matter of time before their spirits break or the flux takes hold again."

Pennicuik was less Christian in approach but his conclusion was the same. "They're stinking up my holds and need to vacate pronto so my men can clean up their mess. And I mean that literally."

Drummond seized on the chance to have a dig at the recently emasculated Commodore. "Ah'm sure they're equally keen to be as far away as possible fae you. For Christ sakes, man, dae ye think they want tae be penned up like pigs?"

Pennicuik shot him a filthy look. Drummond returned it with interest. The atmosphere crackled with barely concealed hatred and almost inevitably it was Pincarton who stepped in. "If you two want to carry on your little feud then take it outside. Jesus, we're talking about the welfare of our people here and all you can do is behave like a couple of spotty schoolboys."

His words hit the mark and both men backed down. Pincarton continued, "I think we agree that it's in everyone's best interests to get the poor souls ashore as soon as possible. But that can't happen until there is adequate shelter. So, until then, get them out of the holds onto the decks and make a start on cleaning their quarters."

Pennicuik grunted something approximating approval.

Cunningham suggested, "Can't we allow them onto the beaches during the day?"

Pennicuik snorted. "And how do you suggest they get there and back? Expect me to run a fucking ferry service for wee trips to the seaside?"

"No, said Cunningham, his face reddening, "I wasn't suggesting… But yes, I see your point. I just wanted to make their lives a little better."

Pincarton saved his blushes. As I believe all of us, well nearly all of us, do so let's get on with it."

The meeting over, Pincarton sidled up to Buchanan. "I hope the natives aren't too precious about that lovely azure water of theirs."

"Why's that then?"

"Well, when we clean out the holds it's going to be the colour of shite for the next few days."

Buchanan chuckled. "Not an idea to go swimming round the bay then."

"Not unless you want to come out looking the colour of our friend Andreas."

CHAPTER 5

Next day a survey party was sent to scout the best location for the township. They explored the lush undergrowth, sought out fresh water sources and tested the soil for its suitability to grow crops. Eventually a spot was chosen and work began in earnest. The ironmongery and wood which had lain idle in the ship's cargo holds were broken out and ferried to the shore. Twenty men from each ship would form the working team and base themselves onshore.

The last surviving Minister, Adam Scott, was rowed over on the third day to bless the land and preached a sanctimonious little sermon to which the exhausted workmen paid little heed. Had he brought food and the promise of a soft bed he would have been far more welcome.

As the labourers toiled away, the other settlers spent as much time as possible on the ships' decks, happy to be liberated from their dungeons. Makeshift awnings were slung from the masts to the deck rail. These gave some respite from the direct sunlight but there was no refuge from the sapping humidity which clung to their skins like a wet sheet.

It also allowed the crew time to clean house. The patina of encrusted shit and spew which caked the floors and walls of the passenger quarters was scraped away. Smouldering fires of burning pitch and brimstone were set and the sailors roared with delight as the fumigation forced the cockroaches, fleas and rats to jump off and drown or perish in the smoke. The expurgated area was then doused with salt water and vinegar.

Shortage of supplies was another big concern. Medicines had been scarce since the moment the Fleet left Leith and this was now matched by the dwindling quantities of food. Fresh meat was non-existent and the pickled pork and beef had begun rotting in their barrels. Efforts were made to hunt some local game and the sight of a wild monkey being roasted on a spit tested the appetites of many. However, if they didn't eat this or the few plantains found near the diggings then the alternative was the hardtack biscuits which now tasted like brittle sawdust.

At the other end of the pecking order, life was still tolerable and Buchanan welcomed the calm waters of the bay, far removed from the stomach churning swell which had accompanied nearly every night's sleep since leaving Scotland.

However, it also meant that Mrs Russell's visits had come to an end. The rise and fall of the ship on the open seas and the noise of a vessel under sail had provided ideal cover for their trysts. Mr. Russell didn't care as long as it remained discreet. But if word of his cuckolding became widespread he feared he'd become a laughing stock. In reality, nobody could give a tinker's cuss if his wife was getting banged behind his back. However, he had put a stop to her little jaunts as soon as Golden Island was reached and, knowing on which side her bread was buttered, she acceded.

Not that this overly troubled Buchanan. At first, the knock on his door in the middle of the night had been welcomed. However, as the journey progressed, she became increasingly challenged in the hygiene department and there was only so much that her expensive French perfume could disguise.

On her final visit, Constance Russell was as enthusiastic as ever, pleasuring herself on top of Buchanan and then finishing him off with her hand before stealing away. His final memory was of her pulling a large flap of skirt from deep within her sweaty buttock cheeks as she slid out of his cabin.

CHAPTER 6

The Council recognised that good relations with the Tule Indians were vital. They inhabited this land and knew its secrets. So, a charm offensive was mounted via a small taskforce comprising Paterson, Cunningham and Buchanan with young Spense as interpreter. Although it expected no trouble, they were accompanied by a small corps of soldiers.

When the contingent went ashore on the third day they were met by the smiling gap-toothed Andreas who ushered them into the small village. There they saw a wider cross-section of the natives. Wrinkled old women who stayed near the dwellings; smiling young girls who moved with easy grace; and pubescent boys who stood sullen and square-shouldered to demonstrate their evolving manliness. Then there were the mothers who posed elegantly as infants darted in and out of their legs and their menfolk, muscled in that whipcord way which conveys both strength and agility. But all of them were small, very small, even compared to the Scots who were themselves no giants by European standards.

The Indian settlement was modest and comprised a long row of huts thatched with cocoa nut leaves. The floor coverings were sisal mats and there were shelves built high into the retaining posts for sleeping. There seemed to be no walls but further inspection revealed several panels of woven palms stacked behind the huts. These could be attached to the superstructure as the weather demanded.

Paterson made notes to take back to the township's chief engineer. He was particularly intrigued by the shelves. The Indians explained that otherwise they would have nowhere to sleep when the rains flooded the lower part of the hut. The Scots knew that there was a rainy season but these beds were five feet above the ground. Paterson pressed Andreas and was assured by the little man that the waters lapped up well past his waist.

In the middle of the little settlement was a fire over which a wild pig was being spit roast. The delicious smell wafted into the Scots' nostrils and triggered their gastric juices. But the meal appeared to be some time off, so the Scots were invited to sit in a circle with Andreas and three other men. Two young girls brought several clay jugs along with some earthen drinking cups. Andreas looked expectantly at the Scots. He almost squealed with delight when Paterson and Buchanan each produced a bottle of wine- not the good Madeira mind- and Cunningham a bottle of whisky.

The Indian jugs contained two liquids. The first was water. The second was an entirely different proposition. Andreas poured each of the Scots a cup, insisting that they drink. Buchanan put it to his lips and took a tentative sip. It was disgusting and took all of his willpower not to spit it out. He couldn't help but screw up his face as he forced down the bitter brew bringing gales of laughter from the locals. Cunningham, Paterson and Spense on the other hand looked none too happy, knowing that polite protocol would demand they follow suit.

Then the oddest thing happened. Buchanan began to feel strangely elated and the circle of men started to move in and out. Everything around him suddenly seemed peaceful and all noise stopped except for the birdsong, the sway of the palms and the music of the breeze. He knew he had been aware of these sounds before but had never heard them like this with all white noise removed. He closed his eyes and let the moment wash over him. His limbs and body felt numb but totally relaxed at the same time. Then, just as quickly, he snapped back to reality and heard the chatter of the Indians, the everyday sounds of the village and the concerned voices of his friends. The elation lingered a bit longer but when it too left, he felt strangely sad.

"Jamie, man, are you alright?" asked Paterson.

"Aye, aye. I'm fine," replied Buchanan hearing his own voice as if it was disembodied and being spoken by an actor.

"We lost you for a wee while there. What happened?" Paterson pressed.

"I don't know. What's a wee while?" asked the alien voice.

"For about five minutes you were just staring into space with a stupid grin on your face."

"Is that a fact? Just seemed like seconds to me."

"Spense, ask Andreas what's in that brew?" said Cunningham, obviously anxious not to have to go through the same experience.

Andreas' response was punctuated by much cackling. He evidently found what he was saying beyond hilarious. Spense was eventually satisfied that he had an accurate enough translation. "It seems that it's cocoa leaves which the Indians have chewed. They then spit the pulp residue into a bowl which is mashed up with some quinoa ashes and cold water."

Paterson furrowed his brow. "But that would just be a stimulant, not an hallucinogen."

"Maybe they stuck in something else they don't want us to know about," said a now tremulous Cunningham.

"Aye, perhaps. There's something nagging in the back of my head which will come to me."

Buchanan having survived the trial by ordeal smiled. "Well, whatever the case, you all need to take your medicine."

Each in turn experienced the same bizarre catatonia as Buchanan. When they had regained their senses, the Indians clapped loudly and then poured themselves sizeable measures which were downed in a single gulp. Had the Scots taken the same amount they would have been out of it for hours. But it was clear that the Indians had built a resistance to the narcotic and returned to normal in no time. Suddenly, Paterson made a little satisfied noise "I've remembered it now. Spense, ask Andreas about *aspira*."

But Spense didn't have to as Andreas' head snapped round at the sound of the word. His face then broke into the trademark grin and he stuck his arms and hands straight out in front of him, made a groaning sound and mimed the wooden movements of a golem. This brought howls of mirth from his companions some of whom copied the actions and fell over at the entertainment of it all.

Paterson nodded his head. "Aspira is a plant in which basically turns its users into automata. That was the hidden ingredient in this lovely cocktail."

Buchanan responded. "Well, the lads here seem pleased enough that we've done their bidding. Time to wash away the taste with some decent whisky and wine."

The Scots offered the bottles to the Indians who immediately threw away what was left of their foul potion and grabbed the alcohol.

The forging of the booze bond with these generous, funny natives was cemented by the dinner that followed. Paterson sent a soldier back to get more whisky. The lieutenant saluted, but as he turned to go he was stopped by Buchanan, uttering the magic words. "And make sure to bring back an extra bottle for you and your men."

The dinner went on for some hours and slowly but surely that great linguistic paradox kicked in. As the consumption of liquor increased, so the need for a translator decreased. Non-verbal communication be it sign language, drawings in the sand or pointing, together with the odd bastardised word of Spanish seemed to do the trick.

They had established a strong bridgehead with the locals. Even more importantly, the Scots learned that Andreas and his group were just a small part of the larger Tule tribe located some miles along the coast.

CHAPTER 7

The township was to be called New Edinburgh. From the outset construction progressed at a snail's pace. It quickly became clear that making inroads into the tough hinterland would be a colossal job. Many of the tools were ineffective against the gnarled indigenous hardwoods and it took an entire day for a team to cut down a single tree and chop it into timber strips. Matters were made worse by the constant assault of the flies which flew in thick black swarms and often disappeared down the exhausted workers' throats.

The promised paradise also had a brutally harsh climate. The entrance cliffs, towering like Panamanian Pillars of Hercules, provided an ideal natural military protection, but along with the steep hills trapped the oppressive heat to create a huge natural bowl in which the Scots gently boiled every day. The water was the only relief, but even that felt like a warm bath.

The lack of wind also caused a serious navigational problem. There was enough to blow a ship into the bay but precious little to help it escape. To make matters worse, the strait between the Pillars was choppy and dangerous with a huge, submerged rock about a hundred metres to the northern side. Far from the ideal scenario for a colony designed to be a trading hub.

Inevitably, there came a new wave of disease. Within two weeks a fresh outbreak of dysentery had taken hold and was accompanied in its ghoulish work by the new mosquito borne terror of yellow fever. To try to stop the spread, anyone who fell sick was taken ashore. This was not so much a Council decision as a direction of the captains who demanded their vessels be quarantined.

The absence of any meaningful quantities of fresh food and medicine meant that the sick didn't get better quickly. Hunting parties were increased, but their lack of expertise in trapping or killing anything in the alien landscape proved an enormous handicap. These were not the rolling, wind blasted hills of Scotland where heather and gorse were the only hiding places. This was a world of dark impenetrable woods where the cotton wool silence was ripped apart by the terrifying screams and screeches of the monkeys and exotic birds.

There were fish in the bay but the catch wasn't nearly sufficient to feed everyone. As the available food declined, daily rations were reduced until they reached near starvation levels. This made it even easier for illness to put people in their graves. Pincarton had ordered that the supplies on the Unicorn be re-distributed to ensure that those still on board were fed at least once a day. The other ships followed suit, even the Saint Andrew, although Buchanan was sure that the Commodore would have held back sufficient of his private stores to ensure he was not personally inconvenienced. The only consumable cargo which remained largely untouched was the Madeira wine which with the linen, tobacco and whisky appeared to be the Scots' only valuable trading commodity.

In that first week ten more settlers died and upwards of one hundred sick taken ashore. They were placed in a makeshift shelter acting as a field infirmary. Most lay silent, stoically enduring the pain, but those gripped in their death throes writhed and screamed in agony. There was little that the doctors could do except hope that the stronger would pull through. It was survival of the fittest, and in their malnourished, depleted state there weren't many of those.

Paterson's son and Pincarton both fell ill on the ninth day. They had each complained of a fever and stomach cramps the day before but during that night the dysentery had taken hold with violent force. Rather than take them ashore to the insect infested beach, the doctor ordered them to be moved to the Great Cabin where there was more light and space.

Young John Paterson lay like a ghost, only moving to wretch spectacular amounts of bile and spew into the bowl which his mother held in one hand as she cradled his head in the other. All pretence of modesty was removed and, other than a cloth covering their privates, the patients lay naked on sheets positioned to catch the running tap of excrement that poured out of their bodies.

Damp compresses were applied to quell the fever but in seconds the raging heat switched to shivering cold and the cloths would have to be removed and replaced with blankets. The doctor tried every trick in his cavalcade of medical futility but all had little effect.

Fearing the worst, Buchanan crouched down to Pincarton and whispered, "Robert, I know you're not a believer, but just in case, do you want to renounce the Devil and his works or anything like that."

Pincarton, lifted his head from the sweat soaked pillow and with a wry smile, whispered, "I don't really think now's the best time to be making new enemies." Then he lapsed into unconsciousness. Buchanan quickly put his hand to his friend's neck feeling for a pulse. There was one, but it was incredibly weak.

Just then Paterson's wife let out a scream. It was the unearthly sound of human grief. As Pincarton had lost consciousness so too had John Paterson. But he was not coming back. Buchanan spun round and saw Hannah clutch the lifeless body of her boy to her bosom. His frail shrunken frame had been unable to take any more and he slipped out of the world in the arms of the woman who had given him life.

Buchanan watched as William Paterson fell to his knees, broken and lost as to what to do or say. He reached across to his wife but she slapped his hand away. "Aye. Well, where's yer all-caring God that would take ma boy away from me?" This meek unassuming woman had been deprived of the main reason for her being and needed someone to blame.

Paterson seemed to crumple in on himself and slumped back, staring blankly at the ghastly scene. Buchanan felt totally helpless. What could possibly be said in the face of such unutterable tragedy? Hannah Paterson sat rocking back and forth, cradling her beloved child in her desperate caress. Then she began repeating a mantra, "No, ma bonny lad, no." Time and again the words fell from her trembling lips as if the incantation would somehow bring him back to life.

Paterson managed to get himself up onto one of the chairs. There were no tears, just a look which Buchanan hoped he would never have to experience. Children were not supposed to die before their parents. The doctor brought over a small glass of whisky and told Paterson to drink it. He looked blankly at the tumbler before swallowing the contents whole.

Returning his focus to his wife he moved back towards her. This time she didn't push him away. She just sat there, her ashen face a hollow mask of grief, all purpose gone. She let Paterson enfold her in his arms and the three huddled together, entwined in a macabre tableau of bereavement.

The hours that followed were tough. Hannah Paterson refused to let go of her son, so Paterson persuaded her to allow him to wash down the emaciated little body in gentle stages so that she was still able to maintain constant contact. He then guided her back to their cabin and laid them down on the bed. Paterson sat beside her for the eternity of that night listening as she prayed to be released from the impossible pain and for Death to take her too.

Buchanan stayed in the Great Cabin with Pincarton. This night would determine the Captain's fate. If he could survive and break the fever then he would recover. Otherwise he would join John Paterson on the list of fatalities. Buchanan spent his vigil mopping Pincarton's brow and sipping away at the whisky to keep himself alert. But eventually exhaustion got the better of him and he fell into a dead sleep.

He was awoken by a shaft of early morning sunlight playing across his face. Sitting bolt upright he stared across to where his friend was lying. "Please God, be alive," he whispered. As the words came out of his mouth he watched as Pincarton slowly opened his eyes and looked at him. "Sounds like you almost meant it, Jamie," he rasped.

Buchanan jumped out his chair and knelt down. He felt Pincarton's brow and knew immediately that the fever had left him. "Jesus Christ, you gave us a hell of a scare."

Pincarton gave a weak smile. "Very sorry about that. By the way, what the fuck happened to my whisky?"

Buchanan bent his head and gently wept. Pincarton raised his right hand and softly laid it on his hair. "It's alright, Jamie. There's plenty more in my secret cabinet."

A few minutes later the doctor arrived and confirmed that while Pincarton was out of the woods, he would need to convalesce until his strength returned. "Thank you," said Pincarton. "Now can you get someone to come and clean me up. You'll understand I'm not exactly thrilled to be lying in my own shit."

When the doctor had left, Pincarton asked, "What about the wee laddie?"

Buchanan shook his head. "Last night. Very sudden."

Pincarton closed his eyes. "Where are they now?"

"In Paterson's cabin. Thought it best to leave them alone."

As if on cue the door to the Great Cabin swung open and Paterson walked in. His face was grey with fatigue, his eyes hollow and devoid of life. Buchanan got to his feet and moved toward him.

"William, I am so, so, sorry. What can I do?"

Paterson looked at him and shook his head. "Nothing to be done," he whispered.

"How's Hannah?" Buchanan asked, immediately thinking how trite and stupid the question sounded.

"She's with him now,"

"Is there anything I can take to her?"

"No, Jamie. She's with him now," he repeated.

His words hung in the air, then the full import of their meaning registered. Buchanan rushed past Paterson and into the cabin. There, lying beside each other under a blanket were John Paterson and his mother. He was still nestled in her arms and her left hand almost seemed to be stroking her child's head. But what struck him most was that her expression was no longer one of impossible loss. It had been replaced by a death mask of serenity. She was with her little boy again in whatever afterlife she had seen when she breathed her last.

Buchanan made his way back into the Great Cabin. He looked squarely at Paterson, scared to speak the words but his eyes asked the obvious question. Paterson returned the gaze. "No, Jamie. It may have come to that, but she just gave up and stopped breathing."

Buchanan didn't know if that was medically possible but he wasn't going to press the matter. Paterson suddenly became shrunken. Buchanan embraced him and let the bereft man cry unashamedly in his arms. After several minutes Paterson regained his composure and forced the steel back into his bones. He rubbed his red eyes and cleared his throat. "I'll mourn them in my own time. But by God, I'll make sure that they haven't died in vain."

Their funerals took place the next morning. Buchanan stood bedside Paterson as he laid his wife and son to rest beside each other in the newly created cemetery. All the Councillors, except the still recuperating Pincarton, were present. The Reverend Scott offered a comforting eulogy and a piper played a lament as they lowered the burial shrouds into the grave. Kind words and condolences were offered by every man. This was a time for putting aside any differences. The stark horror of a life ending had that effect.

They retired to the Great Cabin of the Saint Andrew and held a wake. Pennicuik and Buchanan said a few words and then Paterson rose to respond. He thanked them all for their support and spoke emotionally of his wife and son. As he finished his voice took on a hardness. "I'm not the first person on this journey to have been visited by the pain of loss and I will not be the last. But all the sacrifices made will be for nought if we don't succeed in our mission. We owe it to them to make Darien a reality."

With that, he raised his glass, inhaled the aroma of the whisky and allowed the scent of his distant homeland to flood his senses.

CHAPTER 8

A few days later the Council agreed to take up Andreas' offer to meet the larger Tule tribe. While the Indians might provide intelligence about any Spanish threat on Panama, the main aim was to tap their knowledge about the optimal bridge between the two great Oceans. The Spanish had already done it, so the Scots assumed that it would be well within their capabilities to follow suit. But while remaining confident of their King's protection under the Act the settlers didn't want to poke the Iberian bear. Accordingly their route would need to be sufficiently removed to avoid any antagonism.

The visiting party was to comprise Buchanan, Paterson, Spense and the soldier, Thomas Drummond together with a platoon of his men. The canny Andreas agreed to take them in exchange for more access to the Company's cellars.

The first part of the journey along the coast was made in the sleek native canoes which the wiry Indians powered across the crystal clear water at a speed which the Scots' oarsmen could never hope to match.

Much of the jagged coastline appeared to be an impenetrable wall of mangroves from which, every now and again, would slide the terrifying caimans. Andreas said that they didn't attack humans although there wasn't a single Scot willing to put it to the test.

An hour later, they arrived at a large inlet where several other canoes were tethered. The Scots disembarked and comically splashed onto the shore to avoid any lurking predators. The scarlet coat of the little Indian then struck out onto a path leading back into the dark forest. A route had been hacked through the dense foliage but this had been tailored to the diminutive Indians so the Scots had to continually stoop to avoid banging their heads against the tough gnarled branches which twisted at impossible angles like unset limbs.

Most of the trek was undertaken in a ghostly half-light where shadows moved like living things, darting in and out of the gaps in the gloom. Sweat poured off the Scots in the stifling humidity and all around there was a strange mist which felt almost human, reaching out with invisible fingers and wrapping itself around their skin. It came as an enormous relief when, after about two miles, they escaped the suffocating claustrophobia of the narrow path and suddenly emerged into a large clearing which sat in total incongruity to the unpierceable barrier surrounding it.

Before them lay a Panamanian Shangri La. A meadow of about ten acres was dotted with dozens of large huts, all much bigger than those in Andreas' village. There were rows of crops and a stream running along the edge. Small turkey-like birds wandered around pecking away at some seeds and two horses munched placidly on straw. In the midst of all of this were hundreds of people. Children running around, women busying themselves with their chores, and men skinning game or practising their weaponry skills. In other words a fully functioning community, slap bang in the middle of the jungle.

The sight of their party created no panic as the villagers had known they were coming. Throughout the jungle were invisible sentries, vigilant for any intruder who might threaten their safety. Mimicked bird sounds would have signalled their progress. However, when they arrived every local stopped what they were doing to stare at these giants in their strange attire. A sea of gawping faces fixed them with a mix of curiosity and apprehension. For some it would have been the first time they had clapped eyes on Europeans. For the others it would have been a terrifying reminder of the Spanish.

Andreas held up his scarlet jacketed arm in greeting and shouted out. This elicited a roar from the audience and they began to move as one towards the Scots. The soldiers gripped their muskets. Drummond sensed the tension and the old hand told his men to stand easy and make no sudden moves. "Gently now, lads. We're guests here. Nothing tae get het up aboot. Just keep yer eyes on they big fuckers wi the spears though."

The crowd swarmed the visiting party as Andreas and his men embraced friends and family. Then a path opened through the throng and down strode a man who, by bearing and attire, appeared to carry considerable authority. On seeing him, Andreas broke off from his reunions and went over. They greeted one another warmly and spoke rapidly in their native tongue.

The man then turned to the Scots and said in flawless French. "*Bonjour, mes amis. On ma dit que vous parlez Francais. Je m'appelle Ambrosio et je suis le chef du village.*"

Buchanan and Paterson, who both spoke French, looked at each other in astonishment. How in God's name in the middle of a jungle in a part of the world where the Frogs held no influence could a native Indian speak French? Well, whatever the reason, it was a stroke of good fortune.

No-one was more delighted at this revelation than the hapless Spense who had been dreading mistranslating a crucial phrase and getting them all killed.

CHAPTER 9

The Scots were led to the largest building in the village. It was about thirty yards in length, ten wide and ten high. The superstructure was a combination of hardwood and cane with a thatched roof of palm and plantain leaves tightly bound together by vine ropes. The sleeping quarters were again elevated which left the floor space entirely clear for cooking and entertaining. The ground was covered with ornate rugs made from some sort of hemp which had been delicately decorated with images of birds, animals, the sun and the moon. Buchanan, Paterson and Drummond were ushered into its welcoming cool shade.

Ambrosio then instructed that the rest of the Scots be looked after. He was tall man for a native, standing about five foot eight. The sense of height was accentuated by his upright posture and long neck. He looked to be about sixty but with his weathered skin, the colour of tanned hide, it was difficult to know with any accuracy. His most striking feature were his dark, almost obsidian, eyes, hooded like a reptile. He wore a number of feathers in a head band and a white cloth covered his chest and groin.

Paterson introduced himself and the others. The Scots were invited to sit. As they did so a bevy of young maidens appeared and handed each of them two cups. The first contained water and the second a milky brew. Ambrosio saw the Scots looking askance. "My friends, this drink is called mislaw. Do not concern yourselves. It is not like that hideous concoction which Andreas likes to give his unsuspecting guests."

He translated for Andreas and this brought a cackle of laughter from the impish little man. Mislaw was fermented corn and potato so when Buchanan took a tentative sip he found it akin to a sweet gin. He nodded in appreciation. *"C'est très bon. Merci, chef."*

Assured by his endorsement, Paterson and Drummond followed suit. It was only when the Scots had drunk that the hosts did the same. Buchanan was impressed by this etiquette but then reflected that it wouldn't have been such a politeness had the mislaw been poisoned.

Paterson and Drummond then produced the bottles of whisky and wine which were laid before the Indians. Ambrosio picked up one of the whisky bottles and turned it in his thick hand. "Andreas tells me that you are from the land where this is made."

"Scotland," replied Paterson.

"I know of this place. My French friends tell me of their friendship with it. But is it true that the men wear skirts and play a strange instrument which sounds like a cat being strangled?"

The Scots laughed. Even here in the middle of the jungle the same old stereotype played out.

"Yes, that's true." smiled Paterson.

"Well, we thank you for these gifts."

The two sides then proceeded to ask a barrage of questions. The Scots learned that the Tule had all once lived peacefully near the shore where it was cooler and the fish plentiful. But that paradise had disappeared when then the Spanish arrived. They had attacked their village with unthinking force and either killed or captured the Indians. They came to conquer and subjugate. The natives were seen as an inferior species, fit only to be enslaved or exterminated. Ambrosio himself had been captured and been taken in chains overland to the Pacific coast where the Tule were forced to work until they died in the atrocity of the Spanish mines.

He described how the Spanish would torture their prisoners either to get information, mete out punishment, or simply for grotesque sport. There were whippings, brandings and rackings all learned from those masters of persuasion, the Inquisition. In a flat emotionless tone Ambrosio narrated that he had been forced to watch as the Spanish took his brother and tied long cords to his thumbs and big toes and spreadeagled them to four stakes. The whole weight of his body was held by these digits. Then they beat the cords with sticks so that with every perverse percussion his brother would scream in agony. Then, when they tired of this, they cut him down and placed stones on top of his chest increasing the weight until he was slowly crushed to death, All the while they laughed and made bets as to how long it would take for him to die. At the end, he had longed for the sweet release of death.

The Scots sat stunned. Ambrosio apologised, sensing that he had spoken too much. However, Paterson urged him to continue. Appreciating the interest, Ambrosio explained that initially the Spanish made alliances with the larger more warlike tribes in the region. Then having gained the natives' trust, they broke their word and continued with their slaughter and enslavement. All so these destroyers of worlds could load up their black ships with bloodstained gold and silver to take back to their treasure ports in Spain. He said that even now there were tribes foolish enough to seek appeasement, like a man who keeps feeding a shark hoping it will eat him last.

When an opportunity had arisen for Ambrosio to escape he had seized it with both hands. He was part of the slave train, chained in leg irons, ferrying silver from Panama City to Puerto Bello. But one particular trip had been in the wet season and the Chagres river was running fast. There had been a huge mud slide and dozens of men, both Spanish and Indian disappeared under the torrent of rock, silt and sludge which roared down the mountainside. In the melee Ambrosio had grabbed the Spanish horseman who held the key to his shackles, pulled him from his mount and smashed his face to a pulp with a jagged rock. He had then released himself and ten of his friends, all of them fleeing into the jungle, miraculously freed from their living hell.

Ambrosio had made his way back to the village and since then had been set on a path of revenge. The Indians struck using guerrilla tactics, lightning raids and ambush attacks. The Spanish had tried to find them but their forays into the dense jungle resulted in far more casualties than victims so they gave up and concentrated on guarding their gold and silver trains.

Paterson sat quietly all through this narrative. Buchanan had seen a change in him since the devastating loss of his wife and son. The arrogance and self-possession seemed to have gone. Now he listened patiently.

Ambrosio had obviously taken to him and asked the deformed little Scotsman why he and his countrymen had come all this way to settle in Darien.

Paterson, in an astonishing feat of brevity, explained their recent history and in particular the desire set up a trading hub linking the Atlantic and Pacific Oceans. Buchanan noticed the Indians look at one another. Paterson was about to keep talking when Buchanan tugged on his sleeve. The Indians then began chattering among themselves. Buchanan whispered that they had become agitated when Paterson mentioned the cross-continental trading route.

Ambrosio explained that the Indians were puzzled how the Scots intended to transfer their goods from one side of the Isthmus to the other. Paterson replied that they would create a passage from Darien to the Pacific side and establish another trading port there. Ambrosio fixed Paterson with those mesmerising eyes. "Monsieur Paterson. I have lived my entire life on this isthmus and there is only one viable route across it. That is the treasure road which the Spanish control."

"But we have it on good authority that such a road can be established."

"Perhaps with a thousand men cutting through the forest for ten years."

"No, that cannot be the case."

Ambrosio picked up on the Scotsman's disquiet. "Monsieur Paterson, if you like I can arrange for my best scouts to take some of your people to the interior. They can show you the terrain and you can decide for yourself."

"Thank you. That would be appreciated. We must make our own assessment."

Buchanan glanced at him. There was the old stubbornness back again.

As the conversations continued so did the consumption of alcohol. The Indians might have a high tolerance for mislaw but they were amateurs when it came to whisky. The golden nectar loosened their tongues and it soon became clear that the Tule were keen to enlist the Scots in their vendetta against the Spanish.

"Give me a hundred men," declared Ambrosio, "and we can take Puerto Bello and Panama City. Then you will have your trade passage."

Buchanan laughed. "I can see the merit in your argument, Chief, but I don't believe it would be well received in Madrid."

"Why not? They come here and take what they want without asking. Why should you not do the same?"

Buchanan wanted to launch into a geo-political lecture but two bottles of whisky in, this would probably miss its mark. So he contented himself by explaining that the Scots were here as merchants and not aggressors and that their troops were for protection not conquest. Ambrosio laughed and said it was a pity, especially as the Tule had made a good start on Golden Island the week before. Paterson asked what he meant. The Indian chief narrowed his eyes and said they had killed five Spanish priests who had gone on retreat there and then thrown their bodies off the cliffs for the sharks to feast on.

The Scots looked at each other. Drummond blew out his cheeks. "Aye well, that's no gonnae attract much attention to Darien then, is it?"

CHAPTER 10

The visiting party left the next morning after a breakfast of fruit, corn bread and water. More mislaw had been offered but that was a bridge too far the way they were feeling.

Pincarton was waiting when they arrived back aboard the Unicorn. He seemed almost restored to full health. "Well, well, the happy wanderers return. I trust you enjoyed your wee holiday up the coast?"

Buchanan smiled. "Good to see you back to your normal sarky self."

"Come, tell me your travellers' tales and I'll give you the breaking news from here."

"That sounds intriguing."

They descended into the Great Cabin which felt stuffy and humid, but at least it was out of the baking sun. Paterson and Buchanan both declined the offer of wine and opted for tea. "Bit of a night, was it then gentlemen?" ventured Pincarton, raising a censorious eyebrow.

"One has to do what one has to do in the name of international relations," replied Buchanan as he gingerly rubbed his throbbing temples.

Paterson and Buchanan then spent the next hour giving Pincarton a full debrief. At the end Pincarton just sat shaking his head. "Christ, those Spanish are evil bastards. You did well to make inroads with the Tule."

"Aye, but until we've earned their trust they'll still be wary," said Buchanan. "We might say we're different from the Spanish but how are they really to know? Anyway, what's this great news you trumpeted?"

Pincarton gave a wry smile. "It appears that the English have gotten wind of our whereabouts."

"What! But we've only been here two weeks," spluttered Paterson.

"And it took us two sodding months to find it!" added Buchanan.

"Well be that as it may, yesterday a ship flying His Majesty's ensign was spotted anchored off Golden Island."

"Do we know who it is?" asked Paterson.

"No, but we will later today. Its captain has requested an audience and Pennicuik has invited him for lunch aboard the Saint Andrew."

"How unusually civilised of the Supreme Commander," sniped Buchanan.

"Yes I thought it a bit out of character myself, especially since he's also invited the other Captains and Councillors to attend."

When they arrived at the Saint Andrew, the guest of honour had already come aboard. He introduced himself as Captain Richard Long of His Majesty's Navy. His dark weathered face housed astute hazel eyes which seemed to take in everything around him under a pair of sharply pointed brows. He was of medium height and build but his most notable feature was his voice. This was no low born tar made good though the ranks. This was a man whose vowels oozed Patrician breeding and may have gone some way to explaining the social climbing Pennicuik's eagerness to engage. The table was set for a fine lunch which would have caused a hell of a stir had it been seen by those settlers on survival rations.

"So, Captain Long," asked Pennicuik "what brings you to these waters?"

"Indeed, Commodore," purred the Englishman. It was apparent that Pennicuik had introduced himself using his now redundant title. "I hold a commission to traverse the coast of Central America in search of treasure trove."

"Presumably only from ships that have already sunk," interjected Pincarton.

"Quite so, Captain. As you may have seen my ship, "The Rupert", is not designed for aggression."

"We can only take your word for that without an inspection," angled Pennicuik.

"Well, we shall most certainly have to rectify that."

Long possessed such an effortless charm that it was easy to forget that he was undoubtedly there to spy on the Scots. But how the hell had he known where to look?

Paterson, seeking an insight, asked, "Just out of interest, what was it that brought you to Golden Island?"

"Oh, just part of my routine run up and down the coast don't you know? This stretch of water is ideal for shipwrecks."

"Is that so?" answered a dubious Paterson.

"Tell us, Captain Long. Do you ever run into Johnny Spaniard in the area?" chimed in Jolly, between mouthfuls of the wild turkey which had been caught that morning.

"Not if I can help it. Although we are not currently at War- well I think that's the case this month- the Spanish in this part of the world tend to pay little heed to peace treaties signed in Europe."

Thomas Drummond, the army veteran, crowed. "Well, we won the last war so we can whip their Dago arses this time too."

Long smiled. "Having also been part of that War and seen so many of my friends perish, I'd be more inclined to say that perhaps we just lost more slowly. As far as 'Johnny Spaniard' is concerned, you best to be on your guard. They regard Central America as their fiefdom. Anyone looking to cut in is discouraged with maximum force."

"I think we can look after ourselves Captain Long," countered Pennicuik.

"I'm sure you think you can Commodore. As doubtless did many of the local tribes."

Pennicuik railed at this, "What nonsense to put us in the same category as those natives."

"I'm sure you're absolutely right, Commodore. It's just that I've seen what the Spanish are capable of. They have few boundaries when it comes to protecting their monopoly."

Paterson interjected. "They wouldn't dare attack us when we are under the King's protection."

"How so, Mr. Paterson?"

"It is mandated under the Act sanctioning this enterprise."

Long looked at him with those shrewd eyes. "Well, then I'm sure His Majesty will honour his pledge and you'll have nothing to worry about."

There then followed an uncomfortable pause as the Scots digested the exchange. It was broken by the inquisitive Long. "So, Gentlemen. It appears that you are building yourself something of a settlement here in Darien." He said this with such feigned ignorance that a gullible man might have believed him.

Paterson replied, "Indeed and again with the blessing of his Majesty."

"Well, all the better then. And what will you trade from here? Plantains?" Long said with a little chuckle.

"Well," said Paterson, "certainly we'll be a trading exchange for passing ships and to this end we brought much fine Scottish product with us."

"Seems a long way to set up a corner shop."

"Ah well, that's before you factor in the fine trade to be had in the local Nicaragua wood.," continued Paterson.

"Of course, let's not forget that," smiled Long. "So, no plans to follow the Spanish across the peninsula?"

"Whatever gave you that idea, Captain?" parried Paterson.

"Oh, you know how one hears these rumours in the taverns of the Caribbean."

"Who is foolish enough to believe rumours?"

Long smiled. "I'll wager you never come to a battle of wits unarmed Mr. Paterson."

"I also make a point of never arguing with stupid people in case they beat me with experience."

The Englishman laughed and raised his glass to the wily Scot. "*Touché*, Sir."

Pennicuik watching on felt himself shift from centre stage, and desperately seeking relevance, clumsily re-entered the conversation. "And are you planning on being with us long"- and then there was an awkward gap- "Captain Long?"

"Oh, I doubt it Commodore," he said softly, "It seems you Scots have marked your territory. I do hope you planted a flag."

He had said this as a humorous aside but it did not prevent the oblivious Pennicuik from giving chapter and verse of his titanic efforts in this regard.

Long, with the genteel manners of the upper class, pandered to this cartoonish character's account and gave it due gravitas. "You must be very proud of yourself, Commodore."

The lunch stretched out and a fair dent was put in Pennicuik's precious whisky supply. But all through, Long stuck to his line of treasure hunter for the King. Eventually he declared that he must get back to The Rupert before dark. He thanked Pennicuik for the hospitality and promised to return the favour.

The Scots watched as Long's rowboat made its way back out through the heads just as dusk wrapped its warm embrace around the spectators and the birds and wildlife in the jungle began to whistle and screech their lullabies.

Buchanan turned to his companions. "Well?"

"Well, what?" countered Pincarton.

"Spy or not a Spy?"

"Jamie, for God's sake, were you born yesterday son?"

"Just checking. He's an impressive fellow for all that though, isn't he?"

Pincarton smiled. "That's centuries of breeding. No-one stares into the middle distance quite like the English aristocracy. Wonderful the way they can make you feel so damned insignificant."

CHAPTER 11

The next morning The Rupert was gone.

This didn't come as a particular surprise to anyone other than the self-important Pennicuik, who had been seduced by Long's suavity and the promise of a return dinner on the English vessel. For the others it confirmed Long's true commission. He would by now be under full sail to Kingston to communicate his findings for onward transmission to London. On the upside, at least it would mean that their Royal Protector couldn't deny knowing where they were.

Word from London would also leach north to Edinburgh. The last letters the Scots had sent were from Madeira so, to all intents and purposes, the Company and Scottish population would have no idea if they had reached Panama.

The other side of that coin was that the settlers had received no news from Scotland since departing Leith all those months ago. It was one of the great sacrifices of any colonist, to leave behind an entire life and not know what had become of it. Some, in whose best interests it was to abandon the past and embrace anonymity, would care not a jot. But unused to such separation most would, from time to time, become maudlin and yearn for their loved ones and the smells, sounds and light of their homeland.

The brutality of the journey, the disease and now the heat and hunger of Darien proved too much for a few souls who asked to return to Scotland. While the Council couldn't stop them, it was made clear that if they wanted to leave, they would have to bear the cost and make their own arrangements. So, no-one left.

Mercifully, the buildings onshore had advanced enough to allow the settlers to move in. Paterson also instructed that a weatherproof warehouse be constructed to store their goods and supplies. Establishing what had survived the trip and what had spoiled was a sobering exercise.

The Reverend Scott was delighted to find that the monumental supply of Bibles were undamaged and took this as a sign that the Lord was watching over them. He was perhaps a little premature in his optimism as he fell ill the following week, slumped into a coma and died two days later. He had been the last surviving minister, and if their attrition rate was anything to go by there didn't seem a hell of a lot of Divine support for the venture.

The seedlings were dry and still fit for planting. The hope was that they would take quickly in the fertile soil from which new growth seemed to explode every day. The valuable linens and barrels of whisky were undamaged although it didn't go unnoticed that some of the malt seals appeared to have been tampered with. An investigation found that the angel's share in several was well over its usual tolerance. Most of the heavy woollen blankets and cloths were also relatively intact, but in the oppressive heat of Darien, their commercial worth was questionable at best.

The most spectacular casualties were the prized wigs and leather shoes. Not, of course, that they would have been remotely tradable, even when brand new. The glue on the shoes, while robust even on the hottest Scottish summer day, had melted in the furnace-like heat of the holds, leaving the soles flapping like fish on a dock. The wigs, some blond and others a comical ginger, had fared even worse. Whatever chemical reaction had occurred on the trip had turned them all a bizarre shade of purple. Paterson had plucked several of these from different containers and just shook his head ruefully.

Another significant undertaking was to careen each of the ships to remove the weeds and crustaceans that had taken up residence on their hulls. Each ship in rotation had to be dragged as near to the beach as possible, hauled over on its side and its bottom scraped and repaired. This meant that the crew of the affected ship had to be accommodated elsewhere. Their options were to stay on the land- an abhorrent prospect in the absence of taverns and whorehouses - or find a bunk on another vessel.

As a rule crews didn't associate much with each other and enmities were commonplace. Those on the flagship, Saint Andrew, thought themselves superior, while those on the little Endeavour regarded themselves as better seamen. This did not make a good recipe for sharing quarters, so Pennicuik instituted a savage retribution against anyone who saw the enforced billeting as an opportunity to settle scores.

The first time it happened both men were strapped to the main mast of the Saint Andrew and the cat wielded on their exposed backs. The second time each combatant had one hand strapped behind his back while the other hand was nailed to the mast. They stayed like that until, exhausted by hunger, thirst and the searing sun they chose the only option other than death, to tear the skewered hand from the mast by ripping it apart. After that there were no other fights.

By the end of that third week, many of the Scots, now rested, in better health and with a ready supply of fresh water, could feel a shifting tide of optimism. Their colony was beginning to take shape, and slowly they were becoming acclimatised to the alien conditions in this tropical Eden. All that was missing was more food but with hard work they felt sure they could grow and catch enough to sustain them until a Company supply ship or the Second Fleet arrived. Despite everything, there was a growing belief that they might actually make a go of this wildly ambitious scheme.

Then, in early December 1698, the weather turned. The blue skies blackened and the searing sunshine was replaced with what seemed like an unending deluge. While the cooling rains were welcome they had a devastating effect on the newly planted seeds. The little fields turned into flood plains and the fledgling crops were washed away in front of the settlers' eyes.

To preserve the most useful supplies and goods human chains hauled barrels and boxes through the sludge and up to higher ground for placement under the makeshift warehouse. Anything spoiled or unusable was left in the open so as not to take-up any valuable covered space.

The deluge also increased the menace of Yellow Fever. The mosquitos, plentiful enough in the dry heat, suddenly swarmed in droves in the steamy wet. Settlers fell like ninepins and the death toll began to rise.

The Councillors and elite passengers returned to their weather-proofed cabins on the ships far away from the land bound insects. The Captains agreed to allow back on board those settlers who had not fallen ill but insisted that the sick would need to stay ashore until they recovered. Or died. Such was the tragically binary nature of the equation.

Despite these new setbacks the Scots pushed forward with their building programme. They knew it might only be a matter of time before the Spanish came knocking, so those men still fit to work were put under the command of Thomas Drummond to construct the fort. His reputation as one of the perpetrators of the Glencoe Massacre followed him like a relentless spectre. His stubborn defence that had he only been following orders, carried little weight with many of the Highlanders. However, Drummond had more supporters than enemies and in person was a fearsome proposition. Ox strong, he had as much charm as a war crime and the scars on his face evidenced that he was no stranger to the wrong end of a broken bottle.

But he organised his work team with discipline and was no idle supervisor. Every day Drummond rolled up his sleeves and dug, hacked and strained with the rest of them. All his men may not all have liked him, but he had their respect.

During a break in the weather the Scots welcomed Andreas on board the Saint Andrew to formalise a Treaty of Mutual Protection. Spense, in broken Spanish, explained its terms and the little Indian made all the right noises about abiding by this, bowing theatrically when Pennicuik handed him the parchment. He in turn presented Pennicuik with a quiver of feathers as a sign of his bona fides. However, no sooner had all this been done than Andreas handed the scroll to one of his entourage and immediately forgot about it. He then proceeded to get drunk, passed out and had to be lifted by his bodyguards onto his canoe.

As he watch the chief's undignified exit Paterson showed Buchanan the discarded treaty. "Don't think he's too bothered about the fine detail of our accord."

"I think we'd be better served fostering relations with Ambrosio," suggested Buchanan.

"Couldn't agree more."

"Maybe then we'll be able to organise the survey of the isthmus."

"Already ahead of you Jamie," smiled Paterson.

CHAPTER 12

The Scots battled on with Presbyterian fortitude. Drains were constructed and they began to get on top of the flood waters. There was some limited success bartering for food with the Indians and the Scots hunting parties would occasionally return from the thick bush with a wild pig or turkey. But these were barely enough and unless supplies arrived soon the situation would become untenable.

Then on December 11th, the next excitement arrived. The lookout signalled that a ship flying the French flag had anchored near Golden Island and that a longboat had been lowered and was rowing towards the bay.

Pennicuik ordered the boat to make for the Saint Andrew and then summoned Paterson, Pincarton and Buchanan. They all watched as the little craft came alongside. The first of its occupants appeared at the rail of the deck, a gaunt fellow wearing the smart blue jacket of the French navy. He had startlingly prominent cheek bones and unblinking grey eyes, all of which combined to give the impression of a walking skeleton.

Predictably, Pennicuik introduced himself as Commodore of the Fleet. The Frenchman cleared his throat and replied in an unexpectedly high-pitched voice just like a boy crashing through puberty, "Delighted to meet you Commodore. I am Captain Thomas Duvivier. I command the "Maurepas" and operate under commission from His Majesty King Louis of France to sail and trade in these waters." This was accompanied by so gracious a bow that Buchanan was almost tempted to applaud.

Pennicuik introduced the others and then asked curtly. "So Captain, tell us what brings you to Darien?"

The Frenchman paused for effect. "Perhaps a matter of common interest to us both."

"Go on," pressed Pennicuik.

"The Spanish at Cartagena have recently received orders from King Phillip to cleanse the area of undesirables."

"What do you mean by 'undesirables'?"

"Well, that would be whatever interpretation the Spanish choose to place on it. My intelligence is that they are not overly pleased by the recent spate of raids on their treasure galleons."

Pennicuik shot out his chin. "Can't say as I blame them. But what relevance is that to us?" In this mood, it was easier to have a conversation with a brass band.

Duvivier replied, "Their Caribbean Fleet, the Barlovento, is sweeping the region from Cartagena to Puerto Bello. Any ship deemed contrary to their interests will be seized, taken to Cartagena and their crews imprisoned."

"But under what premise? There's no war footing at present is there?" exclaimed Pennicuik.

"That matters nought to our Castilian cousins. They care little for anyone impinging on their territory and are not slow to take protective action."

All of this accorded with what Long had told them a few days before. A silence fell over the Scots, before Pincarton asked, " Do you know if they're aware of our presence?"

"Captain, everyone from Kingston to Caracas is aware of your presence. "

"I see. Have you any idea about what the Spanish think of us being here?"

"With the greatest respect Captain, they are utterly baffled."

""Baffled," interjected Pennicuik. "Why 'baffled'?"

"My dear Commodore, without wishing to appear rude, they cannot understand what would possess anyone to try to set up a colony in Darien."

"Why?" he snapped back.

"I'm not across those particular details but suffice to say that the Spanish long ago dismissed the idea of settling it themselves."

Buchanan looked at Pincarton, raising his eyebrows.

Pennicuik persevered. "So, why would they attack us? We're not raiders or pirates. "

"That is true, Commodore but they fear you may wish to take a bite out of their precious metal trade."

"But that's preposterous," blustered Pennicuik. "We have no wish to compete with them. We are a trading entrepot."

"The Spanish may not take the same view, especially as you have set up shop in their back garden."

Pennicuik exhaled loudly, his reddening face making him look like an inflated beetroot. "They would never dare attack us. We have a fine fleet, fortifications and more importantly the protection of King William."

"I'm sure all of that is true, but the Spanish are not known to play by the rules," replied Duvivier.

Pincarton lifted his chin. "All that aside, Captain, why are *you* here?"

The Frenchman hesitated, choosing his words carefully. "Let me be candid."

"Please," nodded Pincarton,

"There is no love lost between Kings Louis and Phillip at the best of times. So, any French vessel is an automatic target for the Spanish no matter how innocent its intentions."

"You did say "candid'," Pincarton reminded him.

"*D'accord*. Yes. Well, perhaps my commission from King Louis may have licensed the Maurepas to undertake some operations falling outside of normal trading boundaries."

"So, you are a privateer," barked Pennicuik.

Duvivier gave a small smile and bent his head in acknowledgement.

"And let me guess. You wish to take sanctuary in our bay?"

"Only until the Barlovento has sailed past."

"But why wait? Why not make for safer waters now?" asked Pincarton.

"Were my ship to be fully operational then I would be heading north to the French Antilles as we speak. But we suffered damage in a storm a week ago and need to make repairs. We could only run at half speed as things stand and that would leave us, how you say, 'a sitting duck'."

"I see," said Pincarton. "But if we are discovered hiding you it would not go well for us."

"I believe the Spanish may have bigger fish to fry on their current purge."

"Nonetheless, still a risk that we don't need to take," countered Pincarton.

"That, I fully appreciate. Of course, I would not expect your hospitality to go unrewarded."

This caught their attention. "Go on," urged Pennicuik.

"Just before the storm we took on provisions in Port Royal and our holds have good stocks of meat and wine. I'd be happy to trade some of these for an anchorage."

The danger of colluding with this French fugitive was easily outweighed by the prospect of being able to put some food in the hungry bellies of their countrymen. So the Scots agreed to give Duvivier asylum. He quickly returned to the Maurepas and later that afternoon, Pincarton, Paterson and Buchanan watched as the French vessel sailed through the heads and found an anchorage tucked well out of plain sight.

"A fine looking vessel." commented Buchanan.

"Oh, we've become the expert all of a sudden have we?" ribbed Pincarton.

"Just saying that she's pleasing to the eye."

"Aye that she is. And I'll tell you something else, she doesn't look that damaged to me."

"No, she doesn't does she?" agreed Paterson.

"But look how low she's sitting in the water," Pincarton said his curiosity piqued.

"Well, Duvivier did say she'd just taken on stores."

"Jamie, meat and bread don't cause a ship to look like that."

"So what does?"

"Gold and silver, my son, gold and silver," answered Pincarton, now very much more interested in the Maurepas than before.

CHAPTER 13

Duvivier transferred the supplies to the Scots the next day. Although limited, they were most welcome. The Council agreed to distribute these according to need and not privilege. Any suspicion that the elite passengers or seamen were receiving a more favourable share wouldn't have been well received by the increasingly resentful Landsmen.

Another significant problem had been how to get word to Edinburgh. Numerous letters had been written for despatch but their safe passage relied on the good faith of the captains of the ships carrying them. Even if payment was made there was no guarantee that the carrier wouldn't throw them into the ocean as soon as he was out of sight. The Council decided that the only ironclad solution was for someone to return in person to Scotland via the Maurepas to give a first-hand account of events.

The main issue was who that 'someone' should be since the emissary would have enormous influence on how news of the colony was received in Edinburgh. If he placed a positive spin on events then this would boost the national psyche and increase sentiment for more financial support. On the other hand, if the messenger didn't hold the party line and gave a bleak account of the issues which had plagued the venture then the result would be the opposite. Investment would be pulled, the Second Fleet abandoned and the country plunged into despair.

It was then that Councillor James Cunningham made his move. His staunch Presbyterian faith had been sorely tested by recent events, especially the deaths of his friends, the Reverends James and Scott. He was also no longer a young man and to end his days here, in this God-forsaken hole, was not something he was prepared to countenance any more. The news that the Spanish were now a live threat had been the last straw.

In the middle of a Council meeting he had stood up and declared. "Gentlemen, I want to be the one to leave with the Maurepas." Buchanan noticed Cunningham was pressing down hard on the table with his knuckles.

A hush descended. The departure of a Council member would carry a seriously adverse perception.

"We're all having a hard time of it James," offered Paterson.

Cunningham replied, "I know that, William, but I've lost heart. If I stayed I'd just be a negative influence."

"You've been that for weeks already," sniped Jolly. "Just bugger off then."

"Oh I think not," said Montgomery, his face flushed with anger. "We're not having you go back to Edinburgh and present them with a picture of doom and gloom."

"How can you stop me?" snapped Cunningham, a note of desperation in his voice.

"James, please don't put us to that test," said Pincarton. "You know that we could block your passage if we wanted."

Cunningham bowed his head sensing that his plea was falling on deaf ears. But then, the ever scheming Pennicuik entered the discussion. Normally, he would have told Cunningham to grow a set of balls and get on with it. But he saw the strategic benefit of one of the non-naval Councillors departing, especially one who was so close an ally of the detested Drummonds. His eyes danced at the opportunity. "Perhaps we are being overly precipitous."

Cunningham's head shot up to look at this least expected of supporters. Pennicuik continued. "If our main reservation is the perception of his early departure then it could be easily explained that one of the Councillors was always going to be entrusted with the task of reporting to Edinburgh and then return with the Second Fleet."

"And you'd be happy with Cunningham being that representative?" asked an incredulous Jolly.

Then normal service was resumed. "Christ, no. Montgomery has already explained why not. It would be the death knell if Cunningham was our voice in Edinburgh."

"I'm not following, Pennicuik. Are you saying he should be allowed to leave or not?" asked Jolly.

"It's better to have him gone than have to listen to his pathetic whingeing. But if he went it would be under strict conditions."

"Being?" pressed Jolly.

"That he say not a single word against the venture. He would require to write a letter extolling the hard work which has been undertaken and the successes we have achieved. He would sign and seal this and it would be taken to Edinburgh and presented to the Company by our real delegate. Cunningham's return could be passed off to Edinburgh as a health issue unconnected with the Colony."

This actually made some sense, while also achieving Pennicuik's ulterior agenda. Cunningham seized on the tainted olive branch. "You would have my word on that, Gentlemen."

Pincarton surveyed the room. "Perhaps you should let us talk about this, James."

Cunningham nodded and left, softly closing the Great Cabin door as though this would curry some extra favour. The discussion didn't take long. They knew the only way to deal with an abscess was to lance it so Pennicuik's proposal was adopted. However, that still left the question of who should be the Colony's envoy to Edinburgh.

Eventually the decision was made to appoint Malcolm Hamilton. He was the Accountant-General of the Colony, a man much valued and an enthusiast of the Scheme. His loss would be sorely felt but his credible reporting and positivity would be well received in Scotland.

All that remained was to recall Cunningham. He almost slid through the door. Paterson gave him the news. "James you can leave with the Maurepas but only under the conditions outlined by Pennicuik. Malcolm Hamilton will be appointed our emissary. You will be subordinate to him. Is that understood?"

Cunningham replied in the affirmative. At that stage he would probably have agreed to cut off his left nut. There was then an awkward silence.

It took Jolly only a few seconds to remedy that. "Well, fuck off then and mind and close the door behind you."

CHAPTER 14

As Duvivier grew confident that the Scots had no intention of plundering his vessel or slaughtering his crew, he became more generous with his Gallic hospitality. But he still remained guarded, and the debonair little Frenchman always deftly evaded any question put to him regarding his cargo before quickly detouring to another topic.

Notwithstanding this, Duvivier's company was a pleasure. He was witty, knowledgeable and more than fond of a drink. The sensual charms of Mrs Russell also hadn't escaped his notice. Now transformed as a result of a more regular bathing regime, it was apparent that she was keen to indulge in a little entente cordiale of her own. Mr. Russell seemed more interested in Duvivier's first officer and had fewer others been present, Buchanan was sure that an accommodation could have been reached to satisfy all interest groups.

However, that window never presented as Darien became even more crowded. On December 20th 1698, the lookout spotted a sloop moving towards the bay. It had signalled its intentions as friendly and was granted permission to sail into the harbour.

The appearance of this modest little vessel gave the beleaguered Colony hope that perhaps they had not been forgotten after all. However, the sloop, the "Belvedere", had not been sent by the Company. Rather it was the initiative of Richard Moon, who had been faithful to his pledge to Paterson to arrange for supplies to be delivered to the Scots.

The Belvedere's Captain was someone for whom the phrase 'old sea dog' could easily have been coined. He was a man of indeterminate age due to the abundance of hair which covered every visible surface of his body. His beard was wild, unruly and black as night. His eyebrows were thick and untamed and alarming amounts of fur sprouted from his nose and ears. A leonine mane tumbled haphazardly over his broad shoulders. When he spoke it was with a deep booming voice, as if God himself was talking.

He entered the Great Cabin of the Saint Andrew and announced himself with a percussive explosion of words. "Captain Edward Sands, at your service Gentlemen."

"Robert Pennicuik, Commodore of the Company of Scotland," came the first response, in a voice which sounded positively mouse-like in comparison.

"A pleasure, Commodore, a pleasure. Now, I have not come empty handed," he said, as he produced a bottle of Jamaican rum from inside a capacious gold buttoned black jacket. "This is a mere token. My holds carry supplies of beef and flour for your hungry bellies which our mutual friend Captain Moon asked me to bring to you."

"Then we owe a debt of gratitude to you both," said Pennicuik.

"Well, I'm happy to take your thanks as a down payment, but Moon said that you would have goods to trade."

Paterson stood up. "Didn't Richard draw against the Company account in New York?"

Sands quickly eyed the speaker up and down, his eyes alighting on the deformed shoulder. "I assume you, Sir, will be William Paterson?"

"That is correct."

His laugh delivered a sonic boom almost as loud as his voice. "Captain Moon asks me to deliver his best wishes and to advise that other business has delayed his return to the Colonies. So tell me gentlemen, what treasures have you to barter."

Buchanan winced inwardly at the list which Sands would be given. The precious linens, whisky and Madeira aside, there was not a great deal which would tempt him. The gold in the Company coffers was an option, but that would only be a last resort.

But then Paterson, the great pedlar, came into his own and wove a tale expounding the excellence of the Scottish wool products and how they were prized in any environment especially the cooler climes of Northern America. He was as persuasive as a snake oil salesman and by the end of his spiel the initially sceptical Sands had been sold. The deal was struck, supplemented by some linens and whisky but with the caveat that if the goods proved not to be as valuable as Paterson made out then Sands could return them and get other recompense. The Scots happily agreed to this, thinking that no-one would ever bother to come back to Darien just to return unsaleable goods.

CHAPTER 15

The beef and flour which the Belvedere carried meant that the Colonists enjoyed full stomachs over Christmas. However, the absence of any surviving Kirk Minister made a formal Presbyterian service impossible on Christmas Day. Duvivier offered the services of one of his crew who was a defrocked priest but the offer was declined.

Instead, a secular gathering took place on the beach. Paterson assumed the role of pastor, gave thanks to the Lord and, reverting to form, bored the assembled mass to tears with a ten minute sermon.

Word had also been sent to the Indian villages that the Scots were celebrating an important day and they would be honoured for their Indian friends to join them. Andreas and Ambrosio arrived on Christmas morning along with their entourages. All went swimmingly until Pennicuik produced the Treaty of Mutual Protection which Andreas had left behind on his last visit. He handed it to the little Indian who, now a few drinks in, palmed it off to one of his bodyguards.

Ambrosio, less impacted by alcohol, seized the rolled up parchment. He asked Buchanan what it said. Buchanan glanced at Pincarton, sensing that this might go south quickly. As diplomatically as he could, Buchanan explained its contents and of Andreas' agreement..

Just then the thoroughly inebriated Andreas, let out one of his high pitched laughs and fell off his chair. Ambrosio rounded on him like a vengeful Fury. No need to read between the lines here, thought Buchanan. Andreas had obviously not bothered his arse to inform Ambrosio of the formalisation of the relationship. He ordered Andreas to stand up then berated him in public for a full two minutes. When the evisceration ended, a suddenly sober Andreas bowed and spoke in his native tongue.

Ambrosio translated. "Andreas says that he apologises for any disrespect and begs your forgiveness."

Pincarton quickly cut in. "Chief Ambrosio, we thank you for your words and assure you that no offence was taken. We greatly value the relationship with you and your noble tribe and wish only for continued friendship and mutual support."

The soothing words seemed to placate the agitated Ambrosio. "Thank you, Captain Pincarton. We too value the alliance with you, our Scottish friends. We would not wish this to be jeopardised by any misunderstandings on our side. I accept this Treaty with the reverence it deserves and shall happily carry it to my people."

The flashpoint passed and the revellers, including the chastised Andreas, recommenced their merrymaking on that tropical Christmas Day.

CHAPTER 16

On December 27th, Duvivier sent word that he planned to sail the following morning. The Barlovento had glided past Golden Island the previous day and the French Captain felt sufficiently confident that they would not be back for a while.

As Pincarton read the message to Buchanan and Paterson there was a knock on the door of the Great Cabin. It was Walter Herries, the surgeon. Pincarton looked up. "Mr. Herries. What can I do for you?"

"Good afternoon, Gentlemen. I just wanted to let you know that I'll be leaving on the Maurepas." His tone made clear that this was a statement, not a request.

"This is a surprise, Walter. Can I ask why?"

Herries ran his hand over his face. "Captain, believe me, I haven't taken the decision lightly. But what's the point in going on?"

"I'm not sure I follow you."

"Oh, come on, Pincarton. Our people are dying every day with no medicines to treat them. That ramshackle township is under water most of the time and the fort couldn't repel a banana. As far as the great trading route is concerned we can barely get fifty yards into the jungle never mind cross the peninsula. And now the Spanish are on the move."

Paterson jutted out his chin. "For God's sake, have some faith, Herries."

"Faith? Really? Why not ask the two dead ministers if they can help you out there," he snapped back.

Pincarton, seeing that Herries was not for turning, asked. "Has Duvivier agreed to take you?"

"Only after you'd been informed."

"At least there will be one honourable man on that ship when it sails then," sniped Paterson.

"Christ Almighty, Paterson, can't you see what's right in front of you?"

"I call it desertion, Herries."

"Call it what you like, but it's a sinking ship and I'm not going down with it. I'd hoped to leave on good terms but if that's not possible then so be it."

Pincarton glared at Paterson. They'd had had a similar conversation regarding Councillor Cunningham. Better for anyone leaving to do so amicably. Otherwise the risk of them poisoning the well back home would be greatly increased. Pincarton adopted a more conciliatory tone. "No, let's not end like that Walter. You have our utmost respect for all you've done and deserve our thanks, even if not our absolute blessing."

Herries nodded. "Thank you."

Pincarton lifted the whisky decanter. "Let's take one last glass together and tell us how you persuaded Duvivier to take you with him."

Herries smiled, "No mystery there," he said, taking a little pouch from a secret pocket inside his jacket.

"Let me guess," said Pincarton. "Fairy dust."

"A little sprinkle of this goes a long way."

The surgeon would be delighted to see the back of this pestilential shithole. His work was done. He had gathered intelligence and passed it on at every opportunity be it in Madeira or to Richard Moon. But he prided himself that he had never shirked from his obligations as a surgeon. That he would not do. However, when he gave a full report to his paymasters at the East India Company he was certain that they would be sufficiently pleased to turn his little pouch of gold into something more substantial. Fairy dust indeed!

CHAPTER 17

The following dawn brought a ferocious storm. The rains teemed down and visibility through the blanketing deluge was near impossible. The northerly howled and any ship wanting to exit the bay would have to negotiate not only the wind but also the giant rollers being compressed between the heads.

Buchanan wandered into the Unicorn's Great Cabin and poured a cup of coffee. "Christ, what a day!"

"Not bad enough to stop our Froggie friends taking flight," replied Pincarton pointing to the French sloop.

"Jesus, they're keen," said Buchanan, just as he burned his tongue with the hot coffee.

"Total madness."

They watched as the Maurepas' sails were unfurled, and despite the monsoon they could hear the shouts of the French crew carried on the wind. The ship's huge canvas wings billowed and then caught the gusts. The anchor was hauled aboard and the Maurepas began to move away.

Pincarton subconsciously started to give a staccato running commentary of events. "Easy now... Keep her steady... Not too much topsail... More to starboard... That's it... Steady now, steady... Now your topsail... Push hard and through... Go, go... Oh, fuck... Oh, Jesus no... Not now, not now..."

Buchanan listened, transfixed by the spectacle. "What's wrong, what's happening?"

Pincarton swivelled towards him, eyes wide with dread. "They hit the breakers perfectly, absolutely square on. But then the wind just fucking died and it's thrown them to leeward. They're being pushed backwards."

Buchanan couldn't understand the panic. "So can't they just regroup and go again?"

"No, Jamie, they're heading straight for the rock."

The impact when it came was like an explosion. The ship suddenly stopped as if it had hit a brick wall. Which of course it had except that this was the monumental slab lurking just below the surface of the boiling waters about a hundred yards from the heads. The jolt was so severe that anyone on the Maurepas' deck was catapulted towards the far railing, clutching at anything which might give them purchase. Some of the crates which had been tied down broke their tethers and scattered like tumbleweed before being flung overboard. Cannons, literally loose cannons, careered across the deck flattening anything in their path before hurtling into the maelstrom like enormous iron lemmings.

The vessel was jammed hard and it was impossible to tell how badly she'd been holed, but a collision of that magnitude had to have caused enormous damage. Then suddenly, the wind picked up again and in an instant the ship was off the rock and looked to be afloat. Perhaps there was still hope if Duvivier could bring her round and nurse her into the shallows. But that notion lasted only a few teasing seconds. With the revived northerly came the breakers. Buchanan and Pincarton could only watch helpless as one of these plucked the Maurepas skywards and with a sickening detonation smashed it a second time into the colossal underwater rock.

Pincarton turned to Buchanan. "That's it, she's gone. Quick, let's get the longboats out to her."

The two men rushed up onto the top deck where Pincarton barked orders to launch the boats on their mercy mission. Buchanan noticed the other ships doing the same and soon the water was full of little tenders being furiously rowed through the choppy seas. Sailors from different vessels may harbour grudges, but when it came to a sinking there was one universal law. 'All lives possible must be saved.'

Mercifully the rain began to abate, making the rescue efforts a little easier. It also meant that the view from the Unicorn had improved and from the top deck Buchanan could better see what was happening.

The Maurepas was wedged hard, powerless to manoeuvre. There was a mass of conflicting sounds with the roar of the ocean and howl of the wind mixed in with the panicked human shouts. Buchanan could pick out the spectral figure of Duvivier on the quarterdeck waving his arms and bellowing instructions. With his skeletal frame and long jacket now drenched black by the sea, Duvivier looked every dark inch the personification of the Grim Reaper. He ordered an immediate evacuation and then disappeared below.

The breakers continued to batter the impaled ship and it was only a matter of time before they pounded the Maurepas into submission. Then with an awful inevitably the main mast succumbed to the onslaught. There was a percussive crack as it snapped. The monumental beam with its tons of canvas and rigging turned into a gigantic wrecking ball. Almost in slow motion it toppled straight down the length of the ship. Any man caught in its path was either killed outright or pinned in place to be drowned or slowly crushed to death. As it crashed through the top deck the rapacious ocean surged through the gaping new hole devouring anything in its way.

Buchanan could see the ship begin to disintegrate and heard the timbers of the hull snapping one at a time like knuckles cracking on a finger. Suddenly, Duvivier emerged from one of the hatches conjuring up a chain of figures behind him. Among them were the three Scots passengers, Hamilton, Cunningham and Herries. The French Captain was screaming orders and waving his arms around like a demented puppet. One of his crew began shuttling the Scots onto a longboat. Then Duvivier dived below again and seconds later emerged with a wooden box which he clutched to his chest like a new born baby.

He ran across the deck shouting to anyone still on board to leave immediately. For many this left no option but to throw themselves into the bubbling water or face certain death. Once the ship started to go down it would be sudden and the whirlpool effect would suck anyone too near into its deadly vortex.

The Scots had managed to scramble onto the last of the lifeboats and were joined by the scurrying figure of Duvivier, still clinging on to his precious casket. Buchanan and Pincarton stared mesmerised as the tender started to edge away from the wreck. But not all were so lucky. One of the overloaded French longboats was hit side on by a freak wave and its occupants tossed into the frothing sea. Those unable to swim or too weighed down by their clothes either slid beneath the waves or were smashed against the ship like ripe tomatoes.

And then the little French sloop gave an enormous anthropomorphic wail of pain as it finally capitulated and split apart. The stern and prow were sliced in two. Their ends flipped up and pointing skywards, came together like a pair of gossiping fish wives before beginning their grim descent into the depths of the bay. In seconds, all that was left was the flotilla of longboats circling to drag shocked and spluttering survivors out of the sea.

The Saint Andrew was the nearest to the disaster and all the boats made for her. Dazed and bedraggled, the crew and passengers of the Maurepas were hauled aboard. At last, the heavy woollen blankets proved to be of some use as they were wrapped around the shivering bodies. Whisky was administered but there was little else that could be done. Once the survivors were offloaded, the longboats returned to their host ships. Pincarton stopped the first of these and directed it to turn back and take himself, Buchanan and Paterson to the Saint Andrew. This did not go down well with the exhausted oarsmen until Pincarton made clear that their extra work would be well rewarded with malt.

When the trio stepped aboard the Saint Andrew they made their way up to the Great Cabin. Sitting around the map table wreathed in the blankets were Cunningham, Hamilton, Herries and Duvivier. They made a sorry quartet. Pincarton asked if they were injured, but too traumatised to speak, each could only shake his head. Duvivier still gripped the wooden casket. Cunningham and Herries simply stared into space but Hamilton managed a weak smile as he held up the pouch which contained all the letters and reports which he had been entrusted to take back to Edinburgh.

Paterson went across and laid a hand on his shoulder. "Well done, Malcolm. I knew we'd chosen the right man for the job."

Buchanan could see that Pennicuik was weighing up what to do with these men and the rest of the survivors. He didn't want them on board the Saint Andrew for any longer than necessary, especially Cunningham with whom he had history. Just then, there was a knock on the Cabin door. Pennicuik's first officer entered and handed him a piece of paper. Pennicuik opened it, gravely studied the contents and passed it to Pincarton who in turn scanned the list of survivors. There were eighteen names.

Duvivier extended an open palm and silently intimated that it be given to him. Buchanan watched the anguish flood the Captain's pallid, sunken face as he read the list. The pain came not from the names that were on it, but the ones that weren't. He knew his decision to sail in such atrocious conditions was responsible for the sickening death toll. Duvivier held out the paper to Pincarton and then for the first time laid down the casket, took his head in his hands and wept. Pincarton handed him a whisky and offered some quiet words of consolation. But what really could be said? All that remained that day was to look after the living.

An hour or so later the group from the Unicorn made its way back. The full fury of the storm had passed and as they sat bobbing up and down on the longboat, Buchanan asked. "Why in God's name did he have to leave in such a hurry?"

Pincarton gave a rueful smile. "I'll hazard that whatever is in the holds of that ship made it a risk Duvivier thought worth taking."

"Must have been one hell of a cargo," answered Buchanan.

"Pity we'll never know," said Paterson. "Must be at least twenty five fathoms deep out by that rock."

CHAPTER 18

The next morning a messenger from the Saint Andrew came aboard the Unicorn to ask if Pincarton, Paterson and Buchanan could accompany him at their earliest convenience to meet with Commodore Pennicuik. The polite phrasing of the request meant that Pennicuik must really need them.

Twenty minutes later, they entered the Great Cabin. The other Councillors were already there. Standing by the huge glassed window was Duvivier. On first blush he seemed physically recovered from the previous day's ordeal. His clothes had been dried and pressed and his long ghostly face newly shaved. The razor's work had given his skin the sheen and colour of bone.

Coffee was poured for the newcomers. There was an uncomfortable lull before Pennicuik snapped the tension. "Gentlemen, it appears we have a situation. Mr. Duvivier wishes to make clear that all cargo on the Maurepas remains the property of France and that any attempt by a third party to make a claim on it would be illegal and viewed poorly by his country. I have asked you all here as Council members to discuss this."

It was evident that Pennicuik was not overly impressed with the demand but unsure as to what course of action to take. His usual approach would have been to tell Duvivier to go fuck himself but the threat of French state retribution was not something for which he wished to be unilaterally responsible. He needed some collective accountability.

The first response came from Pincarton. Cocking an eyebrow and looking at the Frenchman he said. "When Captain Duvivier refers to a 'third party' can one assume that, for present purposes, his comment is directed towards ourselves?"

Duvivier replied. "*Mon ami*, it covers anyone, but you are correct that it has most immediate application to your Company."

"I see," said Pincarton stroking his chin. "Now, I'm no expert on these matters but are there not laws governing shipwrecked cargo?" He turned to Buchanan and gave a sly smile.

Buchanan was caught off guard. There wasn't much need to be across the laws of the sea in the Glasgow Sheriff Court but now the entire room was staring at him.

He trawled his brain looking for something, anything. Then a memory flashed. Sandy Baxter- 'Mental Sandy' to his friends- had been up before the court a few years back after he was caught in possession of a crate of tobacco which he claimed he'd found floating up the river.

This had led to a rare esoteric discussion on the topic of lost cargo. The learned sheriff had ruled that if the crate could be legally regarded as flotsam -in other words "fallen off the back of a boat"- then Sandy would have a viable defence. Of course there was as much chance of Sandy's story being true as there was of the sheriff dancing a highland jig naked on the Court roof. But the judge had a soft spot for harmless chancers like Sandy and had given him the benefit of the doubt. The accused, delighted at the outcome had almost curtsied his way backwards out of the Court.

So, armed with the precedent of Rex v Mental Sandy, Buchanan launched into his analysis. "The key is how lost cargo is classified. Anything intentionally thrown overboard and which can be easily retrieved will be 'jetsam' and can be claimed by its owners. However, anything which accidentally falls off and floats away or resurfaces later will be 'flotsam' and that belongs to whoever finds it."

Duvivier snorted, "You are not serious, my friend. Everything on that ship belongs to France and you know it." The Frenchman had lost all of his previous conviviality and was now a very agitated individual.

Pennicuik held up a hand. "Now, hold on there, Captain Duvivier. Let's hear out Mr. Buchanan."

Duvivier gave Pennicuik a look which would have frozen a melting block of chocolate in the desert. Buchanan continued, "Any sunken cargo will be regarded as either 'lagan' or 'derelict.' In short, 'lagan' is anything which sinks to the ocean floor but which has been claimed by being tied to a floating marker to identify it. This can be a wreck or anything in the wreck. The person who attaches the marker has the legitimate claim. 'Derelict,' on the other hand, is anything which has been relinquished by its owner and sinks, such as in a storm. It's then regarded as abandoned and without an owner. So, whoever retrieves it has a rightful claim."

When Buchanan finished his explanation he looked around the room wondering if anyone would call 'bullshit' on him. But he was the one eyed man in the land of the blind and all the Scottish heads seemed to be nodding in agreement with his dazzling assessment. The same could not be said for Duvivier. He slapped his hand down on the table. "Phah! This is absurd. You know that you have no claim to my cargo, despite the weasel words of your jumped up notaire. I warn you, Gentlemen, this will go bad for you."

Pincarton stood up. "Captain Duvivier. If I may?"

The Frenchman gave a peremptory flick of his hand.

"It seems that we find ourselves in something of a pickle."

"A pickle. what is this 'pickle'?" asked the Frenchman.

"A pickle is, a quandary, *un dilemme.*,"

"*Ah, bien. Oui, je comprends.*"

"Obviously, you have our utmost sympathy for the loss of your vessel and your men. The circumstances of that will be for you to reconcile with your masters in France and with your God."

This was a stinging rebuke, couched in a velvet glove. Everyone knew that Duvivier was responsible but doubtless the wily Frenchman would already be working on an exculpatory narrative to prepare, at least, for his terrestrial day of judgement.

Pincarton continued, "Now it is not in the nature of Scots as good Presbyterian souls to take what is not theirs. So, while Mr. Buchanan's comments are compelling it would go against our principles to make an unjust claim on another's property."

Duvivier's face brightened. "Ah, Captain Pincarton. I knew you were a man of honour."

At this point several heads in the room swivelled towards Pincarton wondering what the hell he was up to. The Scots had been given a gift horse and Pincarton seemed to be suggesting that they look it in the mouth, down its throat and out its arse.

"Quite so, Captain Duvivier. Which is why for as long as you are present in our colony we shall of course defer to your claim for ownership."

Buchanan smiled to himself beginning to see where this was going.

"Well, I'm glad that reason has prevailed," said Duvivier.

"Indeed. Now, with regard to the logistics of your continued visit," said Pincarton moving quickly to the endgame.

"Sorry, I don't follow, Captain. What logistics? Surely you will give berth and provisions to my men until we are taken off by a French ship."

"Well, you see that's where there will be a difficulty."

"A difficulty?" said a now wary Duvivier.

"Well, by the time you send word of your plight and a rescue mission is organised I anticipate that at least a month will have passed."

"Yes, that is possible."

"While of course we are happy for you and your surviving crew to remain among us, I'm afraid that as a matter of practicality it will be impossible for us to clothe, feed and shelter you."

"*Mais pourquoi pas*? Why not?" Duvivier spluttered.

"My dear Captain we have barely enough food to keep our own people alive never mind your crew. And with these incessant rains we will need every berth available."

"What are you saying, Captain Pincarton?"

"I'm saying that you and your men are free to remain in Darien but will have to do so onshore in a habitation of your own construction and with food which you are able to forage yourselves."

"But that is not possible and you know it."

"Captain, all I know is that we cannot look after you if it comes at the risk of losing a single Scottish life. You have seen our precarious situation."

"But for us to be put ashore with no provisions will mean certain death."

"That is not our decision Captain."

"Decision. What decision? That implies I have a choice."

"Well, of course you have a choice."

"Meaning?"

"Meaning that Captain Sands will soon be weighing anchor on the Belvedere and I am certain can be persuaded to accommodate your passage to Port Royal for the right price."

"The right price? What on Earth are you talking about? Everything we have is sitting at the bottom of this God forsaken bay."

"Perhaps not everything." Pincarton turned his focus to the wooden casket.

Duvivier looked at Pincarton and then at the little box. He had no option. To remain would be a virtual death sentence. "So, if we were to leave with the Belvedere what would happen to my cargo?"

"Well, as you have pointed out Captain, we are honourable men. However, we are also starving men. So, I trust you'll understand that anything which is washed ashore and which might otherwise go to waste will be employed to save lives. Only fair, given that we saved your lives yesterday."

Duvivier bowed his head. "Yes, I accept that. But what of the cargo at the bottom of the ocean?"

"Well I would scarce worry about that given the depth at which it sits."

"That, as you well know Captain, is not my point. Do I have your word that this will be treated as the property of France?"

Pincarton looked around the room at his colleagues. "Well what say you Gentlemen?"

Montgomery, Pennicuik and Jolly all looked blank. Paterson started to ask a question but Buchanan tugged his sleeve and he stopped. Pincarton was obviously in control of what was happening.

"I shall take silence as consent. So be it, Captain. On the basis that the sunken cargo is in international waters, we will regard it as the property of France."

Duvivier nodded. "In that case I shall speak with Captain Sands."

"The proper choice in all of the circumstances," said Pincarton.

Pennicuik then opened the door of the Great Cabin and shouted down the corridor. "Mr. Collins, can you come in please?" His first officer, an unnecessarily ginger young man from Aberdeen, entered. "Can you please have Captain Duvivier taken to the Belvedere immediately?"

Duvivier got up and shook the hand of each of the Council members. He had recovered enough grace to thank them fulsomely for their rescue efforts of the day before. He also promised to report back favourably to his masters of the treatment afforded by the Scots and their principled resolution of the matter of the cargo. As soon as Duvivier had exited, Montgomery asked. "What the hell was all that about?"

"Two things. First, if we hadn't agreed, when Duvivier arrived back in France the Scots would be painted as pirates who'd laid claim to the cargo. He'd play this up to deflect his culpability and turn the ire of the French on us. The last thing we need is to be held responsible in Edinburgh for Franco-Scottish relations becoming strained."

"Yes, I can see that. And the second?" asked Montgomery.

"What I actually agreed was that we'd recognise their claim on the basis that the sunken cargo is in international waters."

"So how does that help us?"

"What if that cargo wasn't in international waters?"

Montgomery then had his eureka moment. "So if the bay is Scottish, our undertaking would no longer apply!"

Pincarton grinned, "I think you have me now Mr. Montgomery. So, perhaps it would be a good idea to formalise Scotland's claim to Darien and have Mr. Hamilton take this back to Edinburgh."

Montgomery asked, "Is he going back on the Belvedere?"

"Along with Cunningham once we agree suitable terms with Captain Sands."

"What about Herries?" asked Jolly.

"Well, that will be a matter between him and the Captain. I imagine it will greatly depend on whether his little pouch of gold dust survived the wreck."

*

That afternoon Buchanan drafted the Declaration establishing the colony as part of Scotland. However, to be to be legally valid the newly inked document had to be formally 'declared.' In the ordinary course of events it would have been read out in public but that could attract the attention of Duvivier who might cotton on to the ulterior motive. So they decided to do this in the Great Cabin of the Saint Andrew and for a wider ceremony to take place once the Frenchman had sailed into the horizon.

With a certain predestined inevitability the utterance of the seminal words fell to William Paterson as current Chairman. "We Declare that by virtue of the powers given, we do here settle and in the name of God and Scotland establish and claim this land and its seas. In honour of our mother country we will name this colony Caledonia."

The words electrified the room and a reverential silence descended. Despite their varied backgrounds, contrasting personalities and many differences, they were all proud Scots. As the quiet lingered, Pincarton moved noiselessly to the sideboard and poured several drams which he handed to his countrymen. As they raised their glasses, he said simply. "To Scotland."

CHAPTER 19

A gentle breeze and a break from the rain made December 29th far more conducive to navigating the treacherous heads. Captain Sands had agreed to take Duvivier and his surviving crew as far as Port Royal but this had come at the price of lightening the French Captain's casket. Hamilton and Cunningham were accommodated as a goodwill gesture to the Belvedere's new trading partners and Herries was also included but this had come at a cost to his gold dust.

Buchanan wondered what the French sailors were thinking as they passed the sunken rock which had destroyed the Maurepas and sent their crewmates to a watery grave. How many would blame their Captain who had chosen to make a run for it when conditions were so stacked against them? And it was not just the loss of lives and their ship. Whatever was in those cargo holds was gone and unlikely ever to come their way again.

The Belvedere slowly edged its way to safety, tacking against the prevailing northerly and riding the choppy swell. Once out past the heads, the winds strengthened, catching and ballooning the ship's sails. It only took a few minutes for it to disappear from sight.

Attention now returned to the Colony's more immediate problems. Mackenzie's weekly roll call showed that of the twelve hundred souls who had left Leith only six hundred and forty three were left. Disease and illness had taken a merciless toll and unless proper supplies could be sourced, the inventory of the dead would only continue to climb.

Morale in this brave new world was also a serious issue. Just after Christmas two young lads had abandoned the colony and made for the jungle. They didn't make it far through the impenetrable undergrowth and having been caught were led back in chains, sobbing and begging forgiveness. When questioned as to where the hell they thought they were going, they answered that they were looking for the Indian village. The natives seemed to live a lot better than the Scots and they admitted to the added prospect of landing one of the young nymphs.

Buchanan couldn't help but laugh. "Fuck sake, boys, have you had a good look at yourselves lately? The ugliest tarts in Glasgow wouldn't touch you."

Pennicuik wanted to appoint himself judge and jury and seemed happy to speed proceedings along regardless of the finer points of any legal technicality. Buchanan, reverting to his default setting, spoke in mitigation. The Council ordered them to be put in leg irons for a week. They would have punished them with bread and waters rations too, but that was what they were already on. One of the lads, a young pup from Glasgow named Davie Kelso, nodded his silent appreciation to Buchanan as they were led out.

The day after the Belvedere had sailed, the remaining settlers were asked to gather on the shore. Paterson had negotiated his buckled form onto the top of an empty barrel and from there had re-read the Declaration to resounding cheers.

Pincarton then took to the makeshift stage. "Ladies and Gentlemen. While I know that your prayers continue for the poor souls who lost their lives on the Maurepas, there is never a wind blew that didn't fill somebody's sails. So, now that our French friends have left, you will be happy to learn that anything from the Maurepas which either floats or is washed up belongs to the Colony."

This brought a mighty roar. The prospect of some reward from a spot of beach-combing was music to their ears. Pincarton then held up an admonitory hand. "Sadly, that will include some French corpses. I know that I don't have to tell you that these bodies must be treated with respect and given a proper burial."

There was a universal murmur of approval before Pincarton continued. "Now, everything recovered is for the common good and will be distributed fairly. We anticipate there will be quantities of food and wine which will buy us time while we await the arrival of supplies from Scotland. Anything else which might have commercial value will be given to Mr. Mackenzie and preserved for trading purposes. But, a serious word of caution to any of you lured by the wreck of the Maurepas. This is strictly off limits. Whatever may be down there is the property of the Company of Scotland and will only be recovered by organised and coordinated action. There will be no, I repeat no, tolerance of any freelancing. Anyone caught infringing this rule will be severely punished. Is that clear?"

A muted affirmation came from the disappointed crowd.

"Now, before you get all downcast about this, let me say a couple of things. The first is that the water where the wreck lies is so deep that any of you thinking about chancing your arm will almost certainly drown. And let me assure you that this is not a pleasant way to go. But if that doesn't scare you let me throw in this second little nugget. There are about twenty dead bodies trapped in that wreckage which will prove irresistible to the hammerhead sharks. They'll be looking to pick away at what's left of the Frenchies and I doubt they'll stop for a wee chat before taking a chunk out of you. So, enough said, I think. Alright, let's enjoy today. It's a great one for Scotland."

For a few happy hours the animosity between landsmen and seamen was forgotten and they were all just Scots celebrating the establishment of their little slice of Scotland in the Tropics. Permission had been given for a barrel of whisky to be broken out and shared among the revellers. Such was the high mood of the afternoon that the Council decided to amnesty the two runaways who suffered merciless ribbing when brought back into the fold. The bagpipes started up along with the Scottish frame drums, the bodrhans, and the beach resounded to the music of their homeland.

When the whisky had been drained, a cry went up from the beach. As if by Divine providence, the first of the flotsam had made its way into the shallows. A couple of young lads waded out, now careful to scour the water for sharks, and brought ashore a cask of French wine. They looked expectantly at Pincarton who nodded for this to be cracked open. There were going to be some sore heads the next morning, but right here and right now the Scots were having a party and few nations in the world were better equipped to do that.

CHAPTER 20

The truce between Landsmen and Seamen was short lived. The ragged tempers accompanying the hangovers made sure of that as the squabbling began over the spoils from the Maurepas. From the shore the seamen could be seen paddling about in their longboats greedily collecting the flotsam from the French ship. This was then taken back onto their vessels and the well-founded suspicion was that this would not find its way into the communal pot. Untouched in this exercise were the bodies of the French sailors which were allowed to continue their sombre passage towards the beach.

The Landsmen sought to even the ledger by wading out into the shallows to retrieve what had already found its way there. Those that could swim ventured further and pushed anything floating back towards the shore. To their credit this included any corpses and each Frenchman was solemnly laid to rest in the little graveyard.

Over the next few days a welcome stream of barrels containing wine, dried meats, fish and breads were recovered. Some of the barrels of food had not survived completely intact, but for the settlers, who had been eating spoiled food infested with grubs and weevils, a little seawater was no deterrent. The windfall was manna from heaven and if carefully administered the Colony could eke out another month without having to go back onto survival rations.

A bizarre cavalcade of other items also washed up. All sorts of clothing, shoes, and fancy French wigs were fished out. Some ornate chairs and a table had broken free and were set out on the beach in a surreal parody of a dinner party. There were books, their pages ruined and made illegible by the saltwater, along with the poignant personal belongings of the crew-clay pipes, lockets and crucifixes.

*

The question of regular food supplies was one of two main issue facing the Council. The second was determining a route across the isthmus. Both were to be discussed at the last meeting before the new year of 1699.

Pincarton was chairman. "So, Gentlemen, your thoughts on the overland passage?"

Montgomery immediately jumped in. "The mission must be viewed as a military exercise. I've experience of expeditions and would like to lead this one."

Buchanan suppressed a smile. Montgomery had proven to be a poor administrator and this was his opportunity to actually contribute.

"A generous offer, Montgomery. Any comments?" asked Pincarton.

Pennicuik, who had not forgotten his spectacular falling out with Montgomery couldn't keep the snideness out of his voice. "That seems an ideal solution. Perhaps you should enlist Thomas Drummond as your enforcer?"

Buchanan knew it was a no-lose scenario as far as Pennicuik was concerned. Success has many friends but failure is an orphan. If Montgomery carried the day then the entire venture would benefit. If he didn't, then blame would fall squarely on his shoulders.

Jolly immediately agreed, delighted that he hadn't been roped in. Buchanan also nodded.

Paterson took this as an opportunity to park his recent humility. "Fine, but we'll also have to establish its commercial viability. I assume I'm the obvious choice to accompany Montgomery."

Pennicuik let out a derisive laugh. "Are you kidding? You'd not make it more than ten miles."

"I beg your pardon!" snapped Paterson.

"Oh, for God's sake man. Look at yourself. That twisted body might be fine for conjuring up schemes but it sure as hell won't cope with the terrain out there." As he said this Pennicuik pointed back to the dark forbidding mountains lying high above the shore.

"Utter nonsense," fired back Paterson.

"Oh, you reckon? Christ, I heard that you were all but done in from the journey to the Indian village a few weeks back. And that was when the ground was still dry. You'd become a liability within a day. Is that what you want?"

Everyone else knew that Pennicuik was right. Paterson's spirit might be unquestionable but his compromised frame wouldn't survive the rigours of a trek to the interior. But Paterson wouldn't face reality. "No, I must go."

An agonising silence descended on the room. As so often, it was the clever Pincarton who found a way through. "I agree that William is best suited to determine the suitability of any route."

Paterson nodded vigorously. "Quite Robert, quite. I'm glad you can see when others are blind." He shot a disdainful look at Pennicuik.

But Pincarton was not finished. "Which is why I think that the first expedition must be seen as nothing more than a preliminary sortie to lay the groundwork for a larger campaign."

Paterson looked at him. "What do you mean?"

"Well, we know nothing of what lies beyond a few hundred yards of jungle and certainly no understanding of the mountain terrain. So, really, isn't this nothing more than a scouting exercise?"

"Yes I can see that might be regarded as the case," conceded Paterson.

"In which event, your skills and energy would be far better employed on the second crusade when the pathway has been cleared by the advance party."

Buchanan watched Paterson swirl this around in his head. Montgomery interceded. The last thing he wanted as task force leader was the dead wood of Paterson. "Exactly. We can survey the territory, carve out a path and then report back to William to tap his knowledge for the second expedition."

Paterson was not altogether convinced of this but it made sufficient sense for him to accede. "Fine, but only for this scouting mission. I'll need to be present for all others."

"Of course, William. That goes without saying," agreed Pincarton, "but for immediate purposes we will need someone to accompany Montgomery and his men. Perhaps someone with a non-military eye who also knows the Indians. Wouldn't you agree, Mr. Montgomery?"

Given that the threat of Paterson had been removed, the soldier was happy to consent. "By all means."

"Excellent. Well in that case, might I suggest Mr. Buchanan?"

This came as an unwelcome shock for Buchanan. Before he could find a reason to protest the others had endorsed the proposal. Pincarton smiled a knowing smile which seemed to say, 'There you go, son, another opportunity to broaden your horizons.'

The Council then turned to the food supply issue. Pincarton again took the lead. "Even with the French windfall our supply situation is critical. We can't grow crops because of the rain, the fish are scarce and there's only a limited amount we can trade with the Indians. So, we have to access other markets. I've discussed this with Paterson and we have a proposal. If you would, William?"

Paterson stepped across to the map table, unrolled one of the charts and weighed down the ends with two small round stones. "Realistically, our marketplace is limited. While Scotland has no quarrel with any nation, others may have an issue with us. In large part that will be due to our association with England and its moveable feast of enemies. And in the case of the Spanish there will be added spice."

Pennicuik butted in, "Thanks for stating the bleeding obvious, Paterson. We all know we can only trade in ports allied with England or at worst neutral. Just tell us the plan, for God's sake."

Paterson bristled but kept himself in check before stabbing a finger at the map. "These are the ABC Islands. Aruba, Bonaire and Curacao."

Buchanan asked, "What makes them so special?"

"Well, apart from only being three days sail away, they're Dutch. So, unless the state of world affairs has shifted again in the last two months, they're allies of Britain."

"But what about the Spanish Barlovento?" said Buchanan.

"Well, according to Duvivier they're only after privateers and treasure hunters. Traders wouldn't form part of their remit," reasoned Pincarton.

"Makes sense but how do we actually go about it ?"

Pincarton produced a piece of paper from his inside pocket and unfolded it. "Here is a list of our commodities. We've marked those which may be commercially attractive."

He laid it down on the table. Unsurprisingly, the only ones flagged were the linens, tobacco, whisky and the Madeira wines. "Trade enough of these and we can fill our holds with food and medicines."

"And I suppose," said Buchanan, "you'll be wanting me to go on that trip as well."

Pincarton smiled. "I imagine you'll have your hands full picking mud out of your arse on the mountain trails. No, I propose I go with Captain Malloch aboard the Dolphin."

The others looked puzzled. "The Dolphin? Why The Dolphin?" asked Jolly.

"The Unicorn is a fine vessel but its cargo holds are damaged. The Endeavour is too slow, the Caledonia's main mast is compromised and I would never dream of asking Commodore Pennicuik to hand over his flagship."

Pennicuik's glare confirmed the truth of the last element.

"Is it wise to send two Captains?" asked Buchanan.

"I'm not going as a Captain, but as a Councillor. One of us has to be there. Since I know the islands I'm the obvious choice. So, unless anyone else wishes to volunteer, can we have a vote?"

The proposal was swiftly passed and an immediate roadmap for the Company set.

CHAPTER 21

Paterson set the wheels in motion for the inland expedition by asking Andreas to arrange scouts from the larger village. Two days later, the little chief, who had hit the coca and whisky early, greeted Paterson with a high pitched giggle and informed him that Ambrosio himself was coming to the village that afternoon along with some of his best warriors. Paterson made a mental note to reduce Andreas' supplies of liquor and then pressed him about why there was a need for warriors.

Andreas squealed his stupid little laugh before he slurred. "Los Spanish."

Paterson raced back to the Unicorn where the scouting party was preparing for the journey.

Buchanan looked up as he burst into the Great Cabin "Jesus, are you alright William?"

Paterson wiped the sweat from his brow. "I've just had a conversation with Andreas. Well, I say conversation, more an interview with a golem."

Drummond shook his head. "Bin at the funny stuff agin hus he?"

"Aye, but he was still lucid enough to give me some news."

Paterson then recounted the exchange and saw the look of concern ripple around the company. Drummond curled his upper lip and gave the typical soldier's response. "Bring it on. My men are a match for anyone."

"I'm sure they are, but conflict isn't something we really want to court."

"Whit, so we just let them attack us?" snapped Drummond.

"Look, let's hold off making any judgements until Ambrosio arrives," said Paterson.

"Aye alright, but I'll be fucked if I cannae stand up to those bastards."

215

"If we need to defend ourselves we'll do so with maximum force. The trick is not to get to that point."

"Aye, well, you're the politician, no me."

"And you're the soldier, Mr. Drummond and glad we are of it," replied Paterson in an effort to placate the agitated warmonger.

That afternoon there was a commotion on the beach as several large canoes arrived. Buchanan looked through the spyglass and could clearly make out Ambrosio along with about twenty of his tribe. All of them were lean and muscled and didn't look as though they had arrived for tea. A few minutes later one of the canoes headed for the Unicorn. At its prow was Ambrosio, standing upright. It was a mystery to Buchanan how he kept his balance.

Ambrosio came aboard and got straight down to business. The tough, nuggety Indian looked around the table with those piercing brown eyes. "Before we go any further, my Scottish friends, can I have your assurance that our Treaty of Mutual Protection still stands?"

Buchanan thought this about as loaded a leading question as he'd heard in a long time.

"Most assuredly, Chief," replied Paterson.

"Good. I think we may need it shortly."

"Care to elaborate?" asked Buchanan.

Ambrosio explained that the previous week he'd received word that a platoon of Spanish infantry had arrived in Portobello. From there it had made its way south along the coast and rendezvoused with the Boca tribe with whom they had an alliance.

"Do you know what they're doing there?" asked Montgomery.

Ambrosio looked at him as if he was a simpleton. "I think we can assume that they are not practising their jungle survival skills."

Paterson jumped into the embarrassing breach. "I believe Mr. Montgomery wanted to know if the Spanish are here for the Tule or the Scots."

"That perhaps is the better question and one for which I have no immediate answer. Your recent presence may be seen as a threat but on the other hand word may have got back about the incident with their missionaries on Golden Island. Whatever the case, I believe that we both have a vested interest in addressing the issue."

Drummond seizing on the Indian's comment spoke up. "Aye, I couldna agree mair. Got tae take it to the pricks before they get us."

Buchanan roughly translated, bringing a broad smile to Ambrosio's face. "Mr. Drummond is correct. We must meet their threat and take them by surprise."

"Aye, they willnae be expecting us tae come and front them up," said Drummond.

Montgomery then asked, "How many are they Chief?"

"About one hundred Spanish and fifty Boca."

Montgomery let out an involuntary whistle. "That's a large force."

Ambrosio smiled and shook his head. "That was the number that left Portobello. For them to reach Darien they will have to march through the jungle for three days and nights. They will lose men on the way and by the time they reach us will be exhausted and dispirited."

Buchanan then asked, "So where does that leave the scouting mission then?"

Drummond, now delighted that he could get his teeth into some action, made a suggestion. "Why no' kill two birds with the wan stone? We'll huv tae go through the jungle to get to the Spaniards anyway. So wance we've fucked them off we can keep going and let you make yer wee map of the isthmus."

CHAPTER 22

The expeditionary force left Darien the following morning. Ambrosio had taken the rudimentary Scots maps and added some detail including the location of streams and mountain ranges. He then identified the route which he believed the Spanish would take to reach Darien. Buchanan had asked how he was so certain. The response was direct and none too encouraging. "Because that is the only possible way through the jungle."

The Scots beefed up the military detail with seventy veterans of European battlefields now primed and ready. After months of feeling redundant they strode off into the jungle full of purpose, the cheers and drums of their countrymen echoing in their wake.

The Indians took the lead. Moving effortlessly through the dense foliage, they hacked out a path with their curved blades through the tendrils and boughs which twisted around each other like deformed limbs. Swapping out regularly in waves of four each group took on the heavy workload for ten minutes before being replaced by the next surge.

On top of the searing heat, the violent rains had turned the jungle floor into a quagmire so that the Scots with their heavy leather shoes and bulky packs soon slowed. Ambrosio positioned two of his men at the rear to ensure that no Scots fell off the pace or got lost.

They marched until mid-morning when they reached a small clearing where a stream ran down the steep slope. The Scots slumped onto the ground, all facade of discipline evaporating in the suffocating swelter. The Indians found this most amusing and remained on their feet as they compared notes about the feebleness of these strange white men.

The Scots gulped down as much of the stream water as they could and then rinsed out their sweat sodden shirts. Every part of their bodies seemed to be overheating. The sweat dried almost as soon as it escaped their pores and their heads ached with the smothering humidity. Ambrosio allowed them to rest for half an hour until the rumble of thunder signalled the imminent arrival of the afternoon rains.

When the deluge came, giant drops of water pounded down on the jungle canopy like a thousand hammering timpani. It was impossible to hear anything and every ounce of concentration was focussed on putting one foot in front of the other. The path turned into a treacherous slipway and became even more challenging as the gradient increased and the soldiers' calves screamed in protest.

As the afternoon wore on Ambrosio could see that the Scots were unable to continue. To their enormous credit the soldiers had not uttered a word of complaint. They had experienced a different kind of hell in Europe and it left them stoic and hardened to physical discomfort. That of course didn't stop their bodies betraying them and when the order was given to stop they collapsed in utter exhaustion.

Ambrosio had chosen to camp in a small glade which he instructed his warriors to widen with their fearsome machetes. The Scots, feverish from their sweat-drenched clothes, started to gather sticks and leaves to build a fire. As soon as Ambrosio saw this he shouted to Drummond to tell his men to stop what they were doing. Drummond gave the command but then strode over to Ambrosio to ask what the hell was reason for this?

Ambrosio pointed way off into the distance above the tree line further up the mountainside. In the quickly fading light, a wisp of smoke was clearly visible as it spiralled up from the jungle. "The Spanish," was all he had to say. If the Scots could see their fires, then they would be able to do the same. The last thing the Scots wanted was to cede the element of surprise.

Instead, the Indians constructed upright ovens from palm leaves and filled these with dry bark from the inner layers of the giant hardwood trees. They then lit the bark and after a few minutes the ovens started to give out a smokeless, radiant heat which would allow the shivering Scots to stay warm while their clothes dried.

Ambrosio also cautioned the Scots to stay quiet since at night sound travelled vast distances. Any music or singing was banned and to guarantee the curfew, alcohol consumption was restricted. Not that carousing was at the top of any soldier's agenda. All any of them wanted was to stretch out, lay their head against their kit and fall into the coma of the completely knackered.

As dusk fell, a cacophony of bird and animal screams and screeches rent the air. But in an instant, all fell quiet. Silence swamped the men. The stillness carried a sinister malignancy and in the darkness the world suddenly assumed new constrictive boundaries. Despite his weariness, Buchanan slept fitfully, his dehydrated skin stretched tight and his body coiled in tense anticipation of the imagined terrors around him. He felt the giant minutes tick by agonisingly slowly until the new dawn brought blessed relief. When the first shafts of light emerged, he sat upright, ready for the challenge ahead. The challenge that brought with it the threat of death, man's ultimate frontier, and the one he feared the most.

CHAPTER 23

The task force ate breakfast quickly and quietly. The Indians were invited to share but declined. They were happy to forage in the jungle and emerged with various seeds and nuts which they ate with the maize bread kept in the leather pouches which hung across their chests.

Conversation was kept to a minimum and any instructions whispered or in sign language. The soldiers cast envious eyes at the unencumbered Indians and reluctantly began the process of weighing themselves down with their equipment.

They started to march shortly after daybreak accompanied on every step by the maddening mosquitos. As they climbed higher into the mountains the slope became steeper and even more perilous. The Indians nimbly picked their way along the thread of a trail, scything away at the lianas and undergrowth. The Scots on the other hand, slipped and slogged up the muddy scree, constantly falling and caking their already sodden clothes with the muck from the jungle floor.

Buchanan felt like he was trapped in a hothouse as a river of sweat poured down his body. His feet were soaking and the wool of his socks, rubbing against his feet, created blisters which he knew would be almost crippling by nightfall.

But there was no option. This was a race against time. Ambrosio had said they had to reach a certain point where the mountain levelled off to remove the tactical disadvantage of not having the high ground. So they ploughed on. Some of the soldiers, not having been properly fed for months, began to weaken.

During the afternoon, a young Highlander name Donaldson became delirious. He collapsed to the ground and started to hallucinate that he was back home in Oban looking out over the bay. The party rested to see if he could recover, but it was soon clear he wouldn't be able go on.

They were then faced with the agonising decision of whether to abandon Donaldson completely or sacrifice one of the taskforce to get him back down the mountain. Drummond was prepared to put a sword in Donaldson to end his suffering but Montgomery refused to countenance the callous euthanasia and ordered one of the other Highlanders to stay behind. Water and food were left with the two men and the rest of the war party moved on. Within seconds, the Highlanders had disappeared from sight, gobbled up by the dense jungle.

The mood had become sombre and when Ambrosio eventually signalled that they make camp for the night there was a brittle tension among the Scots. As they ate very little was said. Most of them had that vacant faraway expression of men who have reached a point beyond physical endurance.

Montgomery and Drummond tried their best to give encouragement that the worst was over. The filthy Spanish would be met tomorrow and despatched with their Dago tails between their legs. After that the Scots could begin to craft tales of their heroism to mythologise in future years.

Ambrosio came and sat next to Buchanan. "You know, I think you Scots men are crazy with your ridiculous clothes and white skins so ill-suited for this place."

Buchanan slowly lifted his head. "At this moment I couldn't disagree, my friend."

"And the deformed one, Paterson, he says he wishes to trade between the two oceans. Is he mad?"

"That's what we're here to find out."

Ambrosio laughed. "I like you, Scots. You are good men. And better than that, you are good men with muskets and swords who can help kill the Spanish."

Buchanan tried to respond but exhaustion finally got the better of him. He slumped to the ground and the last thing he remembered was Ambrosio laying some huge palm leaves on top of him to give protection from the rain.

CHAPTER 24

The next morning the Scots woke to the steady drum roll of thunder. The skies were leaden and ominous clouds quickly blotted out the dawn. Then in the wake of one colossal peal, the heavens opened and the downpour began.

The expeditionary force took cover under the thickest of the jungle foliage but the sheer weight of the rain bullied its way through the hardwoods and palms. The path became a river and it was impossible to press on until the torrent had stopped. Forks of lightning split the sky and a giant teak tree sustained a direct hit, exploding into flames before being doused by the cloudburst. It was cleaved down its centre like a butcher gutting a pig and as its two halves fell apart it seemed to let out a plaintive arboreal cry.

Ambrosio ran over to where Montgomery, Buchanan and Drummond were huddled. He had to shout above the pelting rain. "The Spanish and Boca are near."

"How do you know?" asked Montgomery.

"Before the rains this morning we saw vultures circling further along the ridge. They would only be there if there was carrion."

"Dead animals?" asked Buchanan.

Ambrosio shook his head slowly. "Dead men. The Spanish wouldn't waste energy in burying anyone so just leave them to the vultures."

Lovely, thought Buchanan. He had seen these grim black scavengers in Darien. Their pointed beaks were too weak to pierce human skin so they started at the eyes, pecking them out to make a hole. Then they painstakingly inched towards the innards and devoured them to leave only skin and bones.

Ambrosio wiped the rain from his face. "Tell your men to make ready. As soon as the rain slackens we'll move into position. Its noise will cover us."

Montgomery nodded and he and Drummond darted quickly among the Scots soldiers to spread the word. Drummond asked Buchanan if he wanted to hang back from the initial engagement. Much as he thought this a splendid idea, he rejected it instantly. Anything else would have meant total loss of face. "No way. We're in this together," he said with as much bravado as he could muster.

Buchanan felt his bowels loosen and he shot into the trees. It gave him some consolation to find he was not alone with half the platoon shitting out their nerves. Drummond laughed when he re-emerged. "Feeling better Mr. Buchanan?"

"Just my normal morning devotions, Mr. Drummond. Very regular, I am."

Drummond smacked him across the top of his back and grinned. "You're alright for a lawyer."

"I can sleep happily for the rest of my days, then."

"Let's just hope there ur many of them. Just remember, son, that a' men die but no a' men live."

Buchanan pondered this odd pearl of wisdom and couldn't work out if it gave him comfort or increased his terror. "So, let me ask you something Drummond."

He cocked his head. "On you go, then."

"When we get into position, do we give the Spanish and Boca a chance to parlay?"

"Ah think you've been reading too many books, Mr. Buchanan. This isnae Greece or Rome or wherever the fuck a' they heroes come fae. This is the real world and they Spanish are right cunts. And anyone who is in league with them are right cunts too. Think they've come a' this way just to politely ask us to leave? I think fucking not. So its bastard rules, Mr. Buchanan. Kill them cunts before they kill you."

"Understood, Mr. Drummond," nodded Buchanan, accepting the perverse logic of the answer.

"Now, sure you don't want to pop off another wee shite before we head out?"

"Fuck off," he fired back, but suddenly thought it might not be the worst idea in the world. Just then, Ambrosio gave the signal to break camp. The rain had abated enough to allow progress but was still sufficiently deafening to mask their movement. The Scots followed the Indians as they crept along the narrow path, slipping and sliding on a surface which more resembled ice than earth.

After about two hundred yards, the lead Indian raised his right forearm. Ambrosio went up to investigate and then came back to consult with Montgomery. "The Spaniards are just ahead in the clearing where they camped for the night. There are about a hundred of them including the Boca traitors."

"What are the tactics, Chief?" asked Montgomery. While experts in pitched battles, the Scots didn't have the Indian experience of jungle warfare.

The Indian whispered. "They're spread out like ducks on a pond. My warriors will move in a semi-circle around them and your soldiers can attack from the front. We'll unleash our arrows and you can shoot them. Keep firing until you see my men take the field. Then join us with your swords and let their blades taste some Spanish blood."

"Will there be an attack signal?"

"The rain is too loud. Watch for the first arrows to land and that will be your cue."

Montgomery nodded and watched as the Chief dispatched his men round the half perimeter. Drummond briefed his troops and Buchanan saw their eyes take on a steely focus. Now coiled and ready, they could unleash all of their pent up frustration and anger.

"God help those poor Spanish sods," murmured Buchanan.

As he edged into position, Buchanan got his first proper look at the enemy. He had expected a well drilled brigade of crack Spanish soldiers, dressed smartly in their yellow and blue jackets, muskets ready and swords by their sides. Why he had assumed this he didn't know exactly, especially given the journey they themselves had endured. Instead, he saw an exhausted rabble shattered by the arduous trek over the mountains. Their jackets, filthy with mud, were either strewn on the wet ground to sleep on or being used as blankets. A pathetic fire, protected from the rain by a makeshift wooden cover, provided the only comfort. Some of them were drinking and arguments could be heard. The Boca Indians sat apart, keeping a suspicious watch on their imperial allies.

The attack when it happened was swift and brutal. A black cloud of arrows rained down from both sides of the jungle like a malevolent army of angels falling on sinners. The heavy arrowheads tipped with metal, wood or fish bones slammed into the unsuspecting enemy with lethal power. Drummond gave the order to fire and the line of muskets exploded in near unison like the Devil's orchestra. The riflemen became momentarily invisible as they were enveloped in the shroud of smoke from the gunpowder flash. When it cleared Buchanan watched as they went through the macabre mime of reloading and firing at will.

The effect on the Spanish and Boca was devastating. The arrows and musket balls scythed through them and bodies seemed to fall like marionettes whose strings had been cut. The remaining troops instinctively grabbed for their weapons but had no idea what was happening. Then the Tule emerged from the undergrowth screaming wildly, their machetes cutting through the air, ready to slice into Spanish and Boca flesh. The Scots in turn raced out of their hiding places, shouting and swearing as the adrenalin coursed through their bodies.

Buchanan slid his sword out of its scabbard and joined the charge. He rushed towards the nearest Spaniard, his blade pointing straight in front of him. As he got nearer he saw to his horror the enemy soldier cock the hammer of a musket and raise it towards Buchanan's head. Suddenly everything went into silent slow motion. He could clearly see the Spaniard's eyes line him up and then the finger gradually squeeze the trigger. It was too late to take evasive action and Buchanan braced for the inevitable impact of the ball in his skull. He watched as the trigger clicked and waited for the flash when the gunpowder ignited.

But nothing happened. No noiseless red flame, no agony of the lead ripping through his brain, no last breath. Nothing. Just the dull click of the hammer against wet gunpowder. Buchanan let out a primal scream as everything came back into sharp real time focus and the roar of the battle returned. His momentum carried him forward and his outstretched sword plunged directly into the Spaniard's heart. The man's eyes widened, bulging like a snails. Buchanan crashed into him and both men slammed the ground. The Spaniard was dead before he hit the mud.

Buchanan got back to his feet just in time to see Drummond's sword slice through the air and land on the exposed neck of a Dago who was down on one knee. The blow almost severed the head from its body and a jet of blood shot from the gaping wound like a grotesque fountain. Drummond laughed maniacally, his eyes blazing like dark tunnels leading directly to hell. "Fuck youse all," he screamed.

Another of his men pounced on a prostrate Spaniard and drove a dagger up to its hilt into the man's groin, completing the emasculation with the next slice of the blade. The Scot let out an unearthly bellow of triumph before moving on to his next victim.

Buchanan recoiled at the animal brutality of what he was witnessing. This was conflict in the raw and beyond anything he could ever have imagined. But the hardened Scots troops had seen plenty and were in their element, gripped by the fanatical madness of close quarter combat.

Neither the Scots nor the Tule were going to stop until the slaughter was finished. All around Buchanan wailing bodies writhed in their death throes or lay draped in stillness. He slashed in a circle with his sword, but had no appetite for more killing. All he was trying to do was stop anyone getting close enough to cause him harm.

He watched the Spaniards and Boca trying to flee but even that mercy wasn't going to be afforded them. Rushing blindly into the jungle they were relentlessly pursued and in that dark place the butchery continued. Buchanan heard their awful screams as they met their savage ends.

He dropped to his knees and hung his head. This was wrong. This was barbarism. Yes, he had killed a man but he knew that it was in self-defence. It was not like the callous, inhumane bloodbath which had just occurred.

The triumphant victors then emerged from the undergrowth whooping in manic delight. The Tule had exterminated the best warriors of the detested Boca and rejoiced in the massacre of the Spanish demons. Buchanan understood why they would have acted this way. But not the Scots. Not his countrymen. Nothing ever preached from any pulpit, no matter how divisive or provocative, could justify what had happened on this wretched killing field. Then the rain stopped. The clouds parted and a shaft of sunlight bathed the clearing and threw the carnage into even starker relief. It was if the Gods had sent this ray to gather the souls of the perished and take them from this hideous place.

Buchanan watched in horror as the Indians went from body to body skewering any which moved or moaned. There were to be no survivors to tell what had happened. The bodies would be left for the vultures. Drummond casually kicked at the legs of a couple of the Spaniards to ensure they were dead. Satisfied, he then took his blade and wiped it on the trousers of one of the victims to clean its gory residue. Here was a man with black ink running through his veins.

Buchanan vomited in disgust.

Then the plunder commenced. The triumphant army feasted on Spanish bread, cooked meats and wines and began helping themselves to anything of value from the corpses. Drummond told them not to worry about that just now as they would be coming back this way later.

The revelry continued for the rest of the day. No longer constrained by the need for stealth or silence the victors cut loose and when the rain returned they frolicked in the puddles as their victims lay lifeless by their dancing feet. Buchanan sat on his own, refusing any of the Spanish spoils. Montgomery came and crouched beside him, offering a flask of whisky. Buchanan looked at it and shook his head. "Alcohol's not the answer."

Montgomery thrust it towards him again. "Aye, but it helps you forget the question."

Buchanan gave a half smile, took a swig and handed it back. The mission commander then looked out at the battlefield and in a solemn voice said. "This is a bad business, Jamie. There'll be a price to pay."

Buchanan glanced across at him. At least there was someone else who felt a flicker of shame. "Aye, but to whom? The Spanish, the Indians, any God you believe in?"

"Maybe all of them, but I was thinking more of our consciences."

"I don't think you'll find too many of them out there."

"Maybe not, but you and I will have to live with being party to this. Old sins cast long shadows."

They both knew that something morally polluting had occurred and, as it sunk in, Buchanan grabbed the hip flask.

CHAPTER 25

The rain had stopped weeping for the dead by daybreak. When an inventory of the casualties was taken it was found that among them were two young Scots. Buchanan thought it desperately sad that this hadn't been noticed before, but in all the ugliness and confusion of the battle, nothing much had made sense.

The Scotsmen were buried side by side in a muddy tabernacle in a ceremony befitting fallen soldiers. This made the indifference to the slain Spanish and Boca all the more repugnant. When the count was complete a total of eighty four Spanish and thirty eight Boca lay dead.

Despite their hangovers and filthy conditions, the platoon took little persuasion to refocus on the expedition. Buoyed by victory and infused with patriotism, anything stated to be for Scotland was instantly embraced.

Drummond also pushed this agenda, but for different reasons. Never a man to turn his back on the main chance, he wanted to discover if the tales of the vast amounts of silver to be found in the mountains were true.

Ambrosio in turn was happy to accommodate his allies. He was delighted with how events had unfolded. Spanish and Boca blood carpeted the jungle floor and his tribe's existence in Darien was secured for the foreseeable future.

The party broke camp about nine o'clock. Buchanan couldn't help but cast another glance at the horrific bloody arena. He instantly regretted it.

The one mercy of the continued upward slog was that as they climbed higher it became cooler and the suffocating humidity decreased. The rain also eased but the path remained treacherous and the Scots slipped and staggered up the slope like new born foals trying to find their feet. Their energy quickly became sapped and Montgomery called a halt after just two hours. The Scots dropped to the ground gasping for breath. Up at altitude the air had become thinner and many were having trouble taking in enough oxygen.

Two days ago the Indians had mocked the feebleness of the white men but now their attitude was different. They had seen these fierce fighters in action and an enormous respect had developed. Giving the weary Scots water carried in broad palm fronds, they then disappeared into the jungle before returning with batches of strange looking leaves which they ripped apart and handed out.

Ambrosio gave some to Montgomery and Buchanan, demonstrating that they should put the leaf between their bottom lip and teeth and hold it there. As their saliva unlocked the contents of the plant, a bitter juice fill their mouths. Buchanan made to spit it out but Ambrosio stopped him and told him to swallow. He almost gagged but a moment or two later was delighted that he had followed instructions. Gradually, his head cleared, his body tingled and he felt strangely exhilarated. He could hear some of the soldiers begin to laugh and when he looked back saw they were all on their feet, their faces fixed in stupid rictus smiles.

Buchanan had experienced something like this at Andreas' tea party on the beach all those weeks ago but this was different. This time there was no stupor, no lapse into unconsciousness. He looked quizzically at a smiling Ambrosio. "Coca, my friend, but without the aspira which Andreas so enjoys giving his guests."

Buchanan guffawed, sending little shreds of mangled leaf flying out of his mouth. Ambrosio slapped him on the back and shouted to his men to press ahead. The coca proved a salvation in the thin mountain air but Ambrosio carefully rationed how it was dispensed. He made clear that only a small amount should be taken as coming off too much of a high would create a problem. He didn't elaborate on what the 'problem' might be and Buchanan didn't want to find out.

The group now made good time, even allowing for the conditions, but at three that afternoon the lead Indian scout ran back down the trail and hurriedly whispered to Ambrosio. The wiry Indian's face darkened at the news. Whatever it was, it wasn't good.

Ambrosio gave some instructions to his men and then came over to the Scots. "There's smoke in the distance"

"Do you know what it is?" asked Montgomery.

"It could be an Indian village or it could be more of the Spanish and Boca. I have sent two scouts to find out."

The news dispelled the light mood as the group was instantly thrown back into combat mode. Silence was once more the order of the day. The thought of having to go into battle again so soon was not one that anyone relished and quiet prayers were offered up that it was a village.

Thirty minutes later the answer came down the line. The scouts talked in hushed tones. Ambrosio listened intently and began shaking his head as the import of the message hit home. It was a village, but that was where the good news ended. The smoke was not from camp-fires but what was left of the huts.

With there now being no imminent danger the party moved quickly up the path to survey the scene for themselves. They emerged from the jungle into a wide clearing and there saw Armageddon.

All that remained of the neat wooden buildings were some smouldering embers whose wispy smoke spiralled upwards. Overhead the vultures were making their sinister circles in the heartless blue sky, screeching a discomfiting welcome, and plainly annoyed at being disturbed from their work.

Strewn across the entire ground were dozens of corpses. Men, women and children. Young and old. No distinction had been made. Hacked limbs lay near their detached owners, intestines spilled out of gutted stomachs and severed heads were jammed on spikes. Most painful were the innocent little bodies of the young. Sliced through in a single blow and all life extinguished.

Buchanan felt the bile rise in his mouth and had to turn away to throw up. He was not alone. They were witnessing the aftermath of an apocalypse. To kill on a field of battle was one thing but to slaughter defenceless women and children was against all laws of nature.

Buchanan saw Drummond suddenly drop to his knees and bury his head in his hands. He couldn't fathom how yesterday's butcher could be so troubled by this scene. Then it clicked. Here he was, six thousand miles away and seven years on, reliving the nightmare of that godless morning in Glencoe.

Old sins cast long shadows, thought Buchanan.

The Tule wandered with reverential silence among the fallen. One of the warriors let out a shout. Someone was still alive. An old woman had been pulled from the undergrowth where the boundary of the village met the jungle. She was barely breathing. Her body was mangled, a broken leg twisted at an impossible angle and her skin flayed. But worst of all was her face. Barely recognisable as human, it had been battered to a pulp, the cheek bones caved in and her teeth and nose smashed. Where her left eye should have been was nothing but a ghastly cavernous hole.

The Indians tried to give her some water but she was beyond all help. She wheezed, her breath a death rattle. With what little strength was left she tried to form some words. Ambrosio knelt beside her and put his ear to her shattered mouth. She muttered something and then in a succession of tightening gasps went limp, her life-force spent.

Ambrosio, placed his hand on her forehead and said some words in Tule before turning to the others. "She said she had prayed for someone to arrive before she died so that she could tell them who had done this and have them take revenge. I can only thank the Gods that we have already granted her wish."

Buchanan paused to take it all in. Some might argue that yesterday's butchery was a form of karmic symmetry. But for him, both were just horrific examples of man's pitiless inhumanity to man.

Ambrosio ordered his warriors to gather up the bodies and arrange them in a funeral pyre. When the Scots saw what was happening they took off their packs and helped in the gruesome task. Ambrosio explained that they could not leave the Indians to the vultures as their souls would not be able to ascend to the Gods. So they would be cremated and their spirits allowed to soar upwards to their ancestors.

The ghoulish work took over an hour. Once the fire was lit Ambrosio ordered everyone to leave. They might not have to watch the incineration of an entire community but there was nothing they could do to prevent the foul stench of the burning flesh lingering for hours in their nostrils.

CHAPTER 26

They struck camp for the night about a mile from the carnage. Because of the elevation it was cold when the sun disappeared and the party was glad for the warmth of their fires. Plenty more drink was taken that evening but this time it was to dull the impact of a tragedy.

When Buchanan woke the next morning the memory of the horror flooded his mind. He looked around and any others who were already up were busying themselves in silence. Montgomery slid across. "You alright, Jamie?" he asked.

"Still pretty shaken to be honest."

"Aye, you're not alone there."

Buchanan slowly shook his head. "What kind of men could do that and live with themselves?"

"Well, we made damned sure that they didn't have to endure that burden for long," replied Montgomery.

"So are we supposed to be excused by casting ourselves in the role of avenging angels?" snapped Buchanan.

"If you like."

"Aye well, we didn't know we were avenging fuck all when we slaughtered the Spanish."

Montgomery laid a hand on his forearm. "I know, Jamie. I know. But best not be too vocal with that thought. It may not play out too well."

"Fine, Robert. I'll hold my peace, but I can't pretend to you that this hasn't changed me."

"That's because you still have your soul, son. Most here lost theirs years ago in France. So don't judge them too harshly."

"Fair enough, but if I ever try to justify what happened, then I'll have lost mine too."

Montgomery let the comment sit for a moment. "Well, we're going have to put it behind us, at least in the short term. We have a mission to complete."

"Aye, but from what we've seen so far there's not a snowball's chance in hell of carving a trade route through this terrain."

"Let's just see how it looks when we get to the top of these bloody mountains, shall we?"

Buchanan gave a weak smile. "Let's do that. After all, I need the exercise."

Montgomery slapped Buchanan's knee and got up to muster the battery. Ahead was another day of slogging up the seemingly never ending peaks. But at least they had now reached an elevation where they could look down on the rain which drenched the lower slopes. They were literally above the clouds and bathed in an intense sun which, although not as hot, seemed to burn them even quicker.

Progress was still painfully slow. The higher they got the more difficult the path. Gone was the incessant mud but in its place were massive boulders which had to be scaled using makeshift ropes sliced from the jungle vines.

The volume of the coca leaves distributed by Ambrosio also increased. It seemed that whatever magical property they contained was metabolising faster in the greater altitude and even the Indians were beginning to struggle.

Then around mid-afternoon Ambrosio signalled a break. He came back to Montgomery and Buchanan and grinned broadly at them. It was the first time they had seen anything other than sorrow on his face since they had left the Indian village. "My friends, we will reach the summit very soon."

Montgomery stared at him blankly. He was completely exhausted and not quite able to take on board what the Indian was saying. He rubbed the sweat from his eyes and looked again at Ambrosio for confirmation.

The chief continued to beam. "My forward scouts have seen it. Only two hundred yards past this ridge."

Montgomery smacked his hands together. "Well, what the hell are we waiting for?" He leapt to his feet, his energy restored and shouted to the platoon. "We're nearly there lads. C'mon!"

This brought a cheer from the soldiers who sprang up, ready for the final push. Ambrosio laughed. "You Scots men are lunatics."

The guides led them over the ridge onto a green sunlit plateau which a hundred yards further on rose to another bluff. Ambrosio pointed. "There's the summit!"

The whole company, Scots and Indians, clambered across those last yards in fevered anticipation. Then with a few final steps all was laid before them like an impossible tableau. On either side of the summit sat the two great oceans of the World reaching out limitlessly to their separate horizons.

Buchanan stood, his mouth agape, scarcely able to take in the astonishing spectacle. He fell to his knees totally overwhelmed by the moment. On one side was the cloudless panorama and blue water of the Pacific and on the other the grey Atlantic, over which a lightning storm was unleashing its extraordinary power.

Buchanan slumped against the stump of an ancient tree and watched as the sun over the Pacific shot arrows of yellow light through the thick forests on the western slopes of the mountains. It was a moment to be savoured and almost made everything worthwhile. Almost, but not quite.

CHAPTER 27

The next morning the view was no less spectacular. Buchanan drank it all in, watching the first rays of the sun seep out from the distant eastern horizon and bathe the world in its light. He felt he was on top of Olympus looking down on the mortal world far below.

The stirring of the others snapped his reverie.

Montgomery wandered over. "Feels like God's waiting room doesn't it?"

"Aye, well if it's all the same to you I'd be happy not to be sitting there just yet."

Montgomery smiled. "Shame we have to leave. Still, we'll see it again on the way back."

Buchanan cast his eyes to the west toward the Pacific and the jungle which sat between then and the ocean. Wreathed in dark shadow it looked menacing and uninviting.

"Think it will be any easier down there?" asked Buchanan.

"Only one way to find out."

It had taken four gruelling days to get this far and Buchanan was not exactly relishing descending into what looked like the abyss. Montgomery called Drummond over and ordered him to have the men ready themselves. Buchanan could see from the soldier's face that he wasn't thrilled at the prospect. "Wi' all due respect Mr. Montgomery, is it absolutely necessary tae press on?"

Montgomery glared at him. "Mr. Drummond. Are you questioning my orders?"

"Not at all. It's just that mebbe we've seen whit we needed tae see."

"Meaning?" snapped Montgomery.

"I hud thought the purpose o' the expedition wis tae assess if we could carve a trade route through the isthmus."

"That's correct."

"Well that's no gonnae be possible is it?"

"It's not for you make that judgement Mr. Drummond. You have no experience in such matters."

"That's as may be Mr. Montgomery, but ah also know when something's impossible without having tae experience it."

Montgomery jutted out his chin. "Just do as I say, Mr. Drummond."

Drummond sniffed. "As ye like Mr. Montgomery, as ye like."

Montgomery turned to Buchanan. "Damned insubordination. I should have him court martialled when we get back."

"Not something you might want to mention right at this moment."

"I'm not afraid of him," he spat.

Fuck I would be, thought Buchanan. Very easy for accidents to happen out here in the wilderness.'

A few seconds later Ambrosio came over. He stretched out his arms and turned in a slow circle to illustrate the entirety of the vista. "Magnificent isn't it?"

Montgomery nodded his agreement. "Sad that we have to leave."

"Yes, but you will always be able to tell your children you have seen it," replied the Indian.

Drummond returned to say the men would be ready in ten minutes.

Ambrosio looked at Montgomery. "Anxious to get back to your settlement, Mr. Montgomery?"

Montgomery, a little puzzled, replied, "Well, yes, eventually Chief."

Buchanan could see what was coming.

"But today we continue our quest," said Montgomery, casting his eyes to the West.

Ambrosio's face took on a look of utter bewilderment. "Continue where, exactly?"

Montgomery pointed to the Pacific. "There, of course."

Ambrosio burst into laughter. "Ah, you Scottish, you are funny men. That is a very good." He turned to his tribesman and rattled off a translation which caused them to dissolve into laughter.

Montgomery stared at the Indian. "I'm sorry, Chief, is there something I'm missing?"

Ambrosio looked at him again and suddenly saw that the Scot was serious. His laughter quickly evaporated. "My apologies. I didn't mean any offence."

"Fine, apology accepted. Let's get on our way then."

Ambrosio looked at Buchanan, his eyes pleading that he say something.

"Perhaps we should ask the Chief for his thoughts before we press on, Robert," Buchanan suggested.

Montgomery saw Buchanan's cautionary look. "Very well. Ambrosio what say you?"

"Mr. Montgomery, it is of course your decision as to whether or not you go there," he said, replicating Montgomery's pointed finger towards the Pacific, "but it will not be with me or my men."

"I beg your pardon!" snapped Montgomery.

"We agreed to help you come here, but no further."

"I remember agreeing to no such thing."

"I can assure you that had to be the case. There is nowhere further to go."

Montgomery opened his palms outwards and directed them West. "So is that a mirage then?"

"No, but you cannot go there?"

"Why not?"

"Because you will never return," came the chilling response.

"What do you mean? We've survived all manner of purgatories to get this far. What else could be worse?" growled Montgomery.

Ambrosio shook his head. "You do not understand. The Gods forbid it."

"Maybe your Gods, but not mine."

"Perhaps your Gods have not been there."

Montgomery looked again at the Indian. "Well, He will be with us now. And that is enough for me."

"I implore you not to go."

Drummond had caught wind of what was going on and had moved within earshot. Obeying orders was one thing, but signing his mens' death warrants was another.

Buchanan interceded. "Why do your Gods forbid it?"

"Because down there exist tribes that know no Gods. They are savages who take pleasure in killing any living creature and then having them for dinner. And sometimes they do not wait for them to die before they start to eat."

Drummond couldn't stay out of this. "Whit, like cannibals?" he asked in his comical pidgin French.

Ambrosio nodded. "Exactly, Mr. Drummond."

"Well fuck that, Mr. Montgomery. Again wi' a' due respect."

"Oh, come on, Drummond. We're well armed and drilled. They would be no match for our muskets and steel."

Ambrosio held up a hand. "You cannot fight ghosts. You would not even see them before you saw your own Maker. Their darts and arrows would come out of the blackness of the jungle and cut you down before you could fire a shot."

Buchanan looked at Montgomery and jerked his head slightly to the side to suggest a private discussion. Montgomery twigged, thanked Ambrosio for his advice and dismissed Drummond.

Alone with Buchanan he asked. "What do you think, Jamie?"

The lawyer looked squarely at the old soldier. "Do you really have a choice ,Robert?"

"What if it's all just bullshit?"

"Want to take that risk? He sounded pretty convincing to me."

"What the old 'Gods forbid it' routine?"

"Look, Robert. Just take a step back here. What Drummond said earlier is true. There's not a hope in hell of establishing a trading route over these mountains. No need to plough on to confirm what we already know."

"Well, the Spanish have managed it just fine."

"Yes, but they went through the mountains, not over them. And they used slaves to do the heavy lifting. So, sure, if you can find another river like the Charges to cut the isthmus in half and then make the Company of Scotland a slaver I'd agree with you."

Montgomery ran his hand through his hair. "Christ, it'll feel like we've failed."

"Are you serious, man? How can you say we've failed? This was only supposed to be a scouting mission. I don't know about you but I reckon we've scouted plenty. Plus we've fucked over the Spanish and their Boca friends which is more than a little significant."

"You think so?"

He laid a hand on Montgomery's shoulder. "No question. Come on, let's go home to Darien and give them the news."

He paused for a moment. "Aye. Alright Jamie. But I want it noted that I was for going on."

"Rest assured on that, Robert."

The news was joyfully received by the Scots soldiers and with some relief by Ambrosio who pulled Buchanan to one side. "It would have greatly saddened me to see you go to your death."

"Thank you."

The Indian gave a little chuckle. "Also, if I'd returned without you I may have been suspected of being involved in your disappearance."

Buchanan laughed, "And you wouldn't want that."

Ambrosio slapped him on the back. "Especially now that I have an ally who knows how to kill the Spanish devils."

CHAPTER 28

The Indians and Scots took one last lingering look from the glorious peak before beginning their descent back to Darien. They slid and slithered into the dense cloud which sat like a grey blanket two hundred yards below the summit. There the air changed from its sharp mountain purity to a cloying humidity which enveloped them like a damp shroud.

By the time they arrived back at the ravaged Indian village the heavens had opened and the rain was pummelling down. Ambrosio, not wanting to relive the pain and horror of the massacre site, paused only briefly to offer up a prayer and ensure that the pyre had done its work.

Buchanan didn't want to look. But he couldn't help it. Maybe seeing the mound of charred bodies, no longer distinguishable as human, would make what had happened easier to live with. He was wrong. If anything it just brought home the extent of the atrocity. The stack of corpses, even though burned beyond recognition, still betrayed its origins. The skulls and bones, especially the tiny ones of the children seemed to make it all the more appalling. Disappointed vultures jabbed at the slim pickings but soon took flight when Drummond stopped their grotesque defilement with a couple of well-aimed shots.

Ambrosio halted a few hundred yards further on in a wider part of the path well sheltered by the thick jungle canopy. He spoke with Montgomery and the two agreed that they would make camp for the night. The memory of the ravaged village cast a melancholy pall and in near silence, the men washed their food down with a mixture of whisky and rainwater. This night was no place for chatter or humour.

The following day dawned bleak and forbidding. The torrential downpour started before first light and didn't ease up the entire morning. By the time the Scots neared the site of the battle they were bedraggled and dispirited. They had been physically sapped by the stinging rain, the oozing mud and the constant attacks of the mosquitos. The soundtrack of their journey were the rolling thunder claps and kettledrum beat of the deluge. Flash floods had turned the path to mush and no sooner did a Scot pick himself up than he was down again floundering in the brown sludge.

The Indians, anxious to return to their homes and families, had again become irritated at the tortuous pace needed to nanny the clumsy, plodding Scots. Ambrosio thought about leaving them to their own devices. After all, they only had to stumble downhill in a straight line. But he knew these Scots would be useful again and abandoning them now would not be beneficial in the long run.

So the Chief moved back down the line to the Scots leaders and suggested that when they reached the battlefield, they stop and use the remaining daylight to pick the Spanish clean of anything of worth. Word of the plan was passed along and instantly the pace picked up.

When they reached the clearing it was apparent that the vultures had been busy. The sound of the expedition arriving had not deterred them from their grisly task and it took a salvo of musket balls to get them to vacate.

The avian scavenging became replaced by the human variety and the Scots and Indians pounced on the carcasses stripping them of their valuables. The prized yellow and blue jackets, the Toledo steel swords and the fine leather boots all found their way into Scottish hands. The Indians seized the Boca weaponry and jewellery as trophies.

The rest of the Spanish provisions were gathered up and split between Scots and Tule. Buchanan declined to participate in the desecration of the bodies but did accept a small cask of Spanish brandy and some Serrano ham.

The enrichment of their wardrobes, arsenals and stomachs brought much needed cheer and the group spent the rest of the day ostentatiously parading their new clothes among the rotting dead while downing Spanish wine. For the first time in a while the Scots brought out their little wooden flutes and chanters and the sound of music could be heard from that terrible slaughterhouse until exhaustion and alcohol took their inevitable toll.

CHAPTER 29

The sore heads the next morning were not helped by the screeching alarm call of the impatient vultures. The rain had stopped and the steam rose in ghostly waves from the ground as the heat began to dry out the soil.

Montgomery and Ambrosio had agreed the previous evening that if they started early enough it would be possible to cover the remaining miles to Darien before dusk. It would be hard work but preferable to having to spend another night sleeping in wet clothes on sodden ground.

So the troop gathered up their spoils and began the last leg of their mission. The prospect of getting back to Darien gave the Scots renewed energy and they ate up the miles despite the crushing heat and extra baggage.

As the ground flattened and the smell of the sea air began to mix with the heady jungle musk, they knew that they were getting closer. Late in the afternoon, there was a shout from the Indian scouts. The bay had come into view through a gap in the tree-line. The Scots could see their ships sitting proudly in the water and the outline of the partially constructed fort up on the clifftops.

A short while later, the party burst through the last of the jungle and back onto home soil. News of their arrival spread like wildfire and they were soon surrounded by the Landsmen. A volley of cannons signalled that the ships had registered their return and a small flotilla of longboats was soon making its way towards the beach.

Ambrosio and his warriors, anxious to get back to their village before dark, bade farewell to their comrades in arms. The men of these two diverse cultures clasped hands in thanks and admiration. The colonists waved as the indefatigable Indians jumped into their canoes and paddled away to their families.

Buchanan noticed that precious little work had been done on the settlement in the seven days they'd been away and the small temporary infirmary looked like it was overflowing. However, before he could dwell on this he heard his name being shouted and turned to see Pincarton and Paterson clambering out of one of the longboats.

"The wanderer returns!" shouted Pincarton as the other adventurers were met with similar welcomes and feted like heroes. But Buchanan didn't feel that way, not after what he'd witnessed. "C'mon, Jamie, let's get you and Montgomery back to the Unicorn. His Commodoreship is meeting us there."

Buchanan turned to say his goodbyes to the soldiers. Drummond gave a mock salute and toothless grin as the rest of the troop shouted friendly farewells. "Seems you made an impression on the rank and file Jamie," said Pincarton.

"They're good men, Robert. They did Scotland proud."

"No issues with Drummond then?"

"None personally. But let's just say I'm glad he's on our side. Hard bastard that one. "

"Aye, that's been no secret since Glencoe,"

As the trio entered the Great Cabin, they found Pennicuik and Jolly already there. The travellers were greeted with a peculiar deference, as if their voyage to the wilderness had elevated them. Whiskies were poured and both Montgomery and Buchanan wasted no time in gulping them down.

"Looks like you needed those," said Jolly.

"You could say that," replied Montgomery holding his glass up to be refilled.

"So, tell us all," said Pincarton.

For the next thirty minutes Montgomery and Buchanan worked as a double act narrating the events of the last week. They left nothing to the imagination in describing the battle with the Spanish, the horrific scenes at the Indian village, the inconceivable majesty of the vista from the summit and the incredible physical obstacles to reach it. The other Council members sat transfixed, taking in the extraordinary story.

Buchanan demurred from injecting his personal emotions. This was not the time. A straightforward recounting of events was all that was required.

Then began the analysis. Pennicuik asked about the Spanish and whether this victory would be an end to it.

Montgomery answered, "Your guess is as good as mine. They were wiped out, so we can't see how word will get back to Panama about their actual fate. I'm sure when they don't return that questions will be asked, but believe me there are many ways to die up there other than at the end of a sword."

Pincarton was more pragmatic. "Doesn't matter why they don't get back. The fact is that they won't and the Spanish commanders will know their mission failed. Think they'll just accept the situation? No, me neither."

They then moved on to questions about the viability of a trade route across the Isthmus. The answers didn't make for happy listening. A disbelieving Paterson asked for confirmation. "You're actually telling me it isn't feasible?"

Montgomery and Buchanan looked at one another to ensure they were in agreement. Buchanan pursed his lips. "Unless there's another River Chagres somewhere on the Isthmus then we can't see how it's possible."

"Sweet Mother of God," said Paterson. He let out a long breath and looked up at the ceiling of the Cabin. In the space of a few minutes his dream of bridging the Oceans had been crushed.

"Sorry to be the bearer of such grim news," said Montgomery.

Pincarton bowed his head. "Nothing to apologise for. At least now we can make an informed decision."

"Aye," snorted Pennicuik, "that this whole venture is a complete fucking waste of time."

Paterson slammed his fist down on the table. "Has there been a single moment since we left Leith when you've not sought to ridicule or undermine everything we're trying to do."

Pennicuik sprang back in his seat before gathering himself. "Aye, well maybe the best thing to do when you're sitting on a dead horse is to get off it."

"Aye, you'd like that wouldn't you, Commodore Pennicuik. You're a vile cancer, spreading nothing but malice. Christ, all you wanted to do was plant the Saltire, take the glory and piss off back to Scotland."

"Fuck you, Paterson!" He got to his feet.

The two antagonists glared at each other, the mutual loathing palpable. Pincarton allowed a few moments for the spat to simmer down and said. "Alright, ladies. Just sit down and take a breath. This is getting us nowhere. We need to concentrate on how we move on from here."

When tempers had cooled they pored over the map to explore possible alternative overland routes. But it was now clear that Darien was in no way suited to being one half of a transcontinental trading entrepot. It was a hammer blow to the entire rationale behind the Scheme. Without this what did the Scots have to offer that dozens of other established ports in the Caribbean didn't already provide?

It was Pincarton who broke the depressed silence. "Well, on the upside we're just about ready to strike out for Aruba. This will give us some idea of the appetite for our linens and whisky."

Paterson, clutching at this ray of hope, cut in. "Then add the Madeira wine and the tobacco and there's the basis for a thriving marketplace."

"And that's the master plan is it?" sniped Pennicuik.

"Unless you've got a better idea *Commodore,*" barked Paterson.

Pennicuik said nothing but it was clear that he would happily hoist the sails of the Saint Andrew and leave for Scotland on the next tide.

Pincarton gave a little grin. "Well, that's all sorted. Let's get on with it then."

"What right now?" asked Montgomery.

"Don't fret, Robert. First, I want to hear the full story of how you kicked Johnny Spaniard's arse."

CHAPTER 30

The Dolphin began its journey to Aruba two days later. It carried a sizeable chunk of what remained of the linen, whisky, tobacco and Madeira wine together with one hundred Pounds in gold coin. This trip would be the litmus test for the Company as a pure trader out of Darien and its future as a single hub port.

"God speed, Pincarton," whispered Paterson as he watched the ship slip through the heads and out into the ocean.

"He'll be fine," said Buchanan. "Couldn't think of a better man for the job."

Buchanan saw Paterson raise both eyebrows. "Well, other than you William, but you're indispensable here."

Paterson nodded and went down below to continue being indispensable.

Over the next few days not a great deal of note happened. The indefatigable Drummond resumed his role as manager of the building works. He thrived on pushing others to the limit and fed off their resentment as some bizarre life force. But the continuing poor conditions and the absence of proper sustenance made progress tortuously slow. Nonetheless, spirits remained relatively upbeat at the prospect of the returning Dolphin.

However, the next ship to enter the bay was a little English trading sloop named the Maidstone. It had passed by a few weeks earlier and briefly stopped to see if any trade could be done. Now the same ship had signalled for an immediate audience.

Its Captain, Ephraim Pilkington, was rowed over to the Unicorn. This was now the command centre for the Company after Pennicuik had made it clear that he had little interest in continuing to host Council meetings and more pressingly to share his dwindling horde of whisky.

Pilkington was a tall rangy man whose clothes looked a size too big for him but the most compelling of his features was his left ear. It was frayed and jagged, almost as if it was constantly rubbed with sandpaper. However, not being a topic of polite enquiry, its demise remained a mystery.

He was met by Paterson, Buchanan and Montgomery, who was now berthed on the Unicorn following his return from the interior. Pilkington spoke in a distinctive West Country burr. "Gentleman. I'm afraid I've some bad news."

These are never the first meaningful words anyone wishes to hear, especially when there hasn't exactly been a golden period of good fortune preceding it.

"We promise not to hold you responsible," said Buchanan.

Pilkington gave a wry smile, aware that his answer was going to sting. "Your ship, The Dolphin, has been taken by the Spanish."

Montgomery dropped his glass on the table, spilling its contents across the sleek mahogany surface. Paterson fell back in his chair.

Buchanan stood stunned, his mind racing. "How do you know?" he eventually asked.

"Two days ago we approached Cartagena to do some business. The Spanish don't mind us as they know we're just traders. But this time we were denied permission to berth. As we sailed past my first officer called me to the top deck and pointed out a ship tied up in the far corner of the harbour. It was The Dolphin."

"Did you see any of our men?" asked Paterson..

"'Fraid not, but I saw a few Spanish sailors on the deck," he said, distracted by Montgomery's effort to try to mop up the splattered whisky.

"For Christ sakes, Montgomery, just leave it be," snapped Paterson.

Montgomery looked up like a chided infant. "Sorry," he mumbled.

"What else?" continued Paterson.

"The Dolphin was holed on her starboard side."

"A cannon hole?"

"No, it was more ragged and longer than that. Like she had run aground or struck something pretty hard."

"Do you know if the Spanish took her on the high seas?"

"Again I can't say, but I doubt it. The Barlovento was tasked with capturing privateers and treasure hunters. They wouldn't waste their time with traders," he replied.

"So how the hell has she ended up in Cartagena?" asked Buchanan.

"All I can think of is that there was a bad storm about three days back. We were south of it near Curacao but God knows what damage might have been sustained by anyone caught up in it."

Paterson puffed out his cheeks. "Jesus Christ."

This was the worst news they could have received. One of its Fleet, twenty of its sailors and two of its best Captains locked in Cartagena along with most of the useful Scottish inventory and a sizeable chunk of its gold.

"So what the hell do we do?" asked Buchanan. "We can't leave Pincarton and the rest of them just languishing there."

"Perhaps they're just waiting to repair the Dolphin, pay the cost and be on their way," Montgomery suggested.

"And perhaps the tooth fairy will come and put a Guinea under your pillow tonight." snapped Paterson. He took a breath. "Sorry, Montgomery. Just a bit overwhelmed by the news."

Montgomery nodded, acknowledging the apology.

"Still doesn't solve what we do," said Buchanan.

"Should we take the Saint Andrew down there and demand some answers?" asked Montgomery.

Paterson ran a hand over his face. "Pennicuik would never agree to that. Anyway, it's too big a risk. What if the Spanish did actually seize the Dolphin? None of our ships have the firepower to prevent further capture."

"So we just sit on our backsides then?" snapped Buchanan.

Paterson turned his gaze towards Pilkington. The English Captain, sensing what was coming raised his hands. "No way. I'm not getting involved."

"Just hear me out," said Paterson in a softer more persuasive voice. "We'd never dream of asking you to put yourself or your ship in harm's way."

"Delighted to hear it."

"But if we made it worth your while would you prepared to deliver a message to the Spanish?"

"What kind of message?"

"To ask if they would entertain a parlay with representatives of the Company and guarantee their safe passage."

"That's it?"

"Well initially, yes," said Paterson.

"What do you mean "initially"?"

"Look, if the answer is in the affirmative it would seem ridiculous that you would then have to sail all the way back here to tell us."

Pilkington's eyed narrowed. "Meaning?"

"Meaning, it would make far more sense to take the representatives with you and if permission is granted they could go ashore."

"And if the answer is in the negative?"

"Then we stay on board the Maidstone and cause you no further trouble other than dropping us off here when you next pass this way."

Pilkington weighed up the merits of the proposal. Seeing no immediate holes he rubbed his whiskery chin and moved on to the next part of the negotiation. "It'd have to be very well worth my while."

"Wouldn't have it any other way," said Paterson. He had his man. Now it was just a question of price.

"What did you have in mind, Paterson?

"Half of any gold and whisky recovered."

"Too risky. I'll need something upfront regardless of outcome."

"Would that I could but what's on that ship is most of what we have. We'll can only pay if the mission is a success."

"C'mon Paterson. I'm taking a hell of a chance. Twenty pounds upfront and five cases of whisky."

"Can't do it, Captain."

Pilkington looked dead at Paterson to see if there was any bluff in those steely grey eyes. Paterson didn't blink.

After more whisker scratching Pilkington tried again. "Ten upfront and three cases and let's be done with it."

Paterson moved across to Buchanan and whispered in his ear. "Just look as if I'm saying something you don't agree with, shake your head and then whisper something back."

Buchanan did as he was asked. Paterson nodded and turned his attention back to Pilkington.

"Seems Mr. Buchanan isn't as hard-nosed as me. I'm not happy about this, but five pounds and one case upfront."

Pilkington dwelt on this for a few seconds. "I'll take your deal."

Paterson raised an eyebrow. "There is one other thing Captain."

"And what might that be?"

"Given that there will be two of us making the trip it's probably best if you leave two of your men here."

"Don't you trust me?"

"Of course I do, but having them here will give you that extra incentive to get us back sooner rather than later."

Pincarton snorted. "Fair enough. Tomorrow morning good for you?"

"Ideal."

Pilkington gave a little salute before leaving the Scots on their own.

Montgomery asked the obvious question. "So, who's going?"

Paterson looked at Buchanan. "Well, I rather thought that if you had no objection it should be Jamie and myself."

Montgomery was delighted to agree to any proposal which didn't include him but added. "For completeness, shouldn't we get Council approval?"

This was the first time that the old soldier had ever raised a governance issue. However if the mission failed Montgomery would be left to carry the can for the decision on his own.

"Of course, Robert." Paterson agreed, knowing that it would be a non-issue anyway given that three of the five remaining Councillors had already consented to the proposal. "Let's get over to the Saint Andrew and collar Pennicuik and Jolly."

As it turned out, the other two had no objection. They were shocked at the news but agreed that Paterson's proposal was sound and that he and Buchanan were most suited as emissaries. Pennicuik was also delighted he didn't have to put the Saint Andrew, himself or his crew in any danger and if there was also a possibility of being rid of the irritating Paterson, then all the better.

As Buchanan laid his head on his pillow that night, he reflected, not for the first time. "How the hell did I ever get myself into this?"

CHAPTER 31

Favourable winds and the affable Pilkington's hospitality made the voyage bearable despite its solemn purpose. It took only three days for the Maidstone to drop anchor in the Spanish port nestled under the cliffs of Cartagena.

Pilkington sent a pinnace ashore with a message requesting that the Governor meet with the Scots' representatives. After an hour the boat returned with news that this was acceptable and when in the future might these envoys be expected. Much to the chagrin of the oarsmen they were despatched straight back with word that the Scots were available for immediate parlay. If a translator was required, one could accompany them.

The Governor replied that he would receive the Scots the next morning and that if they spoke Latin, no translator would be needed.

The following day Buchanan and Paterson made the short row over to the quayside. Buchanan fretted as to how his Latin would stand up. With them they had a copy of the Act and a letter demanding the immediate release of the Dolphin, its crew and cargo.

They were transported by carriage up the steeply winding path to the imposing fort perched on the imposing clifftop. From there the view out over the Atlantic was breathtaking. Buchanan could pick out dozens of ships dotted across the vista and it was easy to see why the Spanish had chosen this location as their stronghold at the top of South America.

The Scots were taken through a set of stone cloisters, deliciously cool in the morning heat. Two enormous mahogany doors then opened onto a large light filled office which looked directly over the ocean. The plantation shutters had been opened wide enough to allow a gentle breeze and the room was infused with the scent of bougainvilleas.

Awaiting Paterson and Buchanan were two men, one of whom was in uniform. He was well built and elegant in a pressed blue and yellow military jacket. He sported a full beard which was fastidiously trimmed and the ends of his moustache were waxed to little exclamation points. His alert brown eyes stared unblinking at the visitors.

The civilian, who the Scots took to be the Governor, was closer to obese than tubby and it looked like a second edition of his chin had already been published. There was no question he enjoyed all the benefits that came with the position.

Using Latin, the Governor introduced himself as Don Diego de Luca. The words barely escaped pursed lips which seemed to move with great reluctance. He then gestured to the soldier, advising this was Major Martin De Saballe, commander of the militia. The Major gave a polite little bow.

Paterson introduced himself and Buchanan and the Scots were invited to sit around a large teak table situated in a shaded part of the room. De Saballe offered them sherry and formalities over, it was De Luca who got proceedings moving. "So, Gentlemen, what can we do for you?" he said, but now in accented English.

Paterson and Buchanan glanced at one another. Paterson replied. "To begin with, can I assume we are to converse in English?"

"Yes, you can assume that," he said. His mouth had a snide cruelty and Buchanan thought that the redundant requirement of using Latin would be indicative of a less than straightforward discussion.

"In that case, please accept these documents," Paterson said, handing over the Act and demand for release.

De Luca, gave a little sniff of irritation and broke the seal of the Letter. He gave this no more than a peremptory glance before handing it to De Saballe. The Governor then flicked through the Act and tossed it across the table in the direction of the commander. De Saballe, at least, had the courtesy to peruse them long enough to glean their import.

De Luca stared at the Scots and shrugged his podgy shoulders. "And so?"

"Excellency, we would have hoped our letter was adequate explanation."

"This demands the release of your sad little ship and its crew, yes?"

"That is correct."

"But that assumes we are keeping them prisoner."

"Well aren't you?"

"That is not the point Mr… Sorry what is your name again?"

"Paterson." he said, clenching his cheeks.

"Yes, of course, Mr. Paterson. The point is that you assumed we were holding them against their will with no proof that this was the case."

"With due respect Governor, from our position perhaps not an unwarranted assumption."

"But an assumption, nonetheless. Do you think we just indiscriminately seize ships and crews of other nations?"

An honest answer would be overly provocative, so Paterson played along with the charade. "Well, I would hope as civilised men that would not be the case."

"Civilised men. How odd you should bring that up. Would civilised men order the slaughter of a squadron of Spanish mapmakers scouting the interior of Panama?"

His words sent a chill down the spines of both Scots. They were walking on eggshells.

"I'm sorry, Señor De Luca but you have lost me," said Paterson.

"We sent men to the interior last month to survey the terrain but not one of them returned. The only possible explanation is that they were murdered."

Paterson kept a poker face. "I am sorry to hear that, Governor. We have heard of barbaric tribes who will not hesitate to kill anyone entering their territory."

"Not in the area where my men were surveying."

"And where might that have been?

"That Sir, is not your business," snapped De Luca.

"Well in that case there is little I can add, Señor. Perhaps if there was a chance that they were lost near our settlement we might be able to assist."

He curled his thin top lip. "Pah. You play your childish word games with me Mr. Paterson. But we both know what happened."

"I'm afraid I really don't know what you are implying. We have come to

Panama with no bellicose intent and merely want to trade in the name of Scotland. It is certainly not part of our remit to engage in any unprovoked conflict."

"Nonsense. We have seen your Fleet. So heavily armed and carrying many soldiers. Is this what a trader does?"

"You seem remarkably well informed, Señor," Paterson said. The Governor said nothing so Paterson went on. "Let us say that it would be a fool who didn't take precautions to protect himself from unwanted aggression."

"And yet you choose to mock Spain by establishing a settlement on its territory. Is this not an act of aggression?"

"With the greatest respect, Governor, we fail to see how Spain has any claim over Darien. Surely had it wished to annex this as part of its Empire it would have established a settlement there."

"Do not pretend with me, Mr. Paterson. You well know that Spain has legitimate claim to all of the land between Portobello, Cartagena and Panama City."

"I must confess that this is news to me, Señor De Luca. Using your principle, all any country has to do is build three separate settlements and then claim all the land within the triangle created by them."

"In Panama that is the case," De Luca sneered.

Buchanan was gripped by the exchange. He could see that De Saballe was also intrigued, but the Spaniard seemed more amused than invested.

Paterson took a deep breath. "Well, let us agree to disagree on that for the present time. I'm sure our respective Kings will be happy to talk about the matter."

Buchanan could see the fat little Spaniard bridle. "Do you think Phillip would give a second thought to your pathetic little enterprise?"

Paterson voice took on an edge. "I don't know, perhaps you should ask him when King William comes knocking at his door demanding answers for your actions."

De Luca and De Saballe both suddenly broke into laughter. They obviously found Paterson's comment hysterical.

When De Luca had recovered his composure he wiped a tear from his pudgy little eye and looked squarely at the Scot. "Well, I tell you this Mr. Paterson you have provided me with some much needed levity. Do you honestly believe that England would risk the fragile peace with Spain over your tinpot little homestead?"

Buchanan didn't like the sound of this at all. What did De Luca know that the Scots didn't? Paterson composed himself and pointed to the Act. "If you had taken the time to read it, all the evidence you need is there."

"Ah papers, papers, Mr. Paterson. Sometimes they are just a waste of ink, don't you think? I always believe that actions speak much louder than words."

"Meaning?" prompted Paterson.

"Meaning, that I have it on good authority that your King has made clear his distaste for your settlement- what do you call it? 'Caledonia.' How very quaint," he smirked.

Buchanan and Paterson were both aware that William was no fan of the Scots colony but for this to be so public was an unpleasant surprise.

"Whether or not that is true, he has pledged to be its guardian," fired back Paterson.

"Oh, I am sure he did, but times change Mr. Paterson, times change. You are now pariahs."

"Perhaps a man's word does not mean much in Spain, Señor, but in Britain it is still valued."

"Ah, but you need to remember that your King is Dutch, Mr. Paterson." This again reduced the Governor to tears of mirth.

"The King would never turn his back on his subjects."

"Alas, I think perhaps he already has," said De Luca. His expression almost showed some pity for these misguided fools, but then his face hardened as he seemed to remember his missing brigade.

"I suppose this also comes from your mysterious 'good authority'?" snarled Paterson.

"Oh please, Mr. Paterson. Do not test me. I've no need for secrecy. You will doubtless know of Admiral John Benbow?"

"Of course. He commands the King's Navy in the Caribbean."

"He also has been a visitor to Cartagena in the last week."

Paterson knitted his brows. "Has he now?

"Yes, indeed. When we told him about our problem with the missing survey team and your little privateer vessel he made clear that he regarded it as a matter between Spain and Scotland."

Buchanan and Paterson absorbed the full import of the words. Surely De Luca was bluffing? But then again why should he? He would know that the Scots would call him out and this didn't look like a man who played cards unless he held the aces.

Paterson gathered himself. "Well, I think Admiral Benbow will find he'll have to answer for that."

"Oh I don't think he's very concerned, Mr. Paterson."

Buchanan could see that this was becoming a futile stand off and decided to step in. "Perhaps, gentlemen we can get back to the immediate matter at hand."

De Luca looked at him with an infuriating smirk which Buchanan sensed he practised daily in front of a mirror. "Ah yes, the matter at hand. What to do, what to do?"

"Well, with all due respect, Señor De Luca, surely that is not really in question?"

"Oh, you think not my young friend? So what would you suggest?"

Buchanan gave the obvious answer. "Simply put, allow our ship to leave with its crew and cargo."

Da Luca smirked once more. "If only it were so easy, Mr. Buchanan. You see I have my orders from Madrid and it would not go well for me if I failed to follow them."

"What orders could possibly allow for the detention of our vessel? We are not at war with Spain."

"Yes, that is the case, but I've been told to seize any ship which is guilty of an act of warfare."

"But what has that got to do with the Dolphin?"

"Don't you think that a heavily armed vessel sailing towards Cartagena constitutes a threat?"

"What are you talking about? The Dolphin was damaged in a storm and sought safe harbour here. How is that a threat?"

"You can have your interpretation of the facts, Mr. Buchanan, and we can have ours. As far as Spain is concerned, a vessel of a foreign power suspected of being involved in the murder of an innocent working party sailed towards Cartagena with no authority to berth. To deter it from attack it was surrounded by our Barlovento and escorted into port. That vessel and its cargo have now been impounded and its crew detained."

Buchanan tried desperately to keep the exasperation out of his voice. "Are you serious, Señor ? Nobody could possibly believe that."

"Oh, I think they will, Mr. Buchanan. I can assure you that in light of recent events it will be a narration which carries a great deal of credibility."

Buchanan looked at Paterson. Which way to jump? Threaten with retaliation or be conciliatory?

Paterson made the decision. "Can I suggest before we embark on any brinksmanship that we attempt to explore some form of common landing acceptable to both sides."

"You can certainly suggest that, Mr. Paterson, but I don't know how far it will get us. From our perspective there appears very little to discuss."

Paterson made his play. "You can keep half the cargo and the ship but we shall not leave without our men."

"In which case, you will not be leaving," said De Luca.

Buchanan wanted to jump across the table and shove the puffed-up ball of lard's teeth down his throat.

Paterson took a deep breath. The Scots had no real leverage, so bravado was a useless tool. He backed off any baseless ultimatum. "So what will happen to them?"

"Oh, don't worry Mr. Paterson, they will be well looked after. Despite what you may have heard, we are not monsters. At least not towards Europeans in any event." He seemed to find this very humorous and broke into another bout of laughter.

Paterson pressed again. "Señor, I'm sorry, but you have still not answered my question."

De Luca looked across at De Saballe who took his cue. "I understand your concerns gentlemen. The officers are being treated with the respect befitting their rank and the ordinary men held in communal custody. They have been fed and watered and not subjected to any physical harm."

"Do we have your word on that?" asked Paterson.

De Luca scoffed at the question but De Saballe looked straight at Paterson. "'As an Officer and a Gentleman', I think you British say."

Paterson nodded his appreciation before Buchanan asked. "Will they remain in Cartagena?"

De Luca butted back in. "Why, are you planning a rescue mission with your little fleet?" Once more he cackled at the apparent brilliance of his wit.

De Saballe answered. "They will be taken to Seville and held there until the terms of their release can be negotiated."

"For ransom you mean?" said Paterson.

"That decision is not within my purview Mr. Paterson. But yes, I am sure that is one option."

"Can we not discuss such terms now?" asked Buchanan.

De Luca sneered. "Would that we were able. But since your little colony has attracted so much adverse attention in Spain, prizes such as your crew are pawns which our superiors wish to have closer to home."

The Scots were in a corner with nowhere to go. If the Spanish weren't willing to negotiate then further discussion was fruitless. They would need to get back to Darien to mobilise the support promised by the King.

Paterson asked. "At the very least, can we see the men?"

De Luca sniffed and said nothing. De Saballe again stepped in. "On condition that you do not try to organise any form of escape."

Paterson looked at Buchanan who gave a 'and how the fuck do they think we could do that' kind of shrug.

"Agreed" said Paterson.

"Then, I shall take you to them now" said De Saballe. He rose along with the Scots but De Luca remained seated as a final insult before saying. "Oh, and please do send word if you come across my missing men, won't you?"

CHAPTER 32

De Saballe led them out through the cloisters and down a series of steep stone steps. At the bottom he stopped and turned to the Scots. "Gentlemen, let me reiterate that your countrymen will come to no harm when they are under my charge."

Paterson studied him. "But can the same guarantee be given when that no longer applies?"

De Saballe tilted his head to one side and gave a slight shrug of his shoulders. "Mr. Paterson, I can only secure their safety in Cartagena and give instructions to whichever Captain takes them to Seville. I would be comforted by two things though. The first, is that ill-treating prisoners is never a good idea, as sooner or later the boot is always on the other foot. The second is that your crew is a valuable prize in a high stakes political game, so they will be looked after in the same way that one cherishes any investment."

Paterson nodded. "Thank you, Major."

De Saballe then paused. "After the sacking by the French, Señor De Luca has been walking on thin ice. The loss of his brigade will not be looked on favourably in Madrid but the capture of your ship, crew and cargo will help offset that. You see how it is?"

"Yes, I see how it is, but that doesn't condone his behaviour. Rest assured representations will be made to King William."

"That of course is your prerogative, Mr. Paterson, but as De Luca said, I would not expect too much. Your King now seems to value his relationship with Spain much more than with Scotland."

"We'll see about that," sniffed Paterson.

"Indeed, Mr. Paterson. Well, let me take you to your comrades."

An armed guard was stationed outside a corridor of cells. De Saballe gave instructions for one of these to be opened. "This is where we are keeping your senior officers. I'll allow you privacy if you adhere to your earlier undertaking."

"You have our word."

De Saballe's dark eyes seemed to glint as he gave a final nod. The guard opened the heavy wooden door, let the Scots pass and then banged it shut behind them. Buchanan took in the surrounds. The room itself was about ten yards by six and there were a series of windows set high into the thick sandstone walls. At one end were two beds and at the other a small square table with two chairs.

Sitting on these were Pincarton and Malloch. The opening of the door had not caused much excitement as it could have been for a routine feed or defouling. However, as soon as they saw Buchanan and Paterson they jumped up.

"Jesus Christ, are we glad to see you!" exclaimed Pincarton, enveloping them in a bear hug before stepping back. "Thank you for coming." The emotion was evident in his voice. Malloch slapped Buchanan repeatedly on the back.

Knowing the news they had to give, Buchanan tried to lighten the moment. "I've seen inn rooms worse than this. Trust you to land on your feet, Robert."

Pincarton held out his arms to the side and half turned in each direction as if showing off his estates. "Welcome to our Kingdom. I'm afraid I've no whisky to offer but De Saballe has furnished us with this bottle of almost drinkable Spanish brandy." He smiled as he poured them all a drink.

Buchanan looked at the prisoners. Both seemed in good health and showed no obvious signs of harm. "How are they treating you?"

"Surprisingly decently," said Pincarton. "De Saballe is rather a good chap. He allows us some exercise each day and has even had us up to his quarters for dinner. Not, of course, that it was anything other than a soft soap exercise to winkle out information."

Malloch butted in. "Aye, not like that little cunt De Luca."

Pincarton laughed. "Definitely a victim of the wee fat man syndrome. But it seems that De La Saballe holds sway over him, so that's good."

"How about the others?" asked Paterson.

Pincarton shrugged. "We've not been allowed any contact but De Saballe has promised they're being looked after. When are you seeing them?"

There was an awkward pause before Paterson replied. "We're not."

Malloch, now slightly panicked, blurted. "Hold on, have you not come to get us all out?"

Paterson looked at Buchanan and then back at Malloch and Pincarton. This wasn't going to be easy. The next five minutes were spent recounting as accurately as he could the meeting with De Luca and De Saballe. He tried to soften the reality but there wasn't too much sugar coating available.

Malloch sat back, the blood draining from his face. "Fucking English cunts," he hissed.

Pincarton casually poured himself another glass of brandy and ran his hand through his thick black hair. "That's not the way it happened at all. A storm hit us and we got holed on a rock. We'd no option but to limp in here. No way could we have been regarded as a threat."

"We assumed that. Pilkington just missed the storm but reckoned it would have crippled any ship caught in its teeth," said Paterson.

Pincarton nodded. "Doesn't really help us though. The Spanish can spin the tale any way they want if they think they're not going to be called to account. Do you think De Luca is telling the truth about King Billy abandoning us?"

"I think he thinks it's true. We'll send letters to Kingston requesting assistance from the Royal Navy and for representations to be made to the Spanish King."

Pincarton gave a resigned smile. "But Benbow is the Royal Navy in these parts and if De Luca is correct then we are literally, 'royally fucked'."

Buchanan slowly rubbed his cheek. "We've given our word to DeSaballe not to discuss any escape plan, but that doesn't mean we can't listen to anything you have to say."

Pincarton smiled. "Always the lawyer, eh Jamie? Now, listen lad, and listen well. Under no circumstances think about launching a rescue mission. While the Spanish may be fairly incompetent, they have a shit load of ships and even more firepower. They'd blow you out of the water and then go wipe out the Colony. If we're to get out of here it has to be through diplomatic channels or the Royal Navy dropping anchor outside Cartagena and training their guns on the Barlovento."

"Robert, I give you my oath that I'll do everything in my power to get you out," pledged Buchanan.

Pincarton came across and put both his hands on Buchanan's shoulders. "Aye, I know you will, Jamie. But you can't treat it as a personal crusade. There are politics involved here which are bigger than any of us. We're just bargaining chips and it will take people with far more influence than us to make a difference."

"So we'll get in their ear and not stop until you're all free," said Buchanan.

Pincarton smiled. "You do that, Jamie. Go and annoy the hell out of them with all those irritating big words of yours. You could do me one immediate obligement, though."

"Anything."

Pincarton went over to the desk and opened a small drawer. From this, he pulled out three letters and handed them to Buchanan. "Can you see that these get to the intended recipients?" Buchanan flicked through them. One was to Pincarton's wife, a second to an admiral of the English Fleet, Edward Russell, and the last to the Court of Directors.

Buchanan looked up and stared at Pincarton. "But how did you know to write these?"

"Jamie, as soon as we were forced into Cartagena we were buggered. No way would the Spanish just fix up the Dolphin and send us on our way. They're hugely pissed off that we've set up in their back yard and even unhappier that they're missing an entire brigade sent to put the frighteners on us."

He paused. "The first letter is obviously personal. The second to Russell is to ask for his support. I served under him and he's a good man with a lot of clout. The last is to your mates in Edinburgh requesting they lobby the King and generate some noise."

"I'll make sure they get there, Robert."

Pincarton then signalled Malloch who pulled out a single letter which he kissed and handed to Buchanan. It was addressed to his wife.

Suddenly there was nothing more to say and a titanic silence settled over the room. Inevitably Pincarton, gallows humour intact, spoke up. "Well, I don't know why you're standing around here drinking brandy when you should be out working on our release."

Even in this dark hour it was a measure of the man that he was trying to remove the guilt Buchanan would feel in walking away without him. The four men embraced and said their farewells. Buchanan heard the door slam behind him and the lock engage. The same familiar sound as the old Glasgow cells, but now a scenario with much higher stakes.

De La Saballe escorted them back to the quay and offered his hand. Despite their fury at the treatment of the Dolphin and its crew they found it impossible to deny the gesture from the gracious Spaniard. If anyone in Cartagena was looking out for their friends it would be him.

Pilkington was waiting for them in the Maidstone's Great Cabin. As Paterson recounted events, he sat shaking his head. When the tale was finished he scratched at the stubble on his face. "I can also tell you this. While you were ashore we traded our goods. The Spanish are convinced their expeditionary force came to a bloody end at your hands and it seems that orders from Madrid are to kick you out of Darien."

This echoed what De Luca had said but to hear that it was common knowledge on the dockside was bad news. Buchanan asked, "Did anyone mention Benbow?"

"Aye, the bold Admiral was here a week ago," replied Pilkington.

"Anything said about him intervening to release the prisoners?"

"Put it this way. When Benbow arrived, the Dolphin had already been impounded and the crew imprisoned. Apparently, it didn't stop him dining three nights in row with De Luca and your men are still not free. Draw your own conclusions."

Buchanan spat on the dock. "Bastard."

CHAPTER 33

When you are the bearer of bad news, the journey to deliver it seems interminable. Buchanan and Paterson had many long hours to chew over how best to do this. It was clear that the Scots were now on their own and if presented in its stark fullness the news would be a hammer blow to the already fragile Colony. Then again it was hard to inject any blue sky into the current scenario.

When they finally reached Darien a meeting was immediately convened on the Unicorn with the remaining Councillors. Of the original seven only five were left, with Pincarton now in custody and Cunningham somewhere in the Atlantic on his way back to Edinburgh.

Before the others arrived they had called First Officer Robb into the Great Cabin and explained the situation. He sat stony faced and when they were done he just bent his head, bewildered and angry. His first reaction was to sail to Cartagena and blow the dirty dago fuckers to hell, but Buchanan explained that although a laudable sentiment, this would inevitably result in the loss of the entire Fleet.

When the other Councillors were informed of the outcome of the mercy mission they listened in stunned silence. Eventually Pennicuik managed to utter, "My God."

Buchanan noticed that the Commodore made no suggestion of an immediate incursion to Cartagena. Either he was a sound strategist fully across the futility of such action or a man who saw the writing on the wall and was now pondering the quickest adieu.

Montgomery on the other hand was all for seeking retribution but Buchanan raised his right hand. "That's not going to happen. And don't forget that we brought part of this on ourselves. We could just as easily have taken some of the Spanish prisoner instead of putting them all to the sword."

Montgomery blanched at the memory of the wholesale slaughter but still countered. "Aye, but it was self-defence. They were coming to attack us."

"Can we be sure of that? De Luca said they were a survey party. Not that I believe it for a moment, but do you really think the number of troops in that brigade was primed to overrun the Colony?"

"Perhaps not, but they weren't wandering over the mountains to have a picnic. They were looking for a route to bring in a much larger force so had to be dealt with."

"Maybe so, but we didn't have to do what we did."

Montgomery snorted. He knew Buchanan was right and had been as disgusted as the lawyer in the immediate aftermath of the bloodbath. But now the playing field had changed and any regret had evaporated. That's how it goes, once war begins, reason and humanity head for the exit doors.

Jolly puffed out his cheeks. "So, what do we do?"

Pennicuik was quick to jump in. "Seems that it's only a matter of time before the Spanish come knocking. Maybe it's time to consider other options."

Paterson's eyes narrowed. "What other options?"

"Well, perhaps we should send a ship to Jamaica to establish the official English position and deliver our letters of representation."

"And let me guess which ship you'd recommend?" sniped Paterson.

"It would make the most sense. The Saint Andrew is the fastest and best equipped to defend itself from attack."

"Aye, and it's also best equipped to defend the Colony, which at this juncture, is perhaps more pertinent. We can easily get letters to Jamaica via Pilkington and until those have their intended effect we need all our ships here."

"What about the Second Fleet?" asked Jolly.

"What about it?" asked Paterson. "It's now the end of March. It's due to leave Leith in July and arrive in September. Nothing in the letters we've already sent will change that position."

"September's a long way off," said Montgomery. "And that's assuming they get here. How do you suggest we survive with no supplies? Jesus, there are already over four hundred Scottish graves in this bay." As soon as the words were out of his mouth Montgomery stopped dead. "Christ, William I'm so sorry. That was completely insensitive."

Paterson waved away the unintended gaffe "No, Robert, you're fine. I know you meant no harm and you're right to make the point. But to give up now would be a betrayal of all those who have died."

"In that case," said Buchanan, "our priority has to be sourcing food and medical supplies. Most of our tradable goods were on the Dolphin and I don't think that the market for purple wigs, winter woollens and left footed shoes has increased too much in recent months."

This brought some much needed laughter before Paterson smacked his hands together. "We've money sitting in bank drafts in New York. Correct?"

The others nodded before Paterson continued. "So, if we can't trade the goods we have left, then we get word to the American Colonies to release funds to purchase supplies."

"Hell of a way to bring supplies when Jamaica is within easier reach." Pennicuik pointed out.

"I'm not advocating the supplies be sourced in New York. Just that we tap into those funds to use elsewhere. "

"Aye, but hold on. Who can we trust to do that?" asked Pennicuik.

Paterson scratched the side of his face. "Well, since Councillors are the only persons authorised by the Company to draw down money drafts, it has to be one of us."

"Who do you suggest?" asked Jolly.

Buchanan could feel that old sense of dread begin to inch up his spine.

Paterson laid his thick farmer's hands on the table. "Well, it shouldn't be Jolly or Pennicuik as we can't afford to lose any more Captains." There was no demurrer to this. "And I feel that my place must be here. We need to push on with building New Edinburgh and organising the Colony. If anyone else wishes to take on that burden then I'm happy to step aside and make the trip to New York."

Jolly, relieved to be out of the frame, spoke up at once. "Nonsense, William. You have to stay."

"Well in that case it's a choice between Robert and Jamie."

As Buchanan scrambled for a cogent reason why it shouldn't be him, Montgomery beat him to the punch. It was masterpiece in self-deprecation. "Gentlemen, while I would regard it as a singular honour to be chosen, it would be doing the Company a grave disservice were I to go. I am a soldier to the marrow of my bones and know little of commerce, banking or legal matters. I certainly couldn't hold a candle to Mr. Buchanan's expertise." Game Set and Match, Mr. Montgomery.

"Well Jamie?" asked Paterson.

Buchanan looked at the four expectant faces. Yes, of course it made sense for him to be the one to go. He wondered if the defence of 'it's not my turn' would carry any weight but he knew there was no other outcome. "Alright, but I'll need to take someone with me who can order the necessary provisions when we get back to Kingston."

Paterson mulled it over for a few seconds. "Take Mackenzie. There's no-one better."

Buchanan tilted his head to one side. Yes, Mackenzie would be ideal. He was competent and, even better, a friend. "Right. But can you give me a few days to recover from Cartagena?"

"We can give you two. The Maidstone leaves for Kingston then and you need to be on it. From there you can take the first available ship to New York."

"Alright. But now that everyone has shown their true colours and we seem to stand alone, shouldn't we also be doing something else?"

"What's that then?" asked Pennicuik, looking up.

"Find out what sits in the holds of the Maurepas."

Pennicuik slapped a fist on the desk. "Excellent idea. If no bastard is willing to help us we have to help ourselves."

Jolly slowly laid his chubby hands on the table. "That may be a little easier said than done."

CHAPTER 34

It transpired that the bold Captain Jolly had already sanctioned some exploratory dives to the Maurepas off his own bat. Pennicuik exploded when this pearl emerged. "Who the fuck gave you permission to do that?"

Buchanan considered this a little rich from a man who had made an art form of doing exactly what he wanted. But he thought better of flagging the irony as the current fire had fuel enough.

Jolly reddened. "Look, I didn't think it would do any harm to see if it was viable. We're anchored nearest the wreck and some of the lads suggested we see what was possible."

"Some of the lads? Some of the fucking lads! You're the Captain of that ship, you piss weak milquetoast. You don't listen to what 'the lads' suggest and then go along with it to be Mr. Popular."

"I know but…"

"There are no 'buts.' We agreed not to touch the wreck unless we all consented."

Buchanan wondered if Pennicuik was peeved because Jolly had had the idea first or was genuinely put out at the breach of the Council mandate.

"Yes, all right. I was wrong. There just didn't seem any harm in it."

"That's your problem, Jolly, you never see the blindingly obvious," snapped Pennicuik.

Paterson then asked the question everyone was thinking. "So, what did you find?"

Jolly shook his head. "Nothing. We couldn't get near the wreck."

"Why not?" said Montgomery. "We can see it clearly from the surface."

"Aye, but we can also see the moon. Doesn't mean we can reach that."

"So what's the issue?" asked Buchanan.

Jolly shifted in his chair. "Well, two problems really. The first is that those big bastard sharks are still swimming around."

Buchanan thought that itself would be reason enough for him.

"The second," said Jolly, "is that even when they were off somewhere else we couldn't reach the wreck. It's just too deep."

"Shit." muttered Pennicuik. "How near did you get?"

"Not near enough to make us think it was going to be possible."

"Can we get ropes down to try to snag some of wreckage and pull it up?" Pennicuik queried. He was itching to get his hands on the French treasure now that the green salvage light had been given.

"Don't know. We didn't try anything that blatant," said Jolly suddenly biting his tongue.

"Aye, in case we caught you at it," fired back Pennicuik.

Paterson held up his hands to bring a bit of calm. "Alright. Just stop the bickering. Now that this is all out in the open let's get the Saint Andrew over to the wreck site and explore the options. Jolly, I suggest that you take the Endeavour to a different spot to avoid any more incidents."

Paterson's tone left no doubt that this was not a request. Jolly had crossed the line of trust and once that happened there was no coming back. It was Pennicuik who pursued it. "Aye, and perhaps you might want to consider your fitness to remain on the Council."

Jolly leapt to his feet. "Me? Given all the crap you've subjected us to over the last six months you ask me to consider my position? You're the one who should go."

Pennicuik's lips contorted in a cruel sneer. "You know, Jolly, your ability to misjudge a situation is quite astounding. Sometimes you should just keep your mouth shut and let people think you're an idiot rather than open it and remove all doubt."

"Fuck you, Pennicuik. What would you know about good judgement? We've all had enough of you."

"Is that right? And who exactly is this 'we' then?" he snapped.

"You ken fine, Pennicuik. Everyone detests you."

Pennicuik shot Jolly a look of utter disdain. "Is that a fact, now. Well, to be honest with you, Jolly, I'm not that fussed what any other tosser thinks about me. Command isn't a popularity contest. You might think I'm a cunt but at least I get things done. Not like you, you pathetic little freeloader."

"You get things done? Fuck me. It's as well you've got a great idea of your own abilities as nobody else has. You only ever leave your precious ship when it's time to stick a flag in the ground. Other than that you sit on your backside sniping at the rest of us trying to build something for Scotland."

Buchanan thought that Jolly's inclusion of himself as one of the architects of the project was a bit rich and Pennicuik seized on it. "'Build something for Scotland'. Oh aye, and how's that going for you? When was the last time you were on site checking how the building works were going? Do you even know where they are? Fuck's sake, you do nothing other than try to look busy. Oh and here's the news. It isn't working."

The truth of this stung Jolly. He could have stepped away, taken his medicine and lived to fight another day. But the fracture was too wide. "Fine. Let's put it to a Council vote. If you want me off then I'll go but if not, then you walk, Pennicuik."

Pennicuik gave a derisive laugh. "Do you ever engage your brain before talking you mewling little quim? This isn't about me leaving the Council. I'm not the cunt who went behind our backs and tried to steal the Frog gold. This is about you and just you. If you're so keen to have a vote about your suitability why don't you just fuck off out the room while we discuss it."

It suddenly dawned on Jolly that his ultimatum was built on a false logic which Pennicuik had called out and was now looking to exploit. "Fuck you, Pennicuik. After that I'm calling for a formal vote of confidence in you."

"No problem. But you do realise that you'll still have to be on the Council to do that. And if I have my way that'll not be the case in five minutes. You stupid little prick."

Jolly turned and with a final, "Fuck you," slammed the Great Cabin door behind him.

Pennicuik helped himself to another whisky and sat back down. "Well, what's it to be gentlemen?"

Montgomery supported Jolly, mainly because he despised Pennicuik. "I vote he stays. He's made a mistake but he's loyal to us. And let's be honest, we can't afford to lose another Councillor."

Pennicuik snorted. "Aye well that just proves that a fool can always find a greater fool to support him. How about you, Buchanan?"

"I'm abstaining. Not because I'm sitting on the fence but I'm fucked if I'll watch this Council disintegrate because you two infants can't sort out your differences. You said command isn't a popularity contest but you've just turned this vote into one. We have to make enough tough decisions without being part of a dick measuring contest between you and Jolly. So mine is a non-vote and you two can grow up and work it out."

"Agreed, Jamie," laughed Paterson, "I'm abstaining too." He got up and opened the door. Jolly, moping at the end of the corridor, was asked to come back in.

"Well?" he said with false bravado.

"One vote for, one against, with two abstentions," said Paterson.

Pennicuik couldn't resist. "Only one vote for. Not exactly a ringing endorsement, Jolly."

"Be quiet, Pennicuik." snapped Paterson, before explaining what had happened.

Jolly weighed it all up. "No. Sorry. If he stays on the Council, I'm resigning."

Buchanan tried to intercede. "Don't be stupid, Jolly. You don't have to do this."

"Yes, I do. I've had enough of him and his high handedness. If you want me to stay then he has to go."

Paterson slowly shook his head. "Unlike you, Jolly, he's done nothing to warrant such action. Stay or go as you wish."

Pennicuik grinned smugly at the besieged Jolly. He had rolled the dice and come up craps. Now it was a choice between tholing Pennicuik and his barbs or walking away. "In that case, you have my resignation with immediate effect."

He placed the glass back on the table, went round to the credenza and picked up Pennicuik's near full bottle of whisky. He looked at the Commodore and snarled. "Consider it a severance payment."

"No problem, Jolly, I've got plenty more," he replied, trumping him once again. His mocking laugh echoed in Jolly's ears as he walked out of the Great Cabin for the last time as a Councillor.

CHAPTER 35

The Maurepas proved to be a real conundrum. When it had been agreed that the treasure was fair game, the pinnaces from the Saint Andrew had swarmed around the wreck like mosquitos on a pond. There was rumoured to be enough gold, silver and jewels in the sunken hold to cover the cost of the entire venture and much more. But that, of course, was just rumour and like most rumours it grew with each telling.

The ship had been split in two but the halves remained largely intact and were clearly visible on the sandy bottom of the bay some twenty fathoms down. However, the crystal blue water contorted the actual depth so the apparent distance to the prize was far less than the reality.

Anything left in the hull was either trapped or too heavy to float to the surface. The treasure wasn't going to come to the Scots. They would have to go and get it.

The hammerheads still occasionally circled in their lazy menacing manner and when any free diving effort was in progress sailors on the other ships threw scraps of turtle meat far from the site to distract the predators.

However it was the depth which proved insurmountable. The best swimmers among the settlers- not that there were too many- would emerge gasping for air, their lungs bursting after not even getting half way. Lines with cannonballs attached were dropped to allow the divers to pull themselves downwards but this again proved ineffective. Then weighted wooden cages were constructed and lowered with a sailor inside. This minimised the need for any effort on the diver's part and reduced the risk of any shark damage. But once more, the pressure and lack of oxygen defeated them.

Finally, an engineer, Alastair Lambie, was brought in to try to find a solution. He suggested a diving chamber similar to one which had been successfully used by the English treasure hunter, William Phipps, some twenty years before to access the wreck of the Spanish galleon the *Nuestra Señora de la Concepción*. The device was simply an inverted cylinder which was open at the bottom and weighed down in order to maintain its equilibrium. The idea was to put a man under the container and as it was lowered, the water would rise but the pressure would result in the water filling only the bottom half with the top half remaining full of air.

Lambie then immediately hedged his bets advising that he had severe reservations a successful attempt could be mounted with the materials available to him and the depth of the water. The Phipps device had been specially constructed at a foundry in London and only had to descend fifteen fathoms.

Nonetheless, Pennicuik had pressed Lambie into service assuring him that if things to go awry, no culpability would fall on him. So Lambie engaged the sole surviving cooper to construct a large wooden barrel sealed with pitch. It would then be girded by iron hoops with lead weights as its bottom circumference.

This had been hauled aboard the Saint Andrew and the Council watched on as a sailor had jumped into the ocean and waited for the barrel to be inserted over his head. The man in question was a ratty little individual called Simpson who had been caught stealing whisky. He had been given the choice of twelve lashes or the role of guinea pig. Having tasted the cat before he had no hesitation in taking his chances in the water. A few trial runs at minimal depth had shown that it worked in theory, so it was now time for the real thing. By then Simpson had started to wonder if the lash wasn't the better option, but his stock had risen dramatically as the Fleet's first aquanaut so he had held his tongue.

The barrel was slid over his body and he gave two knocks to indicate that the descent could begin. The heavy rope attached to the ring on top of the barrel was let out and Simpson slowly disappeared into the clear water, a new attraction for the tropical fish which darted around it in a kaleidoscope of colour.

As the barrel plumbed deeper, the pressure on the rudimentary diving bell began to build. Inside, a petrified Simpson heard the wood begin to groan as it contracted under the strain. Then at ten fathoms there was a sudden explosion as the wood shattered. Bound by the iron girders, the splintered oak had nowhere to go except inwards and straight through Simpson. Only he heard his screams as the deadly shards of the underwater Iron Maiden skewered him. The remnants of the barrel were quickly pulled back to the surface and onto the deck. It was a macabre sight. Shafts of wood protruded from every part of Simpson's body and most grotesquely though both cheeks.

Lambie stormed across to Pennicuik. "It's his blood on your hands, Pennicuik. I telt you about the risks and you wouldnae listen."

Pennicuik responded as one would expect. "Who the hell do you think you're talking to Lambie. I suggest you show some respect or I'll have you thrown in irons."

Not of course, a care for the poor soul who had been so horribly dispatched. Lambie backed down but seethed at the indifference with which Pennicuik had brushed off the death. However, it effectively put an end to attempts on the Maurepas and the Scots had to reluctantly concede that the sea, the sharks and the lack of materials had bested them.

CHAPTER 36

The journey to New York took ten days. The Maidstone ferried Mackenzie and Buchanan as far as Kingston where they secured passage on a little Danish trader. As they headed north the temperature gradually dropped and by the time they reached New York harbour it was damned cold. Nevertheless the fresh clear air was welcome relief after months of suffocating heat and humidity.

Buchanan felt a tingle of excitement as the great city of the Americas had come into view. New York in 1699 was a significant metropolis. From its early days as New Amsterdam under the Dutch, it had exploded when the English took control in 1673 and was now a bustling melting pot of diverse religions, cultures and nationalities.

Stepping onto the quay, they were overwhelmed by the noise and activity. Busy, sweating men worked quickly and the air was filled with the shouts, whistles and laughter of the gainfully employed. The two Scots smiled at each other. They'd missed this. Buchanan had to shout over the din. "Come on, Roderick, let's get going. We've only got two days before our Danish friends head back to Port Royal."

The pair walked down the main thoroughfare of Broad Street and found lodgings in one of the side streets. Once they'd washed and changed they went straight to the Company agent's offices. These were on Wall Street, named for the barrier built across Manhattan Island as protection from the native Indians.

The office itself was located next door to the newly established Anglican Trinity Church, a modest rectangular structure which looked out over the Hudson River. On the front door was a little plaque advising of its construction in 1698 and noting that Captain William Kidd had lent equipment from his ship to enable the stones to be lifted into place. Just three years later the privateer from Dundee was to be found guilty in London on trumped up charges of piracy, hanged and his body gruesomely gibbeted for another two years over the River Thames.

Buchanan and Mackenzie entered the building and climbed up a flight of stairs. On the office door the sign read, 'David Robertson, Commercial Agent' and beneath it were a list of the entities he represented. Buchanan scanned it and eventually found 'The Company of Scotland.'

They knocked and were invited to enter by a muffled voice. The office comprised a single room, at the end of which was located a desk piled high with papers. Behind this sat a man silhouetted by a picture window which gave a view over the river.

He stood and moved around the mountain of documents. Away from the glare of the backlight, he was like a piece of human scaffolding, all angles and protrusions on a bony frame. Long carefully combed grey hair fell smoothly onto the black velvet collar of his frock coat and in the eerie gleam his cadaverous skull and deathly pallor would have led many an undertaker to embalm him on sight.

Buchanan expected a doomsday rasp, but when the man spoke his voice was unexpectedly high and melodic, almost like a bird. He extended a long spindly hand and in a soft Scottish accent announced himself to be David Robertson. Buchanan introduced himself and Mackenzie and advised they were here on business for The Company of Scotland.

"Well, in that case gentlemen," the sing song voice intoned, "please join me in a wee sensation."

"That'd be most welcome after the brandy we've been drinking for the last few days. It may come as no surprise that the Danes haven't cracked the international liquor market," replied Buchanan.

Robertson invited them to sit. "So, tell me all news from the Colony."

"You're familiar with the Colony?"

"Of course, dear boy. I'm agent for many enterprises but the Scots Company is close to my heart."

Buchanan just hoped for his sake that it wasn't close to his wallet. He measured his response. "Well, all continues to progress. New Edinburgh is under construction and the fortress is nearing completion."

"Splendid, splendid. And what of the trading market? Has the great entrepôt been the success we all expect?"

"It's still early days, but certainly our fine whisky and linen are much in demand."

"Ah yes, of course. And what of the bridge to the great Pacific? When do you think that might eventuate?"

"That, I think, is for the future. We've made some preliminary forays into the interior and are exploring options." Buchanan glanced at Mackenzie, beginning to feel a little uncomfortable with the obfuscation.

"You'd make a good salesman, Mr. Buchanan." said Robertson.

Buchanan furrowed his brow. "I'm not quite with you."

"Let's just say that not much that happens in the Caribbean which doesn't find its way back to New York. The word on the street is that the Colony is in trouble."

Buchanan weighed up his options. Total candour or more deflection. He stuck with the latter given that his trust levels had taken a beating recently and he was not about to impart the raw truth to a total stranger. "Naturally one would expect some setbacks in a pioneering venture but we remain positive."

"And yet, here you are."

"And yet, here we are."

Robertson paused to see if Buchanan might volunteer any more information but the lawyer played a dead bat. Robertson continued, "So can one assume your trip to New York is not a social visit?"

"Well, one would hope it won't be exclusively business."

"Indeed. What's the point of a great city having temptations if young chaps like you don't get the chance to yield to them?"

Buchanan smiled. By God, it would be a welcome relief to go out and have some fun but this was not the time to be thinking of that. "Perhaps later. First we have to engage your professional services."

"Well, that's what I am here for." Robertson said, revealing a staggering array of yellowing teeth in what Buchanan took for his best pass at a smile. He hoped he didn't try it in front of young children.

Buchanan handed over the discussion to Mackenzie, who systematically set out the amount which the Company required to draw down and the purposes to which it would be put. Robertson listened intently, jotting down notes in a large register.

When Mackenzie had finished, Robertson looked up. "Two Thousand Pounds is a considerable sum and will enormously deplete the Company coffers."

"We are aware of that, Mr. Robertson, but as I have explained the monies will be put to good use," answered Mackenzie in a calm level voice designed to convey that this was nothing worthy of setting the gossip mill alight.

"Yes, so you say." He re-examined all of the papers and authorities which the Scots had provided. "Well, given that these all appear in order, let me arrange for you to be placed in funds. I assume that you will not wish to carry that amount of money in coin."

Buchanan looked at Mackenzie hoping that the little financial wizard would have the answer. Mackenzie didn't let him down. " Of course not. I suggest we take about one hundred in gold coin and the remainder in tobacco warehouse receipts."

"Excellent," said Robertson.

Buchanan was completely in the dark but knew enough to say nothing.

Robertson made a further note and then said. "I can have these for you tomorrow. Now tell me do you have any plans for this evening?"

Buchanan wanted nothing more than to find an hospitable inn and even more hospitable hostess. But the question courted only one response. "Nothing in particular."

This prompted Robertson to rub his thin hands together. "First class. Well, you must join us for dinner. Here is the address. We shall see you at seven."

Before they left, Buchanan, now comfortable that Robertson was an ally, took the raft of letters from Darien- including Pincarton's- and asked if the agent could arrange their safe transport. Robertson flicked through them and confirmed that he would ensure their despatch the following day. He then shook each of the envoys hands and ushered them out before closing the office door.

"Interesting chap," said Mackenzie.

"You could say that. Looks in dire need of a good feed. Hope he's not reflective of this evening's menu," replied Buchanan. "By the way, what the hell is a tobacco warehouse receipt?"

"Aye, thought that might have stumped you. Basically it's a promissory note for tobacco stored in a warehouse. The bearer of the receipt has a claim on that exact amount of tobacco so he can use it like currency but not draw attention to himself by humping about big bags of gold."

"And that works in the real world?" asked Buchanan.

"Certainly hope so. Otherwise you and me will be smoking ourselves stupid for years."

"Your cleverer than you look you know."

"Well it's better than looking cleverer than you are," Mackenzie said with a grin.

CHAPTER 37

They arrived just before seven at Robertson's house, a well-appointed double storey building situated off Broad Street. It had turned even colder and as the door opened, they felt the rush of warm air with its inviting promise to remove the chill from their bones.

The lanky merchant welcomed his guests and ushered them into a large reception room. A fire blazed in the facing wall and around it were arranged ornate chairs upholstered in red velvet. An intricately decorated table sat between these and next to the right hand wall was a large teak cabinet edged in gold leaf. A soft rug into which Buchanan's shoes nearly disappeared covered the mahogany floor. Apparently, New York was a profitable place to do business.

A manservant, the colour of ebony, emerged with a tray of whisky. Robertson advised that his wife and daughter would be down soon, at which point a commotion from the hallway signalled their arrival. The first to enter was a small fat woman who seemed to waddle rather than walk. She was garishly made up under a bizarre wig which appeared more bird's nest than hairpiece and was wearing what looked like a small cream tent.

Robertson introduced her as his wife. She proffered her hand in a manner which invited some sort of Papal kiss. Both Scots dutifully obliged and watched as she levered herself into a chair which looked very tight about her hips.

Preoccupied with this entertainment Buchanan had failed to notice the entrance of Robertson's daughter.

"And this is Anne," Robertson announced. In that split second before turning round, Buchanan's mind had prepared itself for a younger version of Mrs. Robertson. The reality was quite different. His eyes involuntarily flicked from father to mother and back to daughter. What spectacular trick of nature had fashioned something so beautiful from such an unlikely gene pool?

She was dark and serene and, offering her hand, held his gaze with chocolate brown eyes. She wore a long red dress and raven hair fell over her shoulders in ringlets. He fumbled out his name and her perfect teeth flashed a smile as she extracted her fingers from his lingering grip.

"I'm pleased to meet you, Mr. Buchanan," she said, in a voice which made Buchanan suddenly understand what "sultry" sounded like.

"The pleasure is all mine, Miss Robertson," he replied trying not to squeak like a pubescent schoolboy.

And still her eyes did not waver.

"Come, let us sit," instructed Robertson. "Dinner will be served soon but there is time for an aperitif. Sherry, my darling?" he asked his wedged-in wife.

"That would be *cepital*," she enunciated in a comical parody of a high society accent.

A few minutes later they made their way into a separate room where a magnificent table was set with silver cutlery and fine china. Intricately carved candelabras toyed with anything within their compass and cast gossamer shadows.

Robertson sat at the head, with the ladies on either side of him. Mackenzie sat beside the wife with Buchanan next to Anne. The same manservant and a black maid then ferried in a series of dishes each covered with a silver armadillo. Mrs Robertson fixed these with the look of a tiger who had been on a diet and had just been given the all clear to resume normal service.

The conversation was restrained at first but as Mrs Robertson gravitated from sherry to white wine, then to red her facade of gentility slowly but amusingly began to slip. The *nouveau riche* can only pretend for so long before they are unmasked. By dessert she was asking if "Youse lads huv saw any trouble wi the Spanish."

Mackenzie, the consummate diplomat, paid polite attendance as Mrs Robertson homed in on him. Buchanan noticed that Anne was unperturbed by the unravelling of her mother's social persona.

"I see mother has taken a fancy to your colleague," she said in a soft voice.

"I can't tell if he's enjoying it or not," whispered Buchanan.

"She can become terrifyingly predatory as they evening wears on. Don't worry, she'll be comatose soon and father will wheel her off to bed."

"Doesn't he mind?"

"Not really. He knows she'll never cross the finish line with any of her little passion plays. In any case, his mistress is money and as long as that keeps coming in she's happy."

"Looks like he's been well treated by his paramour."

She smiled that smile again. "He's worked hard, so can now wallow in this gilded cage."

"Cage? That's an odd description."

"Perhaps more a commentary on how I feel."

Buchanan paused. "Wish to elaborate on that?"

"Not the time or place, Mr. Buchanan," she demurred. "So, you're leaving the day after tomorrow then?"

"Indeed. We plan to venture into the badlands of Port Royal."

She chuckled. "Not the cultural centre of the Caribbean, I assume?"

"Satan's parlour, supposedly. I could write to let you know if it's true."

"You can write? What advances Scottish education has made."

He smiled. "You haven't answered my question."

"No, I haven't have I?" She let the sentence hang in the air.

"It's just a letter."

"There is no such thing as 'just a letter'."

"Isn't that preferable to no letter at all?"

"Depends if you want to save your hand from the flame. People come and go through New York all the time, Mr. Buchanan, but seldom ever stay. I've learned never to let someone be my priority, while also allowing myself to be their option."

Buchanan laughed. "Just a letter," he repeated.

She considered it for a few more moments and then whispered. "Just a letter, then," as she brushed her hand gently over the top of his.

CHAPTER 38

The next day dawned bitter cold with a wind so snell that even a Fife farmer would have had second thoughts about venturing out. But out the Scots had to go.

New York was a city gearing itself up not just for the next year or next decade but for the next century. It looked and felt like a cocky young arriviste, all swagger and chutzpah. This was what tomorrow looked like, thought Buchanan, not an isolated insect-ridden sauna in Central America.

When Buchanan spoke his breath appeared like puffs of steam in the freezing air. "Roddy, imagine having the same rights as English merchants to trade tobacco and cotton from here? Glasgow would become one of the biggest cities in Europe."

Mackenzie snorted a laugh. "Aye, well don't get too carried away. There's no chance the English will ever let us tap into their markets."

"Which is why we're in fucking Panama," grimaced Buchanan.

They met Robertson at ten o'clock outside his offices.

"Good morning gentlemen. I trust you slept well," he said with his gentle lilt.

"Like a log. A full belly and fine whisky helps considerably," said Mackenzie.

"Aye, it does that young man. And you, Mr. Buchanan?"

"Absolutely," he lied. For Buchanan had spent much of the night lying awake thinking about Anne Robertson and cursing his knack for poor timing.

"Excellent," said Robertson. "Now, we've got a busy day ahead so let's not shilly shally."

Buchanan thought that if this brief exchange was 'shilly shallying' then God knows what Robertson was like when he was in a hurry. The three men entered the stuffy office and Robertson asked them to close the door. He shifted several piles of paper which lay in front of a large armoire, then got on his hands and knees and fiddled around its side for a few moments. This was a formidable piece of furniture so when Robertson effortlessly moved it the two onlookers thought he'd suddenly been imbued with superhuman powers. It was only on closer examination that they saw that it was not the armoire which had moved but the floor beneath it.

Robertson gave out a strange chortle which sounded like a pig swallowing a turnip. "Clever little mechanism, eh?" he said, pointing to a small lever which now jutted up from the floor.

Beneath the spot where the armoire had stood was a hole which housed a black teak chest. Robertson placed his spindly fingers into the space and pressed on something which caused the chest to rise up like a wooden Lazarus. When opened it revealed a pile of gold and silver coins. Robertson then proceeded to count out an amount of money, closed up the chest, pushed the armoire back and artfully rearranged the piles of paper.

He then divided the extracted gold into several smaller piles while referring to a sheet of paper on his desk. "The tobacco receipts are with different merchants. So, best to come back and forward rather than carry it all in one go. Too many cutpurses and pocket delvers in New York, I'm afraid."

He then donned a capacious black coat with hidden pockets perfect for hiding valuables. "Let's go, gentlemen."

The next several hours were spent shuttling to and from various tobacco merchants located in the intestines of the old docks. As each tobacco receipt was received it was handed over to Mackenzie who jotted down a running total of their value. Finally as the shadows of the late Winter sun began to lengthen they completed their final mission and returned to the office.

Robertson then pulled a purse of coins from his desk drawer and dropped it with a theatrical flourish onto the mound of papers sitting in front of him. "The last piece of the jigsaw. Now you have the means to purchase your precious supplies."

"We can't thank you enough," said Buchanan, in a slightly fawning tone. He didn't want to part on anything but the best of terms with Anne Robertson's father.

"Think nothing of it. Of course you understand that I don't work for free." A chuckle followed.

"We'll report back to Edinburgh in the most favourable of terms," said Mackenzie.

"Aye, I'd be in your oblige for that. A good reputation needs constant upkeep. A bad one just a single aberration."

Then Robertson asked. "So, what are you two young lads up to this evening?"

Buchanan's heart skipped a beat. Was another dinner invitation on the horizon? "No great plans at this point," he quickly replied.

"Aye, well in that case let me recommend a couple of options."

Buchanan's hopes sank. Robertson scribbled down the names of two chop houses which he said were passable but added a warning. "If I were you I'd not stray too far from your lodgings. Word of your transacting will have spread."

Mackenzie looked worriedly at Buchanan. The accountant, skilled though he was with numbers, was not cut out for any rough stuff. "Don't worry yourself on our account," said Buchanan. "A quick bite and then an early night. That fine with you Roddy?"

Mackenzie nodded, happy to minimise any potential physical jeopardy. Robertson eased his angular frame up out of his seat and stretched out his long fingers for the farewell handshakes.

"Good luck gentlemen," he said. "And of course if you are ever back in New York, my door is always open."

"You're too kind," said Buchanan, shaking the bony hand, all the while wondering how and when he might be able to take up the invitation.

At first light they boarded the Danish sloop and as they left on the cold morning tide, Buchanan took a lingering backward look over the black sheet of ocean towards New York.

CHAPTER 39

On the 7th June, 1692, a devastating earthquake and subsequent tidal wave had destroyed much of Port Royal. Until then it had been the principal town of Jamaica with seven thousand inhabitants and rivalling even Boston in wealth. But the natural disasters had killed two thousand with another three later perishing from disease.

The city itself was now a crumbling ruin, the carcasses of its once elegant buildings staring out like stone warts. Kingston, further down the coast was growing quickly and Port Royal was living on borrowed time.

It was also the Sodom of the New World with its pirate culture, grog shops, gaming houses and bordellos. The English governor was in the pockets of the buccaneers and enjoyed a rich additional income from the bribes paid to turn a blind eye to illicit activities in his jurisdiction. But for all that it remained the biggest English trading hub in the Caribbean and it was from here that Darien could be supplied with enough provisions until help arrived from Scotland.

Buchanan and Mackenzie bid their farewells to the genial Danes and headed towards the township, their first port of call being the Governor.

They had half-expected something similar to the civilised scenarios in Madeira and St. Thomas but the reality proved quite different. When they eventually located the consulate it turned out to be a partially destroyed brick building on two levels. It afforded no view of the harbour and part of the bottom level seemed to function as a bordello.

Buchanan double checked the plaque on the wall. "This will be interesting."

The slight accountant was very much out of his comfort zone. "Aye, but not the kind of interesting I'm that fond of, Jamie."

"Don't worry, Roddy. Nobody knows us here so we can transact our business toot sweet and get out of town before we attract the wrong kind of attention."

Mackenzie's eye twitched. "I sincerely hope so."

They walked out of the bright sunshine, grateful for some relief from the heat. A small neat man with a near-bald head covered in freckles sat scribbling at a desk on one side of the room. The Scots announced themselves and asked if the Governor was available.

"Do you have an appointment?" he enquired politely.

"No, I'm afraid not," responded Buchanan. "We've just arrived in town."

"I see. May one enquire as to the purpose of your visit?"

"Indeed, Sir. We are representatives of the Company of Scotland and wish to present our credentials."

The little man scrutinised them over the frames of his eyeglasses. "Gentlemen, you do realise this is Port Royal and not the Palace of Whitehall?"

"That is becoming swiftly apparent."

"I'm afraid the Governor is currently in England on business but the deputy Governor is in town. He is currently engaged but if you wish to take a seat he should be available soon." He directed them to a large leather sofa and continued with his scribbling.

Five minutes later there was a commotion from the other side of the room which served as the brothel section of Government House. A corpulent man with a purple complexion was emerging from one of the rooms, his britches half done up and his shirt loose and unbuttoned. From this protruded an enormous belly which looked like a dropped trifle. He had a wig in one hand and a shoe in the other. Its partner quickly followed in an arc designed to damage its target.

The thrower then emerged, an enraged tart who hadn't taken the time to tether her ample bosoms which bounced around like newly set jellies. "You want to do that then go off and find a sheep you perverted creep. I know you've been round the others but you're not getting it off me."

The fat man gathered up his belongings as she disappeared back inside. Buchanan and Mackenzie sat agog only to be interrupted by a polite cough coming from the clerk. "The deputy Governor is free to see you now, Gentlemen," indicating the specimen who was busy trying to put his clothes back on in approximately the right order.

Buchanan and Mackenzie stood up as the administrator moved in their direction. "And who may you be?" he asked brusquely in a thick Yorkshire accent, obviously annoyed that the little scene had been witnessed by someone outside of his usual circle.

"Jamie Buchanan and Roderick Mackenzie of the Company of Scotland, your vice Excellency," announced Buchanan.

The deputy Governor's astonished expression left them in little doubt that his formal title had been sparingly used.

"Is that so?" he said sticking out a chubby paw. "Arnold Boycott is how I go by." They shook hands, although Mackenzie was quick to put his back in his pocket and wipe it. "I suppose you'd best come upstairs then."

He led them up a rickety staircase and along a corridor to a dingy room. This should have been drenched with sun but the grimy plantation shutters allowed few slivers of light to filter in.

"Sit yourselves down, Gentlemen," he said ,pointing to some faded leather seats haphazardly positioned opposite a desk strewn with papers. Buchanan and Mackenzie sat and watched as the bloated deputy finished stuffing his shirt into his breeches before heading for the drinks cabinet.

"I assume you'll not be averse to some refreshment?" he asked.

"You'd assume correctly," said Buchanan.

"Got this as part of the King's share of the booty from a captured Spanish galleon a few weeks ago." He poured into three glasses and took a long draught of the wine then smacked his lips with his tongue.

The Scots followed suit, without the lip-smacking. "A fine drop," said Buchanan, savouring the excellent red.

"Anyway's up. I expect I knows why you're here."

The Scots looked at one another. "You do?" asked Buchanan.

"We assume word would reach your Colony sooner or later, so you'll be the representatives sent to complain, no doubt. Well, I'm sorry there's not much I can do. The Governor was the one what issued the order and he's back in England."

The Scots again glanced at each other, totally baffled. "What are you talking about? We're here to purchase supplies and only stopped as a courtesy." explained Buchanan.

Boycott took another gulp of wine before placing his glass down. He then rummaged about his desk and after a few moments found a document which he handed over without comment.

Buchanan took the parchment and began reading. "IN HIS MAJESTY'S NAME, His Majesty's subjects shall not correspond with the Scots of Darien, nor give them any assistance, provisions, or any other necessaries, either themselves, or by any of their vessels. Should they disobey they will answer to His Majesty at their utmost peril. Signed Sir William Beeston, Governor of Jamaica."

Buchanan felt his back go clammy with sweat. He handed the document to Mackenzie and heard the accountant mutter "Jesus Christ," as the contents registered.

Buchanan went on the offensive. "Is this some kind of a joke, Boycott?"

Boycott held his hands up in an appeasing gesture. "No point having a go at me. It was the Governor who signed the Proclamation."

"And when is the Governor expected back to answer for this?" snapped Buchanan.

Boycott laughed out loud. "I'm sorry, Mr. Buchanan but I don't think that the Governor would entertain the notion that he has 'to answer' for anything. He was acting on direct orders from the Crown."

Mackenzie spluttered, "But that can't be so. Here's the Act of Parliament promising us protection and assistance." He thrust the document toward Boycott but the deputy simply waved it away.

"That's all well and good but it seems the King has had a change of heart. From what I've heard, he wasn't aware you Scots would be looking to settle a colony in Darien."

"Aye, well he must have been the only one in England that bloody well didn't," snapped Mackenzie. Buchanan laid a hand on his wrist to calm him down.

"Anyways," said Boycott, "seems he recognises Darien as Spanish and doesn't want to put any dago noses put out of joint on account of your Company."

Mackenzie exploded and no tug of the jacket was going to hold him back. "Recognise Darien as Spanish! How the hell can he say that? By Christ, I should have known you English would fuck us one way or another."

Boycott simply shrugged his shoulders. "Decisions way above my head, gentlemen. I'm merely passing on the news."

Buchanan weighed up the immediate situation. With this Proclamation in place how were they going to be able to source any supplies? How venal was this Deputy he wondered?

"Well, let's be realistic now Mr. Boycott. We're men of the world and what goes on over here will never find its way back to London. You seem like a chap who is not averse to a commercial arrangement…" Buchanan let the words hang in the air waiting for some encouragement from Boycott.

"Go on," came the reply.

"Let's just say we have the means to make it worth your while to turn a blind eye to a supply ship leaving for Darien."

Boycott sat for a few moments weighing up Buchanan's proposition. He was obviously giving it genuine consideration. Finally, he spoke. "A tempting offer Mr. Buchanan and one which ordinarily I'd be happy to accommodate. But in this case it's simply not a risk worth taking. There are no secrets in Port Royal. Word would get out and eventually the finger would be pointed at me. And it wouldn't just be slap on the wrist. This is a Proclamation in the King's name. I go against this and I'd end up swaying on the breeze dancing to the hangman's hornpipe."

Buchanan sensed this was a man who was no stranger to corruption. For him to push back so absolutely was not a good sign.

Boycott leaned forward. "Between ourselves, I can tell you that none of the merchants or traders here will give you a second look. All of them have been warned off."

"Christ Almighty," spat Mackenzie.

"Now, if you're looking for some female companionship, a card game or any other vices when you're in town then I'm more than happy to assist," offered Boycott in the apparently genuine belief that this would somehow compensate for the hammer blow which he had just delivered.

Buchanan glared at him. This was not his fault and it would be a dangerous mistake to take their anger out on the hapless Deputy. The Scots were in hostile territory and to get on the wrong side of someone who wielded influence like this obese tosser wouldn't be a good idea. Buchanan took a deep breath. "Thank you, Mr. Boycott. Perhaps another time. We appreciate your hospitality."

He rose to his feet, shook Boycott's hand and hurried Mackenzie out of the office.

They descended the stairs and waved as they went past the little clerk. He peered at them benignly, returned the gesture, and with a small sigh went back to his labours. Then the two Scots were back out into the heat and blazing sun.

"So that's it?" asked Mackenzie. "We don't lodge a formal complaint."

"Roddy, for Christ sakes, be quiet until we get somewhere less public."

Mackenzie looked puzzled. Buchanan whispered, "How long do you think it's going to take fat boy in there to spread word that two Scots are in town looking to buy supplies?"

"Well, we are."

"Aye, I know we are, but what do such men usually have with them?"

The penny dropped. "Shit."

"Yes, Roddy. Shit, indeed. We'll have targets on our backs in no time and there'll be few here willing to concern themselves with the finer details of the Scots Act."

"Jesus. What do we do?" said Mackenzie his voice shaking.

"Get the hell out as soon as we can."

The two men moved quickly through the streets of the decaying city, every passerby's glance now seemingly laced with a sinister message. He hustled Mackenzie back towards the harbour. It was now late afternoon. As there would be no ships out of Port Royal until the next morning their priority would be to find accommodation and lie low.

After ten minutes searching Buchanan saw a sign hanging precariously off a two storey wooden building which sat like a rotting tooth in a street close to the dockside. He quickly ducked inside pulling Mackenzie with him. A wizened old man looked up from behind a battered old desk.

Affecting what he hoped was a passable English accent, Buchanan asked. "Do you have two rooms for the night?"

"Two night minimum," he replied, in a rasping wheeze, which the clay pipe he was puffing was doing little to alleviate.

"That'll be fine," said Buchanan.

"Payment up front. One shilling a room."

Buchanan dug into his jacket pocket and took out a little scuffed purse which was unlikely to attract the attention of avaricious eyes. He handed over the small silver coins and the ancient relic slid him two keys.

"Top of the stairs, turn right and you'll find them at the end."

"Many thanks," said Buchanan as he picked up the keys.

"Your welcome, Scotsman," cackled the old man.

Buchanan looked at him and gave a little smile. He rummaged in his purse and set an extra sixpence down on the desk. "We'll pretend you never said that shall we?"

"Fine by me, sonny," he croaked, grabbing the tanner and sticking it in his pocket.

When he got to his room Buchanan looked around for somewhere suitable to hide their treasure. Nothing immediately presented as a candidate. He went next door to find Mackenzie beginning to unpack his clothes. "What the hell are you doing Roddy?"

"What does it look like?"

"For Christ's sake man. You're not here on your holidays. Chances are we're going to be legging it out of here, so I suggest you keep everything pretty much as is."

A look of apprehension spread over the quiet accountant's face.

"Look, don't worry. I'm just jumping at shadows. Too much time in the Glasgow courts I expect." He gave Mackenzie his most encouraging smile which seemed to calm him down a little.

Buchanan cast his eye over the room. It was at the end of the building facing away from the street. The windows gave on to what at one time would have been an elegant balcony. Now post-earthquake, it was a patchwork of slats which were attached haphazardly to the remaining superstructure. Buchanan ducked his head out and looked up and down. He saw that the far end was more robust but could only be accessed by negotiating some less secure wooden strips.

"Give me your hand, Roddy, and hold my wrist tight," he said.

Mackenzie did as instructed and Buchanan edged out and along the balcony. One of the slats threatened to give way under him but he clutched Mackenzie's hand and managed to hop onto the next one before it broke. A step later and he found himself at the more stable end. Peering around and down to see that no other windows overlooked the space, he began to prod the wooden cladding which made up the outer wall. One of the timbers was loose and he was able to move it to reveal the eaves of the building. There was just enough light left to spot a little recess where the roof joists met.

He turned to Mackenzie. "Alright, Roddy, pass me the gold and tobacco receipts."

Mackenzie carefully lobbed the calico bag. Buchanan stashed the money and papers and banged the timber plank back in place. He then grabbed Mackenzie's outstretched hand and swung back into the room. Closing the windows, he sat down on the bed to catch his breath.

"What now?" asked Mackenzie in the tentative reedy voice of a man who knows the question must be asked but isn't really sure if he wants to hear the answer.

"We go find ourselves a ship out of here on the first tide tomorrow."

CHAPTER 40

The sun was setting as they made their way down to Port Royal harbour. Anywhere else it might have been idyllic, but in this scarred cesspit any positive adjective would struggle to find a home.

Mackenzie stuck like glue to Buchanan as he dodged among the heaving mass of bodies near the loading docks. He watched as the lawyer approached several targets, engaging in easy chat to extract the necessary information. Finally, Mackenzie saw one old worthy point towards the end of the port. Buchanan thanked him and with a tilt of his head indicated for Mackenzie to follow. A few moments later they arrived at their destination. The sign swinging above the door said, "The Captain Morgan."

The inn was blurred with the tobacco smoke which billowed up to the yellowing ceiling and the air hung heavy with the smell of sweat. A sea of faces fixed on the new patrons. This was a world where men were loyal only to themselves and whose primary instincts were survival and profit. If you didn't endanger or enhance either then you would be disregarded. Seeing nothing threatening or rewarding, the locals returned to their drinks.

Buchanan leant over the pitted wooden bar. A large man with an eclectic collection of silver teeth came over. Buchanan asked if there was a Captain Arliss in the bar. The barkeep jerked his head to behind Buchanan and growled that Arliss was sitting in the corner. Buchanan bought a bottle of rum and took it over to Arliss' table.

"Captain Arliss?" asked Buchanan.

A head which had been turned to one side twisted and looked up at Buchanan. Two deep scars ran from the bridge of the man's nose to his hairline almost as if he had been savaged by an animal. A vast black bush of a beard covered most of the rest of his face. One of his eyes was jet black, the colour of a starless night but the other glinted peculiarly in the candlelight of the inn. Buchanan tried not to stare but as the man moved his head Buchanan saw that what was creating the effect was a gold Piece of Eight which had been wedged into the vacant eye socket.

"Who'd be asking then, young man?"

To Buchanan's surprise the voice appeared fairly educated. "Buchanan is the name, Captain. This is my colleague Mr. Mackenzie."

"Is that so, Mr. Buchanan? And what brings you to this august hostelry?"

Buchanan laid the rum on the rickety surface. "I was hoping that was something we could discuss over this fine bottle of rum."

"That, Mr. Buchanan is not a fine bottle of rum." He looked over to the barman and tipped up his chin. The barman immediately came over holding another bottle to replace Buchanan's. "Now, this is a fine bottle of rum. Old Caxton there will ply that cat's piss to anyone who's not a regular."

Buchanan smiled and Arliss invited him and Mackenzie to sit. The Captain shooed away the tart who had been nuzzling into him but an intimidating minder remained by his side eyeing the Scots for any sudden wrong moves.

"So, go on Mr. Buchanan," he said, pouring the superior rum into the glasses in front of them.

"I hear say that you are sailing tomorrow morning for Curacao."

"You hear correctly. No secret in that."

"How would you like to make a small detour to Darien?"

"That sir, is no small detour, and one which I'm sure you are aware is now forbidden to all men who sail under His Majesty's flag."

"But I understand you no longer do so."

Arliss fixed Buchanan with his one good eye. "That's what you *understand*, is it?"

Buchanan sensed that this was no time to show any hesitation or weakness. "I'm told that your letters of commission as King's privateer have been revoked and you've been disavowed."

Arliss continued to stare at him. "An unfortunate misunderstanding which will be soon remedied."

"I'm sure that's so, Captain. But until then, you might not feel yourself unduly constrained by any Royal Proclamations."

"The road to redemption is littered with many obstacles, Mr. Buchanan. Assisting you Scots may be one which is insurmountable."

"Who's saying you're providing assistance? We're paying for passage on a vessel to Curacao. Nothing to do with the Scots Company at all. Of course, after we set sail anything can happen. The winds and tides can be treacherous and ships are often blown off course in that part of the world."

Arliss ran his hand through the thick matted mass of his beard and fixed Buchanan with his cyclops stare. "Taking a hell of a risk trusting a pirate aren't you? What's to stop me taking you on board, slitting your throat and then throwing you over the side?"

"Absolutely nothing. But the very fact you've raised the possibility tells me that you're not minded to follow through with the premise. Had you been serious you would have kept silent and simply done the deed."

Arliss smiled a crooked grin. "A fair point, Mr. Buchanan. Harming those who hire you is not a reputation any sailor wishes to encourage."

"Which only leaves the issue of price and services to be rendered," pressed Buchanan. The clock was ticking and the Scots could ill afford to waste time dancing around the maypole.

"You're a pushy young fellow, aren't you?" smiled Arliss.

"No sir. Just a man who knows what he wants. This is your opportunity. Do you wish to take it?"

"You know, for the right price I just might."

"Five pounds in gold coin for passage. Another ten pounds for any fresh supplies you have on board, minus what is needed to get you to Curacao."

"You do appreciate that some of the fresh supplies are one hundred head of prime ebony. And I'm not taking about wood, Mr. Buchanan."

"I wasn't intending to include them as part of any bargain."

"Well, in that case I think we may be close to striking a deal." He paused and Buchanan waited for the counter. "Twenty five pounds."

"Sorry, Captain, too rich for us. We'll have to look elsewhere, I'm afraid." He moved to get up but felt Arliss' hand grab his wrist. "Not so fast, young fellow. Let's talk a bit longer."

Buchanan sat back down. "I can go to twenty pounds. But for that, you must carry extra meat and vegetable supplies."

"You are an interesting specimen, sir, I must say. You come asking for my help in desperate straits and end up trying to call the tune."

"Not desperate, Captain. That would be if you were my last negotiation and not the first."

Arliss laughed. "I like you, lad. And because of that. I'll do your bidding for twenty three pieces."

"Twenty one," replied Buchanan.

"Twenty two and let that be an end to it."

"Deal." He shook Arliss' hand and downed the rum to seal the compact.

"Now, if you'll excuse me lads, I've some other matters to attend to before we leave this fine city." He snapped his fingers and the mulatto prostitute hurried back to his side. "High tide tomorrow. Six am. Don't sleep in, now."

"There'll be little chance of that, Captain."

The Scots exited through the throng of bodies and picked their way back along the crumbling streets stopping only to pick up some food and drink. Buchanan wanted to get out of plain sight and back to the boarding house as soon as possible. They only had to hold out for ten hours until Arliss weighed anchor.

CHAPTER 41

As they entered their lodgings, the desiccated little clerk held up a hand and put an index finger to his lips. He pointed up towards the rooms and signalled that two men were there. Reaching under his desk, he produced a pair of large wooden clubs. Buchanan nodded and took the weapons, handing one to Mackenzie who grabbed it with shaking hands.

Buchanan mirrored the clerk's action of index finger to mouth as the two Scots slowly began climbing the stairs. He stopped halfway up and turned to whisper to Mackenzie. "When I give the signal, make as much noise as you can so they'll think there's more than two of us. Hit anything that moves other than me."

The doors to both rooms were open but it was clear that the activity was coming from Mackenzie's. The only light was from the moon and a single candle which had been placed in the middle of the floor. Buchanan stopped a few feet away and familiarised himself with the presences scurrying about in the ominous shadows. Yes, two men for sure, obviously searching for the booty. He sensed one of them come towards the door and drew back quickly into the second room, shepherding Mackenzie behind him.

"I'll try the other room again," said the first intruder.

Buchanan raised his club, readying himself. He saw the head sized oval, dark against the outline of the door, and swung hard making square contact with the mass. He heard the sickening crunch of wood on bone and the man went down like a felled oak. At the noise of the impact Buchanan began hollering, followed by Mackenzie wailing like a possessed banshee.

Buchanan rushed into the first room and heard the thud of feet as the second intruder tried to make for the windows. Buchanan swung wildly in the darkness and made contact with something solid but fleshy, perhaps a calf. As the shape reached the balcony, the moon emerged from behind a cloud and Buchanan watched as in slow motion the intruder regained his balance from the blow and grabbed on to the balustrade. The reprieve was only temporary as the thin slat which was supporting the thief gave way and with a scream he fell straight through, landing with a dull thud on the ground below. Buchanan carefully made his way to the edge and looked down. The man lay moaning, but after a moment of two stirred and began to crawl away, soon vanishing into the total blackness of the alleyway.

Buchanan went back to the second room where Mackenzie had lit two candles. In the improved light they could see that the first intruder was out cold, blood coursing like claret from his nose. Buchanan reached down and felt the pulse in his neck. "He's still alive. But he's going to have one hell of a headache tomorrow. Help me drag him over here and put him on his side. Don't want him choking on his own puke."

The two men hauled the body into the centre of the floor. Buchanan stripped the man of his trousers and tied them around his arms and torso. The Scots then surveyed the scene. The rooms had been completely ransacked. Valises had been torn open, clothes strewn on the floor and cabinet drawers scattered in upended confusion. The beds had been stripped and the thin pillows slashed, leaving a corona of goose feathers around the covers. Some boards had been ripped from the floor of Buchanan's room but the thieves had been disturbed before making a start on the second.

Buchanan edged out onto the balcony and called Mackenzie over. They lit two more candles and placed these on the remaining slats allowing the entire structure to be illuminated.

The pantomime of negotiating the treacherous surface was re-enacted and in moments Buchanan had reached the far end. He pulled back the wooden paling and after a few seconds his fingers brushed against the calico bag. Slowly he wrapped his hand around the top and gently extracted it from its hiding place. He held it up in triumph for Mackenzie to see and the accountant, still coursing with adrenalin, silently punched the air in celebration. After he had clambered back, Buchanan laid the bag on the floor and gave it a little pat.

He turned to Mackenzie and saw that the meek bean counter was starting to come off the high. "Stay here and don't move." instructed Buchanan. He hurried down the stairs to the clerk's desk where the gnomish little man sat apparently unconcerned about the night's events.

"All sorted then, Scotsman?"

"Aye my friend, and in no little part to you." He extracted a shilling from his jacket and laid it on the desktop. The clerk's hand darted up and the coin disappeared in a flash.

"I was hoping that would extend to cover some rum," said Buchanan.

The clerk's face broke into a toothless grin and he produced a bottle from the recesses of the desk. "Ahead of you there, Scotsman."

"As far as any damages are concerned, you'll find a gentleman in the balcony bedroom who'll be happy to pay after we've left tomorrow," said Buchanan.

"Fair enough. Just mind and leave the clubs behind before you go. Very important they are to the running of this establishment."

Buchanan nodded and took the stairs two at a time. By the time he got back, Mackenzie was sitting against the far wall, his hands trembling. Buchanan uncorked the bottle and held it to Mackenzie's lips. "Take a swig of this Roddy and you'll be good as gold."

Mackenzie took two large gulps and closed his eyes as the alcohol did its work. A few seconds later he started to laugh. "If my mother could see me now. I always told her accountancy was exciting."

Buchanan helped himself to the dreadful grog and joined in the laughter. After a few minutes respite he kicked into action again. "Roddy, we'll both stay in here tonight. Bring the mattress and what's left of the bedding from the other room. After that we'll drag chummy through and shove him against the inside of the door as a human barricade."

"Do you think we'll be safe?" asked Mackenzie.

"Safer than anywhere else is the best I can offer. Just stay strong for a few hours and we can say *adios* to Port Royal."

They carried out the plan before Buchanan prodded the intruder with his boot just to make sure he was still out cold. "Aye, he'll be no trouble tonight. Time to turn in."

"I don't think I'll be able to sleep much," said Mackenzie.

"Just as well, since you're on guard duty and I've got the bed that's not broken. Wake me if you hear anything."

With that Buchanan clambered into the rickety cot and fell into a dead sleep, the events of the mad day finally taking their toll.

CHAPTER 42

Mackenzie sat awake all night eyes glued to the door. When he woke Buchanan just after five am, his nerves were shot and his hand cramped from gripping the club.

Buchanan on the other hand had slept soundly, confident that they had seen off the imminent threat. They packed their belongings, stowing the bulk of the gold and tobacco receipts at the bottom of their luggage. Buchanan had carefully counted out twenty two coins to hand over to Arliss once they were safely aboard.

Then they dragged the still unconscious thief away from the door and propped him against the adjacent wall before leaving. Depositing the clubs on the clerk's empty desk they slipped silently into the alley. Daybreak wasn't far away and they stole along the edges of the streets towards the harbour where Arliss' ship the 'Pergamon' was loading the last of its human cargo.

The slaves made for a pitiful sight. The Scots watched the shackled wretches shuffle resignedly into the dark hold.

Arliss barked an order for them to stand aside as the paying passengers came aboard. "I trust you gentlemen had a pleasant evening."

"Couldn't have had more fun if I was twins," replied Buchanan.

"Glad to hear it," said Arliss with a knowing smile. "My first mate will show you to your quarters. Make yourselves at home but keep out of sight until I say so."

Their cabin was surprisingly well appointed with two bunks and a small porthole which afforded a good amount of light. They stowed their bags and began the wait.

Thirty minutes later they felt the familiar movement of the sea beneath their feet. There was a rap on the door.

Buchanan opened it and there stood Arliss. "It's safe to come out now."

The Scots followed him down a narrow passageway to the Great Cabin. The Captain held up a bottle of rum in invitation. Buchanan nodded and Arliss poured out three measures. "To beautiful women and following winds."

Buchanan smiled and drained the glass. Mackenzie followed suit before slumping into one of the chairs.

"Your friend looks none too well, Mr. Buchanan."

"Bit of a rough night."

"I can but imagine. Let me guess. Uninvited guests?"

"Indeed."

"Well, you've got out in one piece and with favourable weather we'll have you in Panama in five days."

"Delighted to hear it."

"Now before I'm forced to throw you overboard, perhaps we can transact our business."

Buchanan placed a purse containing the gold coins on the table.

Arliss grinned. "I'll not do you the disservice of counting it."

"Only a fool would short change his rescuer, Captain."

Shortly afterwards, bread and scrambled eggs were brought in by a cabin boy. It had been nearly a day since the Scots had eaten properly and they wolfed down the food.

"Care for a guided tour?" Arliss asked.

"It would be rude not to, but perhaps not the hold," replied Buchanan.

The ship had been converted to accommodate its primary purpose as a slaver, with the storage area enlarged to cram in as many bodies as possible. There was a small but experienced crew, who Arliss advised were all fiercely loyal to him.

"How can you be sure?" asked Buchanan.

"Because none of them want to end up like the last one who wasn't."

The excursion completed, Arliss told them that they were welcome on the upper decks and to dine in the Great Cabin but warned them off exploring anywhere else.

"I don't think that will be an issue," said Buchanan.

"Excellent. Well, enjoy the cruise and I'll see you at dinner."

With that he strode off leaving the Scots to their own devices. Mackenzie leant against the railing watching as the blistering sun began its long ascent and the Jamaican coastline disappeared slowly from sight.

"Scared that the English will send out a pursuit ship to bring us back, Roddy?" asked Buchanan.

"The thought had crossed my mind. By Christ, I'm glad to see the back of that hellhole."

"You're not alone there. I'll wager that Port Royal isn't long as the jewel in Jamaica's crown."

"Nothing that another earthquake wouldn't help," said Mackenzie, smiling for the first time since they'd weighed anchor.

CHAPTER 43

The first day slipped past easily. Mackenzie remained in the cabin for most of the afternoon catching up on some sorely needed sleep and Buchanan edited his notes to ensure that no relevant points would be missed when they reported back to the Council. His encounter with the captivating Anne Robertson would not be part of the briefing.

Around six thirty they went topside onto the quarter deck to watch the sunset. The breeze was at their back and they listened to the lines and rigging crack and hiss as the sails captured every ounce of the Alisio, the easterly trade wind. In the slaving business, time was money. The longer a ship was at sea the more it cost to feed and water the cargo and the greater the risk of some dying.

Arliss waved from the aft deck and signalled it was time for dinner. When they reached the Great Cabin, the Captain's gnarled face broke into a grin. "A nice relaxing day Mr. Buchanan?" he asked in that clipped voice so at odds with his physical appearance.

"Most pleasant thank you," replied Buchanan.

"And Mr. Mackenzie, did you manage some shut eye?" he enquired politely.

"Yes, thank you, Captain. Feeling much better now."

"Excellent. Then let's eat and you can tell me more about the madness that drove you Scots to plant your flag in Darien."

His steward brought in several platters which were piled with pork, potatoes and fried plantains. Arliss asked if they'd like some Spanish brandy.

"I'd prefer whisky, Captain," said Mackenzie.

"Ah, would that I could young Mackenzie. But we only drink what we plunder from the Spanish and sadly their tastes do not run to your native tipple. Perhaps I should consider a raid on Darien." He said this with a smile but Buchanan was not altogether sure just how tongue in cheek the remark was.

Buchanan then gave Arliss a potted history of the Scheme. The Captain listened quietly, from time to time shaking his head at the unfolding narrative. When Buchanan had finished Arliss raised his eyebrows. "But to think a trade route could be established from Darien to the Pacific is lunacy. Why do you think the Spanish never bothered settling it?"

This was the same depressing conclusion Buchanan had come to himself.

Arliss then added. "By the way, the Spanish aren't best pleased with you lot over their Lost Legion."

"How in God's name do you know about that?" asked Buchanan.

"Common knowledge in Jamaica, old son. No coincidence that the King has chosen to issue his Proclamation now. Doesn't want to create any nasty ripples with his new best friend, King Phillip. It's only a matter of time before the Spanish hear that big brother's not going to be looking out for you in the playground anymore. Then you'll be fucked. Or to be precise, more fucked than you are now."

The Scots absorbed this but said nothing.

"Look on the bright side, my friends, there's always a future in slavery," Arliss guffawed.

Mackenzie couldn't let that one go, even if it was said in jest. He regarded the slave trade with a repugnance matched only by his detestation of the English. "Never. Anyone involved in that deserves a special place in hell."

Buchanan looked to calm things down. "Roddy, perhaps wise not to judge others for the choices they make."

Arliss held up his hands. "No need for any soft soap ,Mr. Buchanan. Your young friend is absolutely right. It is a damnable business but until the lawmakers and Kings decide the trade should stop, it will continue on. And if I don't do it someone else will."

"And that's your excuse is it?" snapped Mackenzie.

Arliss levelled Mackenzie with his one good eye and replied in a slow measured voice. "I'm not seeking exculpation or absolution, young man.

Let me tell you a tale. I was a Captain in the English Navy and fought for my King and country with honour, integrity and valour. I filled the coffers of the English Treasury with Spanish, French and Dutch gold and spend ten months of the year away from England. I lost an eye and nearly my life. I was captured and whipped by the Spanish and escaped only by the intervention of my friends. The King didn't lift a finger. But he was happy enough to grant me a commission to privateer for him when I was freed. For the Royals it's all about money to finance their wars and keep their whores and palaces. They don't give a damn about anyone who isn't in a position to enrich them. So, when I was judged not to have handed over the Crown's share of Spanish booty, I was cut loose, had my assets confiscated and told never to come back to England. Privateering magically transformed into piracy at the stroke of a monarch's quill. I could do exactly the same as I used to do for him but now it would be illegal. This life was all that was left to me. We do not live in a fair world, Mr. Mackenzie, and anyone who believes we do is a naive dreamer. So, please save me the sanctimonious sermons."

Mackenzie fell silent, alive enough to the situation not to push the point.

Arliss let the moment linger, massaged the scars on his forehead and then continued. "If it is any consolation, Mr. Mackenzie, I am not in fact a slave trader. I do not buy, sell or own these poor wretches. That is for others far more connected and wealthier than me. The network controlling this industry extends high up the chain of power and don't think that some of your Lords and Masters in Scotland aren't heavily involved."

Mackenzie looked at him disbelievingly.

"Oh yes, Mr. Mackenzie, this is a global game where the very rich ultimately control all of the pieces. I am only a transporter of the goods, a mere pawn."

Mackenzie kept staring, not now sure how to respond.

But Arliss was not finished. "One other thing to bear in mind. I only get paid for the number of slaves that walk off this ship in good health. So contrary to what you might think they are far from maltreated or starved and if you don't believe me I'm happy to escort you below for an inspection."

Mackenzie shook his head mutely.

"I thought not," said Arliss. "Be careful in condemning others Mr. Mackenzie until you appreciate the bigger picture."

Mackenzie remained silent. He abhorred the slave trade but was Arliss really the one to be attacking?

"Perhaps that's enough moral philosophy for one evening, gentlemen. Come tell me more about your encounters with the Spanish. I never tire of hearing about them being put to the sword. And, Mr. Mackenzie, if you want to vent your spleen then our Spanish friends are a more appropriate target. They are an unchecked malignancy, polluting everything they touch."

*

The rest of the trip passed without further incident. The sun rose, the sun set, the wind continued to be favourable and on the fifth evening Panama hove into view.

Arliss had proven to be an excellent host. He regaled them with tales of the high seas which, while probably containing much poetic licence, were highly entertaining. In turn, Buchanan told stories from the Glasgow Courts which the old Captain found hilarious.

On their last evening together he asked. "What are you Scots going to do now?"

"We've been pondering that ourselves," said Buchanan.

"You must realise you've no future in Darien after the Proclamation?"

"Aye, well there will certainly be much for our Council to discuss."

"I'm sure. Just mind that when it starts to fall apart it'll be every man for himself. Someone always has to be blamed, so watch your backs. There'll be plenty of folk happy to point fingers and plant daggers."

"We're becoming painfully aware of that."

"Anyways up, I've taken a liking to you two fools so if you ever find yourself back in Jamaica or down in Curacao then feel free to look me up. I'm also happy to provide my services, but unlike my company, they will not be free."

"You're too kind, Captain," smiled Buchanan.

CHAPTER 44

As they approached Panama the next morning, Arliss told them how the exchange had to play out. "When we get to Golden Island, my men will signal that you're on board along with some supplies and ask for a vessel to be sent out."

"You're not entering the bay?" asked Mackenzie.

"After the Proclamation that would be a bridge too far. I also know how treacherous that entrance is and can't risk any damage to my ship or cargo."

There was no point in pursuing the point. The Captain held all the cards and his position wasn't unreasonable. "That'll be fine," said Buchanan.

The transfer went remarkably smoothly. The little Endeavour was dispatched to meet the Pergamon and the ships tied up next to each other. The provisions were passed across the narrow gap before Mackenzie and Buchanan said their farewells to Arliss.

"Good luck, Gentlemen," he said, shaking each of their hands.

"Thank you for all your help, Captain. Safe onward journey," said Buchanan.

Mackenzie said a simple "Thank you," managing to refrain from any parting volley about the slaving.

They clambered on board the Endeavour and the ropes between the two vessels were released. Buchanan watched as the Pergamon's sails caught the wind and continued south on its voyage of the damned. As it began to disappear from view he swore he saw the sun glint off the golden piece of eight in Arliss' eye socket.

*

When they got back into the bay they transferred to the Unicorn. Paterson jumped up and grabbed Buchanan's hand, pumping it hard. Buchanan thought it questionable just how sustained the welcome would be when they learned of recent events, especially as etched in each of the Councillors faces was the obvious question, 'Where the fuck is the supply ship?'"

Pennicuik fixed Buchanan with his trademark glare. "So, tell us."

Buchanan knew there was no point in glossing over anything. The success of New York evaporated when he narrated events in Jamaica. The blood drained from Paterson's face as details of the Proclamation emerged. When Buchanan finished there was a deathly silence.

"Bastard English," was all that came out of Pennicuik's mouth.

Montgomery just sat staring into space. Paterson, slightly recovered, began to grapple with the consequences of the failed mission. "You still have the tobacco receipts and the gold?"

"Less the tariff paid to Arliss for our passage and the supplies."

"Then you did well, Jamie. At least we still have some capital to play with."

"Aye, but it's fuck all use if there's no-one willing to trade with us," spat Pennicuik.

"Perhaps not in the obvious places. Jamie, does the Proclamation only cover English traders and ports in the region?" asked Paterson.

"I transcribed it to the letter so you can draw your own conclusion. For me 'His Majesty's subjects' goes beyond just the English. But then again, there aren't that many Scottish or Welsh ports in the region."

"Yes, quite," said Paterson missing the humour. "Let's look at the alternatives then."

Pennicuik broke into a mocking laugh. "The alternatives. What fucking alternatives? Are you inhabiting some faerie land where there's always a happy ending? For Christ's sakes, man. When will you grasp that we have just been completely shafted and are now clean out of 'alternatives'"?

"No, I don't accept that," snapped Paterson.

Buchanan stared at his friend. Optimism and drive were one thing but so was a sense of reality. Buchanan wasn't a great devotee of the glass half full or half empty nonsense but he knew when the glass had been taken away. He asked, "What's your suggestion, William?"

"Well, we were desperately unlucky the last time with the voyage to Curacao. It was a good plan thwarted by a freak storm."

Pennicuik snorted. "Are you mad, Paterson? We lost Pincarton and Malloch together with an entire crew, one of our vessels and a huge chunk of our money. No way will I agree to trying that again. Only an idiot keeps making the same mistake and expects a different outcome."

Buchanan nodded. "They're right William. We couldn't possibly sanction another expedition."

Paterson arched his eyebrows and shook his head in the small sideways movements of a man who doesn't quite believe what he's hearing. "Fine. In that case we look to New York or Boston. Plenty of non-English merchants up there who'll accommodate us."

Pennicuik spluttered a response. "You've taken leave of your senses haven't you? For God's sake, Buchanan and Mackenzie have just told us the state of play. You want to go back there in the hope that someone might be dumb enough to defy the English edict and actually trade with us?"

Paterson glared at him. "Have you a better idea then, Pennicuik? You contribute nothing which could ever remotely be regarded as constructive."

"Is that right? Well, let's ask your protege what he thinks. Come on then, Buchanan. Give us your take on this bilge about popping up to the American Colonies to save the day."

Buchanan knew that Pennicuik was right. But he didn't want to give the prick the satisfaction of openly agreeing with him or be used to humiliate Paterson. Plus, the prospect of getting back so soon to New York did hold some ulterior attraction.

He couched his response carefully. "If we are genuine about sourcing supplies then I agree with William that the only viable alternative would be the American Colonies. He is also correct that a number of merchants there are not bound by fealty to the English Crown."

"Ha. There you have it," exclaimed Paterson.

Buchanan held up his hand. "But from what we saw there's no question that the English have absolute control of those Colonies at present. Despite there being a great deal of anti-English sentiment in certain quarters it would be a brave man who would risk alienating the English to trade with us. These people are merchants first and foremost and I doubt they'll sacrifice their long term position for a quick killing."

"And there *you* have it Paterson," sneered Pennicuik. "Even your own man says it's a stupid notion."

"I said nothing of the sort, Pennicuik. If you'd actually been listening I said it was feasible but too risky given our situation."

"'Our situation' is that we're starving, diseased, burying our country-men every day and now waiting for the Spanish to come and finish us off. That's 'our situation'," snarled Pennicuik.

"*Our* situation?" raged Paterson jumping to his feet. "*Our* situation? I don't notice you or any of your sailors on starvation rations or digging graves. Why don't you get off your fat arse and come and see what it is like on the actual settlement. *Our* situation. What a fucking joke."

For an instant Pennicuik moved forward. But he had history of fronting this crook-bodied farmer and knew that it was a battle he would be better fighting with words. "And what do you want me to do? Risk my men to make you feel better? How the hell do you think you're going to get out of this shithole if push comes to shove? Walk home?"

Buchanan held up his hands. "Alright. Enough. This is getting us nowhere. We need to review the position with clear minds. Let's cool off, take on board everything we've discussed and come back tomorrow morning when the dust has settled a bit. Agreed?" He said this in a way which courted no argument. In any event, the others had no appetite to pursue the issues further that day. Montgomery was lost in the arguments and the exhausted Mackenzie just wanted to go back to his cabin and curl up in a ball.

CHAPTER 45

Buchanan slept like he'd been drugged. The long journey had taken its toll and it was well after eight when he finally got up. He dressed for the first time in two weeks in a fresh cotton shirt and wandered into the Great Cabin where Paterson was having breakfast. It still felt odd, wrong even, that Pincarton was not there. His absence had left a huge gap and in hindsight allowing him to make the trip to Curacao was a colossal mistake.

Buchanan was full of questions about what had been happening when he was away. The main headline was that the relationship between the Landsmen and the Seamen had reached breaking point. The Landsmen were living on rations barely enough to sustain life never mind engage in hard labour. Work on the fort had stopped and the township was a motley shambles.

Disease was rife and death a daily occurrence. The little graveyard was not so little any more. All the doctors or surgeons who had accompanied the Fleet were either dead or, in Herries' case, had left. Medicines had been depleted to the point of uselessness. The only thing in any decent supply was alcohol and even among the staunch Presbyterians this was increasingly being used as an escape from their desperate reality. But with the booze came its companions. Resentment, indolence and fighting. Morale was lower than it had ever been, which was saying something given the previous benchmark.

The lot of the Seamen on the other hand was far better. They lived in the normal environment of their ships and were well used to its privations. Not that they were suffering too much. Each vessel still had ample supplies of food and there was no sign of disease or malnutrition.

From the beach the sight of them promenading and laughing on deck had become intolerable.

Paterson had pled with Pennicuik to release some ships' stores but the Commodore had point blank refused. He maintained that all retained provisions were vital in the event that the Scots had to evacuate the Colony. Otherwise they would be out of supplies and perish before they could reach the nearest port which would have them. The Proclamation only strengthened his argument.

The Drummonds and the rest of the Glencoe Gang had demanded an increased voice on the Council. Conflict was in the air and the prospect of civil war was all too real. God only knew what impact the Jamaica news might have on the tinder box.

As Buchanan was absorbing all of this, Robb bustled into the Great Cabin. He looked haggard and drawn. Now the de facto Captain following Pincarton's incarceration, it was clear that heavy was the head that wore the crown.. He welcomed Buchanan back before grabbing some coffee and hurrying off. When he'd left, Buchanan asked Paterson. "Just how bad is the food situation?"

"I don't know how it could be worse, Jamie. We'd been holding out for the supplies from Jamaica." As soon as he'd spoken he held up his right hand. "Before you say anything, there is absolutely no blame being attached."

Buchanan nodded before Paterson continued. "But the few supplies you negotiated won't last more than a week."

"What about the Indians? Have they helped?"

"To the extent that they can. But their crops are purely subsistence."

"Passing merchants?"

"Oh believe me, we've tried but they don't want anything we have to offer other than the whisky and madeira and both of those have almost gone. Aside from that they're not set up for large scale supply. Now, with the Proclamation even that avenue will be closed off."

"What about the Landsmens' claim that the ships have plenty of provisions?"

"Well they do, but though I hate to admit it, Pennicuik is right to insist that enough has to be kept in reserve if we need to abandon the Colony."

"That almost sounded like a compliment."

"Aye, I kind of felt it burn my throat on the way up."

Buchanan smiled before continuing. "Any word on the supply ship or the Second Fleet?"

"Nothing. Absolutely nothing. We don't even know if Hamilton made it back with our letters."

"But surely we'd have heard if they hadn't?"

"How? We're not exactly at the centre of global communications here."

"But still, someone must know something."

Paterson grunted. "Well, maybe if the Company wasn't so damned obsessed with secrecy. They're not exactly going to advertise to the world that there's another Fleet on the way."

He was right. Paranoia was deep rooted in Edinburgh. Buchanan rubbed his chin. He needed a shave. "Do you think news of the Proclamation will have reached the Company?"

"Probably."

"Well, wouldn't that accelerate the Second Fleet leaving earlier or Edinburgh sourcing other assistance for us?"

"Not necessarily. Remember that the picture painted in the letters sent with Hamilton is that everything in the garden is rosy. No reason to panic as far as Edinburgh is concerned."

Buchanan took a deep breath. "But surely they'll make representations to the King to have the Proclamation repealed?"

"I'm sure they will, but that's a separate issue to the survival of the Colony. The Proclamation will be seen as a nuisance but not necessarily result in the total collapse of the settlement."

"Jesus," muttered Buchanan. "So no-one really knows how bad it is here except us."

"That about sums it up. The Second Fleet or a supply ship may be on the way but it won't be a mission of mercy. They'll turn up expecting to find a bustling trading port, with a lovely wee town and a replica of Edinburgh Castle watching over us all."

Buchanan looked out over the bay to where the half-built houses littered the narrow hinterland. He could make out the prone bodies of some of the settlers lying on the ground, either too ill, exhausted or disillusioned to stir. A torpor had settled over the Colony, and for the first time Buchanan knew with absolute conviction that it was doomed. He puffed out his cheeks as the reality registered.

Not Paterson though. "If we all pull together we might still make it."

Buchanan looked askance at him. "Seriously?"

"You've got to believe, Jamie. If you don't, all hope will die."

"Aye, but better for the hope to die than the rest of the settlers, William."

"No, I'll not hear that kind of talk. Come on, let's get over to the Saint Andrew. The Landsmen are coming to visit."

Buchanan realised then that Paterson had lost all detachment. 'Dogma before lives' was not a credo which ever made for happy endings.

CHAPTER 46

As Buchanan, Paterson and Montgomery made the short transfer over to the Saint Andrew they saw Thomas Drummond and three others climbing aboard. Buchanan identified them as Colin Campbell, Charles Forbes and Samuel Leitch. All were soldiers who had served with Drummond at Glencoe and were part of his cabal.

This is going to be interesting, thought Buchanan. It was only a few months previously that Drummond and his brother Robert had been accused of mutiny by Pennicuik. Now the dynamic was very different.

Clambering onto the deck they found Drummond and the others waiting for them.

"Welcome back to the Colony, Mr. Buchanan" said Drummond with a half-smile. "Forgotten tae bring a wee supply ship wi' you?"

"It's a tale I'm happy to tell, Thomas, but let's get below so that it'll only take the one recounting."

As they entered the Great Cabin, Buchanan could see the eyes of Forbes, Campbell and Leitch widen like saucers. This was their first visit and coming from their leaking, mosquito-infested huts it must have seemed like something out of the Arabian Nights. Pennicuik invited the new arrivals to sit but didn't bother with the trifling courtesy of shaking their hands. As far as he was concerned these men were unwanted interlopers who could bugger off as soon as they had said their piece.

On the table sat several bottles of water, but no alcohol. Pennicuik had set out his stall and made this even clearer with his abrupt opening. "You wanted a meeting with the Council. Here we are."

"Aye, that we did Pennicuik, that we did." replied Drummond. There was nothing sinister in the words themselves but they seemed to drip with menace. He let a moment or two lapse and then continued in the same low drawl. "First time my boys here huv seen how the other hauf lives. Widda been nice tae huv bin offered a wee dram to mark the occasion."

Pennicuik jerked his head towards the sideboard. "You know where it is."

Drummond tipped his chin up at Campbell who wandered over and poured out four stiff measures of Scotch. He asked Buchanan, Paterson and Montgomery if they wanted one but specifically excluded Pennicuik. Another three drams were poured and ferried back to the table. Drummond swirled the nectar around his mouth for a few moments before it slid down into his chest. "A nice wee drop, Captain. But then again I wouldnae huv expectit anythin' less."

Buchanan could see Pennicuik seethe. He knew the Commodore hated Drummond and the murderers he surrounded himself with. But now he didn't seemed scared of them. Maybe he thought his crew were a match for the soldiers especially as the latter were so weak.

Drummond finished his drink and placed the crystal glass slowly and carefully on top of the main table. "Now, let's get down tae business. It's clear tae those of us who're actually daeing the work tae create this Colony that wur interests urnae being looked efter."

"Is that a fact?" Pennicuik said with a mocking laugh.

"Aye. It is, Captain. Other than Mr. Paterson, who lives onshore maist of the time and Mr. Buchanan who's done his bit, we've seen fuck all of any of youse. Nae doubt idling on yer lovely wee ships enjoying yer fine wines and food while we starve tae death."

"Aye, the same way that you all just sat on your arses while we got you here. Not up to me to look after you once we'd dropped anchor in the Garden of Eden."

"Fuck off, Pennicuik. You couldnae look efter a bag of messages never mind a settlement. Anyway, we dinnae want you looking efter us. What we dae want is a fair share of the supplies which wur supposed tae be for the entire Colony, no' just you bum shagging sailor boys."

Pennicuik let out a scornful snort. "Bum shagging sailor boys. Is that the best you can do?" He let his mirth subside a little before his tone changed completely. "Listen, Drummond. My task was to get you here and stay anchored while you got on with your job. Which, if I'm not mistaken, was to set up a colony for Scotland. All I've seen is abject failure. Jesus, you can't even grow enough to feed yourselves never mind create a trading hub."

Drummond snarled back. "Aye, like that's wur fault. We've worked wur fingers tae the bone. Maybe if we'd bin properly telt whit it was going tae be like here we might huv had a chance."

Pennicuik shrugged. "Maybe so, but it's still not my problem."

"Nae yer fucking problem. How's it nae yer problem? Is yer precious Council no' supposed tae be looking out fur the welfare of the entire Colony?"

Pennicuik just gave a dismissive sniff. Drummond turned to Paterson. "William, for Christ sakes you know whit it's like. Something's gottae be done man."

When Paterson spoke it was with a slow bubbling fury. "Just listen to yourselves. We're carrying the hopes of Scotland on our shoulders and all you can do is try to score points off each other like wee boys. You want to talk about sacrifices? Christ sake, I've buried my wife and son. Don't you understand that our Nation's future is hanging on what happens here?"

Silence. He repeated it his voice rising to a crescendo. "Well, do you?"

There were compliant nods. Paterson continued, but now in a more measured tone. "Drummond is right about the privations onshore. They are desperate and our people- yes, *our* people- are dying every day. However, if we do need to leave, there has to be enough food on the ships to get us home. So, we need to find a balance and work together."

For a brief moment it seemed that these words might actually have a positive impact. But the next exchange proved it was too late in the day for valiant rhetoric.

"So, Pennicuik, are you gonnae release some supplies tae us?" Drummond challenged.

"Not unless I'm forced to."

"Well, we may huv tae go down that path then."

"Are you seriously threatening me?"

"I don't huv tae. Now, Mr. Buchanan you're the lawyer."

Buchanan nodded, not quite sure what was coming next.

"You'll ken how Edinburgh meant for the Colony tae be governed."

"I do."

"Aye, and is it?"

Buchanan took his time answering. "The Colony was to be governed by a Council. That's where we are now. Then once the Colony was functioning there were to be democratic elections."

"Aye well, we're a far cry fae a democracy then, aren't we?" snarled Drummond.

"But it could also be argued we're a far cry from the Colony being functional."

"Aye, well that'd be a matter of interpretation, Mr. Buchanan, The only decision making power in this place lies wi' whit's left of the Council. That's a lot of power in the hands of four men. So we think it's time the situation wis remedied."

Buchanan studied him carefully. "Remedied how?"

"Well either we huv an election and get ourselves a wee Parliament or we make the Council a bit mair representative of the interests of a' concerned."

Buchanan knew there was also the third doomsday scenario of full blown civil war. Land interests versus sea interests. Whoever came out on top wouldn't matter. It would be the end. "And which do you suggest?"

Arcing his arm to include his confederates Drummond replied. "Well, it seems tae us that the easiest thing wid be fur the Council tae be restored tae its original number with the newest members being Landsmen."

Pennicuik snorted. "What, bring three of you onto the Council just like that?"

"Why no'?" said Drummond with the relaxed confidence of a man sitting on a royal flush.

"Absurd." retorted Pennicuik. He turned to his fellow Councillors for support but it was not forthcoming. Paterson felt a sympathy for the Landsmen and would be happy to see them have a proper voice. Buchanan thought Drummond's position not unreasonable and the best option given that the status quo was unsustainable. Montgomery just wanted to go back to Scotland. But he cared enough never to side with Pennicuik again so he nodded his head, silently saying 'Fuck you Commodore.'

Pennicuik looked blankly at them. "Seriously? You would see three of these men on our Council?"

Paterson spoke. "It's not *our* Council, Pennicuik. It's the Council of the Company."

"Excellent news." Drummond banged the table with his fist in triumph. "We'll look forward tae wur first meeting then to get a few wee things sorted out."

"Aye," Paterson sneered, "enjoy your moment in the sun while you can. Once you hear Mr. Buchanan's news you might not be so fucking smug."

Drummond turned to Buchanan. "The supply ship. What's the story there then, Mr. Buchanan?"

For the next fifteen minutes Buchanan went back over the events of the previous two weeks. Drummond and his men listened intently, their victory smiles quickly evaporating as the ramifications became clear. When he'd finished there was another of those grave silences which seemed to follow any recent Buchanan narrative.

"So, you sayin' we're basically on wur own?" asked Drummond.

"Not unless someone wants to breach the Proclamation."

"Bastard fucking English. Bastard fucking Dutch prick of a King," hissed the soldier.

"Couldn't have put it better myself," agreed Buchanan.

"So whit you gonnae dae?"

"Aye well, it's now more a case of what are *we* gonnae dae. Welcome to the fucking Council, Mr. Drummond."

CHAPTER 47

The expanded Council met several times over the next few days. Since Pennicuik refused to allow the Glencoe men back on the Saint Andrew, they either crowded into the Unicorn's Great Cabin or met in Paterson's hut onshore.

Mackenzie had provided an updated inventory of the remaining supplies. It made for sobering reading. On current estimates there was enough food to last four weeks and still have enough in reserve for any voyage back to Scotland. Pennicuik bowed to the will of the new Council which ordered the release of some provisions from the ships' holds.

For a brief period, day to day life for the settlers improved, but those in the know were painfully aware that they were witnessing the slow demise of a Colony in palliative care. The only thing which could save it was a supply ship or the early arrival of the Second Fleet.

On the morning of May 25th a shout came up that a ship was approaching. Hopes were dashed when it turned out to be the little trading sloop, the Maidstone, which had taken Buchanan and Paterson to Cartagena.

Captain Ephraim Pilkington was rowed over to the Unicorn to be greeted by Buchanan. "Ephraim, very good to see you again."

"Mr. Buchanan," he drawled in his West Country burr. "Made it back from your adventures then?"

Buchanan smiled. It was oddly comforting to see someone outside of the immediate circle of the Scots. "It would appear so. I'm surprised you're happy to consort with us given the pogrom on the Colony."

"Yes, a bit of a fly in the ointment that one."

"It doesn't worry you?"

"Me? What am I doing? Just stocking up my water barrels and then going on my way."

"Of course you are. But what are you really doing here?"

"Apart from a bit of easy trade with you gullible lot?" He then paused and rubbed the foliage of his beard. "I've actually brought some news."

"Good news or bad news?"

Pilkington said nothing. Buchanan gave a wry grimace. "Well, no prizes for guessing which then. Look, Ephraim, we're just about to have a Council meeting so perhaps it would be easier if you could tell all of us."

Just then they heard the other Councillors begin to come aboard. Buchanan introduced Pilkington to the new members and then said. "Don't keep us in suspense then, Ephraim. What's this big news?"

Pilkington took a breath. "When I was in Kingston a few days back, I was told that a supply ship called 'The Dispatch' had been sent out in late January from Leith."

"Aye, well that's great news," said Drummond.

"It would have been if it hadn't been shipwrecked off the coast of Islay. No lives lost but the ship and all provisions gone. "

"How do you know?" asked Paterson.

"An English slaver from Bristol."

"Were there any more details?" pressed Paterson.

"That's all I have."

"News of any other supply ships or our Second Fleet?" asked Buchanan.

"Sorry. Jamie. I've got no other information. At least as far as your ships are concerned."

"Jesus, what else then?"

"The word is that since King Billy has disowned your Colony, the Spanish are actively mobilising to force you out."

"Let the fuckers try and they'll get a taste of our cannons," spat Drummond.

Pilkington looked at him as if he had two heads. "I'm sure they will be quaking in their boots. But they'll not attack you. They'll just starve you out."

The atmosphere in the room darkened as the full import of the news sunk in. The supply ship foundering meant there was no prospect of relief in the foreseeable future and if the Spanish did create a blockade then that was the end. The Scots might be able to stave off a frontal attack, but in a war of attrition they could never hope to survive.

Pilkington studied these haggard and beaten down men, dreamers now living in a nightmare." Listen, I've some extra supplies on board which I'd be happy to trade."

"What about the Proclamation?" asked Montgomery.

"If anyone asks, I was never here," said Pilkington forcing a smile.

"Thanks Ephraim," said Buchanan. "Every bit helps. "

"Sorry to be the bearer of bad news. I'll get back and set aside the supplies. We can strike a price later."

Pilkington rose and negotiated his hulking frame out into the passageway. The entire Council sat in gloomy silence for a few moments. Montgomery was the first to speak. "So, where to now?"

Paterson replied, "We wait for the Second Fleet."

"Aye but whit if they get fucked over like the wee supply ship. Whit happens then?" asked Drummond.

"Well, what else do you suggest?" snapped Paterson. "That we just pack up and leave?"

There was another silence. Montgomery seized on the unintended suggestion. "Why not? Let's be honest. We're done here. If the disease and hunger don't do for us, then the Spanish will."

"No. Absolutely not," said Paterson, "We have a duty to remain and do all we can to prepare for the Second Fleet's arrival."

"And how long are we supposed to hang on?" asked Montgomery, desperation dripping off every syllable.

"For as long as we have to," Paterson barked.

Buchanan watched on, fully aware that Paterson's position was untenable. The Colony was being slowly wiped out and prolonging the agony would be madness.

Pennicuik had had enough. "Well, Paterson, you can stay here as long as you want but as soon as the Saint Andrew reaches the point where it can no longer get back to Scotland I'll give the order to weigh anchor. Those that want to come aboard are welcome. But I'll not sit idly by and put my ship and crew in jeopardy."

Drummond snarled. "You miserable prick. You'd just abandon us here and fuck off back to Scotland would you?"

"I'm abandoning nobody. My ship is available for anyone who wants to come. I think their Lordships in Edinburgh will commend the man who had the clarity of thought to save as many lives as possible rather than wait for certain death."

"Aye, spin it how you like Pennicuik, but you know you're just looking to cut and run," spat Paterson,

Buchanan held up his hands. "Alright, alright. Let's just calm down. Obviously, Pilkington's news isn't what we needed right now. But we've got to take the emotion out of this. Let's just digest the information and work through it in the next couple of days."

There were mutterings from around the table but the consensus was that Buchanan was probably right. The meeting broke up and the various factions went their separate ways with Paterson stomping off to his berth.

Buchanan was left alone in the Great Cabin. The sun was just starting to set over the mountains, its orange rays dancing across the crystal blue water. As he watched nature's grand spectacle he wondered how somewhere so unutterably beautiful could cause so much heartache.

CHAPTER 48

S uddenly it started raining visitors. Two days later, a little sloop named the 'The Three Sisters' arrived. It made a living plying the Panama coastline and had visited Darien before. Its crew were a motley collection, mainly Dutch and Danish, all of whom had left their respective navies in advance of dishonourable discharges.

However, her Captain was English. Peter Soames was a bull of man, probably in his fifties, but then again the sea aged people far beyond their actual years. Burly in the bulky way of a street-fighter, he had a bent nose, which may just have been a coincidence, bushy greying whiskers and long lank hair which was topped by a tricorn hat that never left his head. He used his ship for anything other than slaving and to date had not been particular about who he dealt with.

The Scots were pleased to see him as his arrival usually brought some modest supplies of food. Buchanan and Robb ushered him into the Unicorn's Great Cabin. The Englishman's eyes lit up when he saw the Madeira bottle sitting on the table.

"I 'ope that's for me," he chivvied in his Cockney accent.

"We can still lay on some decent alcohol, Peter. Just sorry there's not much food on offer."

"Not to worry, Jamie. I've got a few bits and pieces which might help."

"Always well received."

Just then the door opened and Paterson shuffled in, dog-tired from his labours ashore.

"'Ard day at the office William?" joked Soames.

"Never really an easy one here, Peter."

"No, I can imagine," said Soames, adopting that concerned look that Buchanan had come to recognise in the faces of recent visitors.

"Anyway, we keep going and remain confident of success."

Soames looked sideways at him from under the battered tricorn and then paused, almost as if he didn't want to deliver the next sentence. "Look, there's no point in me putting this off. I fink you're all mad, but I likes you Scots, and you've always been straight with me."

Buchanan and Paterson waited for the axe to fall.

"You knows about the Proclamation from Jamaica?" he said.

The Scots nodded and Soames continued. "Well, it's not just the Caribbean. Seems it covers from French Canada southwards and the Governors of all English outposts have been told to cut you off."

"The American colonies too ?" asked Paterson.

"Yeah, and not just that. The English navy has been ordered to enforce it with maximum prejudice. In other words, sink anyone what supplies you."

Buchanan and Paterson sat stunned. This was no regional embargo. Tangling with His Majesty's Navy wasn't something that even the greediest trader would chance.

"You're taking a risk being here then," said Buchanan.

"Maybe, but not yet a big one. It becomes big when the English start to patrol the area. That'll be soon enough though, so this will be my last visit with you charming laddies." He gave a rueful smile which revealed a chessboard of gold and silver teeth.

Paterson's head bent in exhausted frustration. He muttered almost to himself. "We can only hope the Second Fleet arrives sooner rather than later then."

An eerie silence descended on the company and Buchanan knew from Soames' face that the axe had only come half way down. Soames cleared his throat. "Ah, that's the other 'fing."

Paterson fixed him with a dread gaze. "What other thing?"

"Well, I was in Kingston before coming 'ere, right? So I 'ears these two blokes chatting to each other and one of them says if he'd 'eard the latest on the Scottish colony. So the other bloke says Nah, and the first bloke says that they've stuffed up their second voyage 'n' all. And the second bloke goes 'After the bollocks they made of the first one? How?' And the first geezer says, they've not paid for the boats and they ain't ready yet. And the second bloke starts pissing himself laughing and calls you all… I don't suppose you need to 'ear that bit. But that was the long and short of it."

Paterson blurted. "Did they have any idea when the Fleet would sail?"

"Months' was all I 'eard,"

Buchanan knew what had to be done. "Peter, if I get you another bottle can you wait until I get the rest of our Council here."

"If it's another two bottles you 'ave yourselves a deal," Soames grinned.

Thirty minutes later, the entire Council was sitting in the Great Cabin. Buchanan gave some quick background and then left Soames to repeat his tale. When he'd finished there was a deathly hush before the inevitable explosions of outrage and cries for retribution.

Soames sensed that given he himself was English that it might be a good time to leave. He pulled Buchanan to one side. "Jamie, I'm going to 'ead orf now. Looks like you gents 'ave a few things to sort out, if you know what I mean."

"Aye, Peter. Thanks for coming. We'll work out the trades later, if that's alright."

"No problem. I'll still be 'ere." With that he slipped away leaving the Council to its discussions.

'Fucking English' and 'How the fuck can they doing this given the terms of the Act?' were the overriding sentiments.

The Council looked to Buchanan as Company lawyer for an answer to the second. All he could do was hazard an educated guess. "It'll be a masterclass in revisionist history. The King will bleat that he was never properly informed of the true nature of the Scots' intentions but if he'd known, then he'd never have allowed the Act to pass, etc, etc."

"But that's bullshit," shouted Paterson. "Of course the English knew our intentions. Christ almighty, the English Commissioner of Trade even advised the King not to worry about us setting up here."

"Fuck, I wish they had now." said Pennicuik.

This brought an unexpected laugh, primarily because it was Pennicuik who had said something funny.

Montgomery best summed it up. "That's it then."

He didn't have to say anything more. Everyone in that little room knew that the death knell had just sounded. Paterson held his head in his hands. Even he, the irrational optimist, realised that staying was pointless.

Buchanan said, "Let's break to work through what needs to be done and re-convene on the Saint Andrew tomorrow."

Everyone knew this would be an evacuation plan. There was a murmur of agreement before Pennicuik added a rider. "Aye, but mind and bring your own drink." His ability to generate laughter hadn't lasted long.

CHAPTER 49

Buchanan slept poorly, which was hardly surprising given Soames' crushing news. But that wasn't the only reason. The other was the sound of Paterson's racking cough coming from the adjoining cabin.

As he lay awake, Buchanan had contemplated his own predicament. It was clear that the game was up. Abandonment appeared the only viable option. But then what? There was still the contract out on him and, as Edinburgh had shown, there was no place in his home country that was safe. But even if he was able to go back to Scotland it would be to face the recriminations from those who'd put their faith- and savings- into the Company of Scotland.

Staring up at the knots in the wooden beams he knew that there was only one realistic path. Head to the American Colonies and try to make enough to keep his father and investors whole. If he could do that then at least he wouldn't have let them down completely. He also couldn't pretend that Anne Robertson wasn't part of the jigsaw. But what would he have to offer her? A refugee from Darien, penniless, with a limited skill set and a price on his head. What a fuck up he'd made of his life. And now he'd be tarred with the infamy of being a Councillor of this laughing stock Company.

A rap on his door brought him back to the present. Robb stuck his head in and said that the pinnace would be ready to take him and Mr. Paterson over to the Saint Andrew in fifteen minutes. Buchanan thanked Robb, eased himself out of his bunk and went into the Great Cabin to grab a cup of coffee. Paterson was already there.

"Morning, Jamie," he rasped. He looked exhausted and deathly pale.

"Morning, William. How are you feeling? Couldn't help but hear you last night."

"Aye. Sorry about that. Just got a bit of a cough I can't seem to shake."

Buchanan cocked his head. "If that's a bit of a cough then I'm the King of Persia."

"Well, Your Highness, there's not much I can do about it given we've no medicine."

"Maybe so, but you don't have to do the work of three men."

Paterson nodded but Buchanan knew that nothing would change. This was Paterson's passion project and he'd die trying to save it.

When they arrived on the Saint Andrew they could hear raised voices coming from the Great Cabin. Unsurprisingly, the two loudest were Drummond and Pennicuik.

The latest spat seemed to revolve around how the whisky was to be split between the ships when they left Darien. Paterson, despite his hoarseness, managed to shout them down. "You're both a fucking disgrace. Spoiled brats arguing over the crumbs of the cake before we've even decided to leave."

Then a coughing fit overcame him and he had to sit down, spluttering as waves of phlegm came up from his lungs. Montgomery brought him a glass of water.

Drummond at least has the good grace to apologise. "Aye, Paterson. Yer right."

Paterson waved a hand in acknowledgement as he tried to catch his breath.

Drummond went on. "So, now that we're all here let's get on with it. William, why don't you give us your thoughts?"

Very clever, thought Buchanan. Ask the person most wanting to remain in Darien to speak first and then work back.

Paterson took another sip of water and then gave an emotional speech, the thrust of which was that despite the setbacks they owed it to their country to never give up. Articulate, heartfelt and superficially appealing, it was a cry to rally round the Saltire, to make those in Scotland proud. But it was also totally without merit or foundation.

The rest of the Council had little difficulty in picking it apart. The odds were now insurmountable and the only consequence of delaying evacuation would be the loss of more lives on that damned shore.

Paterson tried to argue for more time but he was a voice in the wilderness. Buchanan had kept quiet, knowing that what the others were saying was true. Ultimately he could not avoid Paterson turning to him.

"But Jamie, surely you believe we must go on," he implored.

Buchanan took a deep breath. "William. I know this isn't what you want to hear but we have to face reality. All we're doing by staying is digging a deeper hole."

Paterson slowly shook his head.

Buchanan felt an enormous wave of compassion for the man but this wasn't the time for sentiment to rule reason. Drummond seized the moment. "Well it seems tae me that Mr. Buchanan has summed up the situation very nicely. Let's take a vote. All in favour of evacuation?"

All hands but Paterson's rose.

"Against?"

Just Paterson.

"In that case I suggest we begin the withdrawal process as soon as possible," said Drummond.

Buchanan held up a hand. "Mr. Drummond. There will be some method to this process, won't there?"

"Aye, Mr. Buchanan. We get as many bodies as possible the fuck away from here as fast as we can." He then smiled. "Just ma wee joke. Of course there'll be a process. We just have to sit doon and work wan oot."

CHAPTER 50

As it turned out, and consistent with the entire venture, the first stage of the process was a shambles. Buchanan had impressed on the Council that word of the intended evacuation must not be leaked to the settlers until a plan had been properly formulated. That lasted about two hours. As soon as the news got out panic gripped the Colony like a plague.

From the deck, Buchanan watched as the Landsmen swarmed onto the beach, congregating in front of Drummond who was standing on a rock some three feet above the masses. He was all beard and waving arms but the text of his message was not one of salvation.

To have to tell anyone that their dream has ended is a painful task. You see the light go out in their eyes and their bodies slump. Hope is the last thing to die but when it's gone there is nothing left but despair.

These trusting settlers had expected to build a new life far removed from the hardships and prejudices they had left behind. A Scottish Utopia with fields of wheat and a warm climate to soothe their chilled bones. And wealth beyond their wildest imaginings. Wealth from the bridge between the Oceans. Wealth from the Nicaragua wood. Wealth from the gold and silver that sat under the soil like potatoes waiting to be picked.

That had been the promise. But all they had found on that cruel beach was an inhospitable cesspit where mosquitos reigned, torrential rains washed away their crops and death was the common currency.

An hour or so after he'd watched Drummond give his sermon on the Three Foot Mount, Buchanan received a message asking if he and Paterson could come ashore. Although not something he relished, Buchanan knew there could be no hiding place. However, he'd have to go alone as Paterson's condition had now deteriorated.

Buchanan arrived late in the afternoon in the midst of a tropical downpour. Romantics might have portrayed the torrential rain as the Gods weeping but Buchanan thought it was just more shit weather in the land of shit weather. And that was saying something coming from a Glaswegian.

The gathering took place under the ramparts of the fort to give the best protection from the elements. The atmosphere was as subdued as the sodden ground and Buchanan sensed the numbness among the congregation.

Drummond shook his hand in a display of Council unity as he whispered, "Where the fuck is Paterson?"

"Not in a good way. Burning up with fever and in bed."

"Fuck. Let them know he's nae trying tae avoid them."

"Of course. But why am I here?"

"Tae confirm whit I've been telling them."

"Which is what exactly, Thomas? I know you're loud but even your voice doesn't carry over to the Unicorn."

Drummond smiled. "Aye. Fair point. I'll dae a quick once over and then gie you the stage."

Buchanan had to hand it to Drummond. His summary, although not totally balanced, was sensitive. He was at pains to stress that the reasons they were evacuating had nothing to do with them. Instead he focussed on the treachery of the Crown, English envy and the threat of the Spanish. Which of course was only part of the story. But it made for good copy and deflected from the manifold shortcomings of the Company itself. That post mortem would come later but for present purposes the King, the East India Company and the Señors would serve as adequate scapegoats.

Drummond then gave the floor to Buchanan. He immediately apologised on behalf of Paterson. The explanation was accepted at face value as many of them had seen the poor man's health deteriorate before their eyes.

He then spent a few minutes endorsing Drummond's assessment and explaining that the decision to evacuate hadn't been taken lightly. However, there was now no option but to cut their losses and save as many lives as possible. He delivered the message in a frank, open manner and when he'd finished there was no resistance, just questions. When do we leave? On which ship? Where are we going? What about the sick? Will we have safe passage? And so it went on.

All Buchanan could tell them was that the Council was working on the best plan and would let them know as soon as possible. When the meeting had dispersed, Drummond pulled Buchanan to one side along with Leitch and Forbes. "Tell me, Jamie, any thoughts on how this will work?"

"Well, basically isn't it what you've already said? Load the survivors onto the remaining ships and get the hell out of here."

"Aye, aye, I get that. But tae where?"

"Well, back home for most of them," said Buchanan

"Aye, that's maist of them. No a' o' them."

Buchanan could sense that Drummond was as unenthusiastic about going back to Scotland as he was and saw an opening. "For others there may still be a way to salvage something from this."

"Oh aye. And whit might that be?" said Drummond, his interest now piqued.

"New York. The Company has contacts there and it could try to tap into the tobacco boom. If we can establish a foothold then something might be recovered from this mess. But that'd need Council approval."

"The Company wid let us dae that?"

"Thomas, for all intents and purposes the Council is the Company over here. We were given extensive powers and latitude to use them. Granted, New York is a bit of a stretch, but the principle remains the same."

"But whit aboot the English?"

"The Proclamation only refers to the 'Scots of Darien'. Therefore, the embargo shouldn't apply to the Company if it's trading somewhere else."

Drummond rubbed his chin and looked at Leitch and Forbes. They both nodded. Whatever was awaiting them in Scotland was clearly not appealing. "Aye, sounds like a plan. Who'd be part of this group?"

"Anyone who wants but I can't see there'd be too many who'd put their trust in anything the Council tells them after everything that's happened."

"Nae argument fae me on that wan. How many ships wid head fur New York?"

"I'd suggest all of them. New York is a good place to make for regardless. We'll get safe harbour and anyone wanting to stay can do so. The rest can go back to Scotland."

The three men muttered among themselves. Buchanan didn't trust them as far as he could throw them but what other choice did he have? Drummond emerged from the huddle. "Fine then. Let's look at that as the preferred option. How dae we get this agreed?"

"I think we just did. Together we now make up a majority of the Council. But I'd prefer if it was unanimous so that there is no comeback later from Edinburgh if it all goes tits up."

CHAPTER 51

Over the next twenty four hours Mackenzie tried to bring some order to the logistical nightmare of the evacuation. First, he prepared a roll of all remaining Landsmen and soldiery. This made for harrowing reading given that it was not a fresh record but the original list of settlers with the names of those who had perished scored out. The dead now easily outnumbered the living.

The most tragic among the survivors was a group of six terminally ill men. All had requested to be left to die on the land rather than in the nightmarish conditions of a ship's hold. At least on Darien they could breathe their last looking at the stars and comfort themselves that they were on Scottish ground.

Those being evacuated were divided so that the remaining ships carried proportionately the same passenger numbers. Mackenzie was careful to keep family and friends together and had split the soldiery according to background and allegiances. Paterson had then given this to the Council for review. Almost inevitably, the first hand to grab the list was Pennicuik's. He was damned if he was going to have any undesirables on his vessel especially those Glencoe curs. He cast a beady eye up and down the names and finding no-one repugnant, grunted his acceptance. The list then did the rounds of the others.

Mackenzie, attuned to the rivalries and vendettas among the Colonists, had done a sterling job and there wasn't a single objection.

The one unexpected twist came when Robert Montgomery requested that he be allowed to leave with Captain Soames aboard the Three Sisters. Ostensibly this was to expedite word back to Edinburgh of the evacuation and try to stop the Second Fleet from sailing.

It was a clever ruse for an early exit as it did actually make sense. Who, other than a Councillor, would have the gravitas to explain to Edinburgh why the Second Fleet should be kept in port. This had become a priority and there was a much better chance of Montgomery making it back to Scotland on his own before the rest of the First Fleet. The Council agreed to let him go.

Soames had no objection to taking him to Kingston and built the cost of passage into the price of the beef and flour he sold the starving Scots. Buchanan wrote two letters which he gave to Montgomery. One was to his family explaining what had happened and his intention to make good.

The other was to the Company. This gave a frank and honest account of events of the last few weeks and would paint a very different picture from the rose coloured missives which Hamilton had carried. It made clear that the Second Fleet should not set sail for Darien and referenced the potential plan to establish a foothold in the American Colonies. But most pressingly, it reinforced the need for the Company to negotiate the release of Pincarton and his crew.

Montgomery tucked the sealed letters into his jacket and shook Buchanan's hand before boarding the Three Sisters. They had been together on that dreadful expedition to the interior. Perhaps the savagery of what Montgomery had witnessed went some way to explaining his recent erratic behaviour. Perhaps he had just audited his soul and found the ledger short. Whatever the case, Buchanan could see that he was hugely relieved to be leaving. He departed without fanfare or fuss, his exit a mere sideshow to the main event.

Of more immediate concern to Buchanan had been the health of Paterson. He was wracked with illness and spent four days in a state of delirium. Buchanan did what he could to help him but there was no silver bullet for yellow fever. Only sleep and fresh water could trigger whatever was left of the body's defences.

Mercifully on the fifth morning, the fever broke and Paterson regained a bemused consciousness. He lay weak and drenched in his sweat-soaked sheets looking around like a trapped animal suspicious of its surroundings. His skin still resembled a cold fillet of veal but he was out of immediate danger. Buchanan held a cup of water to Paterson's cracked, parched lips but after a few sips, the patient slumped back onto his pillow exhausted by the effort.

"You had us worried there, William," whispered Buchanan.

"Did I?" croaked Paterson "Ma faither would say I was just malingering to avoid getting the crops in." A weak smile played across his face. "How many days have I been out?"

"Four."

"Jesus. What have I missed?"

Buchanan took a deep breath and filled him in. As he spoke he saw Paterson's drawn, pained face become imprinted with sorrow.

"William, believe me. There's no alternative. If we stay, we die. Leave now and we live to fight another day."

"Fight?" he rasped. "This was the fight and we lost it."

"Maybe this battle, but we can still win the war."

"What in the American colonies?" croaked Paterson.

"Why not?"

"Because they're English, Jamie. Do you honestly think they're going to let us set up shop there?"

Buchanan started to explain his reasoning but Paterson flopped back into an exhausted sleep. Maybe that was the best place for him just now. But his last comment gave Buchanan pause for thought. If they did meet resistance in America, the Scots' money would be of little use without a marketplace. A private venture outside the umbrella of the Company wouldn't be a target but that couldn't be financed using the tobacco receipts and gold. Christ, what a mess.

*

Paterson recovered slowly. All he could do was sit on the deck of the Unicorn and watch as the worldly goods of the settlers, both surviving and dead, were ferried to the ships. The seamen were none too pleased to see the disease ridden refugees. Now, all the tortuous fumigation would be for nought and the sickness would return.

Amazingly, the enthusiasm to leave wasn't universal. Despite all its extraordinary challenges, some of the settlers had come to love this inhospitable place. A small faction of ten men and women made representations to the Council to remain. It was agreed that they should be allowed to choose their own destiny and would be left their portion of the rations and alcohol.

CHAPTER 52

At first light the following morning, the next caller came knocking. A French ship, the Le Havre, pottered into the bay. Its Captain was named Duclos, a dapper little Breton who sported a well-groomed goatee.

The Scots assumed the ship was there to provide a progress report to Versailles about the Maurepas but it turned out to be carrying a very different message. Duclos was asked to make for the Saint Andrew and was sitting sipping a glass of wine by the time Buchanan and Paterson arrived. Introductions were made before Pennicuik took the bull by the horns. "Gentlemen. Captain Duclos has something to tell us."

Buchanan took from Pennicuik's grave demeanour that whatever it was wouldn't be good news. The Frenchman stroked his elegant beard and in heavily accented English began. "My colleague, Captain Duvivier spoke highly of you and the kindness shown to him and his crew. Because of this I have made a detour to come here with news."

Is that right, wondered Buchanan, or have you just come for a sly peek at your treasure ship?

"I have just been in Cartagena." He paused to allow this to sink in. All eyes were on him. "There is a new Governor who has taken over from Don Diego. This man, Hernando de Montoya, has come direct from Seville carrying orders from the King of Spain to mount an offensive against your settlement. When I left, the Barlovento was being readied to attack by sea with a force of some seven hundred soldiers to be deposited further down the coast to make an overland assault."

The Scots looked at each other. This to an extent confirmed what Pilkington had told them a week or so back, but this was no mere blockade and its immediacy made it even more worrying.

Drummond was first to respond. "You're sure of this Captain?"

"I witnessed the preparations myself." His sincerity did not appear in doubt.

"How long?"

The Frenchman shrugged his narrow shoulders and turned down his mouth in that very Gallic way. "That I cannot tell you. But my best guess is that they would not be more than five days behind me."

This was the final slash of the Scots' death by a thousand cuts.

Duclos got to his feet. "Gentlemen, I sense that you'll have much to discuss and I'm anxious to catch the wind before it changes. So, I shall take my leave and wish you *bon courage*."

Buchanan suppressed a smile. Obviously Duvivier had briefed him well about the seagoing lottery of the exit. All the Councillors thanked Duclos who politely shook each hand before bouncing out of the room.

Drummond was the first to speak. "So, dae we believe hm?"

"Why wid he lie?" asked Leitch.

"Fuck's sake man," said Drummond, looking at him as you would a dull child. "Didn't you see how he came intae the bay?"

Leitch shook his head, cowed by the chastisement.

"Aye, well, ah did," said Drummond. "Straight past the wreck of the Maurepas where he stopped for a wee look-see just tae make sure we hudnae taken its precious cargo."

"So you think he's trying tae scare us aff?"

Drummond snorted. "That's exactly whit I'm putting out there."

Pennicuik, who had spent much time fawning over the suave Duvivier, disagreed. "I see no reason to doubt his word." It was said with conviction but wasn't backed up with anything more tangible than his Francophilia.

"Uh uh. And based on what exactly?" said Drummond.

Pennicuik hummed and hawed for a second or two before Buchanan stepped in. "Well, it's not exactly a bolt from the blue is it? We've known about the Barlovento for months and when we were in Cartagena it was made clear that it would only be a matter of time before the axe would fall. Now that there's a new Governor, it seems the tipping point's been reached."

Despite the logic of this, Drummond was still sceptical. "Aye. Mr. Buchanan. Fair enough, but how come a Frenchie has just come fae Cartagena? I thought them and the Spaniards wur at each other's throats. Seems strange that suddenly they're a' loved up."

Paterson, his voice still not fully restored from his bout of fever, knocked on the table to signal he wanted to speak. "The Le Havre is just a trading ship and poses no threat regardless of its flag. I mean look at us. We've done business with anyone."

Paterson then took a gulp of water to soothe his raw throat and sat back. It was clear from his grey face that he was struggling. However, his words rang true with Drummond. "Aye. Alright Paterson. Let's suppose whit Duclos says is legitimate and that his wee detour isnae just a ploy."

Pennicuik threw up his hands. "What the fuck does it matter? We've tried and failed to get at the treasure so why should we care if someone else has a go?"

"It matters," spat Drummond, "'cos it was wur last hope of salvaging something worthwhile oot of this bastarding venture. You might've understood that if you'd been payin' attention."

Stung by the words, Pennicuik went on the offensive. "Is that right,, you jumped up prick. At least I've done my job. Got you all here and if necessary, I'll get you back. What about you then? Half built a useless fort and slaughtered a battalion of Spanish and their Indian guides. Old habits die hard eh, Drummond?"

Drummond hurled a glass at Pennicuik, narrowly missing his head, and began his lunge towards the Commodore. But Pennicuik was prepared and reached behind him to pick up the flintlock which he'd placed on the credenza. He pointed it straight at Drummond and snarled. "Come on then Drummond. Just keep going and I'll show you the ultimate in self-defence."

Drummond stopped in his tracks. "As God is ma witness Pennicuik, I'll huv you."

"No, you won't Drummond. Your card is marked. Everyone knows you're a murdering dog and sooner or later you'll hang. But until that day, if I'm around, there's always going to be a gun trained on you."

"Did you hear that, boys?" smirked Drummond to Leitch and Forbes, his Glencoe cronies. "The Commodore here thinks he's protected." This brought uncertain laughs from the other two. They knew they were supposed to side with Drummond but they were streetwise enough to understand that you don't want to piss off the person in charge of the ships that'll take you home.

Buchanan knew he needed to bring this under control. "Oh, for fuck's sake. Will you two just stop all this hard man bullshit. Jesus Christ. We're talking about the realistic possibility that the Spanish are going to turn up here in a few days and do to us what they know we did to their raiding party."

This stark truth seemed to restore some order before Paterson croaked. "I don't think it's a ploy. I believe Duclos and like Pennicuik says, the treasure is beyond our reach anyway." This was the definitive word. If Paterson, the arch proponent for staying, thought the threat real then that was enough.

Buchanan stepped in again. "So we'll need to accelerate what we're doing. By the way, if we believe the Spanish are coming, then any possibility of any healthy Landsmen remaining is off the table."

"Agreed," rasped Paterson.

"Aye, agreed." echoed the others.

"Fine then," said Buchanan. "Let's press on. We don't want to spread any unnecessary panic but we need to tell the settlers what we've just heard."

Drummond and Paterson were closer to the Landsmen then any of the other Councillors. They quickly exchanged glances and Paterson gave an imperceptible nod. Drummond delivered the answer. "Aye. Only right and proper."

Suddenly there was little else to say. The immediate death warrant for the colony had been signed by the new Spanish governor. The Scots now had a deadline to meet.

CHAPTER 53

Paterson and Drummond sombrely made their way over to New Edinburgh.

When the message was delivered that the Spanish threat was now imminent the mood became desperate. Not only had they to evacuate, but now they had to do so urgently to avoid annihilation. None of them had signed up for this. They were exhausted, broken and in most cases weak with illness. They were the real victims of this debacle, the errors and wrecks of others dragging them down. Sure, there would be a heavy financial price for Scotland but at the sharp end of the Scheme these were the poor bastards who had suffered most.

Paterson and Drummond fielded myriad questions about the process but most were a rehash of what had been asked a few days previously. Both Councillors were pragmatic and honest and did all they could to prevent widespread hysteria. Eventually the crowd drifted off and the settlers went back to the melancholy task of gathering up their goods and boarding their allotted ship for the journey home.

What would be waiting for them in Scotland though? Every tavern strategist would point out the flaws in the grand Scheme and human nature would demand that somebody be held to account for the debacle. Certainly, the English, the Spanish and the King could all be held up as villains. But it was not they who would have to look into the eyes of those who had entrusted them with their dreams. That would be the fate of those who had the temerity to return empty handed and beaten.

Drummond went off to order the soldiers to dismantle the cannons and drag them down from the escarpment back onto the ships. He was buggered if he was going to leave them for the Spanish jackals, especially as they were worth a pretty penny.

Paterson shuffled to his little mud hut on the beach and began to pack up his possessions. Buchanan knocked on the rudimentary door.

"Ah, Jamie. Come to help me with the flit?"

"Something like that," Buchanan replied.

"Hard to believe it's actually come to this."

"Aye, it is."

"Christ, I had such hopes and just look at us now."

"Listen William, you can't blame yourself. It's......"

"Stop, Jamie. I know what you're going to say and I appreciate it. But we're the authors of our own misfortune just as much as the English or Spanish."

He stared at Buchanan almost daring the lawyer to contradict him. But Buchanan realised that this was not the time or place. It's only when the tide goes out that you can see who's been swimming naked and the Edinburgh autopsy would inevitably deal with all of that. The Company would be too big to fail in the eyes of the Scottish public so its demise would inevitably be attributed to malicious foreign intervention, regal neglect and commercial dirty tricks.

However they both knew the truth. The lack of planning. The disastrous location of the Colony. The woeful provisioning of supplies and medicines. The list could go on and on. But right here, right now, what was the point in any of that? Today, all that mattered was survival and getting as many poor souls as possible away from this misbegotten bay before they were overrun.

"C'mon, William, let's take a saunter along the beach before the sun goes down."

Paterson nodded and the two padded slowly along the sand, enjoying the warm blue water washing over their feet. They strolled in silence, feeling the balmy air gently stir around them. The rains had stopped and the air was infused with the ozone of the lightning strikes. Paterson stopped for a second and pointed over the bay. "Look, can you see the Tule camp fires begin to burn?"

Buchanan screwed up his eyes. It was still light and difficult to see the flames. But then he caught a flicker of them and nodded to Paterson. When the Scots left, the Tule would just go on living as they had before these strange white people had arrived. The Scots would warn them of the Spanish threat and in the short term they would probably just disappear into the jungle until the coast was clear. Buchanan doubted the Señors would spend more than a few days razing the deserted Colony before returning to their whores and fine wines in Cartagena.

Paterson turned to him. "Jamie, would you mind coming with me to the graveyard. I don't think I could face it on my own today."

"Aye, of course William."

The pair wandered the twenty metres or so off the beach to the little cemetery where several hundred Scots now lay buried. Paterson's evening ritual was to visit the graves of his wife and son. Now there would be few more occasions when this would be possible.

Buchanan looked at the little white crosses. Every burial had been undertaken with Presbyterian reverence. Rich or poor, Scots or French, no death was treated differently from any other. When the chess game ended, the King and the pawn were returned to the same box.

Paterson knelt beside the graves of his loved ones and offered up a silent prayer before slowly getting to his feet. "C'mon, Jamie, let's leave the dead to their peace and see if there's any whisky left in that bottle under my bed."

Buchanan smiled and placed a comforting hand on Paterson's warped shoulder. "Now, there's a good way to end a shit day."

CHAPTER 54

In the frantic few days before the Fleet sailed Roderick Mackenzie undertook a brutal stocktake of any Company goods still ashore. The equation was simple. Take what was of value and leave everything else behind.

Bequeathed to the Indians and the elements were the mildewed Bibles, rotten leather shoes, discoloured wigs, laddered hosiery and empty barrels. Ferried to the Fleet was the balance of the linen, tobacco, some ironmongery and the last of the whisky. The precious Madeira had remained on board throughout. Mackenzie had the goods divided up so that each vessel carried its fair portion. This would ensure that if the ships became separated there would be a cargo of some value available to every Captain.

The Council met aboard the Saint Andrew on June 20th 1699. This was to be its last recorded assembly. Paterson was the current Chairman. Not yet fully recovered from the fever, his voice was still a croak. "Gentlemen, let's finalise where we're going."

There was a murmur of agreement except, almost inevitably, Pennicuik. "Are we not also forgetting one other little detail, Mr. Paterson?"

Paterson frowned. "What other little detail?"

"The tobacco receipts and Company gold"

"What about them?" Paterson rasped.

"Well, if we're dividing up everything else shouldn't these also be split?"

"Your faith in your fellow man is touching, Pennicuik" Paterson wheezed.

"Not a question of faith, Paterson, Just fairness."

Paterson grunted, "I scarce thought I'd ever hear you use fairness as the basis of an argument."

This brought some snide appreciation from the Glencoe brigade. Paterson cleared his throat. "Each ship has been allocated more than sufficient funds to ensure re-supply for the passage to Scotland. As far as the New York gold and the tobacco receipts are concerned, they will be divided between Mr. Buchanan and Mr. Mackenzie into whose hands they were entrusted."

Pennicuik sought to pursue the point but was cut off by Buchanan. "Gentlemen, let me be very clear. It was impressed on us in New York that any other option would not be palatable to our masters in Edinburgh. So, if you want it reported to their Lordships that you are challenging their orders, please make yourself known."

The spectre of retribution from the Edinburgh potentates was enough for Buchanan's statement to be taken at face value. In reality there was no concrete basis for the assertion, but Buchanan knew that in the absence of trust- a commodity now in very short supply- the best way of maintaining control was to hold the purse strings.

Paterson took a sip of water. "If that's settled, let's focus on the more pressing business of our destination and route."

Now that the Fleet was about to go back under sail, Pennicuik decided to re-assert his position and call the tune. But Thomas Drummond was having none of it. "Now just haud on a wee minute there *Commodore*." His enunciation of Commodore dripped with contempt. "Ah've been talking wi' Mr. Buchanan and some of the others and we've come tae an agreement on whit's best."

"Oh, is that right Mr. Drummond? Pray enlighten us as to this grand plan."

Buchanan smiled to himself knowing that if Pennicuik didn't like what he was about to hear he'd conveniently hive off from the rest of the Fleet at the first opportunity and go his own way.

"Our main job," said Drummond, "is tae get as many bodies and ships back tae Scotland. Given whit we've bin telt about the English embargo and the Spanish dislike o' our wee colony, it's obvious tae us that the safest way hame is via the American Colonies and across the North Atlantic."

This was exactly what Pennicuik himself had intended to propose so he now found himself stuck in the dilemma of agreeing with the detested Drummond or finding some spurious reason to raise an objection. He pondered the situation. "And what's the route to the American Colonies then? You appreciate that we may have insufficient food and water to reach New York or Boston without re-provisioning."

"Aye, well we've thought about that as well. We need tae avoid any Spanish ports which really only leaves Jamaica."

"Aren't you forgetting the Proclamation."

"We're no stupit, Pennicuik. Mr. Buchanan, want tae tell the Commodore whit you telt us?"

Buchanan cleared his throat. "To my mind, the sentiment behind the wording of the Proclamation is to stop any help getting to our Colony. If that's been abandoned and we're sailing for home then the threat has been neutralised. All we'll be requesting are supplies for our onward journey and having seen the appetite for trade in Jamaica, our gold will trump a stricter interpretation of the Proclamation."

"Are you sure Buchanan?" asked Pennicuik.

"After what we've been through, I'm not sure of anything anymore. All I can give you is my best assessment. And that is my best assessment."

Drummond took the reins again. "Aye well that's good enough fur me and ma boys. Mr. Paterson, whit say you?"

"Agreed," said Paterson, wearily rubbing his eyes.

Drummond smacked his hands together. "Aye, well there we huv it, *Commodore*."

Pennicuik, pleased enough with the proposal anyway, made great play of holding his hands up like a benevolent Caesar. "If that is the will of the Council, then so be it."

Drummond then flagged the second part of the equation. "There's also bin some talk about part of the Fleet mebbe staying in the American Colonies."

Pennicuik almost choked on his whisky. "What the fuck are you talking about Drummond?"

"Me and some of the lads huv bin discussing it and seems that trying tae get something going in the Colonies might no' be a bad idea."

Buchanan wondered just who 'some of the lads' might comprise.

Pennicuik couldn't resist the opening. "Aye, well that's probably the only alternative left to you and your gang as you'll no' be welcome back in Scotland."

"Whit's that supposed to mean Pennicuik?"

Pennicuik for the second time in a minute held up his hands, but this time it was in the 'I don't think I need say any more' kind of posture.

Paterson, slammed his palm down on the table. "Enough of this bullshit! For Christ' sake, let's just concentrate on getting out of here in one piece. New York is the obvious destination given our circumstances. Once there we can decide if any of us are going to stay."

"Aye well good luck with that folly," said Penicuik. "You can count me and the Saint Andrew out. We'll be headed back to Scotland."

Paterson glared at him but he was just too damned tired to argue the toss with this arrogant buffoon. To all intents and purposes the meeting was done, so Drummond, uninvited, opened Pennicuik's drinks cabinet and removed a bottle of his whisky. Half-hearted toasts of good health and safe voyage were made but as soon as the bottle was drained the participants went their separate ways.

CHAPTER 55

At first light, the Saint Andrew, Caledonia and the Endeavour conducted a final check of their passenger manifests. Other than the six unfortunates too weak to sail, all the Scots were now on board.

However, the Unicorn was behind schedule. When the rigging on the topsail had been unfurled, part of it had broken free and crashed to the deck. Mercifully no one had been injured, not even the young sailor who had been holding onto it when it had come loose. He had had the presence of mind to spring out on a different trajectory and landed unharmed with an almighty splash in the sea.

Robb had quickly surveyed the damage and determined that repairs would be better carried out in the lee of the bay. The delay would only be a few hours but would mean one more night in Darien. However, the benign weather that June morning presented the perfect opportunity to exit the treacherous heads. Therefore the decision was made for the first three ships to take advantage of the conditions and then wait for the Unicorn to emerge the next day.

Paterson watched the sails of the other ships catch the light wind and slowly edge out of through the choppy channel until they disappeared out of sight past Golden Island. Buchanan came up beside him. "How you doing, William?"

Paterson was about to reply when he jerked his head and stared at the beach, suddenly becoming very animated. He shouted to Robb to hand him his eyeglass. Paterson began to focus on a spot some way down the shoreline. "What the hell?"

He handed the telescope to Buchanan and pointed him in the same direction. Buchanan adjusted the device and caught the unmistakeable figure of Andreas in his scarlet jacket together with a dozen of his men paddling towards the shore in their dug-out canoes. They hadn't been spotted in a few days but obviously had been keeping a close watch on events.

"Bloody scavengers. Didn't wait long to pick over the carcass did they?" growled Paterson.

Buchanan watched as the Indians came ashore and pulled the canoes up onto the beach. But instead of heading for the fort where the Scots anticipated they might first scrounge, they made a beeline for the shaded retreat where the six invalids had been placed. Buchanan didn't know what to think. He had spent time with these kind, civilised men but he had also seen their savagery first hand.

Paterson was not having it, though. "Robb, lower a longboat, give me a crew and some armed soldiers and get us to shore immediately."

Paterson turned to Buchanan. "Well, are you coming?"

Buchanan clambered into the pinnace alongside the agitated Paterson. If these heathens were going to finish off his countrymen he would make them pay. It took about ten minutes of hard rowing to get to the shoreline. Their efforts had not gone unnoticed by the Indians. Buchanan was uncertain how this was going to play out but sensed it could go south very quickly. However as Andreas began walking towards them with arms outstretched in welcome, the immediate crisis passed.

But what the hell were they doing on the beach? Why had they not just waited until the Fleet had gone and had the whole bay back to themselves? The reason soon became apparent.

Through broken Spanish and hand gestures, Andreas explained that they had watched the Scots prepare to leave and knew that some men were to remain behind. So they had come to take them to their village to give shelter and care until they passed away. Paterson went over to the little Indian and placed a hand on his gold epauletted shoulder. "*Gracias*" he murmured, his voice full of remorse.

Andreas just grinned his usual grin but then spent some more minutes trying to convey to Buchanan that he wanted him to come to his village.

Buchanan initially resisted but the Indian became increasingly insistent. He looked at Paterson. "What do you think William?"

"Why not? I mean we're not going to come to any harm unless Andreas is playing false."

"And we don't think he is, do we?"

"No, we do not."

So the Scots helped the Indians lift the wretched six into either the longboat or onto the rafts and began the paddle to the Indian village further along the bay. Throughout the journey, Buchanan and Paterson speculated on why Andreas was so keen to have their company. They could come up with nothing.

When they arrived at the collection of little huts the sick men were gently lifted and taken into a shaded nook carpeted with palm fronds. The Indian women gently dabbed the men with cool wet cloths and gave them fresh water. Paterson ordered the soldiers back into the boat but to be prepared for anything.

Andreas then began tugging impatiently at Buchanan's arm and led him and Paterson inside one of the huts. The light, although much dimmer, was still sufficient to be able to make out the figure of a man lying in the corner.

Buchanan let out a gasp. "Jesus Christ. It's Kelso."

Davie Kelso had been one of the young lads Buchanan had spoken up for when he'd absconded months before. He was lying under a thin blanket on top of a mattress of palms and was in obvious distress.

Buchanan knelt down beside him. "Hello, Davie," he said softly.

The young lad stirred into consciousness at the sound of the voice. His glazed eyes focussed in the half-light. "Ho, Mr. Buchanan is that you?"

"Aye, Davie. It's me and Mr. Paterson."

"Christ, I'm awfy glad you've came. Got masel' into another wee bit of bother, ah'm sorry tae say."

"No problem, son. We're here now. So what's the story?"

Kelso coughed violently and grimaced in pain. Then Buchanan saw blood begin to seep through the blanket. He shot Paterson a look. This was no fever. Gently, Buchanan pulled the blanket back from the young man's body and stared in horror at what lay beneath. His thin torso was ripped open from the left side of the waistline to just under his armpit. It looked like a huge chunk had been taken out of him and blood was leaking from under the dressings and unguents which the Indians had applied.

Buchanan drew in a sharp breath. "What in the name of God?"

But Paterson knew. "Shark," was all he said.

"Fucking hell," muttered Buchanan. "Davie, how did this happen?"

Kelso pointed to the little wooden cup beside him. Buchanan reached across and as he lifted it to Kelso's lips smelled the pungent aspira. The Indians were sedating him to ease his suffering. Kelso sipped it greedily. A few seconds later the pain which had been etched on his face fell away and he lay back in a state of herbal euphoria.

He turned his head to Buchanan. "When the Colony began tae go tae hell naebody kept any tabs on anyone anymair. So ah was able to duke off a' the time and come here. Ah've got a lassie you see." He hacked again and for a moment was reminded of his wound. But it passed and he carried on. "When the Indians saw youse messing about the sunk Frenchie ship I telt them whit we were trying tae dae. They thought it was all hell of a funny and couldnae understand how youse didnae know how tae dive proper like."

Buchanan stared at him. "But we tried, Davie. We tried everything."

"Aye well, maybe Scots urnae designed fur the water. But the Indians got down there nae bother."

Buchanan and Paterson listened to all of this, their eyes widening as the story unfolded. Buchanan asked the obvious question. "But how could they without us seeing them?"

"Aye, well that's the clever bit," he croaked. "They dived at night when the moon was oot. Gave then a' the light they needed."

Buchanan looked again at the gaping hole in the boy's side. Kelso saw him and let out an ironic little laugh. "Aye, I ken fine whit yer thinking."

"What happened son?"

"When I knew that the ships wur gonnae leave, ah thought that ah'd try for one last wee haul tae top up whit ah'd got. So me and one of the young Indians went out on our ain three nights back. He was bringing some stuff up to the surface where ah was waitin' when ah saw a shark coming at him. Ah manage to hit it wi' a paddle but ah fell in and couldnae get back on board before the bastard came back and took a bite oot of me. Ma mate pulled me in and brought me here."

Kelso spluttered out some phlegm and this time blood came up with it. He signalled again for the cup and Buchanan put it to his lips. The young lad took a deep breath. "Listen, Mr. Buchanan, ah' know ah'm dying. Ah'm just glad that you're here. You were awfy good tae me when naebody else wis so I want tae tell ye something."

"Aye, alright son. Take yer time."

"Time isnae something ah've got much of," whispered Kelso with a weak smile.

Buchanan took the boy's hand knowing that he was on his way out.

He looked at Buchanan and whispered. "A' the treasure ah got is in the grave of ma pal Billy Simpson."

"I'm sorry, son, what?"

"Ma treasure is in Billy's grave. That's where ah hid it. Ah want you tae huv it."

Buchanan looked at him in astonishment. He could feel the boy's hand grip him tighter. "Alright son. Alright. But have you no family I can get it to?"

Kelso shook his head. "Ma ma's deid and ma da's a prick." He gave out a peculiar little chortle at this and then lifted his head in a desperate attempt to make his words more audible. "The Indians got their fair share. Ah want you tae huv mines."

"Aye. Thanks, son. It's much appreciated."

Then, content in the knowledge that his wishes would be fulfilled, he began to tremble uncontrollably. Buchanan lifted the head and shoulders of the boy and cradled him in his arms. A few seconds later Kelso shuddered one last time and died.

Buchanan laid him back down on the palms and swept the sweat-matted hair from his face. The boy's eyes were wide open in a ghastly death stare. Buchanan gently closed the lids and whispered. "May your God grant you peace, Davie Kelso." He stayed there for a few moments and then eased himself back to his feet. Paterson was looking at him.

Buchanan returned the stare. "What the hell do we do now?"

"There's no 'we' Jamie. He made clear that he wanted you to have what he's buried. What you do is make sure this boy is laid to rest and then go and find Billy Simpson's grave."

Buchanan let Paterson's words sink in. "I can't do that. The treasure wasn't his to give so it can't be mine to take."

"Oh, for God's sake, Jamie. Don't be such a Puritan. Alright then. Just hand over whatever is there to the Company. Or maybe the French. Or perhaps the Spanish. As far as I'm concerned, whoever managed to recover that treasure deserves it."

Buchanan mulled it over. Paterson was right. Perhaps it was just that a Scotsman getting a windfall was anathema to the national psyche.

"Fine, but I'm not taking all of it. You and I will split whatever it is."

Paterson began to object but Buchanan held up a hand. "No, William. We split it. Comfort yourself with the thought that you'll be halving my guilt."

Paterson gave a faint smile. "Who am I to stop you doing what you want with your property?"

"That's it settled then. In any event, there'll probably be next to nothing."

"Well, there's only one way to find out."

The two men left the hut and blinked at the brightness of the outside light. Andreas came over and they told him that Kelso had died. The Chief nodded and barked an order. Two of his men entered the hut. They wrapped the body in the thin blanket and waded out to gently place the corpse across two of the longboat's seats.

Paterson and Buchanan then went to the other sick Scots to say a final farewell. All were painfully weak but being in the care of the Indians would make their last days tolerable. When Paterson and Buchanan moved back towards the longboat, Andreas gave them a theatrical salute which the Scots returned before he embraced them in a fit of giggling.

As they rowed away Buchanan watched the entire village wave goodbye. The Indians would simply return to their happy, carefree existence. Sure, other settlers might come and temporarily disrupt their idyll, but once word spread of the Scottish debacle this would be far less likely. There were plenty of other places better suited to colonisation than this flawed paradise.

CHAPTER 56

The journey back to New Edinburgh was made in near silence. This was mainly out of respect for the body of Davie Kelso lying in its shroud among the oarsmen. However, for Paterson and Buchanan it was also the anticipation of what might be waiting in the grave of one Billy Simpson.

When they reached the shore Buchanan asked two of the sailors to help carry the corpse to the cemetery and then told them to go back to the longboat. They looked at him blankly, puzzled that they had not been tasked with the grunt work of digging the grave and interring the body.

Buchanan got round the issue by saying that Kelso's last wish had been for the two Councillors to lay him to rest. Paterson then added that he wanted to spend some time at the graves of his wife and son. As he didn't want to be rushed in this final vigil he suggested they return to the Unicorn and he'd signal when he wanted collected. The sailors nodded, happy not to have to toil in the heat, and left the two men to their tasks.

Their first duty was to bury Kelso. Buchanan and Paterson picked up two of the discarded spades dotted around the graveyard and selected an appropriate spot. Stripping down to their waists they plunged the shovels into the soft yielding soil.

Carving out the grave took a good twenty minutes and by the end of it they were dripping with sweat and caked in mud. They then took the body and reverentially placed it into the dark hole. Both bowed their heads and Paterson said a few words, consigning the deceased into the hands of his Maker. After they had replaced the soil Buchanan used some palm sisal to tie two pieces of wood into the shape of a cross and planted it in Kelso's last resting place.

Buchanan looked at Paterson. "Are we happy about what we're about to do?"

"And deny the last wish of a dying man?"

Buchanan nodded, reassured by the justification. "Right then, where the hell is Billy Simpson?"

Mercifully, the ever efficient Mackenzie had insisted that for a Christian burial to be complete the name of the dead had to be scratched on the little cross placed on each grave. Suddenly remembering this, Buchanan scrabbled about and found a sharp flint which he used to carve the name "Davie Kelso" on the marker which he'd just created. They then turned their full attention to the quest for Simpson.

To streamline the process they split the graveyard between them. Every marker had to be carefully scrutinised as some of the inscriptions were barely legible. It was painstaking work but after ten minutes Buchanan heard Paterson's excited shout. "Jamie. Over here. I've found it!"

Buchanan bounded across to the far corner of the cemetery grabbing the two spades en route. He stared down at the marking. Etched into the wood was the name 'Billy Simpson.' The earth on top looked like it had been recently turned over, giving further credence to Kelso's story.

It only took about a minute of careful excavation before the iron tip of Buchanan's spade hit something hard. The two men stopped and looked at one another. "The moment of truth," whispered Buchanan.

They got on their hands and knees and began to scrabble in the pungent earth. Thirty seconds later they had uncovered a square wooden box which they hauled out of its hiding place. It was unexceptional and would have attracted no attention were it not for where it was located.

They laid the box on the ground in front of them. "Jesus, my heart's pounding," said Buchanan.

Paterson looked at him. "Do the honours then."

Buchanan reached down and brushed the remaining earth from the top. There was no lock and when he lifted the lid it came away without resistance. As he opened it, he leapt back as if a viper had sprung out and launched itself at him.

"In the name of God," muttered Paterson.

"Fucking hell!" was all Buchanan could manage.

Both men stared in disbelief at the contents. Before them lay an astonishing array of treasure. Gold doubloons, silver coins, emeralds, diamonds, rubies and jewellery of every description. They sat in incredulous silence until Buchanan started to laugh. An almost hysterical cackle which turned into a joyous howling whoop.

Paterson just continued to stare, wide eyed and dumbfounded. Buchanan put his hand into the cornucopia and began to caress the treasure with his fingers. What the box contained was beyond the imagining of all men other than kings. Paterson joined him in groping the fortune, allowing the jewels and coins to run through his hands.

"Sweet mother of God," whispered Paterson.

"Sweet mother of God, indeed," echoed Buchanan.

They sat there transfixed trying to take it all in. The spell was only broken by the sound of a parrot screeching in the nearby palms. Now, suddenly alert, the two men became paranoid. Had someone come back? Were there Indians in the trees watching them?

"We have to move quickly," snapped Buchanan..

They closed up the box and covered over the grave. Paterson gave up a prayer for Simpson's soul and apologised for their defilement of his mausoleum.

"Can we risk taking it back like this?" asked Buchanan.

"Too dangerous. I've a better idea. Follow me." His leg cramping from the unusual posture, Paterson began to hobble towards the abandoned settlement. After a few moments he found what he was looking for. A large empty chest lay in a corner of one of the half-completed huts.

"Grab one end," he barked to Buchanan and they lifted the container back over to the graveyard. "Now put the treasure box in it and cover it with soil."

Buchanan looked at him quizzically.

"Jamie, for fuck sake, just do as I tell you. I'll be back in a second."

He hirpled off into the undergrowth and a few minutes later emerged with an armful of native cuttings- palm stalks and flowers stems. "Now plant these in the soil on the top of the chest and then leave it open."

The penny suddenly dropped. If they were to return to Edinburgh then the botanists would welcome some samples of the native flora. Well, at least it was a plausible enough story for them not to attract any difficult questions when ferrying the chest back onto the Unicorn. Once there, no-one would care a jot about the fate of some local plants.

"Right, let's get this to the shore and get cleaned up," said Paterson,

It was an ordeal to haul the heavy soil-filled chest back down to the beach, but both knew that a thousand times the effort would be worth it. When they had positioned it near the gently lapping waves they waded into the bay and washed the sweat and grime off their filthy bodies. Paterson then told Buchanan to signal the Unicorn. The whole exercise had taken no more than forty minutes but it felt like an eternity.

Buchanan stood on the shore waving his arms and a single musket shot from the ship confirmed that his gesturing had been noted.

Paterson turned to him. "Do you mind waiting here, Jamie. I'd like to go back to the cemetery and spend a few moments with my family."

"Of course, William. Take your time."

Paterson smiled. "This won't take long. I've grieved them enough. Now I want to thank them. I'm sure they're watching over me and that a part of this was their doing."

Buchanan returned the grin before Paterson said. "In any event, we need to get back to the Unicorn before the heavens open. If that chest is exposed to the rains for too long then the soil will wash away and we'll have some explaining to do."

"Hell's teeth. That hadn't crossed my mind."

The afternoon storm clouds were massing quickly and the downpour wouldn't be long in arriving. He looked back at the Unicorn and saw that the longboat had started making its way over to them. "Come on, you fuckers! Row like your lives depended on it."

Five minutes later the little vessel arrived in the shallows. Paterson, now returned from the graveyard, shouted for two of the sailors to come ashore and assist them with a special cargo. He instructed them in a calm, even voice. "Now, be careful lads. These plants are more precious than you could ever imagine."

The sailors looked at one another totally bemused. But they just shrugged compliantly and did as they were told, lugging the box through the knee deep water and gently manoeuvring it onto the floor of the longboat. "Thanks lads," said Paterson. "Now, let's get back to the ship before we all get drenched."

Buchanan cast worried glances at the sky throughout the short trip. Please God, hold off for a few minutes more, he silently beseeched. Then, just as they came alongside, the first fat drops of rain started to fall.

Buchanan leapt out of the boat and up the ladder onto the deck. He shouted at a couple of the sailors to bring some ropes and drop them over the side into the longboat. Galvanised by the urgency of his voice, they produced them in seconds and Paterson then began supervising the most important freight transfer of his life.

Tugging at the bindings to ensure they were secure he gave the order to slowly haul away. By now the rain had stared to teem down and Paterson could scarcely take a breath as he watched the chest agonisingly make its ascent. Buchanan was craning over the rail shouting instructions to keep it steady and stared in horror as the deluge began to wash away the topsoil. "'C'mon," he muttered to himself, "C'mon. Just a few more feet."

Finally, the chest was eased onto the deck. Buchanan studied its contents. Although battered down by the storm, the palms and flower cuttings were still in place and there remained a sufficient layer of earth to obscure what lay hidden beneath. He offered up a silent prayer.

"Well done, lads. Now, take this to Mr. Paterson's cabin immediately. And be very careful."

The sailors, oblivious to the massive subterfuge, nodded and shuffled along the narrow gangway to Paterson's quarters. Buchanan followed them terrified that with one slip the whole thing would go over. But the sure-footed tars completed their task without incident. Buchanan slumped down into the little chair which sat in the corner, mentally and physically spent.

Seconds later a rap on the door was followed by Paterson himself. He looked anxiously at Buchanan. "Well? Everything alright?"

Buchanan theatrically waved his hand over the top of the drowned flora and broke into a wide grin. "Behold, all the treasures of the earth."

CHAPTER 57

Leaving the Aladdin's chest inside Paterson's cabin, the two men tried to go about their business as normally as possible. Thankfully, with everything else that was happening, no-one really paid them much attention. They had a quiet dinner with Robb who then excused himself to oversee final preparations.

A little time removed from the frantic events of the afternoon, the enormity of the situation began to sink in. Buchanan and Paterson looked at each other not quite sure what to say. Eventually Buchanan asked. "So, do we tell anyone? No, sorry, stupid question. Of course we don't."

Paterson nodded. "That would be like signing our death warrants."

"Keep it quiet then?"

"Absolute secrecy."

"But somehow, it just doesn't sit right."

"Jamie, when was the last time anything sat right since leaving Leith?"

Buchanan looked at Paterson not wanting to make the obvious comment of, 'Well Darien was kind of your idea.'

But Paterson was not insensitive to what he'd just said. "Yes, I know that sounds ridiculous coming from me but if we'd been properly provisioned from day one then things would have been different."

Buchanan nodded but didn't say anything. What would be the point? However, if Paterson thought that a few more supplies would have turned the expedition from disaster to triumph then he was delusional.

After a slightly awkward silence, Paterson asked. "Any idea how much it might be worth?"

"Pick a number, William, but I'm not going to be rummelling about in the chest trying to put a value on it. Best keep it under the soil until we get to New York."

"Yes, that's a given. But what do we do with it when we get there?"

"That shouldn't be an issue. From what I saw it's not a place where people require certificates of provenance. The value of the gold and silver will be easy to establish and we can trade or sell the jewels as needed."

"Then?" asked Paterson

"What do you mean? Then?"

"Well, aren't you going back to Scotland?"

"Jesus, William. I can't go back. You know I've a price on my head."

Paterson shook his head. "Sorry, Jamie. I'd forgotten about that."

"Aye. Well, I haven't. But there's nothing stopping you from returning."

Paterson snorted. "Apart from my crucifixion you mean. Every disaster needs a scapegoat and I'm under no illusions who the most obvious candidate will be. I'm not ready to face that just yet."

"So we stay in the American Colonies?"

"Does 'stay' mean the same as 'hide'?'"

"More 'out of sight' than 'hide,'" replied Buchanan.

Paterson smiled. "What will you do?"

Buchanan didn't hesitate. "Use the money to parlay it into a bigger pile. A lot of people my father is involved with were relying on the Scheme succeeding and I'm going to make damn sure they get their money back."

"How will you do that? And how the hell do you explain where you got the capital?"

"The *how* is simple. I've seen the future, William, and it's the tobacco industry. The plantations in Virginia are growing the best leaf in the world and the demand is insatiable. As for explaining the money, well, as I've said, New York isn't a place where too many questions are asked as long as you're prepared to grease the right palms."

"What about the Company? We talked about using the New York money with the tobacco and cotton businesses in mind. Are we going to give up on that?"

Buchanan looked at his hands. Christ, this was a lot to try to digest. "William, I really don't know, but why use the Company money when we can use our own? All I can tell you is that we've been given an opportunity which I'm not going to let go to waste."

Paterson nodded slowly. "Agreed. Christ knows I love the Company and I've given it my all, including a wife and son. But I don't owe it or those fat slobbering Lords in Edinburgh anything anymore. Those pricks have shafted me at every turn and I'm sure they'd happily do so again." His voice had been slowly rising with his anger.

"Wheest, William, for God's sake." whispered Buchanan, as he put his hand on Paterson's arm.

Paterson halted his diatribe, but even in its brevity it revealed his bitterness. Alright, he'd made plenty of mistakes and been his own worst enemy at times. But he'd been treated appallingly and Buchanan doubted if he could have put up with what Paterson had endured.

"William, the best payback is success. So, let's use what we've been blessed with and show them all."

The words seemed to resonate. "Aye, Jamie. That's the ticket. Let's show the bastards."

CHAPTER 58

Despite their physical exhaustion, neither man slept much that night. Their minds whirred and spun with the impossibility of what had happened. Fate is a fickle mistress rarely coerced into service by those asking her favours. Then perversely, when all seems lost, she takes pity, extends her hand and offers deliverance.

Both were relieved when the first tentative light of the new day began to finger its way into their cabins. They got up almost simultaneously and made for the Great Cabin where they looked out of its huge windows over the still, flat ocean. The heat of the day would soon build but at this early hour they watched as eerie ribbons of mist crept across the water and wrapped around the rails of the ship like the tentacles of a sea monster.

"Think the Gods are plotting to keep us here?" asked Paterson as he sipped gingerly at a cup of coffee.

"Nothing would surprise me, William. But don't you think they've had enough amusement for a while?"

"I'd like to hope so," Paterson said, smiling that peculiar lop-sided grin of his.

A few minutes later Robb breezed in. "Morning, Gentlemen." His demeanour conveyed that there was nothing a mariner liked more than getting back to sea.

"Good morning, Captain," answered Buchanan. "Are we all set?"

"As we'll ever be. Rigging up and running and the tide turning as we speak."

"How long until we depart?"

"About half an hour." He then walked across to the chart table, rummaged around for something, and left.

"Will we go up and watch the proceedings?" asked Paterson.

"Only right and proper."

They clambered up to the aft deck and leaned across the railing. The haze was already lifting. In the distance they could see the tell-tale wisps of smoke rise up from Andreas' village and thought of their stricken countrymen and the kindness of the Indians. For the natives it would be just another day. For the Scots, it would be their last in this crippled Utopia.

The oyster coloured sky was now giving way to shafts of sunlight which cast their long early rays onto the shore. At seven thirty everything was in readiness. Robb shouted his orders and cries to heave cables, halyards and lines filled the morning air. As the first draught of wind pinched and pulled at the unfurled canvas, they felt the little ship start to lurch ocean-wards.

A sudden, irrational sense of loss swept over Buchanan. The experience in Darien had been almost exclusively nightmarish but this land had a beauty which transcended all reason.

He comforted himself with the thought that maybe one day he would return, but until then all that was left was to watch the shore gradually recede from view. As they inched nearer the Heads, the ramshackle collection of huts and abandoned fort looked utterly surreal against the verdant landscape.

The two men stood side by side. Nothing was said. Nothing needed to be said. The palette of the sky had shaded orange to blue and the Sun had begun its imperious ascent. But as it did, Buchanan thought with bitter irony that what he was actually witnessing was that same Sun going down on the great Scottish Dream.

Daniel Pollock was born and brought up in Glasgow. After several years practising criminal law he moved to London where he worked in the oil industry. Following numerous postings overseas he now lives in Australia with his family.

www.ingramcontent.com/pod-product-compliance
Ingram Content Group UK Ltd.
Pitfield, Milton Keynes, MK11 3LW, UK
UKHW040702010525
5718UKWH00012B/143